Firefly

By
Barbara Fitz-Vroman
With
Kim Vroman-Pence

Sequel to:
"Tomorrow is a River"
- 1977

This is a historical novel based on the Tomorrow River country in Wisconsin and references some local towns of the time. This information is mapped at the end of the book. The references to The Old Soldiers' Home, also known as the Grand Army Home or the Wisconsin Veterans Home facilities, are located at King, Wisconsin.

However, this novel is a work of fiction. Any references to events or businesses are intended only to give a sense of reality and authenticity. Any resemblance to actual persons, living or dead is entirely coincidental.

"Scripture quotations taken from the King James Version (KJV): KING JAMES VERSION, public domain in the United States."

"Scripture quotations taken from the New American Standard Bible® are referenced as (NASB®), Copyright © 1960, 1962, 1963, 1968, 1971, 1972, 1973, 1975, 1977, 1995 by The Lockman Foundation. Used by permission. www.Lockman.org"

ISBN: 978-1-54663-065-4
Printed in U.S.A.\

Cover Watercolor Illustration by: Liudmila Vakulenko, Kaukauna, WI
milla.vakulenko@gmail.com

Print interior design by www.jimandzetta.com

Table of Contents

Dedication

In memory of my mother,
Barbara Fitz-Vroman, the author of "Firefly",
a sequel to "Tomorrow is a River",
I miss you every day.

Kim Vroman-Pence
****
She was the prettiest flower on the prairie.
Ryan Vroman

****

To mom, our spiritual and creative light.
Marc Vroman

Acknowledgements
by Kim Vroman-Pence
***

I became acquainted with Barbara Rosner after my mother passed in May of 2012, and I learned that she had been a neighbor and was a long-time friend of my mother's. Barbara quickly became a source of comfort and inspiration to me during my grieving period. Our friendship grew and Barbara became a steadfast partner in helping me move forward with finishing the work for publishing my mother's manuscript "Firefly", written as a sequel to "Tomorrow is a River", a book she co-authored with Peggy Hanson-Dopp.

My deepest and heartfelt thanks to Barbara Rosner and her daughter Lisa Rosner. They both contributed endless hours of support and extensive research to help me validate the history of Tomorrow River country, and encouraged me and inspired me with their suggestions and guidance to help finish "Firefly". I must also mention Barbara Rosner's husband, Don, who scrounged up Wisconsin Extension maps that helped Lisa recreate the Tomorrow River country map for this book. This information provided important Wisconsin historical foundational information which is the backdrop of both "Tomorrow is a River" and "Firefly". I would not have been able to get Firefly to publication without their help.

Special applause to my sweet, smart, and beautiful 27-year-old niece Nicole Vroman and my sister-in-law Doreen Vroman who came to my rescue with one last final edit to help me meet a book proof deadline.

My exuberant thanks to Julie C. Eger, an extraordinary Wisconsin author and friend to my mother. Julie's kindness and friendship to me has also helped inspire me to finish "Firefly" and embrace my mother's writing legacy.

Thanks to my family who entrusted me to finish my mother's Firefly manuscript after her passing in May 2012; Dale Vroman, Marc and Doreen Vroman, Ryan and Faye Vroman.

My mother was thrilled to have Mary Rae Johnson complete the editing of the first draft of the Firefly manuscript.

Texas size gratitude to Billye Johnson (Dallas, TX), creative writing instructor and freelance writer, for her additional editing of punctuation and spelling, and editorial skills. Her writing group provided incredible support and feedback to me on how to move forward on this project. A writing colleague, Paul Paris, business owner and author of four non-fiction books, generously provided critique notes on the manuscript to help validate the story flow and consistency.

My heartfelt appreciation to April Kain-Breese, Unity Minister, for her revival of interest in "Tomorrow is a River" through her church book club. April is an incredibly creative, inspirational, and a gifted speaker. I am grateful for her inspiration kindness to me.

Last, but not least, my devoted and loving thanks to my incredible husband, who has supported me every step of the way on this journey. His generous love and support fills the sails of my life with laughter, joy, and adventure. His incredible patience and assistance with the final book production requirements helped me finish an important and sentimental life goal from my bucket list.

Kim Vroman-Pence
Plano, Texas (2017)

Foreword

Barbara Fitz Vroman co-authored with Peggy Hanson Dopp a book entitled, Tomorrow Is a River, published in 1977. It is an engaging historical novel set in the Tomorrow River country near Waupaca, Wisconsin. The story features a young couple, Adam and Caroline Quimby who move to a desolate wooded area where the minister husband intends to "save souls." Very soon, he disappears and his wife becomes the main character in the story, along with a Menominee Indian woman named Kemink and their children. Throughout the story runs an inspiring thread of hope and healing, despite some major challenges. The setting includes the Tomorrow River area, the Civil War, the Great Chicago Fire and the Peshtigo Fire. At the time of the publication, the Milwaukee Journal described this novel as "Wisconsin's Gone with the Wind."

Peggy Dopp conceived of most of the characters in "Tomorrow is a River".

Barbara completed the manuscript for the sequel to "Tomorrow is a River" titled "Firefly". The book continues with many of the characters from "Tomorrow is a River", however, many new characters were developed by Barbara and added to the story of "Firefly.

"Firefly" is the story of Felicity Quimby-Jacobson haunted by her first love Dan-Pete, and overwhelmed with her new responsibilities to her husband, Hans Jacobson and life at the Old Soldiers' Home in King, Wisconsin. Hans is a man desperately in love with his wife, but proud and bull-headed, lacking the tenderness and patience of Dan Pete. Felicity's first child, Jason, struggles to earn his father's accolades, while finding solace in his fascinating friendship with Colonel Maxwell Harrison. Jason turns out to be a musical genius and relishes his musical progress, while battling with his father's expectations. The story is set in the late 1800's and early 1900's in Tomorrow River Country of Wisconsin. The story culminates in a spoiled young girl reconciling her childhood love and becoming a mature devoted wife and mother.

Barbara was unable to finish the book publishing prior to her death in 2012. She gifted Pearl-Win Publishing and all her literary works, including her remaining manuscripts to her daughter, Kim Vroman-Pence. In memory of her mother, Kim completed the publishing production of "Firefly".

Although the setting of "Firefly" takes place from approximately 1870 – 1937, the journey of the characters' parallels many of the same challenges, struggles, conflicts, disappointments, jealousy, hopes, fears, courage, love, healing, forgiveness and celebration of life today.

Note: The Old Soldiers' Home is also known as the Grand Army Home and the Wisconsin Veterans Home -- King, Wisconsin.

Dr. Frederick Marden was a Civil War Navy veteran and a Grand Army of the Republic (GAR) member. He was chosen by the GAR to head a five-member committee to establish a veterans' home in Wisconsin and is credited with drawing up the plans that helped Wisconsin repay its debt of gratitude to veterans. Dr. Marden originated the idea of making the home a true retirement community for veterans, allowing wives and widows of veterans to live at the home, as well as the idea of allowing members to live in cottages. Dr. Marden died on September 24, 1887, just a year before he could see his dream of a veterans' home become a reality. The Wisconsin Veterans Home was dedicated on August 19, 1888.

Reference: *Wisconsin Veterans Association of Wisconsin* WDVA B3402 (11/11) *(dva.state.wi.u)*

Prologue

Firefly Timeline

1871 - Peshtigo Fire

1873 - Felicity wedding plans go astray

1887 - The Grand Army Home (King/Waupaca County)

1892 - Felicity marries Hans Jacobson

1893 - Felicity's first child is born; Jason Jacobson

1896 - Felicity's second child is born; Seena Jacobson

1898 - Felicity's third child is born; Jacob "Jake" Jacobson

1900 - Felicity's fourth child is born; Saran Jacobson

1902 - Felicity's fifth child is born; Rasmeena "Meena" Jacobson

1906 - Colonel Maxwell Harrison dies

1906 - Jason Jacobson moves to Appleton

1937 - Boston Symphony Hall

Characters

- Adam Quimby – Caroline's first husband
- Caroline Quimby-LeSeure – Adam's first wife; second marriage to Baird LeSeure
- Baird LeSeure - Caroline's second husband
- Felicity "Firefly" Quimby – Daughter of Adam and Caroline Quimby, wife to Hans Jacobson
- Dan-Pete Tartoue' - Son of Pierre and Kemink Tartoue'
- Pete Tartoue'
- Kemink Tartoue'
- Danny Quimby – First born son of Adam and Caroline Quimby
- Robert Anderson - Felicity's "husband to be"
- Hans Jacobson - Husband to Felicity "Felly/Firefly"
- Henry Collins – Union veteran at the Old Soldiers' Home
- Colonel Maxwell Harrison – Retired Commander and Jason's Confidant
- Dr. Bentley – Jacobson's Family Doctor
- Mrs. Isabel Bentley – Dr. Bentley's Wife
- Grace Ott Benjamin – Married Adam Quimby – April 1902
- Mrs. Howard – The Jacobson's Housekeeper
- Maggie Grasslee – Daughter of Mrs. Mary Grasslee
- Mrs. Ellie-Bee Neffer – Bawdy House Owner
- David Bernstein – Friend to Jason
- Mrs. Charlotte "Lottie" Carthington –Mr. and Mrs. Hubert ("Lottie") sponsors of Appleton's city anthem music contest

CHAPTER 1
Wedding Day at Harbour Hill

"Better is the end of a thing than the beginning thereof: and the patient in spirit is better than the proud in spirit."
(Ecclesiastes 7:8)

Dan-Pete stood in a small hotel room. He had left behind the sharp rustle of hawk wings, the scent of pine needles, massed trees swaying in unison to the music of the wind. Yellowed, wallpapered walls closed in on him, the board floor was unforgiving, and the stale smell of tobacco smoke from previous residents assaulted his nose.

The young man, who had earned the name of Iron Heart, slid the moccasins from his feet. He took off his leather leggings and raised his doeskin shirt over his head, then flung it on the rumpled bed where he had slept the night before. His bare torso rippled with muscles gained from bow hunting and reining in strong horses.

He drew on black gabardine pants and pulled a white, starched shirt over his arms. Once, such garb had felt familiar and unnoticed by him. Now the materials seemed stiff and abrasive to a body more used to the softness of animal skins.

The morning darkness still pressed against the window. He slung a tie about his neck trying to remember how to knot it. He was a handsome young man, with dark eyes, a proud nose, and full lips with a hint of tenderness, however on this morning, it was beyond a somber face. His eyes looked like those of a man about to go into battle— a battle that might contain his death, but that he could not avoid.

He was going to a wedding. He would have preferred the battle.

****

Felicity Quimby, dressed in her chemise and petticoat, lay atop the coverlet on her bed, fanning herself with a palmetto fan. Her dark curls slipped from their topknot, uncoiling around her shoulders. Her face was passive, emotionless.

She studied the bedroom that had been hers since late childhood as if she was seeing it, for the first time. At various times, the walls

1

were covered with blue cornflowers, yellow roses, and painted pink bows. Now they were covered with daisies. Her eyes slid over the familiar chest of drawers holding her childish treasures, shifted to the porcelain commode from her wealthy Aunt Ann, and on to the wardrobe. Ribbons and ruffles streamed out of half-closed drawers.

All of this had seemed second nature to her, as familiar as the hand that brushed her hair and buttoned her boots. All of it had been simply the background of her life. Now it seemed strange this would no longer be **her** room. Someone else would move into it. Her mother, stepfather, brothers, baby sister, 'second' mother, Kemink and all the rest of the lively household would no longer be part of her daily life.

In three days, she was to be married. The entire household was astir with preparations. Her mother was cutting yards of white satin ribbon for decorations. Beneath her window, her stepfather Bay LeSeure was building the arbor under which she would make her vows. His voice, and that of her half-brother, Jimmy, mingled as they prepared the lawn and rose garden. She heard them laughing together as they worked.

From the kitchen warm, rich fragrances of baking wafted through the house reminding her of all the efforts for her happiness, but she felt sad as she looked around the room. The hand swaying the fan dropped, a sigh swelled her small bosom, her eyes traced the shadows that danced on the walls from the swaying tree branches outside her window.

"I should be thinking about Robert," she told herself. She tried to imagine the face of her husband-to-be, but it wavered and would not focus.

She sat up, her lower lip sulky, her eyes near tears. "I don't feel like a bride at all," she cried, hurling the palmetto fan at the wardrobe. Was this the way all brides felt? If it was, it was a wretched way to feel.

But he is coming. Dan-Pete is finally coming home!

She leaped from the bed, half pinned up her straggling curls, and pulled on a pinafore. Barefoot, she ran down the stairs to the kitchen.

Kemink, who had been part of their family as long as she could remember, her dusky fingers stained with raspberries, smiled at her. "You always could smell when the pastries came out of the oven," she teased.

Pretending nonchalance, Felicity wandered about, commenting on the dinner preparations. She stole a radish and nibbled a bit of a biscuit. Only after this circumvention did she get to the point that had brought her to the kitchen.

"Dan-Pete is coming, isn't he, Kemink?" She slid the words out casually but the end of the question trembled, betraying her.

Kemink shook her head. "I've told you seventeen times he's coming. In fact, Danny just drove off with the buckboard a half hour ago to pick him up from the hotel." She smiled but her dark eyes became thoughtful. Kemink stood, tall and silent, a magnificent Indian woman into whose hands Felicity had been born twenty two years before.

"Oh," Felicity cried, her hands becoming fists against her chest. "Danny's gone for him already. Oh!" In a flurry of pinafore, she was gone, concerned now about her bare feet and drooping curls.

On the landing, she paused, her eyes filling with tears, this time a different kind of tears. *He's coming home. Dan-Pete's finally coming home.*

It had been three years since Felicity had seen him. Kemink went often to visit her son, but Dan-Pete did not return the visits.

"Gret!" Felicity called over the banister, catching sight of a fourteen-year-old girl below her. "Fetch me up a tea kettle of steaming water, and hurry about it, would you please?'

Gret nodded and went off at her own pace. She was one of the dozen or so children Caroline LeSeure, Felicity's mother, sheltered at Harbour Hill. Each of them suffered from some physical and/or mental incapacity, which made it hard for them in less kind environments. Under Caroline's loving care, many had found healing and gone on to normal lives elsewhere.

Within minutes, Felicity turned the room, which had been merely untidy, into shambles. She pulled out one costume after another and discarded it. She dumped whole drawers, spilling hairpins, overturning boxes. The formerly listless girl had become a dervish.

None too soon, she had scarcely buttoned the last button of her pearl-pink waist-coat and secured the last curl when she heard the buckboard, and then through the open window, her mother's joyous squeal.

"Dan-Pete!"

Felicity drew toward the window, afraid to look out.

From her vantage point, she could see her mother embracing Dan-Pete, Bay, Jimmy, and Kemink were next to reach him among a stream of other people converging on him from the house. All she could see of Dan-Pete was his dark suit with a high collar and the top of his head. His black hair was shining in the sun.

How she loved this half-Indian son of Kemink and her French fur-trapper husband, Pierre Tartoué. From childhood, they had been like brother and sister, growing up in the same households. Dan-Pete saved her life when the ferocious Peshtigo fire raged around them. Ever since, he had been the dearest person in the world to her. Now he had arrived after a long three-year absence to watch her make her vows to another man.

Her heart was like a tom-tom of *Dan-Pete, Dan-Pete, Dan-Pete*.

She forced herself to walk down the stairs.

When she reached the garden, she saw him coming toward her. Dan-Pete had an arm around Caroline on one side and Kemink on the other. Jimmy was tugging at his sleeve and everyone else was mobbing him, all talking at once. Then he saw her. Their eyes met, and everyone else in the garden melted away. He stopped. She ran forward.

"Dan-Pete."

"Fly." He used the diminutive of the childhood nickname "Firefly" he had given her and everyone else had picked up. Ever since she had reached young womanhood, she had been trying to break her family from calling her that, but on his lips, the name was sweet.

"My little sister, all grown up, a bride-to-be." His voice was of a deeper timbre than she remembered; the voice of a man not a boy.

He leaned forward to brush his lips on her cheek, and then the group pulled him onward toward the house. She stood alone in the garden, her hand on the place his lips had touched, feeling a trembling all through her.

At the dinner table that evening, Bay was seated in the place of honor at the head of the table. On his right was Dan-Pete, Danny and Emily. Mother was seated next to Bay on his left, along with Kemink and then Felicity. The seating arrangement did not allow for Felicity to have the private conversation she had hoped to have with Dan-Pete.

At any rate, he was so engrossed in conversation with Bay, the rest of the assemblage got few words in. Both men were in the lumbering business. Though each in a very different capacity. Bay had his own lumber mill and was thinking of extending into the growing and prosperous Menasha area. Dan-Pete, half-Indian half-white, had chosen to return to his Menominee nation and was trying to help his tribe set up a lumbering operation of their own.

Their discussion concerned Dan-Pete's trouble with white lumbermen to whom the tribe sold timber. Because of the reverence for all life, the Indians wanted only the dead or dying trees to be harvested, but the white men were notching healthy trees to make them available for cutting. Dan-Pete himself would have liked to see more trees harvested, but he was bound to the Indian traditions.

"Cutting the timber could ensure full stomachs and warm

4

wigwams. Surely wanting those things for my people is not greed. However, when I try to urge more cutting, some of the elders say it's my white blood speaking. They feel I'm trying to make the Indians like the white man."

"Well, in a sense I suppose you are," Bay said. "However, white men or Indians, people must change with the times. You've chosen a difficult road for yourself, son," Bay said.

Felicity could not help but reflect how handsome Bay looked with the candlelight highlighting his almost white hair. When he returned from the war a few years before he was a rack of bones; Caroline's and Kemink's bountiful table had filled him out, and it was becoming. However, Felicity was frustrated that she could not see Dan-Pete's face because he was turned toward Bay.

"When my people wanted me to be their leader, after the death of the great Sashwatka, my head swelled," Dan-Pete went on, laughing at himself. "I'm finding it is not so easy to lead where others do not always wish to follow."

He finally glanced Felicity's way and their eyes met. His fork slid from his fingers and clanked against the china plate. The blood coursed so red beneath his dusky skin as to be noticeable.

Felicity's dark eyelashes fluttered downward. Ah, perhaps, Dan-Pete was not as cool and indifferent to her presence as he pretended.

They lingered over the meal, until the dessert dishes were taken away and the chairs pushed back. As everyone drifted toward the veranda, Felicity darted after Dan-Pete and caught his arm.

"We haven't had a moment to talk. Can't we..."

"Fly, my journey has been long. I'm very weary and I want to spend some time alone with my mother this night," he said. Then he touched her cheek, "I promise you tomorrow I will find time alone with my little sister while she is still Firefly." His manner now became the old, teasing way of their childhood. He tugged at a curl and winked at her, putting on a pompous tone, "before she becomes Mrs. Robert Lindsey."

She could do nothing but acquiesce, but her eyes burned with tears held-back. She feigned a yawn. "Well, I'm tired, too. See in you in the morning."

After 'goodnights' to the rest of the family, she escaped to her room.

"Please, God," she prayed. "Don't let me lie awake all night." However, so many storms were raging in her, she feared her prayer would not be answered.

CHAPTER 2
Oconto Falls
***

"Let nothing be done through strife or vainglory; but in lowliness of
mind let each esteem other better than themselves."
(Philippians 2:3)

Felicity's prayer was not answered. After lying awake, most of the
night, she woke with a start, dismayed to see how long she had slept
once it had finally come. The quality of golden light flooding the room
told her the day was well under way.

She flung aside her covers and ran to the window. A survey of the
grounds below showed no evidence of Dan-Pete. Perhaps he, too, had
slept late.

Gripped with urgency she could not explain, she washed quickly
with cold water, dressed in haste and hurried downstairs to seek out
Kemink.

Kemink was in the kitchen as usual. The Indian woman liked best
her gardens and the wooded areas around Harbour Hill. However, if
she was in the house, it was the kitchen she chose for her domain. She
ruled there happily among her copper kettles, iron skillets, drying
herbs, and wondrous harvests from field and wood.

This morning, the kitchen was a whirl of young women carrying
out preparations for the wedding feast. The smell of roasting geese
vied with the scent of vanilla and fresh strawberries.

"Where is Dan-Pete?" This time she asked forthrightly without the
pretense of nonchalance.

Kemink shook flour from her hands, then wiped them on a towel.
"He had to leave, my child."

"Leave?" Words wrung with anguish spilled. "Is he coming back at
once? Surely, he's coming back!"

"Last night—late," Kemink explained, "a rider came from
Keshena. He had ridden half the night to bring bad news. There was a
fire on a large acreage of Menominee timber. The white men helped
put the fire out, but Dan-Pete's close friend, Tall Elk, had seen these

6

same men start the fire. The half-burned timber could no longer be harvested. They took advantage of Dan-Pete's absence to do this deed to make trouble for the Indian loggers."

"Oh. That's all terrible," Felicity said. "He can't do much about it now. Couldn't he have stayed just until--?"

"Tall Elk accused the white men of the deed he had witnessed. A fight ensued. Now they have Tall Elk in jail in Oconto Falls, and there is talk he may be lynched without a trial or given only a mock trial and scuttled off to the penitentiary. In the fight, a man was killed. My son had no choice but to go to Oconto Falls quickly to see what he can do to help his friend. You must understand that, child." Kemink's tone was firm.

"Oh, I suppose he couldn't help it," Felicity raged, "It makes me so angry. Why do things like this always happen? He's not been home for three years and he's hardly set his foot in the door then--"

"Fly, Fly," Kemink chided, "You are no longer a child who becomes upset with every disappointment. Even though I still call you a child, you are a woman now and must learn to ride with life's storms. Dan-Pete was sorry, too. He left a message and his wedding gift for you."

Didn't Kemink know this was more than just a small disappointment, Felicity thought, not able to quell the rage inside her.

"Dan-Pete said to tell you he is a poor Indian without money to buy you the kind of gift he would like to give," Kemink continued, drawing Felicity a little away from the others in the kitchen to a more private spot by the pantry.

Kemink drew a small leather pouch from her apron pocket and opening it pulled out a copper necklace.

"One of his friends is a metalsmith. He had him fashion this gift for you." She handed the necklace to Felicity.

Attached to the copper chain were curious amber colored stones. Viewed one way the stones were dull, but viewed another way each caught the light with a golden glow. "Fireflies," Felicity breathed.

Kemink smiled. "Yes. My son bade me tell you he knows it is not suitable jewelry for so fashionable a lady as you. He asks you to wear it sometimes for love of him and to keep it always. 'Tell her,' he said, 'if she ever needs me, to send this necklace and I will come, even from the farthest corner of the earth.'"

"Oh, Kemink—Kemink." Felicity's white fingers closed around the stones and chain while tears slid down her cheeks. "Was ever there such a beautiful gift as this?"

"Now, enough of tears," Kemink said, her voice firm. "This is the day before your wedding and there is much to be done—by me, if not by you." She gave the younger woman a small spank. "Off with you."

Clutching the necklace, Felicity turned obediently and left, but she walked with dragging steps. The beautiful day had turned leaden for her.

Back in her room she sat, lost in a daze, staring at the curious amber stones that flashed light off and on like a firefly when it moved until she heard a tap upon her door.

She looked up to find her mother coming into the room, a huge white box in her arms, her eyes sparkling.

"Darling—Emily finally finished the dress. It is a gorgeous wedding gown. Even more beautiful than the one she made for herself when she married your brother. Just look!"

She was drawing out reams of white satin that fashioned the gown.

"Look at this yoke, Felicity."

Emily had hand-sewn tiny seed pearls and cut-glass beads on the bib of the dress and the little stand-up collar. The beads sparkled like ice crystals on new snow.

Felicity suddenly burst into tears again. "Mother—it's the most beautiful dress I've ever seen. But—I can't, I can't wear it."

Caroline stared at her weeping daughter. "Can't wear it? Whatever do you mean? Emily has spent over a year making this dress for you. You know that."

"I know—I know and yet it does not matter. I can't wear it, because---Oh, mother, I can't marry Robert. I can't."

Caroline draped the dress across a chair and came to sit on the bed beside Felicity's drooping figure.

"What is it, darling?"

"You know how I feel about Dan-Pete. When I saw him again—I just, I just... Well, I know I can't marry Robert. I can't."

"Fly," Caroline said sitting down beside her, "Dan-Pete has told you that his destiny lies in a direction that cannot include you, other than as his beloved little sister. You know that, Fly, and you know that he's right."

"I know."

"And Robert is a very fine young man."

"I know. But that's just it, don't you see, Mother, Robert is too fine to...to do this to him. I don't love him as I should." She burst into a new outpouring of tears.

Caroline held her and patted her.

"Felicity, you don't have to marry Robert if your heart tells you not to. You must please think about it carefully. All brides feel jittery before their weddings."

She drew back from her daughter with a little smile. "Why—I was wildly in love with your father when I married him—but on the night before our wedding, I actually considered climbing through a window and running away."

Fly wiped her cheeks with the back of her hand and managed a wry smile through her tears. "From what I've heard of my father's early life, you would have been smart to have done it."

Caroline laughed, "Oh, no. Then I wouldn't have you and Danny, would I?"

"Oh, Mother, I don't know what to do. I can't marry Robert, but I feel trapped. All those people coming from as far away as Chicago and Green Bay. Emily's made the dress. Kemink's got the geese in the oven and the cake. And how can I face Robert? Oh, Mother, help me. Please help me."

"Darling, it's much better to stop the wedding now than to be unhappy for the rest of your life and to make Robert unhappy too. If you're sure that this isn't just bridal jitters, then you will find the courage to do what's right. And of course, I will help you." Caroline smoothed back damp curls from her daughter's tear-flushed face.

"Mother, it isn't just jitters. I know it isn't."

"All right, I'll go then and stop the flow of events to the extent I can. We won't be able to stop everyone from coming, but we'll cross that bridge when we come to it. We'll have to talk to Robert."

"Mother, I want to go see Dan-Pete."

"That's the one thing you mustn't do right now," Caroline said. "As Kemink must have told you, he has urgent problems of his own right now."

"Mother, I've got to see him."

"Believe me, Fly, that wouldn't be wise. First things first. We have to call the wedding off." She kissed her daughter's forehead and left.

On the following morning, Felicity Quimby did not oversleep. She was up at first light. Below her, the grass and garden roses still sparkled with dew.

The sky was just turning from violet to blue. It was going to be a beautiful day, this day that was to have been her wedding day.

It had become clear to her that weddings were like babies—once conceived they could not be wished away, nor could wedding cakes become unbaked once they were decorated. Within hours, carriages would be rolling into the yard below her window, and over and over again, people would have to be told that the nuptials were not to be celebrated.

She wanted to escape. Yet more even than that, she wanted to see Dan-Pete. She knew her mother's counsel to her was almost always wise and that she usually got herself in trouble when she went against it, but she felt as if her very life depended on seeing this man she loved, as indeed, in a way it did.

Felicity dressed in a pale, peach-colored suit with a lace blouse beneath, the suit that was to have been her going away outfit for her honeymoon. Her fingers trembled on the many tiny buttons down the front, but the face reflected in her mirror was determined.

Softly she stole down the steps. The rest of the house still slept, except for Gret who was stoking the fire in the kitchen to heat water for the morning wash-ups. She was too busy to notice Felicity's departure.

Felicity bartered for a ride in to Peshtigo with Burt Miller, who drove the milk-wagon route. She told him if he would take her to Pestigo she would have a fresh blueberry pie waiting for him the next time he delivered milk at Harbour Hill.

She was determined to get to Oconto Falls before Dan-Pete went back to Keshena. It was at least 30 miles to Oconto Falls and by horse and wagon it would take most of the day to get there. Felicity knew she would have to try and barter some more with Burt to take her on once they got to the end of his milk route in Peshtigo. She might have to try to hire someone in Peshtigo to take her the rest of the way to Oconto Falls.

She figured she best offer to pay Burt for his time and hope out of the kindness of his heart he would agree. She really didn't want to have to negotiate to get another driver in Peshtigo, which surely would just raise more questions that best not be answered.

Felicity proceeded to plead her case to Burt. "Burt, I know you know this is my wedding day and I'm sure you are wondering what is going on. There is some unexpected business I must take care of and it would mean so much to me if I could trust you to drive me on to Oconto Falls.

"We can stop in Peshtigo and give the horses a quick break. I know this is a special favor and I will make sure you are paid handsomely for your help."

Burt noticed the distress in her voice and the anxiety on her face and could not refuse her. Besides, she was the daughter of Caroline and Bay LeSeure. "Well yes," he stuttered, "I guess I could do that for you, Miss Felicity."

Normally Felicity loved to go to Peshtigo to shop for a new frock or hat. Everyone in town was aware of who Miss Felicity Quimby was. There was always lively interest in everything that went on at Harbour Hill. The daughter of the house was something of a local celebrity and folks had already garnered rumors that her wedding—weeks in preparation—was being called off. The young woman's arrival in town was a curiosity to passersby. There were knowing and disapproving glances as she rode by in the milk-wagon with Burt. Felicity told herself: "Well I don't care. Let them buzz."

As the wagon bumped and swayed along the path to Oconto Falls, scenes of surpassing beauty succeeded one another—a herd of golden cows scattered like buttercups in a green field, a cataract of white water beneath an aging wooden bridge, great dark green pines along with birch on the side of a hill. Felicity saw nothing of the splendor of the day. Cheeks flushed, eyes large and dark, her vision was fastened on some inner panorama that no one else could see.

It was late afternoon when their carriage reached the city of Oconto Falls.

Felicity was thirsty and hungry, but she knew she had no time to get either drink or food. Her priority was to find Dan-Pete and get headed back to Peshtigo.

Her pale, peach suit was now rumpled and was damp from perspiration from the strenuous long ride. When the wagon had stopped, Burt started unbridling the horses to get them to water and food. "Felicity, you know it's already late and we won't make it back home tonight unless you get your business done quickly. I'll wait for you in the General Store."

Felicity knew Burt was right. She needed to try to find Dan-Pete and tell him of her decision not to marry Robert. Her heart started swelling with anxiety as she knew her time was short. She hoped he was still here and had not headed back to Keshena yet, as she dared not spend another day travelling to Keshena. Her mother would already be distraught and probably angry at her for leaving the house today.

With a dainty hand, Felicity lifted her skirts and stepped out of the wagon and up on to the wooden sidewalk in front of the General Store...she glanced around in search of signs of where the county jail might be.

Every eye watched her.

"What're you doin' here, miss?" A harsh challenging tone made Felicity's lips tremble.

She had to swallow twice before she could get her words out. The man was huge, with hair like a bear on his chest and a pockmarked face.

"I'm looking for the County Jail." Felicity realized her voice was trembling as she was caught off guard by the sudden appearance of this large man coming out of the General Store.

"And why would a young lady like yourself be interested in the County Jail?"

"I'm looking for Dan-Pete Tartoué. He's-- he's my brother." It was only a half-lie she reasoned. Hadn't they been raised as brother and sister? Didn't he still call her his little sister?

"He's—he's a Menominee Indian chief—he works in lumbering."

Now there was a slight murmur of recognition.

"Iron Heart?" the pockmarked man gave the name a derisive twist.

"I don't know—I don't know what they call him," Felicity said.

Other men seemed to appear from nowhere and were gathering more closely around her, a circle of large, sweaty men, many of them wearing only underwear tops over their trousers with the sleeves either rolled up or cut off. She looked at them with troubled eyes, feeling a menace which she could not understand.

Jim Moriarty grunted. This girl struts in with her twenty-one-inch waist, her porcelain skin, lace at her throat, smelling of eau de Cologne and lavender soap and is looking for the county jail and her Indian brother. Jim knew immediately this had something to do with Tall Elk.

God's britches, I'd like to throttle her, he thought. She was like a bomb that could go off at any time. Now to say that she was looking for that half-breed—Iron Heart so called—that uppity Indian already resented by a lot of the lumbermen, that was enough to detonate the bomb on the spot.

Moriarty barked, "And why would you be thinking your half-brother could be found at the jail?

The man who had barked at her was now madder than a bull. Felicity became flushed with fear. She did not want to provoke him further and yet she knew without an answer she wasn't going to get past him. She swallowed hard to calm her voice before she answered forcefully, "He's here to help a friend and I need to talk to him. Now are you going to help me or not?"

Moriaty grunted and then growled, "Follow me." There seemed nothing else she could do but follow him as he strode ahead of her.

CHAPTER 3
Fate Awaits

***

"But if ye have bitter envying and strife in your hearts, glory not, and lie not against the truth."
(James 3:14)

Jim Moriarty had half a mind to give the young woman beside him a good tongue lashing about her stupidity, but he could see she was already rigid with fear, and there was something about the set of her pale lips that touched him.

I've been tough with my judgment of her, he thought. Maybe the girl knows she shouldn't be here but had to come for good reasons, even though it seems there could be no good reason for her coming to the county jail and getting involved with Tall Elk.

As they reached the end of the boardwalk, Moriarty pointed toward the jail and growled again, "Just around the corner here to your left."

She flashed him a grateful look, hoping he would now depart.

He offered his burly hand to her and said, "I'm Jim Moriaty. I think I should wait here for you in case you run into any trouble."

His response startled Felicity. "Oh, well, suite yourself."

She could scarcely breathe with the tension of hoping she would find Dan-Pete. Suddenly, there before her eyes, was his horse and just as she started moving toward the jail steps, the door opened and Dan-Pete stood in front of her.

His torso was bared except for a vest and a tangle of beads and amulets. He wore brass bracelets beneath his biceps and a braided band around his forehead. As she rushed toward him, Dan-Pete was startled at the sight of her.

"Dan-Pete." As he embraced her, his touch as always both pleased and disquieted her.

"You want me to wait and take her back or is she going to stay a

13

spell?" Moriarty demanded.

Dan-Pete looked up in angst at the unexpected stranger. "She will not stay long. You don't need to wait. There will be no trouble here." Dan-Pete nodded and Moriarty walked away.

"Fly, you should not have come here," Dan-Pete whispered to her with intensity. "Tall Elk is in great danger and I may be as well. You need to leave.

"Dan-Pete, I had to come."

"How could you come today? Today is your wedding day." He had been conscious of this since dawn, the knowledge intruding on important considerations that should have claimed his whole attention.

"I couldn't marry Robert. We've called the wedding off."

"Oh, Fly, no." Dan-Pete threw his head back and made a groan that was deep and painful.

"Dan-Pete—I don't care; I'll even live with you on the reservation if that's what you want. The other night at the supper table it sounded as if you might feel your Indian clan think your part white and don't accept you quite as you expected either—and--"

"Fly, this is my life. I have burned my bridges. I cannot turn back now."

"Dan-Pete, that's not true. Bay is going to open a mill in Menasha. He's going to need all kinds of new help. Why, he'd welcome you with open arms? He would...."

"Fly..." the way he said her name was filled with anguish, reproach, tenderness, desire, regret and something else so final it halted her tumbling eager words. "You should not have come, but perhaps it is for the best you did."

He did not take her arm, as he would have at Harbour Hill. He walked ahead of her and she was obliged to follow behind, Indian style. "Come," Dan-Pete said gently as soon as they were out of the sight of Jim Moriarty. "Let us sit on the bench here beneath this tree. There are things I need to tell you that you must understand."

Dan-Pete took her hands in his and held them tightly for a moment as he gazed into her eyes with love and kindness. "Dearest Fly, you know you mean the world to me and that I will always be there for you if you need me. You also know that in life, we cannot always have what the heart yearns for. I ask that you take the love you claim for me and honor me by letting me go without any anger or resentment.

"Fly, I have not wanted to hurt you, but you have hurt yourself by insisting on a life that is not ours to live.

"I was waiting to tell you until after your wedding to Robert. The time has come that I must tell you that I have a wife, Spring Moon, and I have a baby boy. My life is with my family and my tribe. I have responsibilities and you have always known that I would walk in my father's shoes. Our ways are not your ways."

It seemed to Felicity that time had stopped. There was silence except for the soft rustle of the tree branches in the breeze. She felt as if ice water had been splashed on her face. Then a waterfall of tears poured down her cheeks as she sobbed out words with a bitter tone.

"You should have told me, Dan-Pete. You should have told me. How could you be so cruel?"

He looked over her head with empty eyes. "I could not tell you."

"It's—it's the child that hurts the most. Dan-Pete."

"Fly--"

"You must have taken this woman the moment you turned your back on me."

He had tried not to touch her, but now his hands grasped her shoulders, hurting her with their grip.

"Spring Moon did not come to my wigwam until the second year. Even then, I did not take her out of love—or even lust. I took her because it was expected of me. I am a chief and I must have sons. How is it that you refuse to understand my responsibilities?"

He loosened his hold on her shoulders. "I have come to have reverence for her. I have come to love her as the mother of my child."

Felicity winced as if he had hit her with a whip.

Again, he took her shoulders in his hands, this time with infinite tenderness. "Fly, listen to me. I never stopped loving you, never. I still love you. Don't you know that? You must feel it. You know the heart has many ways of loving."

She lifted tear-filled eyes to meet his. "I will never love anyone but you, Dan-Pete."

"Don't say that," he implored. "Go home, Fly, and make up with Robert. He is a fine man. You will come to love him as I have come to love Spring Moon."

She shook her head, pulled herself away from him. "I'm afraid my love is not as perfidious as yours, Dan-Pete. I'm stuck with it. You never loved me anyway," she went on, a sudden flush of anger climbing up her neck to her cheeks. "All you ever really cared about was your 'destiny'. Well, you've got your destiny. I hope you're happy with it!"

Her eyes swept away from Dan-Pete in the hope he would not see the anger in her eyes. She jumped up from the bench and then whirled with a great flouncing of skirts and ran from him.

He stood motionless, making no attempt to stop her flight. She had not gone far when she halted of her own accord, stood trembling for a moment, then turned. The expression on her face was so pathetic it would have wrung a heart far less vulnerable than Dan-Pete's. Her eyes begged him to come to her and he did.

"Dan-Pete—forgive me. I hate my vicious tongue. It's always saying things I don't half mean. You hurt me so. I wanted to hurt you back."

"Oh, Fly--"

She was choking on held-back sobs. She was acutely aware that Jim Moriarty might be hovering around the corner and she did not want another confrontation with him.

"What I said earlier I meant. I will always love you, Dan-Pete. Always. Goodbye." Fly rubbed away the tears from her face to regain control of herself. Fly felt numb with pain as she realized, undeniably, that her insistent plans for a future with Dan-Pete were not within her immediate reach. She could not reconcile the desires of her heart and the truth she must accept.

They wanted desperately to touch each other, but they both knew if they did, there would be havoc. One last time their eyes met and held an anguished communication. Then she whirled and was gone. This time, she did not turn back.

Jim Moriarty had been an interested spectator. Although he could not hear the conversation between the two, he had made his own assessment. That had been no brother-sister scene. The girl had come on some fool romantic quest. He felt both contempt for her— what in the hell did a girl like that want with a half-breed? --and sympathy—she was so damn young, aren't we all fools when we're that young?

When she reached the sidewalk, she swiped at her face again with both hands in the hopes that Moriarty did not see her tears.

Some would have described Jim Moriarty as a hard, gross man, but he was not without his sensibilities. He gave the pale girl her privacy. Nodded and walked away.

She was not oblivious of his kindness and called out to him "Thank you sir." At the last moment, he turned around and waved. With relief, Felicity ran to the General Store to find Burt.

As the wagon headed homeward, Felicity tried to hold the tears back, but a slow wet stream rained down her cheeks. Burt was not sure what to do and opted for being quiet. He wasn't sure it was his place to ask her what was wrong and did not want to make whatever ailed her worse.

"I guess the feeding and the visiting sort of went on anyway even if there wasn't a wedding," Burt offered.

"I suppose," Felicity said.

"I suppose that's why you wanted to get away, huh?"

Silence.

"I suppose."

"Yes. Thank you, Burt. I appreciate the ride."

By the time they returned to Harbour Hill all the hospitality of the day had been completed and only a few lights twinkled through the windows. It was almost midnight. She sighed with relief while hoping she could slip up to her room and deal with the all the questions tomorrow.

Exhausted by her trip and her emotions, she threw herself fully-clothed on her bed and slept.

When she awoke, it was still dark outside, the lamp by her bedside was lit and Kemink was unbuttoning her boots. Felicity sat up, removed Kemink's hands from their task, and looked at her with betrayed eyes. "Kemink—why didn't you tell me? You must have known. Why didn't you ever tell me?"

"Yes, I knew," Kemink said. "I wanted to tell you, little daughter, but the words were not mine to say. Dan-Pete had made me promise I would not tell you. He promised me in return he would tell you in his own time. He knew Robert was courting you and he felt once you were married, his words would no longer be any pain to you. We thought to spare you. Instead, we hurt you more."

"Kemink, tell me one more thing. Are you—are you pleased with Spring Moon?"

Kemink sat down beside Felicity on the bed and took her hand. "Yes, Felicity, I am pleased with Spring Moon. She is a fine young woman."

Felicity pulled her hand away and flung herself back on the bed burying her face in a pillow. "I hate you, Kemink. Right now, I hate you."

"I know," Kemink said, stroking the young woman's hair.

Felicity sat up again and threw her arms around Kemink. "Oh, Kemink--I love him so much. I love him so much and I can never have him—never. I can't bear it...-"

"You will bear it. You have no choice," Kemink said, wiping Felicity's tears. "This only can I promise you, sorrows well-borne bring forth unexpected and beautiful fruit."

"I'll never be happy again."

Kemink stroked Felicity's cheek, but her voice was firm. "That, Fly, is up to you."

* * * *

Firefly—Firefly—You exasperating girl, how could you leave your home on your wedding day? How could you chase after me when you have always known we cannot be together? Dan-Pete's heart cried out.

If he had chosen to live in the white world for her sake, there would be many conflicts that he knew neither Firefly or he would be equipped to deal with. Dan-Pete also knew Firefly would have given him things Spring Moon never could despite all her Indian goodness and her dearness to him.

That night Spring Moon felt his desolation and knew well what was behind it, she knew she had won the battle, and in her generosity held no rancor that there had been a battle. She drew her husband into the solace of her firm young arms.

Even in the comfort of Spring Moon's arms, Dan-Pete felt as if part of his spirit had fled to a high rock outcropping to howl like a wolf driven from its pack.

CHAPTER 4
Transitions

***

*"If I say, I will forget my complaint, I will leave off my heaviness,
and comfort myself:"*
(Job 9:27)

Mother looks older than Bay, Felicity thought, as mother and daughter sat together in the garden swing and the bright afternoon sunlight revealed all the tiny etchings of lines on Caroline's cheeks, and illumined the silver strands in her hair. Although she had not long been forty years old, there were more silver strands now than dark.

Yet Felicity envied her mother. With Caroline, the lines and gray hair seemed not to matter. At parties and social gatherings, her radiance eclipsed younger and more beautiful women. Men and women alike always crowded about her mother.

"They ate all the ham, geese, and pate' and we even served the wedding cake. There seemed no reason to let it go to waste." Caroline was recapping the day before. "The string orchestra played and Robert appeared. He was very charming and managed to joke a little, but I can't conceal from you in private he was crushed, especially because you didn't face him yourself. That was unconscionable to run off like that, Felicity."

The younger woman gave a savage push with her foot, which set the swing going back and forth at a wild rate.

"Mother, please don't lecture me. You know I've suffered enough for not listening to you and running off to see Dan-Pete."

Caroline planted a firm foot to stop the swing from rocking so violently. "Nevertheless, Fly, you must see Robert. You owe him that much."

"I don't feel as bad about Robert as I might, Mother," Felicity admitted. "He's so good looking and charming, and the banker's son.

19

Every girl in Peshtigo wanted him. I know the news wasn't out five minutes we weren't getting married, before half a dozen of them were all a-twitter and had set their cap for him. Robert won't be 'broken hearted' long."

"And when you see him walking down the street with some other pretty girl on his arm—will it bother you?"

The daughter met her mother's eyes. "No, Mother, it won't, that's what tells me more than anything that I don't love Robert."

Her gaze dropped and she plucked at her skirt with uneasy fingers. "I'm ashamed to admit it, but it was all the other girls wanting Robert which made me flirt with him in the first place. I guess I just wanted to beat the competition—and then—then something else, though I didn't think it out this clearly then. I think somewhere deep inside of me I believed Dan-Pete would never let me marry another man."

She sighed and gave the swing a desultory push. "I had some silly idea that at the last minute when the minister said, 'Can any man give just cause why this marriage should not take place?' Dan-Pete would appear and whisk me off. Well, I got disabused of that idea, didn't I?"

"Don't be bitter, Felicity."

"Oh, I don't know if I'm bitter, Mother. I just feel lost. So lost. Where do I go from here?"

"Bay seems set on moving to Appleton. Come with us there. It should be a very exciting milieu for a young woman. The city is becoming a culture center from all I hear."

Felicity turned pleading eyes on her mother. "I don't know what I want to do. I feel like sawdust inside, Mother. Can you understand?"

"Of course, I can. But life will have to go on, you know. By the way, your father is still here."

For a moment, the young woman's eyes lit up. "Oh, how could I have forgotten about Papa! Where is he?"

Bay had been a surrogate father for Felicity long before Caroline had married him. He had always been so good to her that despite her love for her real father, Felicity had felt only Bay could take her up the aisle. The problem of stepfather versus real father had been solved by asking her real father to perform the ceremony since he was an ordained minister. As it turned out, neither man had to play a role.

"He's at the Peshtigo hotel. Even after all these years, Adam and Bay aren't easy with each other. He felt he would be more comfortable at the hotel than at Harbour Hill, but he promised not to leave without seeing you. In fact," she turned in the seat, "I think I hear a carriage coming now."

She rose from the swing and called to Rosalie, the little daughter who had been born to her and Bay. The child had been playing nearby with new kittens the mother cat had just brought out into the light of day.

"Time for your nap, Sweetkins."

The child came to her mother, her blond hair bleached by the sun, a black and white kitten clutched in her arms.

"Can kitty come?"

"No, honey, I'm afraid not. Kitty is still too little to be away from her momma. When she is bigger, you can bring her into the house."

Caroline replaced the kitten with the others and picked Rose up. Halfway up the garden path, she encountered Adam.

"Good afternoon, Caroline."

Years of preaching had given his voice a magnetic resonance which still touched some chord in her she could not explain.

"Hello, Adam. Firefly's in the garden. She's looking forward to seeing you."

For a moment, their eyes held, then she nodded and passed him. He turned and watched her retreat for a moment before continuing to the garden.

"Papa!"

He heard Felicity's glad cry as she caught sight of him. She bounded to her feet and hugged him.

He was a broad-shouldered man, still trim in his dark well-tailored clothing and flawless white shirt. Half his face had the texture of pink satin ribbon, scar tissue from the burns he suffered during the Great Peshtigo Fire. The ribbon of scars gathered and puckered, drawing the corner of his mouth out of alignment in a way that made his face grotesque. He had lost the sight of his eye on that side from burns as well but he was able to hide that disfigurement with a black patch.

Felicity's fingers traced the scars on her father's cheek. He wore those scars because he had wanted to save her life on the terrible night of the fiery holocaust.

"I'm so glad to see you, Papa. Let's stay here so we can be alone. Do you mind sitting in the swing?"

"Of course not." He settled himself beside her. "Your mother told me you ran off to see Dan-Pete. She said you would come home with a broken heart. Are you broken-hearted?"

"Yes, Papa. I am broken-hearted." His tone had been light. Hers was not.

"Ahh, I see. I haven't seen much of Dan-Pete since he became a grown man, but he was a plucky little boy. That he was."

"I'll never love anyone else, Papa."

Adam laughed. "Of course, you will. A beautiful girl like you, they'll be fighting for your favor in squadrons and one day you'll..."

"Papa, can I ask you something?"

"Of course."

"Do you still love Mother?"

The teasing light went out of his eyes. "Of course, I love your mother. Everyone loves your mother."

"That's not what I mean, Papa, you know it isn't."

"Okay. You deserve an honest answer. I adore your mother. But it's like loving a star in the heavens—or loving George Washington. She's beyond my reach. All it can be is an abstract emotion just as Dan-Pete is beyond your reach now, Felicity."

"Why then have you never remarried, Papa?"

"I married Sally."

"But Sally's dead." For a moment, both father and daughter remembered how Sally had perished in the fire.

"Who would have me?" Adam demanded, laughing with a gesture toward his mutilated face.

They both knew this was not true. Adam Quimby had become a legendary figure in the Tomorrow River country where he carried on an unorthodox ministry. Some people called him Queer Quimby because of his grotesque face and because it was known he was a wealthy man with gold mines and a mansion in San Francisco yet he chose to wander forever homeless in the Tomorrow River country.

His ministry was no longer from the pulpit, and now without exhortation. Where there was trouble he would mysteriously appear and stay if needed. A hard-pressed farmer would find Adam beside him getting in the hay. A widowed mother would find an unexpected hired hand while she was trying to get her bearings. The old and the sick would find a nurse looming above them.

There were tales of how he had nursed a little boy run over by a wagon until the child walked again; of a young woman who had lost three children in a fire and gone mad—of how he stayed with the family for months until he had restored the young woman's sanity and returned her to her husband's arms. There were stories of money given to those who did not ask and refused to those who petitioned for it.

Adam well knew in his heart that in many of the lonely, isolated farm houses where he stopped, overworked, neglected women had seen past his scars and yearned for someone like him. He was aware of his own magnetism. In his younger days, he had used it to his own ends, and doing so had led his spirit to a black and devastated place, until all his soul cried out for was redemption and restoration. At first the covert glances of these sad, tired women had filled him with dismay. He had not come to fuel their romantic fantasies and leave them emptier than before. Then gradually he had relaxed and left it in the hands of God, for he saw the men of these households were not unaware of their wives' soft sighs and warm glances. Adam's gentleness and kindness to their mates awakened in them a realization of their own neglectful or brutish behavior. Sometimes when he left, a husband and wife were on a tentative but new and promising footing with each other.

"Oh, Papa, plenty of women would have you and you know it. I hear stories about you all the time. You're becoming a legend. It's disgusting," Felicity was saying.

"Disgusting?" Adam laughed.

"Yes, disgusting," Felicity insisted. "It's bad enough to have a mother who everyone considers practically a saint without my father becoming one, too. And Danny—my brother's just a beautiful person. And your Jimmy—he patterns everything he does on Danny so he's going to be a beautiful person, too. And Rosalie—oh, Papa sometimes I'm just wickedly jealous of her. She looks exactly like Bay, but she's Mother over and over again in disposition. It's natural for her to be good."

Felicity put her arms around her father's neck and buried her face against him. "Oh, Papa, why do I have to be the only one who's selfish and wicked and mean-tongued? Why is it always such a struggle for me?"

"Why, Firefly—Fly, darling," Adam said. "What's all this?"

"I—I want to be like Mother, but no matter how hard I try, I just can't be like her."

He took out his handkerchief and, tilting her face up, mopped at her tears.

"Dear child, all of the qualities you have are wonderful qualities," he assured her. "Your mother has some qualities you don't, but you have a lot of qualities she doesn't. The things you feel are so dreadful about you are some of the qualities most marvelous when they're channeled in the right way—passion, enthusiasm, ambition."

Her father's words were of great comfort, but his words also reminded her that she needed to live up to these words and strive to be less selfish.

She rested her head on his shoulder. "Papa, you always make me feel better. Maybe I should come back to the Tomorrow River country with you for a while."

He smoothed her hair. "I'm afraid that wouldn't work. I don't even have a house to take you to."

"You could buy one."

"No, little girl, I couldn't. All the money I have is really Sally's money. God and I have a pact about her money. It isn't mine. If anything, I was a worse husband to Sally than I was to your mother. At least I loved your mother. And my ministry takes me first here then there. I can't give it up, Fly. It's the only thing that gives me rest—propitiation for sins more terrible than even those you know of. See to it you use your gifts well. Don't end up as your father did."

"Well, nevertheless—you give me hope, Papa. If you were such a blackguard and now are up for sainthood in Tomorrow River country maybe there is hope for me."

They laughed together and the tears dried on her cheeks.

"What will you do now? Would you like to go to San Francisco? Your mother says you are very talented musically. Would you like to study at a musical conservatory?"

"Mother and Bay may move to Appleton. She says it's very exciting there and I should come along."

"Sounds good."

"I don't think I will go, Papa."

"Why?"

"Because if she goes they will need me here."

"If you had married—"

"I was still going to come back here to teach music and language and run the school."

"Bay's wealthy, they can hire someone."

"I think I want to stay here, Papa."

"Don't do that, Fly," he said. "I think it's important you get out into the world for a while, learn new things, do new things. Don't stay here and brood about Dan-Pete."

Felicity's face went woe-be-gone again. "Wherever I am I will brood about Dan-Pete, Papa. I can't help it."

"Make up your mind you're not going to and you won't," her father's voice was stern. "Now, dear, I suppose I'd better see if I can find Jimmy and spend a few minutes with him before I leave."

Jimmy was Adam's son by Sally. Caroline and Adam had once waged a fierce legal battle over the boy's custody. Caroline had cared for the child when Sally wanted to be free of him while Adam was in the war. Adam longed for his son's approbation. It was hard to come by.

"You're not staying for supper?"

"I think not. I'll keep in touch with you, dear. I love you a great deal."

"I love you, too, Papa."

They embraced and then she watched with regret as her father left. She wished he would have stayed for supper but she knew it was best for him to go. Bay would not have been too pleased to see him at the table.

CHAPTER 5
A Good Gardner

***

"Trust the LORD with all thine heart; and lean not unto thine own understanding. In all thy ways acknowledge him, and he shall direct thy paths."
(Proverbs 3:5-6)

Caroline felt troubled. She was concerned with Felicity's problem and there were other things disturbing her as well. For months, Bay had been taking the train to Appleton and Menasha searching for just the right site on the rushing Fox River to furnish power for a sawmill. The more his lumber business had thrived, the more he could see he needed a mill of his own. Now he had found the site—what he called the "perfect site." Caroline was joyous for him. His business was flourishing and he had exciting dreams and plans, but they presented a wrenching problem to her.

The lumber business in Peshtigo was well set up. Bay had good men under him, and it could almost run itself. The sawmill, on the other hand was going to be an ambitious undertaking which would require Bay's constant attention. Running back and forth on the train was impractical. He was planning on moving to Appleton and it never occurred to him she wouldn't go with him.

Every time he came back from the city, he brought new blueprints of the mansion he intended to build her and reports of all the delights Appleton and Menasha had to offer her. He was like a kid getting ready for Christmas. The sawmill site had been purchased and the foundation stones were being laid for the house. Instead of being filled with happiness, Caroline felt somber and torn.

She loved Harbour Hill. She had expected to live all her life there. But that was not what tore her heart. She would have gone with Bay to the ends of the earth and been happy except it meant leaving her children behind. Not just her blood children—Danny and her troubled

Felicity were old enough to buck their own tides. Little Rosalie and Jimmy, of course, would go with her--but not those other children who were part of her heart if not of her blood.

Some of them, like Jenny and Josh and Gret, were older now and had gained strength enough over their difficulties. They could fend for themselves, but the thought of some of the younger and more fragile ones—blind Patrick, the two little German boys the world would have labeled imbeciles, Mary who had been disfigured by smallpox and who would not face the world now, little Paulie who had lost both legs in an accident—these children were like spikes nailing her to Harbour Hill. How could she leave them? How could she make Bay see a life in society, however cultured, would seem empty to her compared to this work which seemed so vital?

"Bay, the house is going to be so big," she had said, studying the blueprints, "Can't we move the whole household to Appleton?"

"Yes, Caroline, we could," he had said, quiet disappointment in his voice. "I'm tired of you working yourself to a rail. I want to give you a life of leisure and luxury for a change. What does all my success mean if I can't translate it into the things I want to give you—the experiences I want to share with you?"

Oh, Caroline thought, *if I could just divide myself into two people.* She did not want to deaden Bay's dreams and joy. She knew Harbour Hill had not been fair to him. From the moment he had married her, he had had to share her with two dozen other people in a demanding schedule which left them precious little time for each other. Bay had never complained. He had given unstintingly of himself to the Harbour Hill situation. Now he was asking for some time with her. He was asking her to let him do all those things he longed to do for her. She felt as if she were tied to two horses running in opposite directions.

In all the years of their association, Kemink had never once interfered in Bay and Caroline's affairs but now she, too, had spoken.

"Your destiny is with your husband, Caroline. You must go. Danny and I will continue with Harbour Hill. All will be well. If there are special problems Danny will come for your counsel."

Caroline could not have asked for more from her loyal friend, but this, too, was a bludgeon to her heart—to be separated from Kemink? This majestic Indian woman was more to her than a sister. She was like Caroline's other half. She worried too, this was not fair to Kemink. The burdens of Harbour Hill were heavy and Kemink was no longer a young woman.

As for Danny—Danny was marvelous. Harbour Hill was, and had to be, a self-sufficient farm because all but a few of the children were charity cases and had relatives who could pay little. Danny had long assumed the responsibilities of the dairying, haying, and crop productions. She knew it would be a burden for Danny to take on all the duties of the household, which would inevitably wear him thin.

The worst of it was Danny's wife, Emily, would not be able to help and support him in this hard endeavor. She had only recently come into the "land of the living." A strange, beautiful little girl, she had lived in a world of her own, refusing to speak or perform any of the functions of normal life. Her prominent father had brought her to Caroline in desperation. Even Caroline's dedication had brought scant improvement over the years. It was Danny's love which had at last unlocked the crystal cage which had held her apart and made her willing to enter the realities of his everyday life. Emily was still shy and fragile. Expecting her to take over a household like Harbour Hill was impossible.

Caroline took a walk through her garden, which always soothed her. Then she sat on a small bench and closed her eyes, going deep within to the place where she always found answers and peace. She wanted Bay's happiness as much as her own. There had to be a way.

She met Kemink on the path. "Mr. Gorsuch is waiting for you," she said.

"Oh dear, I had forgotten all about him." Caroline said in consternation. "Thank you, Kemink."

Mr. Gorsuch was a reporter for a prestigious monthly journal in New York. He was well-known for his biting articles that debunked the rich and famous or the notorious and revealed their foibles. Caroline suspected he wanted to interview her because her darling Bay was so clean and upright Gorsuch could find no dirt on him. While Caroline, as a healer, might be suspect.

She wanted no publicity about her healing work and had wanted no part of being interviewed by him, but the magazine's promise of thousands of dollars to charity made it difficult to refuse. She had at last given in.

She gathered up her skirts and hurried to the porch where she found him rocking in a rocking chair.

Frank Gorsuch was waiting for her with his well-manicured fingers tapping the table beside him and one-foot swinging in annoyance. He was short and portly with quick dark eyes, a full moustache and well-barbered hair. He leapt to his feet at the sight of her.

"Mrs. LeSeure, I presume."

Caroline smiled and invited him to reseat himself. When she had settled herself in a chair, he leaned far across the small table that separated them and looked at her with narrowed eyes.

"You are purported to be a healer, Mrs. LeSeure, someone who affects miraculous cures. Is that true?"

"No, Mr. Gorsuch I do not 'purport' to be a healer. At best, I am a channel for God's healing, and in a certain sense, even that is untrue. In truth, not even God is a healer."

He stared at her. "Are you saying that even God cannot heal?"

Caroline sighed. It was always so hard to explain, especially since she didn't fully understand it herself, and she knew he was likely to twist her statements and bring calamity upon her.

"God doesn't heal because there is nothing to heal," she tried to explain.

"Nothing to heal? But you yourself have been credited with miraculous cures of terrible things like smallpox, consumption, and cataracts. Are you trying to tell me that none of these things exist?"

"They do exist to our human sense, Mr. Gorsuch, but the moment we lose that human sense of their existence they are gone. I don't know how to explain it to you."

"Well, perhaps you can explain this to me, Mrs. LeSeure," he said with a growing tinge of sarcasm in his tone. "You tell me that you are not a healer and that indeed there is nothing to be healed, and yet you run this school—or home, you call Harbour Hill, especially for crippled and other unfortunate children. Isn't it true that you lead the poor parents of these children into false hope?"

He did not wait for her answer but began to riffle through a briefcase pulling out papers which he waved at her. "These are interviews I have had with people as far away as Chicago and San Francisco. People who came to you believing you could heal and were disappointed. People who, in fact," he paused for effect, "believe that you, Mrs. LeSeure, are a charlatan."

"Mr. Gorsuch, you know I did not want this interview, you forced me into it. One of the reasons I did not want to do it is because of what you just said to me. Every time an article is printed about my work, I soon find throngs of people at my doorstep begging to be healed. Some of them have spent a great deal of money and come a long distance, expecting me to pull fire from heaven. When they don't get a healing, it is heartbreaking. And please, Mr. Gorsuch, by all means do quote me, for perhaps it will discourage a repeat of such happenings."

"Are you then in fact confessing, Mrs. LeSeure, that you are a charlatan and have no power to heal?"

Caroline felt a rising sense of irritation heating her cheeks. "I have never claimed to have healing power, Mr. Gorsuch," she said, forcing herself to be patient by reminding herself of the money for charity. "It has sometimes happened that I have been able to be a channel for healing, but the power is not mine. God knows that I wish I knew why some people are healed and others are not.

"I wish it were as sure as putting a kettle on the stove and having it boil. But if you are familiar with the verse in the Bible that says Jesus did no great miracles in his own country because knowing he was a carpenter's son they did not believe."

"Faith—so it comes to Faith Healing," Gorsuch cried, triumph in his voice, as if he had finally backed her into a wall.

This stupid ox, Caroline thought, *he is never going to understand and why must I sit here with him when I have so many more important things to do? This stupid o ...* Then abruptly shame flooded her. *What am I thinking? Please Father God let me see him with the eyes of love.*

"You are saying then that it is the fault of the people who come to you for healing if they are not healed?" he was pressing her. He was excited. His face was flushed. And suddenly she did see him differently. She saw a small, anxious man fighting it hard, he *wanted* to believe. He needed to believe. He had come for this story because somewhere deep inside of him he was sinking into despair.

Now it was she who leaned across the table. She took one of his hands between her own and said in a tone now suffused with love and warmth, "Dear Mr. Gorsuch, you really do want to understand, don't you? Will you come into the garden with me? Maybe I can explain better there?"

He followed her down a brick path. She stopped now and then to pick a rose, a daisy, other flowers whose names he did not know, always taking his hand again and leading him on until they came to a large, neat vegetable garden.

Her eyes swept the plot and came to rest on a plant at the end of a row. "Ah, yes, there." She drew him closer, pointing out a bean plant somewhat shriveled and yellow beside the more flourishing plants in the row.

"Within each seed there is a pattern of perfection, Mr. Gorsuch. God has done his work. This plant too has that pattern of perfection. But if you look closely you will see that the soil at the end of this row is rocky and there are several weeds around this plant that got missed."

She knelt and laid her bouquet down. She pulled the weeds and stirred the soil around the plant with her fingers. "We do not know, Mr. Gorsuch, why this plant was planted at the end where the soil is

30

not good. But the pattern of perfection is in this plant also."

Caroline looked up at him. "Now that the weeds have been removed and the soil stirred I will tell the children to give it extra water. This plant too will begin to flourish. Within a few weeks, you will not be able to tell it from the others."

She stood up and brushed the dirt off her hands and picked up her bouquet. "If you come back and the plant is like the others, will you say it is a miracle? Of course not. You will say that I am a good gardener."

She smiled at him and took his hand again to lead him back. "People are like that plant. Only the weeds are things like fear and anger and the soil that needs stirring is their faith in themselves and in God. And the love we pour out to them here at Harbour House is like water. Do you understand now?"

She stopped and looked at him and he felt her love surround him as physically as if she had put her arms around him. He found it disconcerting, unbearable. He could not believe his own emotions.

"The only person who ever loved me was my mother. She's been dead for thirty years." How could he have said such a thing? He was amazed at himself.

Now she did indeed put her arms around him, locking her radiant eyes on his she said, "Frank, you are loving and lovable," with finality that settled it for all time.

"I assure you, I have no desire to be either lovable or loving," he snapped. "I will promise you one thing. I will be fair."

Caroline laughed. "I cannot ask for more than that. Let's get these flowers into some water and, of course, you will stay for dinner."

"I think not," he said, "but I will escort you back to the house." He extended his elbow; she laid the fingertips of her unencumbered hand on his arm and they promenaded back to the house.

****

Later, aboard the train that would carry him back to New York, Frank Gorsuch scribbled in his notebook. "What a damn, charming woman Caroline LeSeure is. Ten more minutes with her and she'd have wrapped me around her finger like a ribbon."

He did not, of course, put that in his article, but as he promised, he was fair. He began by describing how beautiful Harbour Hill was and acknowledging that though some of the children did not look quite normal, they all seemed healthy and happy.

His article went on to quote people who gave grateful accounts of the 'miracles' attributed to Caroline, followed by an equal number of quotes from people who had been disappointed and disgruntled and were quite willing to call her a charlatan. He tied this together with a few accurate quotes from Caroline, then ended the article by saying, "I must confess there is not enough evidence to prove that lumber baron, Baird LeSeure's charming wife, Caroline, is either a charlatan or a female Jesus Christ. All that I can conclude for you is that she is a very good gardener."

Caroline gave the article to Bay to read and he groaned, "I thought he was going to do a hatchet job on you. Now we're going to find throngs of people pounding on our doors again!"

"He really is a lovely man in his own way," Caroline said. She did not tell Bay that she was grateful to Frank Gorsuch because he had helped her find peace with her dilemma of moving to Appleton. If God did indeed want to use her as a channel for healing, people would find her in Appleton, as they had in Chicago and Peshtigo. She trusted her life to God.

She also repented for thinking that the handling of Harbour Hill would be too great a burden for Danny. He had worked hard in the fields and with the animals. It was time that he hired that kind of help and took over the reins of Harbour Hill. He was a magnificent young man and should now have the right to expand to his fullest capacities. It was after all, his love, not hers, that had freed Emily to rejoin the human race. Danny too was a healer.

Caroline felt a return of peace. For the first time, she began to take a real interest in the house plans when Bay brought them to her and his gratification was sweet to see.

* * * *

Danny loved his work at Harbour Hill but he always felt a keen sense of joy when it was time to return to his own cottage, the cottage he had built for Emily on a wooded section of the property. Although along with his joy and anticipation at returning each evening there was a slight edge of trepidation, too. He was angry at his fear but it was there.

He was never quite sure what he would find when he got home. The strange inner world from which he had coaxed Emily still seemed to threaten at times to lure her back. There were times when he came home and the house was dark, silent, no meal cooking. He would find Emily sitting in the darkness, her hands folded, her face expressionless and his heart would leap with fear. But always his voice, his gentle touch would rouse her.

Once he had come home and found the house empty. He had run out to the sheds and then into the surrounding woods calling her name. When at last he found her, it was deep into the woods, and she was on her hands and knees under a gnarled tree, sobbing.

That time and only that time she had tried to tell him about her "other world." Back in the cottage, he had wrapped her in a blanket, brought her hot tea, and chafed her small hands in his to bring them to warmth. She had clung to him sobbing out incoherent words. Then as she grew calmer in the circle of his arms, she talked more lucidly.

"When I get frightened here, Danny, it's nice to go back there."

"There?"

"When I get anxious and upset and feel I can't do things right, they call to me. They say— 'Emily—Emmmilly, and I know I can go back there and nothing in the world can touch me or hurt me."

"Oh, Emily"

"No, no, it's all right, Danny, I don't want to leave you ever." She covered his face with feverish kisses, "And besides they lie you see—that's the thing—they lie."

"They?" He wanted so to understand.

"Yes, they make it very beautiful and safe at first so you want to go, but if you stay there—Oh, Danny," she clutched onto him, "it's worse—worse than anything. There are all those voices screaming at you," she shuddered and buried her face against him.

He held her close caressing her hair. "It's all a lie, Emily," he told her. "A bad dream. It isn't real."

Now as he turned the buggy along the curve of the driveway he saw a light in the kitchen window and felt the fine little feathers of fear inside him unfurl and relax. He unhitched the horse and led him into the barn. He would feed him later.

When he opened the kitchen door, he was greeted with the wonderful aroma of fresh baked bread and the sight of Emily, one curl dangling across her cheek, a white apron covering her gown, buttering the tops of the crusts.

"Emily! You've made bread—it smells wonderful." He came in and whirled her into his arms.

She laughed and shook her head. "No. I didn't. Kemink came this afternoon. She made it, but I watched. Next time I think I can do it."

Danny blessed Kemink. Kemink was the one person besides Danny whom Emily felt comfortable with. Emily was shy even with his mother, gentle and loving as she was, and was frightened of Felicity with her high voltage energy and passionate ways. Silences with Kemink were never threatening, and both women shared a love of the forest and the creatures that lived in the wooded area. Many a day, Kemink would come and take the girl with her into the forest or spend an afternoon showing her how to do things in the kitchen.

"I made soup to go with the bread. It's ready if you want to eat."

"You're so beautiful," Danny said. His mother had always told him beauty was only skin deep so he sometimes felt guilty for reveling so in Emily's beauty. It was like owning a living masterpiece to watch her, he thought, the golden light of the lamp modeling her cheeks, the little shadow under her chin, the sheen of her hair.

"I could eat you up," he said.

"I should eat you up," she said. "You're late."

"I know. I'm sorry. But you know how it goes at Harbour Hill some days. Anyway, I brought you a present for amends." He reached into the pocket of the light jacket he wore and pulled out a small brown-wrapped parcel. "I'll give it to you after we've eaten."

She gave a squeal of joy. "Oh, Danny, it's the poetry book I wanted, isn't it? Oh, let me have it now, please, please."

He held it out of her reach, shaking his head. "Not until I'm fed."

She launched an attack on him in a flurry of white apron and bouncing curls trying to snatch it from his hand. "No, you don't!"

He led a merry chase all through the house, dodging behind settees and darting around doors. But it was after all a small house and who can say he did not want to be caught, for they ended up in a tangle in the big sofa, laughing and out of breath with her in possession of the book.

He kissed the back of her neck as she bent her head to unwrap the parcel.

"Oh, it is," she breathed. "It's the new volume by Wordsworth. Oh, Danny, I love you so. Thank you."

"We'll read from it together later," he promised her, "but right now I am hungry. The smell of that bread is tantalizing." Arm in arm they went back into the kitchen to eat.

After they had eaten, Danny helped with the clean-up and then Emily put a shawl around her shoulders and went with him to the barn. While he curried and fed the horse, she played with the two black and white kittens he had brought her from Harbour Hill.

"The kittens are growing so," she said to Danny. They rolled before her in the hay, their round little bellies taut with the milk she had given them earlier, their pretty white paws flailing at the piece of straw with which she tickled them. "They're so adorable."

"All baby things are cute," Danny said. "You should come with me tomorrow to Harbour Hill and see the new calves."

"Danny—when are we going to have a baby?" It was not the first time she had asked, and always Danny's heart had sunk like a weighted anchor. There was an edge of fear. Was she ready for a baby? Could she be trusted to take care of it? Then the quick rush of shame at feeling that fear. It was his love and faith in her actual wholeness which brought her healing this far. If he doubted her—

He had spoken to his mother about Emily's desire for a child and his own struggles with fear. She had said, "Give it some time, Danny. She's getting better."

"In due time, in due time," Danny told his wife now, tossing the last forkful of hay into Brubaker's stall and then leaning his chin on top of the fork handle and regarding her with tenderness, "I want you all to myself for a little while yet."

She was not fooled. Her eyelashes drooped, her lower lip trembled.

"Emily, don't cry," He squatted down in the straw next to her. "We'll have a child. I promise you."

"Soon, Danny?"

"If God wills it."

He tickled the cats with his finger, laughing at their antics.

"What have you named the kittens?"

"Mew and Meow."

"That's ridiculous."

"No, it isn't. It's appropriate."

"You're right. Which is which?"

"Meow is the boy."

They put Mew and Meow back into the box of straw Emily had fixed for them and went back into the house. Emily served Danny tea made from the pretty teapot they had received for a wedding present and then cuddled in his arms as he began to read to her from the new poetry book.

"Give all to love:

"Obey thy heart" and so the evening passed.

* * * *

Danny and Emily were pleased a short time later when Felicity consented to take over Caroline's work with the young people living at Harbour Hill. Caroline had established a small classroom and study hall, with a large glass window in the partition between. Felicity could work with a child and monitor the activity of other students who were playing together.

Caroline spent most of her time in Appleton now, overseeing the completion of the fine home Bay was having built for them. Rosalie and Jimmy completed the family, and Caroline began to feel rested and content. The fact Felicity was proving sensitive and competent in working with the children gave Caroline the needed assurance that the move to Appleton was blessing her more than she could have imagined.

And for the first time, Felicity felt her life might be worth something. Several busy years soon passed. Overseeing the care of the children, their squabbles, their progress in speaking, etiquette, and even in basic education gave her a fulfillment she never dreamed of wanting or having.

Part of her was still Firefly—and quickened and then ached unbearably every time she heard Dan-Pete's name.

CHAPTER 6
Hans Jacobson

***

"Pleasant words are as a honeycomb,
sweet to the soul, and health to the bones."
(Colossians 3:14)

Seven years later:

"Felicity, I want you to meet Hans Jacobson." She had been so busy she had not noticed her step-father come into the room. Bay was visiting Harbor Hill on business. "This young engineering genius has designed a sluice gate for the mill which is going to solve untold problems for us."

Felicity looked up from her desk to give a perfunctory greeting and then was surprised by the powerful figure of the man standing before her. He was not as tall as Bay—few men were— but close. He was young and flush-cheeked with red blond hair, wide gray eyes, and strong facial features. He wore a loose white shirt and his neck rose out of it from broad shoulders like the neck of a bull. An energy emanated from him in a wave, like an intrusion. Wherever he was, he would be the kind of man who could never be ignored, Felicity thought.

She was polite, even though she was not pleased to be interrupted. "How do you do, Mr. Jacobson?"

A huge hand grasped hers. "I am well. And you?"

"He'll be staying for dinner, Fly," Bay said. He still forgot and used her old nickname. "Will you please tell the kitchen?" I think this needs clarification. Some might not understand it means 'the help'...

The two men left but it was as if someone had thrown a huge boulder into the still waters of her mind and ripples were still spreading. Felicity's attention had been broken. With a sigh, she got up and went to the kitchen to tell Kemink and the cook there would be an extra person for the evening meal.

At dinner, Felicity felt Hans Jacobson's intense gaze. She was no stranger to admiring glances. She had been used to them, and indeed expected them ten years ago, but it had now been some time. And even then, she had never enjoyed or suffered such steadfast and unashamed scrutiny. She was more amused than flattered or offended.

"So, you are an engineer, Mr. Jacobson. Did you go to Harvard?"

"No, Ma'am."

"Mr. Jacobson has been in America a short time," Bay offered. "He came over from Denmark about three years ago."

"Oh, then you studied at a European university?"

"No, Ma'am."

"Hans has a natural genius for engineering, Felicity. He has picked up by himself everything he knows through observation and experience."

"Ahh, well that's even more laudable," Felicity said. A great conversationalist he is not, she thought to herself.

Jenny came in bringing a silver tray of apple tarts.

Felicity folded her napkin. "I don't believe I will have dessert tonight. If you gentlemen will excuse me I have a great deal of work to do."

The young giant bounded to his feet, bowing.

Felicity ducked her head at him and was glad to escape to the privacy of the library and her waiting work. She had just begun however, when she felt someone looming behind her.

She looked up with a slight irritation. "Yes?"

"Miss LeSeure?"

"Miss Quimby. Bay is my step-father."

"Miss Quimby. Do you think I speak good English?"

Her irritation was tempered again by amusement. "Why yes, Mr. Jacobson, you speak English very well. The lovely lilt to your voice is the only clue you are not a native.

He looked pleased. "May I sit down?"

Thinking of the work still to be plowed through, she did not want him to sit down, but she didn't want to be rude to Bay's friend either. She nodded.

He pulled the nearest available chair even closer, so close his knees were almost touching hers when he sat down.

"I worked hard to learn to speak this well. I was determined. The spelling and writing of English I do not have down so well. My pride prevents me from going to school with the little children. I went to the school mistress here in Peshtigo. I asked if she would instruct me in the evenings. She is old and her health is frail. She was regretful but she said her energy would not permit her."

He looked at Felicity with an expectant expression.

"Mr. Jacobson, I'm sure there must be other tutors in the community who will be glad to help you."

"Your step-father thought perhaps you would help me." His deep-set eyes were fixed on her in a penetrating way. In any other eyes, she would have said, with pleading, but there was not so much plea in those eyes as command. She felt her irritation flow back.

"Ahh, Mr. Jacobson, I am not old and frail like Miss Pritchard, but my time, too, is congested with many responsibilities." She nodded toward the reports she was writing to families of the children. "As you can see many of my evenings are already taken up with school responsibilities. We all cherish a little time for ourselves." She gave him a winning smile to take the edge off her refusal. "I'm sure you can appreciate and sympathize with my dilemma. Why don't you contact Reverend Burke's wife? She's well-read and their youngest child has just left home so she might have time."

"Miss Quimby, I want you to teach me." The unwavering flame of his glance burned with an intensity she could not ignore. To refuse his kind of desire would be an insult she knew. Confound the man! She would have liked to throw a shoe at him and tell him to get out. Instead she found herself saying in a weary tone, "If you insist, Mr. Jacobson, but I can't give you more than one night a week. I will give you enough assignments to keep you busy the rest of the week on your own. Would that be satisfactory?"

A slow smile spread across his face, crinkling at the corner of his mouth, revealing strong white teeth. The smile of a charming boy softened the blunt masculinity of his features.

"That would be most satisfactory."

She could feel his happiness fill the room like water gurgling around rocks. She found herself smiling back.

"All right, what day would you like to come?" She pulled out her little notebook to write it down.

"In the evening."

"Yes, which day?"

"Saturday."

"Saturday? Are you sure? Everyone goes to town on Saturday. That's when they have all the parties and dances and picnics. You're a young man..."

"Saturday." he said.

"Very well. From seven until nine o'clock. All right?"

"Forgive me," he said, face flushing a sudden red. "Perhaps you...you will miss the parties and picnics."

"No. I don't attend parties often. I was thinking of you."

"Seven until nine. Then it is so."

She nodded and waited for him to leave.

He continued to look at her. "Would you begin with me tonight?"

"No," she said, not caring anymore if she was being polite or not. "Can't you see I have all this to do?" Again, she gestured at her desk. "Saturday. Next Saturday."

A sigh swelled in him and escaped with windy sadness. The happiness in the room drained away. His face was bereft without its smile. But he stood, took her hand and kissed it, his full warm lips lingering longer than necessary against her skin. Then the radiant smile crept back. He bowed.

"Saturday," he said, and left.

The minute he was gone she was the one that sighed and shook her head in frustration. "Why did I tell him, yes," she scolded herself. "I don't even think I like him." She remembered his smile. "On the other hand, I'm not sure I don't like him," she comforted herself. Still she was angry for not having found a gracious way out. Wait until I get hold of Bay, she thought, and bounced up to find him. She was too agitated to work on her papers now anyway.

Bay was closing the door on his guest when she attacked him.

Bay met her sputtering and fuming with his usual laughter and charm. "Oh, come, Fly. He's a good fellow. You will enjoy him. He's brilliant. He's going to be a great asset to this country. And you will have helped. That should make you feel good."

So, it began.

On Saturday, he arrived a half hour ahead of time, his red-blond hair darkened with water and rose oil in a vain effort to make it lay smooth, a bouquet of daisies clutched in one large hand. His collar was high and starched, his jacket impeccable.

She put the flowers in a bowl and took them along to the library where they would begin their work.

He at once flung off his coat, loosened his cravat and unbuttoned the top buttons of his shirt. She was disconcerted. Catching her amazed look, he smiled his disarming smile. "I cannot work well, unless I am comfortable."

"I see," she said. If he gets too impossible I don't have to go on with this, she promised herself.

She sat down beside him at the small table she had provided. "The first thing we must do is find out what level of proficiency you have gained," she said. "Let me get a teacher's manual...I will start with the fourth-grade test. If you have no trouble with that we will go on to a fifth-grade test."

He worked hard, his jaws clamped, his head bent low over the papers she had given him. Within twenty minutes, he handed her the completed sheets.

"Sixth grade," he said.

She looked at the work he had done and agreed. "We will start with the sixth-grade text."

It was the first of many evenings sitting together in the circle of light cast by the large kerosene lamp, the grandfather clock in the library ticking a slow accompaniment to the passing hours. The only other sounds; the stirring or shuffling of their papers and their two voices on occasion murmuring a litany of grammar.

"Have...has...and had."

"Have...has...and had," his deeper voice echoed.

"Present, past and past participle."

"Present, past and past participle."

He was a quick and eager student. When comprehension came, he would redden with pleasure and his engaging smile would come. He was a joy to teach. She could not have said at what moment her disgruntlement over this new chore became a pleasure. She only knew she came to look forward to Saturday evenings.

CHAPTER 7
Joy Comes Softly

***

"That I may come to unto you with joy by the will of God,
and may you be refreshed."
(Romans 15:32)

Spring came in a sudden rush. One day the earth was blanketed in graying snow and hoary icicles hung from every building. The next a warm rain, then fog came dissolving the snow like magic, and sending icicles crashing and filling the day and all night with gurgling's and drippings of symphonic majesty. On the third morning, Harbour Hill was an ark floating in a lake, and the horses in the barn were snorting and rearing at the smell of spring. Two days later the lake drained into the soil leaving a muddy morass and, from such primeval material, spring arrived overnight. On the seventh day, a new world had been completed—grass, buds, singing birds, buttercups in the meadows, and cowslips in the muck along the creeks.

Harbour Hill, like most of the other homes in the area, was torn apart with the arrival of the new season. Every window was thrown open to evict the stale air of winter. The boys of the household grunted and huffed as they manipulated mattresses and feather ticks down stairways and narrow landings to air in the sun. Clotheslines were lined with carpets which both boys and girls beat with wire whisks sending out clouds of dust which made them sneeze.

All the women in the household were swathed in head cloths and aprons, armed with vinegar rags, scrubbing brushes and Fels Naptha soap. Kemink scrubbed, then polished the stoves with stove black until they shone like patent leather while Danny supervised, carrying soot-filled pipes out for emptying. In the back yard, the boarding children, Gret and Jenny, soaked and scrubbed all the bedding and curtains, then helped Kemink pin the lace panels on frames to dry.

Felicity, sleeves rolled up and a smudge of dust on her cheek, was examining paint swatches Mr. Carleton, of the Peshtigo General Mercantile, had brought out in person for her inspection.

"Hmmm—no, Mr. Carleton, I don't want green for the library. We have a blue Aubusson carpet in there. And the walls have been blue for so long I do want a change—so not blue. Something light"

"How about oyster?"

"Oyster?"

Intent on the paint swatch Mr. Carleton had handed to her, she was not aware Hans Jacobson had come into the room and was standing before her. When she lifted her eyes he was there, she was startled.

"Hans! What are you doing here? It's not Saturday." Then she flushed at how ungracious that sounded. She laughed, patting at straying locks and rolling her sleeves back down. "Forgive me—you've caught us in some disarray."

There was an air of suppressed excitement about Hans. His color was high and there was a smile on his face that wouldn't go away.

"May I talk to you alone for a minute, Miss Felly?" He had given her his own nickname.

Felicity looked at Mr. Carleton, "Uh—well"

"It's all right," Mr. Carleton assured her. "I'll get Kemink to give me a cup of coffee. I'm not in a hurry to get back to the store anyway. We're spring cleaning there too."

"Thank you, Mr. Carleton. I'll be back soon. Come then, Hans, we'll go into the library."

Because the library was one of the rooms to be painted it had been stripped of furnishings and carpet. All the windows were open and the room felt bare and chill. Hans' voice echoed off the empty corners.

"I've been offered a wonderful position. I'm to be the chief engineer at the Grand Army Home near Waupaca. The water, the heat, the lighting will all be my responsibility. I will make everything operate with perfection."

His face was like a child who has just been given a train set for Christmas.

"Well, Hans, I'm very happy for you. Proud for you. I will miss our study sessions, but you are doing so well I think you will have no trouble going ahead on your own."

"I want you to come with me today to Waupaca to see what they've established there, Miss Felly. It's like a small kingdom, a paradise, you'll see."

Felicity shook her head. "Hans, I couldn't possibly go. You can see what a mess we have here."

All the joy left his face. "Miss Felly, you cannot know what it would mean to me."

Why did this man always think his convenience mattered more than hers? Felicity thought with resentment.

"Hans, dear, I would be happy to come sometime, but not today." She put a firm hand on his arm to guide him out. "Why it must be ninety miles from here. I doubt we'd even be able to get back by tonight."

"Of course, you must go, Fly." It was not Hans' voice. Felicity turned in surprise to see her brother, Danny, in the doorway. "I didn't mean to eavesdrop but I couldn't help overhearing. You haven't had an outing all winter. You need to get away sometimes too, little sister. Go get your things on. Go with Hans and have a good time. It's a beautiful day to play hooky."

"But Danny," Felicity protested, feeling beleaguered with her brother joining in Hans' well-intentioned but ill-timed demand, "I can't go today. I have no intention of going off and coming home to find the library has been painted purple or something. Mr. Carleton is waiting right now."

"I'll send Mr. Carleton home, and we won't put an inch of paint on until we have your approval tomorrow. Everything can wait until tomorrow."

"Danny. Look at the time. We'd never get back tonight."

He was propelling her toward the door.

"I can't go off with Mr. Jacobson and stay all night."

Danny was grinning at her. "We trust your morality, Felicity. I'm sure Mr. Jacobson will find proper quarters at an inn if you can't make it back tonight. I want you to go, Firefly. You work too hard and have too little fun."

Danny was always supportive and kind to Felicity. He seldom made a request or command, so when he did she found it hard to refuse him.

He had propelled her as far as the stairway now and with a small shake of her head, she gave in. Why not? Yes, she would go. Run away from it all for one day.

"Tell Hans I won't be long," she called back as she ran up the stairs.

In the back of her closet, she found a dimity dress printed with bluebells and trimmed with lace. It had been a long time since she had worn it but it seemed suited to the day. The last time she had worn it with blue ribbons in her hair, and her fingers touched her ribbon drawer.

44

She stared at the face in the glass above her bureau. "You are beyond the stage of ribbons in your hair," she told her reflection, her expression becoming stern. "But—not so far beyond," she told herself with more kindness. The little girl roundness was gone from her cheeks but her eyes were still bright, her skin unlined. In two more months, she would be thirty-five.

She compromised by stringing a locket on a blue ribbon and wearing it around her throat. She found a warm shawl to take along, tied on a leghorn hat and ran down the stairs with something of the eagerness of the old Firefly.

Hans was waiting for her at the foot of the stairs. All the children in the vicinity stopped what they were doing to stare at her. They had never known her to go out with a man. After the first surprised silence, there were titters and giggles as Hans took her arm. She could have shaken the lot of them!

"Children can be so silly," she said.

He smiled in answer.

Hans did not have a horse of his own yet so he had rented a carriage from the livery. The horses pranced in their harnesses, eager to move on this warm and sunny spring day.

He lifted her into the carriage with solemn care, as if she were something fragile and precious that might break.

The roads were still muddy. The horses' hooves made a sucking sound as they tried to trot smartly despite the uncertainty of their footing. Farmer neighbors were already in the fields with their work teams and waved a greeting as the carriage passed. The air was exhilarating. It seemed charged with the burgeoning growth of spring surrounding them, with just enough sting in it to bring color to their cheeks and for Felicity to be glad she had the shawl to wrap around her. She was glad she had come.

Hans said little at first, but every time he looked at her, he smiled with a contagious joy.

By noon, they were hungry. There was no inn close by so they traveled another hour until they came to a prosperous looking farm and stopped there, offering to pay for a sandwich. The good farm wife would have none of that. Her food was free to sojourners for the exchange of news and the novelty of new faces. She brought them cold frothy mugs of milk and frizzle-fried ham on thick slabs of homemade bread.

When Felicity had eaten the huge sandwich, she was sure she would never eat again she was so full, but Hans assured her by the time they reached Waupaca, she would be famished again, and they would dine at the famed Delavan Hotel.

As they continued their way, he became talkative, telling her things he had never told her before.

"My mother's name was Rasmeena," he said, "I was twelve when she died but I remember her well. She had blond hair, the longest of any woman I ever saw. Even braided it hung below her waist. She wrapped the braids round and round her head. At night, she would unbraid it and brush it out before the fire. My father used to call her hair 'dwarf's gold.'

"My father was not rich, but our family is of good stock and well respected in Lolland where we lived. Lolland is a large island, which lies just below Sjilland where Copenhagen is located. He had a small but prosperous farm and was a sexton of the Lutheran church. A devout, God-fearing man. You would like Rodbyhavn, the village nearest our farm, Miss Felly. There are cobblestone streets, and though the houses seem a bit crowded against each other, they are all neat and well painted and everyone plants flowers in their window boxes and on their doorsteps."

"It sounds lovely, Hans. Why did you come to America?"

"Had I been the oldest son I would not have come," Hans said, his face grown serious. "The love of land and family is deep in the Jacobson's culture. But I was the youngest, and though they would have shared with me, my father knew, and I knew, there was not enough from the farm for Jake, Nels, Christian and me all to raise families. After mother died, he asked if I was willing to be an apprentice and I said I would be happy to do so. He found me a good master, Pieter Hansen. Pieter was the cartwright for the village. He made wheels for every purpose, including the waterwheels which ground our flour and sawed our wood, and he was of an inventive mind, always trying this and that to see if he could make something work better. I learned a great deal from Pieter.

"When I was twenty, though I loved Pieter, I began to get restless. I wanted to be my own man. He understood. He took me with him to a Science Fair in Brussels, and there I saw the most wondrous thing of my life."

There was a dramatic pause. She had to urge him to continue.

"Well, tell me Hans—tell me what was so wondrous."

"Electricity, Miss Felly. Electricity. It was—it was like seeing God."

"E-lec-tri-city? Is that what you and Bay talk about so much? Some new kind of power you are going to pull out of the water?"

"You pull it out of the sky—out of the air. It's like stealing lightning from the sky. In Brussels, they had a bell jar all hooked up with coils and wires, Miss Felly. They threw a switch—and that was the wondrous moment—the moment like seeing God. A light came on, a light brighter than the sun, because the sunlight is golden and this light was white. Brighter, brighter than anything you can imagine. So bright you could not look at it any more than you can stare at the sun. The closest thing would be lightning. But this was not a flash across the sky. This was lightning captured in a bell jar. It lasted about as long as a flash of lightning in the sky. But it was within the control of man, and that changed my life, Miss Felly. From then on, I was no good to Pieter, or to anyone else for that matter. All I could think of was I had to learn to capture lightning in a bell jar like these men in Brussels had done."

Felicity was caught up in the excitement of his narrative. To think I thought he was no conversationalist, she berated herself.

"Did you do it, Hans? Did you learn how to capture the lightning?"

"Yes, I did. But it was years before I could do it. For six years, Pieter put up with me and my coils and jars and experiments. He got a new apprentice to help with the wheels. He was himself fascinated, you see. He told me, 'Use your mind, Hans. Find out these new secrets and someday you will make us both rich.' In the meantime, he was content to feed me and to help me. I had once helped him and learned from him. Now he helped me and learned from me. "

"Six years is a long time, Hans."

"Yes, it is a long time. A very long time for an impatient young man. Yet the time did not seem long. I lived in a constant state of excitement. And when the day came I finally got a spark into my jar— when I finally made the light, ah, Miss Felly, I could have gone to heaven right then."

"Did this knowledge make you rich as Pieter expected?"

"Not yet. But in time it may. Already I am to have this fine new job because of my knowledge learned in those years."

The sun was sinking, beginning to cast rose shadows over the landscape, ribboning the horizon with amethyst and gold. The horses were no longer trotting smartly, they had come a far piece and they were tired. Felicity was surprised she was not tired from the long journey although her body ached some from the unaccustomed jolting. She was glad however when Hans told her they were not far from Waupaca. They would be there before dark.

The Delavan Hotel was as elegant as Hans had promised. There were thick carpets, real linen napkins, candlelight. Felicity had to admit to herself it was pleasant to be dining on sumptuous fare with an attractive man. Danny was right, it was doing her good to get away for a day or two and see new sights.

Over the meal, Hans went on with his story explaining how he had come to America.

"Mr. Frankbaum, a visiting American from Chicago saw my experiments and he invited me to come to America and work on a project in Peshtigo. He had half interest there in a sawmill. So, it was I came. Me and my younger sister, Seena. The two of us we came. For Seena, he arranged employment in a rich man's house in Chicago. There was also at the house a young man who took care of the horses, Joseph Armilen. Within a year, he had asked for her hand in marriage. He is a good young man, and I was pleased enough about it. Now Seena has someone else to look after her and I no longer have to worry about her alone in a huge city."

In the warm dining room, full now of food, Felicity found she was surrendering to weariness after all. "It has been a lovely day, Hans, but I am growing tired," she confessed.

"I've arranged for rooms," he said, "And we should retire anyway. We will have to be on our way early, or we'll not make it back to Harbour Hill tomorrow."

He walked with her to the door of her suite and kissed her hand in parting. "Bless you, Miss Felly, for coming with me."

The bed was soft, the linen impeccable, the room was neither too hot nor too cold, but Felicity Quimby spent a restless night. She dreamed of Dan-Pete and Robert Anderson and strange white lights.

CHAPTER 8
Tomorrow River Country

***

"Oh that I might have my request;
and that God would grant me the thing that I long for!"
(Job 6:8)

The morning dawned as beautiful as the day before. They had an early breakfast, eager to make the last few miles which led to the Soldiers' Home to be on the road together for as long as they could before they would reach home. The sky was a tender blue, heaped high with confections of clouds. Rock outcroppings and water along the way were spangled with sunshine. The edges of the road they traveled were red with last year's pine needles still damp with ice melting beneath the leaves and needles the winter winds had picked up.

The horses, refreshed, stepped lively again and Hans had to rein them in on many curves of the road. The farther they went, the thicker the trees became until they were traveling through great avenues of trees filled with a greenish light with an occasional wink of blue sky above them. Red and gray squirrels spiraled barky trunks. Except for the jingle of harness and pound of hooves? the morning was unusually silent.

Felicity felt as if she had entered a fairytale kingdom remembered from her childhood, for this was the Tomorrow River country where she had been born. She had been taken from the area while she was still too little to remember but perhaps some infant memory still stirred—or was it the many stories Danny and her mother had told her?

There was a smell of fresh water and pine and damp leaves and earth. She kept inhaling deeply like a thirsty person filling a cup.

"Oh, Hans," she said, "it's a wonderful morning to be alive."

He smiled at her exuberance. "We've not far to go now. Would you like to stop and stretch for a minute?"

"No, I'm fine," she said, which was a bit of a lie because her body still ached from the travel of the day before. "What a curvy road this is."

"That's because it's following the river," Hans said. "Water always takes the path of least resistance and so did the Indians. Many of these roads were once Indian paths and the Indians made paths to the places where the river could be forged. The Indians have not been great bridge builders. That is interesting to me. The red man bends to nature's way. The white man bends nature to his way."

Hans said it with pride but Felicity rode in silent thoughtfulness for a time. She remembered Dan-Pete's frustration that his Indian people preferred to live in poverty rather than cut down living trees.

But who could say what poverty was? Perhaps they had a richness the white man would never know.

"Why so silent?" Hans asked after a time.

"I was thinking of Kemink," Felicity said. "I was thinking of the mystical rapture she has with the earth and all the things in it. I was thinking she and Thoreau are peers and she and Emerson would understand each other at once."

Since coming to America, Hans had acquired the prejudices against the Indians rampant among many of the white settlers. He had been puzzled at Harbour Hill to find Kemink treated as if she were a goddess. He did not understand. To him she appeared to be an aging, heavy-set Indian woman who did some cooking for the family. Why she was paid such continual homage by the entire household was beyond him.

Thoreau and Emerson were mysteries to him as well. Though he read English, his time for reading was short and his natural inclinations led him to read scientific and political journals and texts rather than more literary compositions. He had no ready answer to her comment and simply nodded.

"We're but a stone's throw now," he told her. "Right around the next curve then a straight road to the Old Soldiers' Home."

They left the river and the pine forest grew less dense. The horses banked around the curve into a flood of sunlight which dazzled a large white building in the distance. In a few more minutes, they arrived at what seemed like a white fortress or a low-slung castle standing carved out against a deep evergreen background. A moment later, they were at the hitching post near the front entrance. A long columned porch stretched between two rounded turrets at each end.

"Here we are," he said with pride as he drew up the horses. They sat for a moment, contemplating the scene before them. The morning's silence was broken now by a sound of hammers and the whine of saws. In the trees, crows screamed while woodpeckers made sharp staccatos. A dog barked.

"It's still being built," he explained. "When it's complete, the Grand Army Home will be bigger than most villages. Like...like a world all its own," he ended with satisfaction. He jerked the reins and chirped to the horses. "See all those little buildings going up across from the main building? Those will be separate cottages for the soldiers well enough to care for themselves. There will be a post office, a store, supply buildings, a chapel."

A Mr. Winters, who was to be the Commandant, met them at the door.

"Mr. Jacobson, Mr. Jacobson, we are so glad you are here," he said, jerking Hans' arm up and down as if it were a pump handle. He turned his pleasant, pink face toward Felicity. "And this is your lady? How do you do?"

"I'm...I'm..." Felicity growing pink herself was about to say she was Hans' tutor not "his lady" but found herself stuttering because she wasn't sure Hans wanted it disclosed he needed a tutor.

"Miss Felicity Quimby," Hans rescued her.

"...happy to meet you," Felicity managed.

Mr. Winter took them on a tour of the main building where soldiers of the Civil War were already in residence. Then Hans and he disappeared into the recesses of space beneath the building leaving Felicity with a cup of tea and one of the old soldiers for company. The man, named Henry Collins, was thin and hollow-eyed but blessed with a merry smile and a gift for gab.

"It's a good thing the people of Wisconsin have done to put up this place," he said with enthusiasm. "The men who are here and the ones who are coming have need of this haven, and believe me, young woman, they deserve it. The Wisconsin fighting men had no peers, the commanders will tell you that. There was a saying that one Wisconsin regiment was worth six ordinary regiments."

"Really?" said Felicity, intrigued. "To what do you attribute such superiority?"

"Why, we're just naturally a better lot," Henry Collins said, laughing.

"Tell her the truth, Henry," a laconic voice spoke from the center of the porch. A man older than Henry was sitting on the steps, whittling staves.

"Awright, the truth," Henry said, swiping across his heart with a horny forefinger. "We had good leadership. Most of the other states divided their fresh troops into regiments and sent the poor greenhorns into battle. Our commanders were wiser. The new troops were dispersed among existing regiments. Our recruits had the advantage of being with veterans who knew the score."

"Going to war must be terrible," Felicity said.

Neither man spoke for a few moments and Henry Collins' eyes had a momentary glazed and far-away look.

"I...I didn't mean to say the wrong thing," Felicity apologized.

Henry leaned forward to pour more tea into her cup, forced himself cheerful again.

"Yep, the Wisconsin regiments were the best, though some of the other states would give you a fight about it. And few of us started out with any notions of being heroes, I'll tell you. For myself I went for selfish reasons. Had a nice little farm up near Marshfield and my wife was carrying our first child. Enlisting was the only way I knew to get some cash to buy us some land and a team of horses to break it. I figured I could stand anything for ninety days. That's what we enlisted for—ninety days. That's all we figured we'd need to whip those rebels."

"You talk too much, Henry," the other man said, "always running off at the mouth."

"Did you get out in ninety days?" Felicity asked.

"Hell no...oops, excuse me, Miss, I guess I ain't use to being around ladies anymore." Henry apologized. "No, by the time my ninety days were up I was in the hospital with dysentery and in no shape to go anyway. Then when I did get back on my feet," he looked down, his fingers plucked at his suspenders, "well, I got word my wife had died of pneumonia. Took the 'little one' with her of course. Didn't seem much reason to go home anymore. I stayed for the whole show."

"Just goes to show you Henry's crazy," said the voice of the man on the steps.

Henry gave a good-natured chuckle. "That commentator down there is named Willis Hawkes and he was in for the whole war himself, so he must be as crazy as I am."

A man at the end of the porch lifted his hat to Felicity and she bowed and nodded in acknowledgement. Two terrible things had become clear to her at the same time; this "old" man talking to her was not old at all in terms of years, he was maybe forty, and Henry Collins had no legs.

When she had first come, he was sitting at a table at one end of the porch. He had nodded to her but not risen. Now sitting next to him, she understood why. A gust of wind had lifted the tablecloth which had hid his stumps from her view.

She was rescued from her pity and confusion of whether to say anything or not by the return of Mr. Winter and Hans.

"I'll show her the cottage myself," Hans said to Winter. He took Felicity's hand.

"Goodbye, Mr. Collins, Mr. Hawkes," Felicity said, "thank you so much for..." she had been going to say, "for keeping me entertained" and broke off at such shallow words.

Henry grinned and waved, "Always enjoy a pretty face. You come and see us any day!"

Hawkes said nothing, his head bent over his whittling.

"Come back at noon. We'll serve you lunch in the main dining hall," Winter called after them.

Felicity clung to Hans' arm, still moved by Henry Collins' incapacity.

"Oh, Hans...I thought he was an old, old man...but he was just a boy when he went in with a young wife expecting their first child. And now...now he hasn't any legs."

Hans stopped to stare at her. "You're crying."

"I can't help it. He...he's so cheerful and gallant, not complaining or feeling sorry for himself."

Hans took out a handkerchief and brushed the tears from her cheeks. "Today is to be happy. Only happy," he told her.

She nodded and tried to comply. After a few moments, it wasn't hard. The grounds were so beautiful, the spring day so heady, it was indeed a day made for happiness. The smell of fresh wood and sawdust hung in the air now as they passed buildings under construction. Workmen waved to them from doorways and rooftops.

"That will be the engine room of the power house," Hans said, pointing out a large square structure which was just in the process of being painted. "That's where all the turbines and machines will be located."

Felicity wasn't much interested in machines but she nodded and tried to be enthusiastic as he waxed eloquent about the magnificence of the machinery which would provide heat, light and water to this kingdom. The light of joy in his eyes meant more to her than his descriptions of the machinery.

"I'm glad for you, Hans, so glad you have found something to do which excites you so much."

"Now," he said, steering her to turn on yet another path, "here is the cottage which will be my home."

Set back among the leafy new green of some big deciduous trees, was a large cottage of new construction, freshly painted. Hans drew her inside.

There was a big kitchen, beautiful hardwood floors throughout, and a handsome fireplace in the living room. Felicity loved the large windows in the dining room and the long-mullioned windows in the library; but the most impressive thing to Hans were the indoor bathrooms—two of them. He delighted in showing her many times how the flushing mechanisms worked.

They did not have indoor plumbing yet at Harbour Hill but Felicity was not unaware of the concept for Bay had installed indoor plumbing in the home he had built for Caroline. Felicity was a little embarrassed by Hans' concentration on the china fixtures and the sewerage system to go with them. She was glad when his attention was diverted to lead her up the open stairway to show her the three bedrooms upstairs.

"I know it is not as elegant as Harbour Hill," Hans said to her, "but it is a nice house wouldn't you say? A nice place to raise a family."

"It's a charming house, Hans," Felicity agreed. "Anyone should be pleased to live here."

"Would even you be pleased to live here, Felly?"

"Of course. It's a beautiful house," Felicity said, not at all absorbing the import of what he had just said to her, bending her head to peer through a little window, and running her finger over a bit of sawdust.

He grasped her shoulders with his hands and turned her to face him. "Felly, did you hear what I just said to you?" he demanded, his tone deepening with emotion.

She was startled by his taking hold of her in such a way. "No...what?" she said in confusion.

"Do you want to live in this house...with me?"

She was shocked. Her face went white. Even Hans could see her amazement was unfeigned.

"You cannot have been so blind to my feelings for you all these weeks?" he demanded, his cheeks burning.

"Oh Hans...I'm sorry, I didn't know...didn't. I never...You were my student, my pupil. I'm older than you are. It didn't occur to me"

"Don't tell me that. Don't tell me you had no idea."

"Well...yes, I guess...I guess I did think maybe you were a little 'sweet' on me. But Hans, dear Hans, I had no idea you were serious about me."

"And you felt...feel nothing for me?"

Her eyelashes lowered. "I...I don't know. I'm older than you are,

Hans. I haven't thought of you in that way."

He gave her a little shake. "Felly, look at me. Don't look down. Look at me. You have not had any awareness of me as...as a man?"

Felicity found it impossible to lie to Hans. She met his burning eyes and dredged up the truth she had not even admitted or examined herself.

"I am aware of you as a man, Hans."

He relaxed his strong hold on her shoulders.

"All right. We will start from there."

"Hans, I'm too old for you..."

"I don't ever want to hear that again," he said. "You are not so much older than I am, maybe five, six years. That's nothing. It doesn't matter."

She could see he was bitterly disappointed. He had constructed this happy scene in his mind of bringing her to this lovely home and having her accept their future together with joy and excitement. To discover she had never even considered him in this light was bruising to him.

A loud gong sounded interrupting their private and emotional scene.

"The dinner bell?" Felicity guessed.

"Yes. We might as well go back and have a meal before we start home," Hans conceded. His face was a deep red, his pale eyes fired with inner emotion.

Felicity walked by his side, outwardly subdued, but inwardly filled with a maelstrom of emotions of her own.

"Hans," she said in a low voice just before they reached the main hall, "please forgive me for my stupidity. I should have known."

"You know now," he said, a note of gravel in his voice. "We will take it from there."

CHAPTER 9
Dance of Happiness

***

*"That I may come unto you with joy by the will of God,
and may with you be refreshed."*
(Romans 15:32)

Hans Jacobson and Felicity sat in the library, which had ended up being painted oyster. Rain slithered in silvery streaks against the windowpanes, and thunder growled above the roof like a prowling animal. A small smoky fire struggled on the grate. The clock's ticking seemed unusually loud.

Hans sat rigid in his chair, his eyes riveted on Felicity's face. Her fingers smoothed the ruffles at her throat with a nervous gesture. All I can do is be honest, she thought.

"Hans, we haven't known each other very long. I need more time."

"I begin my new job at the end of April. I want to take you there then as my bride."

"That's too soon, Hans."

"Once I've moved there will be many duties, and I will be far from you. I will not have the opportunity to make such a long trip often to court you."

"We could write to each other."

"Either you want me or you don't." The room was filled with the tension of his masculinity and his emotion.

"I like you very much, Hans, but...but I'm not sure I love you," she said forcing her honest words out, knowing they would wound him. How could she tell him her heart was still all tangled up with Dan-Pete, and that it always would be?

The fire sputtered, the clock ticked while he absorbed what she had said. He got up and moved to the settee to sit beside her.

"But, you're not sure you don't," he said.

"That's it...I'm not sure of anything." His presence beside her was overwhelming. She felt suffocated. She wanted him to go away.

"You will come to love me." It was as much of a command as it was a statement of belief.

"But what if I don't?"

"Then..." with a sudden deepening of tone, a tenderness she had not suspected him capable of, "the love I have for you is so great it will be enough for both of us."

He put a hand on her back, and then with the other on the back of her neck drew her mouth to his. His lips nuzzled hers leisurely but with an intensity that at last caused her lips to part. He pulled her closer, hard against him, and she began to struggle, frightened by the currents of physical sensation he was evoking. His lips slid from her mouth to her neck and followed it down to the beginning curve of her breasts. He turned his head a little and looked up at her. Looked at her dilated eyes, her flaming cheeks. "You love me," he said.

At that moment, she knew that if he had gone on she would not have stopped him. She didn't want the sensations he was arousing in her to end. She wanted more and more of what was happening to her. Hans Jacob Jacobson knew how to kiss.

The test was to have been whether he would wait for her or not. He would not. Either you want me or you don't.

* * * *

Hans Jacobson and Felicity Quimby were married on April 28, 1892 at her mother's home in Appleton. Without sentimentality or regret, she wore the dress Emily had so lovingly made for her years before; quite pleased with herself she could still fit into it.

The wedding was a large social affair in keeping with the prominence Bay and Caroline had achieved in the area and was reported in detail in the Appleton newspapers. The newspapers did not report the passing sadness the bride felt as she looked at the assembled guests. A few were friends of Hans, most of them were friends of her parents. She had not realized how isolated she had let herself become. She had few friends left of her own.

Her half-sister, Rosalie, was her bridesmaid, so blond and gorgeous at fifteen she almost stole the show from the bride. But Felicity felt with deep regret she hardly knew Rose. She had always harbored a slight jealousy toward the younger girl. Bay was an utter fool over his daughter and although he had always been the soul of kindness to Felicity she had often watched them at play together with a secret pang. Once he had made over her like that, called her his "little princess of Chicago." She knew her jealousy was unworthy and hated herself for it. After all, besides Bay's unquestioned devotion, she had the love of her own father. She wouldn't have given Adam up as a father for any other in the world.

"Are you, all right?" Adam asked, gazing into her eyes, as they waltzed midst the roses and pink streamers and glittering table of punch bowls.

"Why of course, Papa," she said, "I'm wonderful. I'm a married woman at last and everyone can stop worrying about me."

"You didn't marry Hans Jacobson just so everyone would stop worrying about you?" The frown of concern was deepening in his brow.

"Of course not, Papa." She gave him a roguish grin. "Hans kisses very well."

The lines of concern softened and he laughed. "Are you trying to shock your father?"

"Don't you like Hans, Papa?"

"I haven't had much chance to find out, Firefly."

For some reason, the old childish nickname brought sudden tears to her eyes, a burning to her throat. The music had stopped. She gave her father a quick kiss and turned away.

"Papa, I want to see Kemink a moment. I'll find you again soon." She didn't want him to see the treacherous shine in her eyes. Besides, it was true, she did want to see Kemink.

She found the Indian woman as she had suspected she would be working in the kitchen. Kemink smiled when she saw Felicity approaching. The two women embraced for a long time and there was tear shine in the eyes of both.

"Kemink, thank you for all you did for my wedding...for both my weddings...for all you have done for me all my life."

"You are as my own daughter."

"I know, and I can't thank you enough. I often haven't deserved it."

Kemink shook her head. "From the time, you were born you were a dear little girl, and now you are a dear woman."

"Oh, Kemink thank you for believing in me. Sometimes I don't believe in myself." The tears were coming now.

Kemink's warm, strong fingers wiped the tears away as they had so often done in her childhood.

Felicity laughed a shaky laugh. "I don't know what's wrong with me. I'm so emotional today."

"It is a very special day in your life. A day which will bring great changes. It is not unnatural you should feel strong emotions and some fear," Kemink said.

Felicity looked out the window. "Does Dan-Pete know?"

"Yes."

"What did he say?"

"He is happy for you."

"No. I want to know his exact words, Kemink. Tell me."

Kemink hesitated for a moment. The pressure of Felicity's fingers on her arm told her how much she needed to know.

"He said, 'I am glad for her. All I have wanted for her was to be happy.'"

"Yes. He has borne a large burden of guilt about you for many years, thinking that you were unhappy. Dan-Pete feels at peace with you now knowing of your happiness."

"Yes, I'm sure he does," a deep sigh escaped from Felicity. She turned back toward the window. Thank God. What Dan-Pete had felt at her marriage was relief, as she had felt relief when Robert Anderson had married. All these years she had imagined Dan-Pete loved her. Maybe he never had. And what did it all matter anyway? Her mood had turned bleak.

"Where is my bride...where is my wife? Where is Mrs. Hans Jacobson?" Hans' strong voice sang out behind her.

She turned, hoping the tear stains did not show on her cheeks.

"Here I am, dearest," she said, walking into his outstretched arms, smiling into his eyes.

* * * *

Deserted by his daughter, Adam Quimby's eyes swept the scene before him, looking for a familiar face.

He saw his son, Jimmy, so much like himself as a young man, dancing with a dimpling, laughing Rosalie. Jimmy and Rose, like Felicity and Dan-Pete, had been raised as brother and sister though in actuality there was no blood kinship. They seemed devoted to each other but without any of the dangerous romantic complications which had blighted Felicity's life. Rosalie was already the center of an admiring male coterie though still so young she appeared not to realize it. While Jimmy, twenty-seven now and a rising young star in his stepfather's lumbering affairs, was becoming serious about a young woman, Julia.

Adam longed to reach out to his handsome younger son, but his overtures through the years had taught him Jimmy would reject any such advances. Pursuing the boy had not worked. If Jimmy was ever to seek out his father it would have to be on his own terms and in his own time.

Danny was kinder to Adam, but their relationship too, was superficial. There was no doubt Danny considered Baird LeSeure his real father. Adam reflected the only one of his children who loved him was Fly. The irony was she was the one he had wronged the most, once giving her away to cruel strangers. He was grateful she did not seem to remember, grateful that Caroline had moved heaven and earth to get her back.

At last his eyes found the face he sought. Caroline was presiding at a punch bowl. Her hair was silver now, but for some reason it made her look younger. Or was it because these last years had been such happy, relaxed ones for Caroline? Adam could not gainsay Bay had been good for and to her. She was flushed with the excitement and joy of the wedding, her cheeks as rosy as the satin gown she wore.

She had been Baird LeSeure's wife now longer than she had ever belonged to Adam, but this occasion was after all, the celebration of the marriage of the daughter of their long-ago-love, which had been valid in its time. Once Adam had thought dancing a wicked sin. He had mellowed through the years, and he wished now he could take Caroline in his arms one more time and dance with her on this special occasion.

She felt his eyes on her and looked up. As if she read his thoughts (or perhaps it was the mute appeal she read in his eyes) she smiled, handed the punch ladle to someone else and made her way through the crowd to him. To his pleasure and surprise, she put one hand on his shoulder and held the other out.

Adam led Caroline onto the dance floor, and mother and father of the bride danced together to the strains of a Strauss waltz. When the music ended, he let go of her with lingering regret. Bay was already waiting for her.

"I say my pretty wench, what is this?" Baird asked. "The moment my back is turned I find you consorting with this blackguard?"

Caroline laughed. "I have to keep you on your toes. I wouldn't want you to take me for granted."

She was starting back to the punch bowl but Bay put his arms around her and led her back to the dance floor.

"I never take you for granted," he said with sudden seriousness, "Every morning when I wake up and find you beside me I am still filled with wonder. You are to me heaven and home on this earth."

"Oh, Bay...Bay," she said, "and you to me."

They had started to dance when the waltz was broken off abruptly, followed by a fan-fare and the appearance of Hans with Felicity in tow.

Hans' hair, slicked back for the wedding ceremony, was falling on his forehead now, he had loosened his cravat, his eyes were fever bright. Felicity looked a little pale.

"In my village in Denmark, when two people get married it is the custom to share with them a dance of happiness with the bride and groom dancing in a ring formed by their friends. Good ladies and gentlemen, will you join me now in perpetuating this custom in my new country." He stomped his polished boots and held out his arms to his bride.

Whooping and laughing, the guests joined into the spirit of the ring dance. When at last, with everyone out of breath, the music came to an end, even Felicity was no longer pale, but hot-cheeked and laughing.

Clinging to Hans for balance, Felicity thought, *it's going to be all right. It is. I will be happy. I'm sure I will.*

CHAPTER 10
Christmas

***

"When they saw the star,
they rejoiced exceedingly with great joy."
(Matthew 2:10)

The first year of marriage to Hans Jacobson was one of the hardest in Felicity's life. The change from Harbour Hill to the Old Soldiers' Home was dramatic. She had always felt she worked hard at Harbour Hill, and indeed she had, but hers had been a privileged position. There were so many other people at Harbour Hill to share the everyday burdens of life she had been able to pick and choose the jobs most compatible with her nature.

In mid-life, she had gone from the position of mistress in a household where she told many other people what to do, to the position of a wife subordinate to her husband. She did not come down to a beautifully set breakfast table replete with Kemink's delicious cooking. She was the one who must come down in the chill of the wee hours and shake the grate and coax the kindling to light. She was the one who must skim the cream for Hans' cereal and fry the bacon and set the bread.

No longer did she find piles of clean clothes on her bed to put away in her bureau drawers. Now it was she who must fill the copper boiler with water and keep the stove stoked so Hans' white shirts would boil snowy white. It was she who had to put her slender white hands into the galvanized washtubs and scrub the clothes on the washboard. No one else spent hours ironing all the pretty ruffles on her clothes. She was the one now who stood sweating and red-cheeked on hot July days transferring sizzling flat-irons from the range to the ironing board.

She had envisioned days of leisure in this pretty cottage under the leafy trees; days of embroidery and poetry and perhaps late afternoon picnics with Hans. She was amazed at the amount of physical work required to keep a household for just the two of them.

The transition from teacher to a domestic was hard. Even harder was the loneliness. At Harbour Hill, her problem had been to find privacy and solitude when she needed it. Seldom could she retire to her room without being interrupted by some servant or child. Besides her duties with the children, which kept her involved with the youngsters all day, there had been the constant nurturing companionship with Danny and Kemink. Oh, how she missed it.

This was a demanding year for Hans too, as he engineered, installed and smoothed the kinks in the systems needed to make this small kingdom function. He left before dawn, came home for lunch but gobbled his food as if he were in a marathon and bolted away. The sky was dark before he returned home for the night. He was tired then and often taciturn, immersed in his own thoughts of how to solve some engineering problem.

On the few occasions when Hans did become garrulous, Felicity found her eyes glazing over. She had no real interest in amperes, wattages, turbines and water diversion. And he found the interests she wanted to share with him even less palatable. Nothing more than that. I would say, that hurt her the most.

Hans had been such an eager student those long quiet evenings at Harbour Hill. She had been filled with excitement of all there would be ahead to share. She would introduce him to Shakespeare and Dickens...to the poetry of Browning and Tennyson and Keats. She had savored the thought of the delight he would experience as she brought Mozart and Bach into his life. She would help him learn to love great art. They would go to Milwaukee to the ballet and opera.

No shock of the new life felt harsher than the gradual realization that Hans had no time for such things. He operated in a sphere beyond her understanding, a world of practicalities and pragmatism. The excitement and charge in his life came from grappling with real and concrete problems and making them bend to his will and his knowledge. Literature, music and art were all right as occasional flourishes, they were fine for women and the effete; but men engaged in the real work of his world had little time to waste on such frivolities.

What had happened to the man who had spoken of his mother's hair as "dwarf's gold" and of "lightning in a jar" and of "seeing God?" What had happened to the poetry she had felt was in Hans?

When she came to him eyes a-sparkle and full of delight with some literary gem she had found, he was indifferent. She felt like a child who comes running from a meadow with glad arms full of dandelions, to have its mother toss them away saying, "Darling...these are weeds."

Adding to all the newness and difficulty was the greatest transition of all. Felicity was now sharing her body with another being. She was pregnant and the second half of the first year of her marriage was a nightmare of morning sickness, lassitude and leg cramps. In Caroline's house, no one had ever been ill, or if they were, it was quickly over. Though she had been born with a deformed arm, it had healed in early childhood, and Felicity had no memory of childhood diseases or even a fever or cold. The worst discomfort she had ever faced was the burns she suffered in the Peshtigo fire and even those seemed to heal miraculously. To be gagging, weak and out of sorts for days on end was almost unbelievable to her.

By the fourth month of her pregnancy, however, she began to feel better. The morning nausea ceased. She felt a resurgence of energy. Her reprieve was short. By the sixth month, she was ballooning to a size of discomfort, and by the seventh month every bend or stoop or stretch in her tasks was arduous. In bed at night, she did not know which way to lie to accommodate this ever-growing mound of herself. By the eighth month, the burden seemed unbearable.

Felicity marveled at other women who accepted this great extension and disruption of their bodies with equanimity, not seeming to notice anything was going on, indeed quite radiant with their approaching motherhood. Felicity hated herself for not being able to carry it off in such a nonchalant way. She was ashamed it was so hard for her.

But the wonder and marvel of the life growing within her was not lost on her. She would stand for many minutes with her hands on her swollen abdomen feeling the piston-like kicks of the child forming within her, transfixed with the realization she was carrying life. Every spare hour she spent preparing the nursery and the layette. Perhaps her anticipations and eagerness were among the ingredients which made her pregnancy seem so onerous and grindingly slow.

Impatient by nature, she wanted the baby to be born and in her arms. Above all, she wanted her body back to herself.

This arduous and difficult first year was mitigated by hope. Once the baby was born, things would be better. Once Hans had all the systems installed and needed only to maintain them, things would be better. As they prospered, they would be able to afford a servant to relieve her of some of the drudgery.

There were also joys along the way. On a cold, snow-covered night in November, Hans came running in charged with energy and élan.

"Felly it's done! The whole electrical system is hooked up for lights. We've tried each section one by one and they all work, but we're ready now to throw the master switch. We're going to brighten this night like a cluster of stars!"

Felly looked up hopefully...there was the hint of poetry in Hans again. He wasn't always official, busy, or completely pragmatic.

He wrapped a shawl around her. "Come on, Felly, I want you to throw the switch. I want you to have the honor."

"Oh, Hans..." she said, startled by the responsibility.

He was pulling her boots on her feet. "Come on, everyone's waiting."

They ran through the cold darkness like children, Felly holding her huge stomach with one hand as if it were a melon which might burst under this sudden strain.

Everyone was waiting. Faces were full of anticipation and delight at what they believed would be an awesome moment. The officials of the Home, the workmen, the ambulatory veterans, even the cooks and laundresses, waited inside the powerhouse and outside it.

The babble of voices ceased when they saw her. Everyone seemed to hold their breath, waiting for the great moment. Inside the powerhouse, the electrical cables and wires and switches looked formidable to Felly. She turned wide eyes to Hans.

"Oh, Hans, I'm afraid...what if...what if I electrocute everybody?"

Hans laughed. "Silly. Would I ask you to do anything dangerous?"

She could feel the impatience of the waiting crowd. Shivering with the cold because the shawl Hans had thrown about her shoulders was not a warm one and giggling with nervous excitement, she threw the switch.

A shout and cheer went up outside. Hans put his arm around her and drew her to the doorway. The main building across the way was blazing with lights, a whiter light than she had ever seen, as if they had indeed captured starlight in every window, light that spread across the snow in long columns like candles of gold.

"Oh, Hans," she breathed, "oh, Hans." For the first time, she had some sense of the magnitude and rewards of the work which so absorbed him.

Afterward, there was punch and nut bread and a celebration in the main hall. Near midnight, they excused themselves to get Felly home to bed. Hans kept his arm around her to keep her warm as they traversed paths homeward to the cottage. She could almost feel the energy and joy coursing through him as electricity coursed through the cables and wires he had brilliantly installed.

The cottage was not yet wired with the new marvel, so when they had turned out the lamps and got into bed he took her in his arms and said, "Felly, I'm so happy. I'm so happy. I love you so much, and I'm so happy."

She longed to say back to him. "And I'm so happy too, Hans." Somehow, she could not. She was not sure. But happiness did seem a possibility.

She dreaded the approach of Christmas. Ever since Bay and Caroline had moved to Appleton, it had become a tradition for them all to return to Harbour Hill for the holidays. Weeks of preparation resulted in the most festive, traditional and heartwarming Christmases one could conjure. Felly's doctor and Felly's husband both decreed her pregnancy was too far advanced for her to make the long trip this year to Harbour Hill for Christmas.

Felly was disconsolate. No great silver dish at the door filled with nuts and candies? No sixteen-foot tree resplendent with candles and baubles? None of Kemink's roast geese and plum pudding? Not to be there when Bay's beautiful tenor led them in singing the Christmas carols? Not to be part of the frosty cold Christmas morn, when Bay relit the yule logs and all the children came scrambling down the stairs to claim their bulging stockings? Not to be there at the late Christmas breakfast replete with Danish Kringle and coffee made from fresh ground beans?

Every day, she thought of some new loss. Who would ride out across the snowy fields in the cutter with Danny to pick the tree? That had always been her privilege. Who would decorate the puddings with white sauce and cherries now she wasn't there? Who would rehearse the older boys and girls in reading the Christmas story?

Most of all...not to be with her mother and Kemink at Christmas. Not to be with Danny and Bay and all the other people she loved. She knew now what homesickness was.

Her mother's letters tried to comfort her.

> ...they depend upon us coming to Harbour Hill for the holidays so much, I feel we can't break the tradition and disappoint everyone, darling. But I shall come to you right after the holidays to be with you at the time of birthing. Perhaps even Kemink can arrange to get away.
>
> In the meantime, my sweet, don't feel sad. You can make this a most precious Christmas for just you and Hans. You can begin your own traditions.

* * * *

66

Felly threw a pillow at the fireplace. Just she and Hans...that was the problem. She could not conceive of how you could have any kind of proper Christmas with only two people!

She tried. Even though her back ached with the weight of her pregnancy, she spent hours baking Kringle and plum pudding only to have Hans disappointed because she had not made some strange Norwegian Fattigman Bakkels "poor man" cookies he called them. She had never even heard of them.

Then something unexpected happened which made Christmas all a-sparkle again. Days before Christmas Adam Quimby came sweeping in with the most resplendent pair of bay horses anyone in the area had ever seen, and a carriage of black patent and red leather, bells jingling from every harness, his face wet and cold from the long drive. He swept his daughter joyously into his arms regardless of her amazing bulk.

"I've come for Christmas!" he announced.

CHAPTER 11
Pride's Sting

***

"Only by pride cometh contention:
but with the well advised is wisdom."
(Proverbs 13:10)

Hans, returning from the powerhouse, stopped on the path, arrested by the sight of the magnificent horses, silvered by the star-brindled, crescent-mooned sky, their plumed breaths blowing like steam in the wind.

"What beautiful animals," he exclaimed, "I've never seen the likes anywhere!"

Adam laughed. "You like them, do you? That's good, for they are for you Hans...the carriage, too. My Christmas present to you and Fly."

"Oh, Papa!" Felly was ecstatic, "They're grand! And the carriage...I shall feel like a queen!"

Hans' face darkened. "Your generous intentions are appreciated, Sir, but no, we could never accept such a gift as this."

Adam laughed again. "Not accept them. Of course, you're going to accept them. Come and get acquainted with them, Hans. Their hearts are as fine as their hides. Come on..."

Against his will, Hans drew closer, his eyes gleaming. The nearest horse was making nervous jerks of his head, perhaps longing after the lengthy trip to be free of his harness. Hans' hands went out to the shining neck, the velvety muzzle. He talked in a low voice to the horse and the horse quieted.

"See, already he has an affinity to you," Adam said.

"Beautiful, beautiful animal," Hans said, his voice reverent". That one is called Smoke, the other Cloud. But you can name them what you will, of course."

Hans moved to the other horse, also stamping in the snow and snorting, and tossing its head. His hand felt the withers, his eyes

68

admired the well-formed haunches.

"These horses are all any man could dream of," he said to Adam, "but I tell you, I cannot take such a gift. They're worth a king's ransom."

Felly was shivering. "Hans, Papa's traveled a long way. Can't we go in now and offer him something hot to drink and some food. I'm freezing."

Adam put his arm around his daughter again. "Fine. Take me in and bring me all those good things you are talking about. I trust Hans can take care of his horses."

Hans swore under his breath at his father-in-law's back. The older man was not going to take no for an answer. It riled Hans to have to be beholden to anyone, and especially to Felly's father. He felt as if Adam had just stolen something precious from him...his right to earn such a pair of horses on his own. Yet there was no denying he had lost his heart to the pair the moment he had seen them, which complicated his feelings of resentment. Nor was he pleased Adam had come crashing uninvited into the Christmas he had expected to have alone with Felly.

All the same, he crooned to the horses like a new mother as he led them into the shed, removed their bridles, watered and fed them.

The following afternoon brought further excitement for Felly, and a secret resentment for Hans. A wagon tied down with tarpaulins and padding arrived from Harbour Hill. The driver said the wagon contained a present for Felly from her mother and step-father and she must be brought out before the tarps were released.

Dressed in a warm cloak with a fascinator around her head, Felly's eyes danced about the wagon in excitement.

"Whatever can it be?" And then, as the tarp was loosened and pulled free and the pads slid off... "Ohhh, Hans, I can't believe it! Look...look...it's a piano. A beautiful piano. Oh, I'm so happy! Mother must have known how I missed the piano at Harbour Hill. Oh, Papa, look...isn't it a beautiful thing?"

Adam was laughing and joining in his daughter's excitement, but Hans' face was dark.

"How will we ever get it in the house...it's so big? Oh, please, don't scratch it."

"Don't bring it in the cottage for tonight," Adam instructed the men sent to unload. "Take it up to the main hall. My daughter is a wonderful pianist. Tonight, she will share her gift with the old soldiers. We'll make this a wonderful Christmas for them."

The men drew the wagon up to the main house and began the unloading there. No one had asked Hans. He felt a sting of hatred for this father-in-law who came in and took charge with no by-your-leave from anyone. Who did he think he was, anyway?

Hans grabbed Felly by the shoulders. "Stop whirling around, you'll bring the baby before its time."

Felly looked up at Hans surprised to see his tight jaw and angry forehead. "Hans, aren't you pleased for me? Can't you see how happy the piano makes me?"

"Well, I'm not pleased," he admitted. "What is your family trying to prove? First the horses and carriage from your father and now this, presents extravagant beyond reason." He dropped his hands from her shoulders and strode away from her in anger.

She ran after him and caught his arm. "Hans, please listen. Neither my mother nor my father thought in any way to hurt you. They're just trying to express their love to both of us. Hans"

"All right, Felly. All right. You can have your piano. You can keep the horses, but you talk to your parents, do you understand? You tell them I want no more of this."

"Hans, I don't understand. I just don't understand," Felly said, tears coming into her eyes. "I should think you would be..."

"Grateful? I don't want to be beholden to anyone. Will you try to understand my feelings? If you want to be my wife, you will live on what I can provide. Is that clear?"

Once again, he strode away from her. This time she did not follow. Adam who had been assisting in moving the piano had come up in time to hear the end. She turned her hurt and bewildered face to him.

"Pride," Adam said. "Not such a bad thing for a man to have, Firefly. I'm sorry I stepped on his toes."

"Oh, Papa...both presents are the most beautiful thing I could ever have happen to me. Why must he spoil it?"

"He can't spoil it unless you let him," Adam said. "His mood will pass and in the future your mother and I'll try to respect his wishes. In the meantime, I suspect he needs a little extra attention from you. Go along. I'll be in a little later."

"Papa, you are the dearest, dearest man." Felly gave her father a hug, then went after Hans, though it was hard for her to obey her father's injunction since she felt she was the injured party.

She found her husband putting logs on the fire. He picked up a huge package by his feet, turned to her and thrust it at her belligerently.

"Since your father has already arranged for how our evening is to be spent, you might as well have my present now," he said.

Felly had to stifle an impulse to throw the present back at him and break into angry words. She knelt and undid the wrapping and then her heart melted and she was glad she had restrained her first anger. She found a beautiful hand-made rocking cradle.

"Hans, it's lovely. Just lovely. Did you make it yourself?"

"No. I designed it, but a friend made it."

She stood up and kissed him on both cheeks and on his lips. "Nothing...nothing could have pleased me more."

"It does not stack up with pianos and horses and carriages," he said with sarcasm. Then more softly, "But I'm glad you like it."

"Nothing could have touched me more," she said. "Let me get my present for you."

She had made him a velvet jacket for chilly evenings and had ordered him some special tools he had wanted for his work. He was well pleased, and as her father had predicted, his mood ameliorated enough so Christmas was not spoiled for Felly.

That evening, Adam gave the Christmas Eve service at the main building as only Adam could—bringing hardened men to the edge of tears and the next moment making the room rumble with laughter.

Felly played and sang for the old soldiers (many of whom she had already discovered were not old at all, just ill and disabled), and then everyone joined in singing the great old Christmas hymns: "Silent Night," "Come all Ye Faithful," and "O Little Town of Bethlehem."

Looking over the top of the piano into her father's eyes, Felly smiled. What a thing her father had taught her tonight. She had thought she and Hans would be alone at Christmas. In her narrow vision, it had never occurred to her what it might mean to these men, from whom so much had been taken, to have someone share with them. She had felt so homesick for so long for Harbour Hill. On this Christmas Eve, her father had given her back a sense of community. She felt the love of the men in the room flooding to her. Her eyes touched their faces one by one. Handsome faces, ugly faces, wasted faces, old faces, faces still touchingly young, round Dutch faces, square German faces, lean English faces, a few dark Italian faces, but all faces that had known pain.

She recognized a few of the faces by name, but she vowed she would get to know each one of them in the future. They would be her extended family, as the children at Harbour Hill had been her extended family there.

After the singing, there was punch and Christmas cookies, German Stollen bread and leftover turkey. Many of the men came up to thank Adam and Felly. The Christmas she had dreaded had become an exalted Christmas she would never forget.

Henry Collins teased Felly about adding so much weight since the first time he had seen her and said, "If the baby comes tonight, you'll have to name it Noel."

"Not for a month yet," Felly said. She put a sprig of holly in Henry's hair, and kissed him on the forehead.

"I had no idea the men would enjoy music so much. We must get our own piano," Mr. Winter said. "You play divinely Miz Jacobson; would you consider teaching my little girl?"

"I would love to," Felly said.

She walked home through the snow-sparkled darkness with her arms heaped high with little presents the men had found for her somewhere, Hans on one side of her, Adam on the other. For the first time in a long time, she was happy. Hans and Adam found things to share in conversation, and so all hearts found peace and joy in the season.

But Adam had just departed when Caroline and Kemink arrived.

"I know the baby's not due for several weeks, but sometimes babies come sooner than expected and I wanted to be sure and be with you," Caroline said breathlessly with the unloading of box after box from the carriage "And besides, Kemink wants to visit old friends in this area, and so do I."

Inside the boxes were beautiful little gowns embroidered with rosebuds by Emily's clever needle, soft as a puff of eiderdown quilts made by Kemink, beautiful French bonnets and little satin shoes from Caroline, a bunting made of rabbit skin to wrap my 'baby Bunting in...' from Bay, and to Felly the most wonderful gift of all...her great-grandmother's rocking chair.

"So many nights I rocked you and Danny in this chair, just as your grandmother rocked me and Ann, even as her mother had rocked her babies. Now you will rock your little ones," Caroline said, her eyes misting.

"Oh, mother, I will cherish it, I do already," Felly said, sitting down to demonstrate at once how she would rock her babies in it.

Hans came in to find the women among a welter of tissue and ribbons, still exclaiming and squealing over the tiny clothes and rattles and knitted sweaters. He nodded curtly and went upstairs without greeting them.

Caroline looked at Felly questioningly.

Felly shrugged. "Hans doesn't approve of my family giving me so many expensive gifts. Papa says it's his pride and I shouldn't let it worry me too much."

"I hope he doesn't mind us coming like this," Caroline said.

"Of course, he doesn't!" Felly said, but her cheeks burned hot, and anger toward Hans flooded through her to think he might make her mother and Kemink feel unwelcome.

Later in the evening in their bedroom, she confronted her husband on the matter.

"Your family has always spoiled you rotten," he snarled back at her, "That's why you're never happy."

"I'd be happy right now if you didn't keep spoiling it for me!" she hissed back. She wanted to slam the door and storm out of the room, out of his house, but she did not want her mother and Kemink to know they were quarreling.

They both lapsed into a sullen silence and lay down beside each other, seething with tension and anger, wanting to shout at each other, but aware their voices would carry to adjoining rooms.

At length, it was Hans who made an overture toward peace. His hand stole out to caress her. "Felly...I do love you," he whispered hoarsely.

"You don't act like it, sometimes," she whispered back after a pause.

Another long silence, and then, as if his gesture of reconciliation had relieved his tension, Hans began to breathe deeply and was soon asleep.

Felly turned in restless patterns, trying to accommodate her heavy, unwieldy body, her eyes wide in the darkness. What was her life with this man going to be like?

CHAPTER 12
Jason Jacobson

***

"Humble yourselves therefore under the mighty hand of God, that he may exalt you in due time: Casting all your care upon him; for he careth for you."
(Peter 5:6-7)

"It has been fifteen years since I have stood by the grave of my husband," Kemink said. "It is my desire to go there once more."

A sudden storm during the night seemed to thwart her desire, leaving four to six inches of fresh snow in the roads, and making travel by carriage difficult.

As if to make up for his previous coolness, Hans was more than solicitous and kind. "There is no reason why you can't go. You can take the cutter, and the horses Felly's father gave us, they would go through drifts ten times as high. I'll send Arnold and Japhet, the stable boys from the main house, with you in case you should encounter any difficulty."

"Who would tend the horses then? And what if the baby should come and you didn't have the cutter here?" Caroline worried.

"I will tend the horses myself," Hans said, "and we have another cutter at the main building we can use to fetch a doctor if Felly's time comes. Though it's not likely. She's not due until the end of the month."

"You'll be all right, Felicity? We'll only be gone overnight," Caroline said.

"Of course, Mother. I want you to go." Felly leaned over and kissed her mother's cheek, but added, "You don't think it will storm again, Hans?"

He shook his head. "It's going to be clear and cold."

Caroline and Kemink, bundled in fur hats and muffs with hot bricks for their feet and thick lap robes, set off for Weyauwega with

Arnold and Japhet.

With the perversity, babies sometimes have in these matters, Felly's labor began the following day.

As a young girl, she had always felt impatient with the tales' women told about giving birth. Every time a group of women got together, it seemed they had to give harrowing accounts of how they had brought their children into the world. Even her mother had seemed to delight in accounting her own unusual birth—how Caroline had been stricken with labor in the woods and stalked by a hungry she-wolf. How only Kemink's arrival and her courageous fight with the wolf saved Caroline's life, and how Kemink had delivered Felicity after hours of travail.

Felly had tossed her young curls and thought disdainfully, I'm never going to make such a to do about having a baby. I'm going to have my babies like a cow or a cat and be up the next day as if nothing happened. She had heard tales of peasant women in Europe who worked in the fields until a few minutes before the birth of their children, went home, gave birth, and within an hour or two were back at their work. If peasant women could do it, so could she.

Now her cavalier young attitudes came back to haunt her as twinges of her labor grew more severe. Hans borrowed a Camp cutter and went for the doctor. Felly paced from window to window, trying not to moan, feeling very young and alone, even though Anna, one of the laundresses, had come in to sit with her until Hans came back with the doctor.

Hans was gone for an hour and returned white faced.

"Doc Bentley is delivering Mrs. Baxter's child. She's having difficulties and he wouldn't leave right now. He says we are not to worry. A first birth usually takes hours. He said he should be here shortly."

Hours yet! Felly let out a sob. Her misery was turning into agony. She couldn't believe this might go on for hours.

"Go upstairs. Lay down, child. I'll put a knife under the bed to cut the pain," Anna said in her cheerful, guttural voice.

Felly leaned against Hans, sobbing. "Hans, I want my mother, I want my mother. I don't care about the doctor. I want my mother."

"Felly...I don't know where your mother is. They should be on the way home right now."

"Oh, Hans, send someone for my mother."

"Yes, I will, I will," Hans said. He helped her upstairs and laid her on the bed, covering her, touching her cheek with tenderness, holding her hand, while she rolled back and forth moaning and yowling.

Anna came grunting up the stairs with a butcher knife. Hans ran down the stairs to find someone to go to Weyauwega for Caroline and Kemink. He stopped at the doorway, his muttered prayers stilling on his lips. Praise God, the cutter was just turning in the driveway! His legs were trembling as if he had been in battle, sweat was rolling down his neck.

"Mother," Felly said, "Oh, Mother."

Caroline sat down on the side of the bed and spoke to her in soothing words. She had Felly turn on her side and she rubbed her back. Soon after, the baby was born. A boy.

Kemink made the actual delivery which her mother said was very fitting, "...just as she delivered you so many years ago."

When the baby had been bathed and Caroline had wrapped him in a heated square of flannel, she looked down at him and said just two words, "Little Adam."

She put him in Felly's arms. Felly blinked down at him. He had lots of dark hair like his Grandpa Adam but Felly could not see any other resemblance. The baby was as tiny and wrinkled as a little old man. She had thought he would look like the cherubs on Christmas cards. He was tinier than anything she had imagined. She stared at him in wonderment. He seemed to stare back at her in wonder too. The floodgates of her heart opened. "My baby...my baby."

Kemink came halfway down the stairs. She smiled at Hans. "You have a son. All is well."

A son! For the first time, he noticed how beautiful the Indian woman's face was, how beautiful her smile was. He leapt up the stairs.

In the room growing dim with the winter darkness, stringent with the soap and pungent smell of Lysol they had used to clean up, the bed glowed white. Felly, propped up with pillows, held his son, her dark hair curling on her shoulders. She did not look up when he came in but she knew he was there for she said, "Hans, I want to name him Jason."

He stopped five feet from the bed. His feet seemed so loud on the bare floor. "I had thought we would call him after me if it was a boy...the first born...Hans."

"If we have other children you can name all of them anything you want," she said, "this one I want to name Jason."

She still did not look up at him. She and the baby seemed lost in contemplation of each other. He felt as if there were a glass wall around them shutting him out. He had wanted to throw himself on his knees at her bedside, to thank her for his son. He had wanted to touch his newborn child. He had heard a new baby will clutch a finger. He had wanted his son to clutch his finger. But he could not go through

76

the glass wall.

After a while, he left. He was sure she did not even know when he was gone. She never called after him. He would have been glad to have the child named Jason Hans Jacobson, but he never got to tell her this.

CHAPTER 13
Jason's Talent

***

*"As every man hath received the gift,
even so minister the same one to another,
as good stewards of the manifold grace of God."
(Peter 4:10)*

When Jason was three, Felly's second child, a precious little girl destined to bring light to her father's eyes, was born. This time Felly saw in Hans' eyes a gladness as he came to her with his arms outstretched to embrace his daughter. First, he kissed Felly, with the same warmth she remembered from their first embrace and kiss. Then he lifted the swathed baby from her arms, and clasped her to his heart.

"Did you mean it, Felly, I could name all the other children you give me?"

"Of course, Hans...what shall we call this one?"

"Seena, Seena, after my oldest sister. I never show how much I miss my family but just hearing this name will remind me of my younger days in Denmark. How does 'Seena' suit you?"

"Seena is a nice name, Hans. When I first saw her my thought was she will be a beautiful woman."

"Like her mother," Hans said with emotion. Felly smiled her thanks.

"Welcome to our family little one," he said. He touched his lips against the baby's forehead before placing her back in her mother's arms.

Two years later, Felly presented Hans with another son. "A son, Hans, you have another son," said Dr. Bentley when he came out of the bedroom.

"I thought so," grinned Hans. "How's Felly?"

"It was an easier birth than the others. She's waiting for you," Dr. Bentley said.

Hans went in to Felly who looked drained.

"Doc said it was an easy birth."

Felly shook her head, "The birth was easier but I'm not so comfortable now. Dr. Bentley said this will pass when I rest a while."

Hans was leaning over the baby, smiling. "So, Jacob Hans Jacobson has arrived. He's a big baby, Felly, and I thank you for this son."

Felly thought—he's mellowing...this husband of few words. He does love having children.

"Jacob Hans Jacobson," she said. "Your father's name?"

"It is," Hans replied, "and he's got my build, hasn't he...thank you, you're the perfect mother for my children."

Hans bent to lay his cheek against hers.

"Shall we call him Jake?" she asked.

"Jake, it is," Hans said.

The fourth child fought against coming into the world. The labor was long and arduous. Felly was worn out afterwards. Hans tiptoed into the room, exhausted himself from the long vigil, worried about his wife.

The baby was in the cradle Hans had made for Jason. Hans bent over to inspect her, then whispered, "A daughter, our family is balanced now. This one I name Saran, after my second sister, not Grace, Saran...almost the same, yet enough difference to suit her daddy's Danish heart. I am glad you consented when we discussed this baby's name. Sleep now Felly, rest sweetly. I am grateful to you for this daughter."

Felly was already sound asleep, when Hans kissed her brow and tiptoed out of the room.

Two boys, two girls, Felly considered her family complete and stood in awe of the miracle of birth which gave her motherhood responsibilities, satisfying her yearning to pour out love like she had learned from her own dear mother. She tried hard to keep secret the special love she felt for her first born, but he controlled her heartstrings more than any of the others.

Jason seemed a child of great sensitivity and talent. Every day was intense and exciting to eight-year-old Jason Jacobson. The Old Soldiers' Home property was a pleasure trove for him that no day seemed quite large enough to explore. He was always up before anyone else in the household. He ran off without breakfast, leaving a smear of jelly across the table, his hands clutching a fat sandwich he'd made himself or a leftover piece of cake or some cookies.

He often forgot to come home for lunch and was invariably late for dinner, habits which irritated Hans. The father was further enraged that disciplinary trips to the woodshed availed nothing. Still, the boy would come home with torn shirttails and muddy feet, and a great smile, clutching a jar with a frog in it or a bird's egg he had found in the woods, bubbling over with the adventure of his discovery, his face falling only as he realized everyone else was already sitting at dinner and he was late again.

Jason had long ago come to accept trips to the woodshed philosophically as the price he had to pay for his freedom to be where he wanted to be when he wanted to be there. From his earliest experience, he found he could never please his father, so though he never thought it out in words, there was a feeling deep inside the child...a decision... he would not break his heart trying.

But even for his mother, whom he wanted to please with every atom in him, he could not be punctual. It was just not in his nature.

His pleasures in "Camp," as the residents of the Old Soldiers' Home called it, were twofold, private and social. The private part of his day began with those early morning risings when the mist was still hugging the breast of Rainbow Lake and the screech owls were still hooting in the forests around Camp and the lakes.

He loved the woodlands with the shafts of early morning sunlight just starting to break through the great ragged branches above his head. He would sit on a rock, hushed and rapt, listening to the stirrings of all the hidden things which lived in the forest coming to life or settling down to daytime sleep as their various natures demanded.

Here were many mysteries to be unraveled. Here were thousands of small dramas and events. Here was magic and wonder no lifetime would be long enough to witness. What were in those small white packages the ants were carrying? What kind of cities and houses did they have inside the great pyramids of sand they built? He was consumed by curiosity. Jake, his five-year-old brother, would have taken a stick and dug the mound open to see. Jake took everything apart to see how it worked, even his toys. Some sensitivity in Jason would not allow him to destroy the ant hill to satisfy his curiosity no matter how burning. The ants were living creatures, too; he felt for them.

Rainbow Lake, the beautiful ever changing, never changing lake, lady of many moods, had both private and social pleasures to offer. The early morning hours were the private ones. Often, he had the lake all to himself, at least as far as humankind. The lake, like the forest, swarmed with strange, exotic life forms: frogs, fish, dragonflies, odd little crabs, large bad-tempered turtles, sinuous snakes, otters and sometimes a beaver.

His mother and father both had forbidden him to swim alone. He disobeyed them, disregarding their fears because he had none of his own. He loved the sharp chill of the morning water, the soft lapping sound of his limbs breaking the surface of the lake's liquidity, the sensuous envelopment of himself as part of the lake's entity.

Sometimes if he was early enough and still enough, he could watch the deer come to drink. Once he had seen a moose. This had almost stopped his heart, the creature which was so huge with great moss-covered horns and eyes of brown fire. Its hooves had stirred the leaves, warning of danger.

Then he would begin to hear Camp itself come alive. Banging of doors, sleepy voices, the clop of the milkman's horses, the cries and callings of children: sound transformed and eerie as it drifted over the lake.

His private time dwindling, he would start homeward. The livery stable on the corner of Camp, the next stop on his itinerary, was a fair distance. He would start off at a good trot anxious to be in time to see the horses get their morning feeding, but sometimes dawdling on the way despite himself. The field he journeyed through had its own seductions.

In the spring, the meadow gave a thousand dandelions. He loved to gather the cool, green stems, and bend them into circlets, linking the circlets together to form necklaces and bracelets for his sisters, Seena and Saran. In the summer, the meadow was full of grasshoppers that spit brown tobacco juice and leapt like kangaroos. They fascinated him. In the autumn, the milkweed pods were turning to silk, and when butterflies were skipping and dipping to find late blooming flowers, the monarch cocoons were hanging ready for winter dormancy.

Always there were wonders awaiting his alert eyes and curious mind. At last, he would make his way to the livery stable. He loved everything about the stable. The smell of horses and dust and sweet hay, of liniment and leather and manure. Rich, satisfying, masculine smells.

The horses knew him and welcomed him. There was pride, too, in knowing though his father's matched pair were growing old, they were still the finest in the stable.

He liked Willie and Asp and Jorge, the stable boys. He liked their tenderness with the horses and their coarseness. They smelled of sweat and they swore. They drank straight from whiskey bottles and played cards and talked about women.

The horses made a chuffing sound, loved talking to him,

beckoning with their velvet noses, straining their necks toward him. This was his moment of ecstasy. Only one thing was more wonderful than the warm, powerful, silk-covered flesh of these horses, those were the moments when he nestled against his mother and smelled her hair and the sweetness of her skin.

Still, it was not the livery stable he loved best of all. What he loved best of all sat in the Entertainment Hall. The other children in the Camp were not allowed to go in there except for "doings." Jason Jacobson alone had carte blanche to go in and command the thing he loved best of all, the piano.

His mother gave lessons on her piano in the house so it was often in use. When she was not using it, his brothers and sisters were all about to distract him. Most of all if his father was there, he was always commanding him to do something else. In the Entertainment Hall, the piano was his alone in the hours before noon, all its potential harmony and melody waiting to be evoked by his touch.

He often had pulled the carved panel apart to stare at the dusty hammers which made the sound and yet the hammers seemed to him to have nothing to do with it. Music lived inside the piano. Music lived inside of him. When they were joined, the music came magically from somewhere, but not from the hammers.

His small fingers played with the keys, lingered, chopped and slid. Every new sound was a thrill. He tried to draw from the keys sounds he heard in the silent morning forest, the mysterious sounds of the lake, the masculine sounds of the stable. All the wonderful things inside of him wanted to be born as sound.

The adults let him trespass here because they were amazed at what he did. They said he was "composing." Their eyes were round with astonishment as they said, "Did you hear that? And he's only eight?" He did not understand their awe of what came so naturally to him, but he welcomed it for it gave him access to the piano. Even his father didn't try to keep him from those morning hours at the piano. His talent must be served, the other adults said. They treated him as if he were special because of the sounds he could evoke from the piano. Jason basked in their admiration, and preened a little too, if the truth must be told.

Sometimes one of the other boys in the Camp would "drub" him for his preening. Jason never won those fights, he had little violence in him, but he was nothing if not resilient. He managed to come out of them still unabashed and unbowed, however bloodied and battered physically.

Lost in the music, often he would forget lunch, and realizing what

82

he had done belatedly he would prefer not to go home and get a scolding. He ran to the main dining hall and Cooky would always give in to his charm and end up handing him a sausage or a hunk of cheese, some crackers or cookies, even though Hans had expressly forbidden it.

When his private day ended, he would begin his social rounds. He knew every one of the sixty-six veterans living there. Knew them by name, knew their temperaments, their idiosyncrasies, their stories of past glories and present pains. He had his favorites but he loved them all, even the worst curmudgeons. The latter fascinated him in the same way the tiny crayfish and the tobacco spitting grasshoppers did. Some veterans tried bitterly to reject him. He sparred with them and kept coming. Grudgingly, they succumbed, one by one. It was impossible not to love him.

He didn't visit every one of the veterans every day of course, but now this one and now that one. He had his own reasons for whom he visited each day. Some of the reasons were altruistic. On rainy days, he visited Old Sam because Sam's rheumatism always hurt worse then and Jason's visits distracted him from his pain. Some of his reasons were selfish. He visited Gregory Paulson the first Thursday of every month because Gregory got a check then, and if Jason took it to be cashed for him, he got a courier fee of six cents for penny candy.

Every day he could, he visited Henry Collins. Henry's skin was a dark chocolaty color, almost black. He had lost his legs in the Civil War. He was a special friend of his mother's, and Jason loved him best of the veterans, too. Henry was funny, made him laugh and teased him. Henry gave him quarters and carved wooden toys for him. Henry hoisted him up and gave him wild rides in his wheelchair down the length of the Marsden Hall porch.

The first time Henry had swung him into his lap for a wheelchair ride, Jason had been somewhat horrified of Henry's stumps. Now he no more recoiled from them than the tree stumps he sat on in the woods. Henry wasn't always feeling strong enough to give him rides but when he did it was great.

On one summer day, Jason was surprised to find Henry dressed in his Civil War uniform, all brushed and pressed, polishing his musket. At the far end of the porch, other veterans, also dressed in their uniforms, with some bearing drums and bugles, were clustered. Most of them also had guns.

"What's happening, Henry? Why you all dressed up? Why's everybody dressed up?"

"Everybody's not dressed up, Jason. Just the veterans of the 98th

Division who are here."

"Why are they dressed up? Why are you polishing your gun? Are you going to war again?"

Henry smiled, his thin face crinkling in beautiful patterns. "No, lad. We're fixin' to be a welcoming committee to a very special man. Our old commander, Colonel Maxwell Harrison, is coming to live here at the Grand Army Home. He's the bravest man any of us ever knew, Jason."

"What did he do, Henry? What did he do that was so brave?"

The smile faded from Henry's face. He looked over Jason's head and his face grew ashy.

"More things than I could ever tell you, lad. He gave us courage when we were young, untried soldiers and had to go into battle. He led us gallantly and never let us down. At the Battle of the Wilderness, we were fighting in a brushy wood and the damn thing caught fire from all the gunpowder going off...hundreds of wounded men were burned alive in the fire, Jason...but not one of the 98th Division, because of Maxwell Harrison. He went into the fire again and again, with great cost to his own personal safety, until he had every man out and accounted for. He won a medal for his courage."

"Did you ever win any medals, Henry?"

Henry's lost, faraway look dissolved. He laughed. "No, Jason, I didn't. But I shoulda. By cracky, I ought to have a whole chest full of 'em, the kind of soldier I was. You believe me?"

"Yes, sir, I do."

Henry laughed again and ruffled the boy's silky hair. "Ahh, Jason, I'll bet you do. You're a good lad. But where have you been? I haven't seen you for three days?"

Jason looked down. "I was naughty, Henry, so Papa said I had to stay in for three days."

"Naughty? You?" Henry shook his head. "Well, what did you do this time?"

"Jake was pestering me all day. I finally hit him. Jake's Papa's favorite. He won't have nobody monkeying with Jake."

"Well...Jason," Henry drawled, "Jake is considerable smaller than you, you know. Your Pa doesn't want you to go around hitting people smaller than you are."

Jason lifted his eyes and looked square into Henry's. "Pa's bigger than me, Henry, and he hits me."

Henry cleared his throat. "Well, now that's different, Jason. He's your Pa. He's just tryin' to make a good person out of you."

"I was just trying to make a good person out of Jake, Henry,"

Jason said.

Henry put his hands on Jason's shoulders and gave him an affectionate shake. "Jason, if you got one fault, lad, it's you won't ever owe up to being wrong, 'n we're all wrong sometimes, Jason."

"What about Jake, wasn't he wrong, too?" Jason asked.

"Well, you paid your penalty. Let's let it go at that," Henry said. "How'd you like to come along to welcome Colonel Harrison?"

"Oh, could I, Henry? Could I!"

"You can push my wheelchair. The ground is still soggy after the rain and makes it hard going for me."

The boy's eyes, not Viking-blue like Hans' but midnight blue, shone with delight.

"Gee, thank you, Henry. When do we go?"

Henry gave one last swipe at his musket, pulled out his big railroad watch and squinted at it. "Right now, lad. Right now. He's supposed to arrive around two."

The cluster of soldiers at the other end of the porch had been growing. There were perhaps twenty-five men assembled now. They were looking at their watches too, and then starting off.

Jason pushed Henry's wheelchair fast, hurrying to catch up with the group so Henry could be right out in front where Jason was sure he belonged.

* * * *

Fly's family had grown quicker than she had anticipated. Her time was filled with the demands of the house and four children; Jason, Seena, Jacob, and Saran.

CHAPTER 14
Colonel Harrison

***

"Thou hast heard; see all this; and will not yet declare it?
I have shewed thee new things from this time,
even hidden things, and thou didst not know them."
(Isaiah 48:6)

The day would have been hot except for a strong breeze coming off the lake. The breeze brought with it the smell of water and fish, hemlock and pine, sun-hot grass and sweet clover.

The men waiting for Colonel Harrison were grateful for the breeze. Their Union jackets felt heavy, their faces grew red and warm even with the wind which snapped the flag and fluttered the grass at their feet.

Mercifully, they did not have to wait long. The rented carriage from Waupaca arrived first. Behind it came the dray wagon drawn by four powerful horses, laden with crates and boxes of the Colonel's belongings.

John Middman leaped forward to open the carriage door. The drummers rattled their sticks. The buglers put their horns to their lips. Colonel Maxwell Harrison stepped out of the carriage to a rousing, if somewhat uneven and thin, rendition of "The Battle Hymn of the Republic."

The Colonel straightened to his full height, a tall, spare, wide-shouldered man with thick, white, wavy hair blowing in the wind. Despite the heat of the day, he was wearing a gray cape which also lifted and gusted in the wind, revealing beneath it an impeccable pearl gray suit and snow-white stock. His face was angular and stern with deep-set eyes and lips unexpectedly full in such an ascetic setting.

His eyes surveyed this small assemblage of men in fading Union blue, their aging, depleted bodies straining to hold the old military stance, and his eyes glinted for a moment with tears. His hand shot up in salute.

"Men of the 98th," he said, "I expected nothing like this. I am touched and honored."

Then he smiled. All the sternness left his face. It mellowed like a meadow in the sun, and Jason understood why his men loved him. He went from one to the other, gripping their shoulders, shaking their hands.

"Robert Fallon, by the gods, I never expected to see you alive again!"

"Didn't think I was going to make it myself, Sir."

"Dave...John. Wilbur...Wilbur Finnegan—what a time you led me, man...but I forgave it all when you carried me off the battlefield at Shiloh. George...Herman...Lars Olson...Jim Davis...Emmet Jones..."

He seemed to remember each man by name until he got half circle, then he gripped a middle-aged and stocky man by the shoulders and said, "I ought to know you, lad. I do know you...but I can't put the name..."

"Nathan Long, Colonel."

"Nate...Nate, of course! But where did your round face go? Where are all those freckles?"

"They got blown off my nose at Shiloh, Sir."

Everyone laughed.

"Henry...Henry Collins...you've still got your smile, I see. Never saw the like of a man to smile in the face of danger as you did."

His eyes fell then upon Jason, dark gray, piercingly intelligent eyes. "And who are you, little soldier?"

"I'm not a little soldier," Jason said forthrightly, "I'm a musician. My name's Jason Jacobson and my father is chief engineer here."

The Colonel's smile broadened. "Oh, indeed. I see. Well, then I have something in one of those crates which might interest you. Would you like to help me unpack later this afternoon?"

"Yes, Sir!" Jason said with alacrity, his heart pounding with excitement.

The remnants of the 98th Regiment and their long-ago commander began the trek up to the dining hall where there was to be a special luncheon and an address by the Colonel. The flag and the Colonel's cape crackled in the wind, the sun glinted fiercely on the lifted bugles and flutes, and they marched to a rousing chorus of "Yankee Doodle Dandy."

Jason felt joy swell inside him to bursting. It was a grand day.

The boy was waiting on the threshold of the cottage which would probably be the Colonel's home for the rest of his life, when the gentleman arrived, finished with lunch and the welcoming formalities.

Most of the veterans lived in small rooms in the various halls scattered about the grounds: Marden Hall, Houston Hall, Marston Hall, Fairchild Hall, Jerry Rusk Hall. There were also a series of cottages provided for those old soldiers who had brought their wives with them, or who had been of sufficient rank to accord them the honor of separate and private quarters.

One of the largest and most desirable sites had been set aside for the Colonel's use; even so, the house was small. Since he would take his meals at the main dining room there was only one large room with a small adjacent bedroom, a dressing room, a bathroom, and a tiny kitchen.

The dray men were struggling to get the largest crate from the wagon to the ground. Even with a breeze the men were sweating by the time they got it lowered. They began pounding on the crate with their hammers and prying with pliers.

"Easy men, easy," the Colonel instructed. He took Jason by the hand and went inside to inspect the cottage.

The walls were white. There was a modest fireplace and two fan-shaped windows.

"Well, what do you think, lad?" the Colonel asked surveying the room.

"I don't think it's grand enough for you, Sir," Jason blurted.

The Colonel laughed and squeezed his hand. "Then we shall have to make it grand enough," he said.

"How are you going to get all those boxes in here?" Jason marveled. It seemed to the boy the crate the men were pounding on was so large it alone would fill the room.

"How are we to get all those boxes in here? With dispatch, Jason. The army always does everything with dispatch," the Colonel said.

There was a sound of splintering wood as the crate gave way outside. Jason ran to the door to look out and gave a shout of incredulity.

"Wow...whillikins...a grand piano! But how'll you ever get it in here?" Jason worried.

"It's not going to be easy," the old man acknowledged. "But we can always take the legs off if we have to"

Which proved to be the case. Late afternoon sunlight was striking the lake and forest shadows were creeping across the sand by the time the sweating dray men got the piano into the room and reassembled. The Colonel gave them a bonus with which to buy a pail of beer and sent them off telling them he and the boy could manage the rest. "We can finish up," he said.

"We." To Jason's soul, the word was like a sparkling diamond given to him. He turned it this way and that way, reveling in it. "We." He, Jason and the Colonel, were a "we."

He stood before the grand piano, awestruck with its splendor. He touched it with a reverent hand. "Do you play, Sir?"

"Do I play? Of course, I play," the Colonel said, seating himself on the bench. His long, nervous hands poised for a minute over the keyboard, then fell like devouring birds, flashing and flying, drawing out a crescendo in D-minor which overwhelmed Jason.

When at last the Colonel stopped, he saw the rapture on the boy's face. "You like my style, huh?"

Jason nodded, wordless with wonder.

The Colonel slid over on the bench. "Now you play something."

Jason shook his head.

"Come now, you've been wanting to get at those keys from the moment you saw the piano; don't tell me different."

"Yes, Sir, that's true."

"Well then?"

Jason looked down and ran a forefinger round and round his kneecap.

"Ah, I see," the Colonel said, "I have intimidated you." Then with sudden sharpness of tone, "Look up at me, Jason, don't hang-dog. Now listen. Never be intimidated by excellence, be inspired by it. There will always be someone way ahead of you in whatever you do. Don't let it deter you from going forward. Now sit yourself upon this bench and show me what you can do."

Diffidently, Jason seated himself beside the Colonel. He touched the keys with tentative fingers. At the rich responsive tone, his fingers evoked he could not help but flash a smile of joy at the Colonel.

"Wow."

Now his hands became eager. He forgot the Colonel. He forgot everything, lost in the joy of this wonderful instrument.

"That's quite beautiful, Jason. I've never heard it before. What is it?"

"It's a piece I made up, Sir."

The colonel's eyebrows climbed in surprise. "Have you made up many such pieces, Lad?"

"Oh, lots and lots of them." He finished the piece with a flourish.

"You were right, Jason...you are a musician," the Colonel said. "I will want to hear all of your pieces. You must come often."

Jason glowed.

"But for now, I suppose we must get back to work. We are not accomplishing this unpacking with dispatch, and I promised dispatch, did I not? A soldier keeps his word. Would you like to put the books in the bookcase for me?"

"Yes, Sir!"

"We will have to make this room grand then to match the piano," the Colonel had said, and as his personal possessions began to come out of the boxes, the room did become grand.

There were three narrow mirrors with gilt frames which they spaced between three tall mahogany bookstands. There was a curious carved table from India and a great silver samovar from Russia. There was a red velvet box with a dueling pistol. Six black and white etchings of war machines framed in gold were unwrapped. Jason helped to hang them above the elegant pale green velvet settee. There was a marvelous painting of the sea crashing against a rugged shoreline, which they hung over the fireplace.

Jason was putting books in the bookcase when a shadow in the doorway blocked the late sunlight and he looked up to find his mother there.

"Jason...I've been looking for you for hours. I've been worried about you. You didn't come home for lunch and..."

Felly looked hot, and tired, and cross. Her cheeks were moist and red. There was a smudge of dust on her forehead and her hair had loosened from the knot in which she now wore it, letting tendrils escape about her face.

"Mother," Jason said with excitement. "This is Colonel Harrison. Henry says he's the bravest man who ever lived...and look at his piano, and he's got an ivory tusk and a gold bullet and..."

"Jason," the Colonel's voice, ringing with sudden sternness, cut him off, "you must never again come without telling your mother where you are going. Can't you see you have caused your mother pain, Jason?"

Jason looked at his mother, contrite. It had not occurred to him he was causing her pain. He thought Felly had long ago accepted him as he was. "I'm sorry, Mother."

The Colonel made a courtly bow. "Please, Mrs. Jacobson, won't you sit down and rest a moment."

"Thank you, Colonel, but I really can't..."

He waved her protests away. "Here, Jason, run to the main dining hall and bring your mother, yourself, and me, some lemonade. There's an extra quarter there for you in payment of all your help."

"Oh, you didn't have to pay me. Golly winkers I was just..."

"Go, Jason, and hurry back."

Jason trotted off, and Felly found herself sinking down onto the green velvet settee with a sigh. It had been a long hard day. Perhaps she would claim this small moment of respite.

"Your son is a remarkable boy. He played for me," he said smiling.

"Of course, I think so," Felly smiled back, confessing her motherly pride. Her eyes were sweeping the bookcases Jason had so lately arranged. "I see you like Dickens."

"I do."

"Poor Pip."

"Tragic Miss Haversham."

"Oh, the Artful Dodger."

"And Scrooge!"

They were laughing together, sudden friends because of their mutual fictional acquaintances.

"I think there is no other author who has made practically every human foible into a character, as has Dickens," the Colonel said.

"Oh, and you have Rumi. I've heard about his poetry. But I haven't read any of it."

"Take it with you."

"Oh, I couldn't."

"But, of course, you must. Then we'll talk about it."

Jason came back with the lemonade, and at his request, the Colonel played for Felly. She was as overcome as Jason had been.

"Would you allow me to give Jason lessons, Mrs. Jacobson?"

"Allow you? Allow you? Oh, Colonel, I should be so grateful."

And so, it was thus that Maxwell Harrison came into the lives of Jason and Felly Jacobson.

CHAPTER 15
The Old Soldiers' Home Celebration

***

"Hope deferred maketh the heart sick:
but when the desire cometh, it is a tree of life."
(Proverbs 13:12)

Felly was pregnant again. She did not feel like getting up to face the day. It was an important morning and was therefore going to demand a lot of her. Even though it was only a quarter past five, the hour was already late in terms of everything she needed to do.

The Women's Relief Corps had been instrumental from the beginning in helping establish the Grand Army Home and continued to support and embellish it in important ways. The group had raised over three thousand dollars to build a chapel on the grounds. Now, the completed chapel was to be dedicated at a special service on this day.

The event was expected to draw hundreds of people from all over the state. Many of the families and relatives of veterans had begun arriving the night before. Carriages and farm wagons (some with hayracks) were already hitched to trees along the lake and, from former events, Felly knew they would be stretched for a mile down the road before noon.

The Waupaca band was coming and the drum corps from Weyauwega and even a large uniformed band from Omro. A distinguished Army Chaplain from Milwaukee was to address the convocation.

Many of the families brought picnic baskets and would eat under the spreading trees on the grounds. Others would squeeze into the main dining hall. Felly, with other women in Camp, had been pressed into service to ladle out lemonade and cookies during the afternoon.

Once she might have been excited at this special celebration. Now her heart was not in it. She was tired. The Chief Engineer and his family had been afforded a pew of honor, third from the front on the right; they would be expected to occupy that pew for the earliest service which would take place in a little over two hours at half past eight. The Chief Engineer's wife would be expected to be warm and welcoming to the visiting dignitaries and their wives. Some of them might be invited back to their own table for breakfast.

Felly thought of all the little boots and shoes still waiting to be polished. *Oh, I know I should have done it yesterday but the whole day was such a rush.* She thought of the struggle of getting all her children washed and brushed and stuffed into their starched best, while still trying to get herself ready and meet Hans' quick demands. She could just imagine the hubbub which would ensue. "Where is my watch fob with the gold bar, Felly? Felly! I can't get this collar buttoned, come help me." "This coat has a loose button, Felly". "Couldn't you have given my shoes more shine?"

And what was she to wear? Six months pregnant, her body was as shapeless as a potato. None of her good clothes fit. The loose aprons which hid her condition on a day-to-day basis would not do for a special occasion. There had been so much preparation for the others for the dedication she had not thought about her own clothes.

She longed to sink deeper into the featherbed and sleep forever, forgetting all the responsibilities and anxieties of the day ahead.

"Felly!" Hans jerked to a sitting position beside her. "Look at the hour. We're going to be late!"

He leaped from the bed. Still she lay.

"Felly, are you coming? Get some water on for my shave. Where are my linens?"

He managed to find them on his own and hurried out the door. "Jason, get up! Seena...Saran...get Jake up!"

The creak of bedsprings, feet running on bare boards, the sound of her children's voices. Still she lay, like some creature turned to stone. That was what she felt like. A boulder. So huge, so heavy.

"Mother?" Jason had come to the door. His face was serious, his deep blue eyes questioning why she was not yet up. Her eyes caressed his dark silky hair, his sweet child's mouth. He was so beautiful—her Jason.

She raised herself on her elbow and smiled reassurance at him, the sudden fusion of love flowing through her held the day's freneticism at bay for a moment.

"I'm coming, dear. Give Jake a biscuit and butter to hold him over 'til breakfast. I'll be down in a minute."

"Mama, I can't get my curl-papers out," Saran was wailing.

"I'll be there in a moment."

She got up, closed the door against their sounds and demands, and looked in her closet.

"Half my problem is vanity," she scolded herself with a wry smile. "If I thought I was going in fine fettle and everyone would stare at me and think how grand I looked, I'd no doubt be itching to go. Well, Miz Jacobson, you better get over such childishness."

She settled on a long-sleeved lavender dress which large pleats that began at the square neckline and flowed to the hem, leaving the dress as loose as a Monk's robe. It would conceal her lumpiness all right but I'll be roasting before the day is over with those long sleeves, she thought. There was no help for it, she couldn't find anything else suitable and the decibel rate of noise coming through the door assured her there were crisis's everywhere to be solved.

"Mama, Jake won't let me wash him."

"Mama, she's trying to wash me with cold water!"

"Mama, I can't find the shoe button-hook."

"Felly! Are you getting up, or aren't you?"

She closed her eyes and leaned against the door for a moment before taking a deep breath, opening it, and walking into her lion's den.

Somehow, as always, they were at last ready on time. Hans, looking positively handsome, so brushed, and proud, and autocratic. Seena's silver-gold hair, undone from the curl-papers, making her look like a Christmas Angel, with Saran her smaller replica. Jake, sturdy, starched, red-cheeked, and Jason, so beautiful in his best clothes but looking somehow as if he did not belong to this family of blond, red-cheeked cherubs. Jason was pale, dark-haired, intense. My Jason...my Jason. It was not that she loved him more, it was that in some way she could not understand, she hurt for him more.

"Felly...where are you going? We're going to be late."

"I have to get my bonnet, Hans. I can't go to church bareheaded."

She tried to run up the stairs but she could not make it. She had to stop, hold her stomach, and go more slowly.

In the bedroom, she looked at her bonnet with loathing. They were not wearing bonnets this year. They were wearing hats. Only old women wore bonnets. Oh, I don't want to be old...not yet, something in her cried out.

Hans made good money but he was close and careful with it. He did not see the need for fashionable garments for her.

"Your closet is jammed with clothes!"

How was a man expected to understand her clothes were long outdated and outgrown? Felly would never have a twenty-three-inch waist again, but she was too proud to tell her husband none of her clothes fit.

With a sudden inspiration born of anger, she tore off the bonnet strings, rummaged in her drawers until she found an over-blown cabbage rose which had been attached to a dress she had once owned. She bent the brim of the bonnet back on one side and fastened it there with the rose. Now it looked like a hat, not a bonnet. She tilted it down a little in front, secured the hat pin, smiled at herself, felt better...and marched down to her waiting family.

Hans met her halfway on the stairs. "Felly!"

"I'm coming, Hans," she said, pulling on her white kid gloves.

They were almost the last ones to crowd into the chapel. Everyone stared at them as they promenaded to their reserved pew. Hans shot her a frowning side-glance to show his displeasure in arriving late and being put under scrutiny. Felly just stiffened her neck and held her head at a prouder angle as she ushered her beautiful children into the pew.

"Look at Mrs. Jacobson's hat," Thelma Vesper whispered to Mrs. Maddox. "I'll bet her rich mother bought it for her in Paris."

"Well I can't say I like Mrs. Jacobson's dress," Hester Maddox hissed back.

"It's very high fashion," Thelma whispered back under the cover of the shuffling of hymn book pages for the first hymn. "High fashion always looks a little odd until you get used to it."

"Well, if you ask me, she's in the family way again," Thelma whispered just before raising her voice to "Praise the Lord and Hosts Entire."

"I would like to begin this service with the reading of a statement by the Board of Trustees of the Grand Army Home regarding the wonderful women of the Women's Relief Corps whose efforts have made it possible for us to sit here today in this beautiful new chapel..." the Reverend Arnold Palmister began.

Jake began to kick the toes of his boots together. Felly laid her hand on his shoulder and gave him a warning glance. Even in church, there was no respite from motherhood.

"What would the Grand Army Home be today if it were not for this noble band of ladies? In every nook and corner of the institution can be found the handiwork of this association, there is not a resident of the Home but has received some token of their work and efforts."

The minister's voice droned on in a pleasant, kindly fashion. Felly tried to listen. The Women's Relief Corp work was exemplary, they deserved to be honored, but her mind could not seem to halt its harried circles. She wished she knew how many people Hans had invited back to the house. He had been so vague. "Oh, several couples, Felly." Would she have enough chairs? Would the ham be large enough? Should she serve the biscuits hot on such a warm day?

The minister's voice intoned:

They talk about a woman's sphere as though it had a limit.
There's not a place in earth or heaven, there's not a task to mankind given:
There's not a blessing or a woe,
There's not a whisper, yes or no,
There's not a life, or death or birth
That has a feather's weight of worth,
Without a woman in it.

Already her dress felt heavy. The afternoon ahead loomed so long. Jake was kicking his boot toes again. Oh, next time she must remember to put him next to Hans. Jason had always been so good in church, and the girls, too.

Then finally, blessedly, the last "amen" and people began filing out of the chapel. Guilt flooded Felly at her sense of relief. Oh, where was her spiritual self? What thought had she given to God or being good? How much had she even listened to the minister's words? Instead she was caught up in hams and Jake and how hot and tired she felt.

The new little chapel was beautiful. Sunlight came in the stained-glass window making prisms of the colors so they lay on black clad shoulders or wrinkled old faces like small colored butterflies.

I must come back by myself someday when it is empty and pray, she thought.

Hans' hand was firm and hard under her elbow steering her.

"Dr. and Mrs. Mosier, this is my wife, Felly. Felly, this is Mr. and Mrs. Swen Anderson and their daughter, Lise."

That's five...Felly was counting mentally, hoping her smile and responses were not too wooden.

"Mr. and Mrs. Karl Davenport."

"How do you do..." "Very pleased to meet you..." "I've heard so much about you," Eight...nine...ten...oh, please Hans, no more—

"Mr. Felberg... and this is Rev. Brook from Springfield. You remember Rev. Brook?"

If men knew what it felt like to be six months pregnant. Hans kept promising he was going to get her some help, but every time he did he was dissatisfied. They had had a querulous old woman for a while. Hans could not abide her bossy ways and had dismissed her. They had tried a young girl. Hans thought she was slovenly and dismissed her, too. Felly was past caring if they were slovenly or bossy. They had been another pair of hands.

She looked at Seena, so beautiful this morning with her angel hair curled and her cheeks red from the warmth, and her heart caught. She relied too much on Seena, piled too much on her. She was just a child. Felly saw by Seena's sulky mouth she had been counting, too. Twelve. They would have twelve guests. There would be enough chairs. Now if the ham would stretch to feed them all.

* * * *

"You're tired my dear...so tired, and you're with child, aren't you?" Mrs. Davenport said, staying behind to help Felly clean the table after the meal. She was a tiny old woman in a rusty black dress with eyes like faded pansies planted in the wrinkles of her face. "You shouldn't have had all of us."

"Oh, no...no I'm fine," Felly lied. She could bear anything now but sympathy. Sympathy would make her cry. Sympathy would break her down. She rushed away from Mrs. Davenport calling to Seena to come and help.

Later, the shade of the great old trees which arched over the lemonade table was thick, and a slight breeze was coming in off the lake, but still shameful dark blots were beginning to spread under Felly's arms. Her dress was much too heavy for the day as she had known it would be. Ladies weren't supposed to perspire, especially not when they were serving lemonade. Streams were trickling down her forehead, too. She felt humiliated.

"You shouldn't be here standing on your feet," Thelma Vesper said, "You shouldn't have been asked in your condition. Why didn't you speak up?"

Thelma was a notorious gossip with a malicious tongue. Felly had never liked her, so she was more than touched to find the sprightly, rather ugly old woman, wiping her face with a handkerchief and taking the ladle from her hand.

"Go home and rest, Mrs. Jacobson. I'll take over."

This time the tears did come. Her mouth quivered uncontrollably.

"Go," Thelma ordered in a tone which for her was kind.

Felly found she could not speak so she just squeezed the woman's hand in silent gratitude and escaped. How kind other women could be. They understood.

She went back to the house, tore off the awful hot dress, buried her face for a moment in a basin of cold water. The house was so quiet, so empty. How wonderful to be in the house all by herself, to be alone.

It was seldom she got to be alone. She pressed a linen towel to her wet face and stared in the mirror.

Felly Jacobson. Who was Felly Jacobson? Once she had been a little girl named Firefly, a little girl who wore blue velvet and ribbons in her hair and was always petted and spoiled. Then she had been Felicity Quimby, a spirited, flirting young woman who had teased and danced and always had her own way. Where had those selves gone? Now she was Felly Jacobson...somebody else.

She went to the bureau drawer and reaching far back drew out the little box with the Firefly necklace Dan-Pete had given her long ago. The copper and stones felt cool in her fingers. Holding the necklace seemed to give her back something of herself. She laid down on the bed with it still in her hands and let her great weariness overcome her. She slept.

Hans found her still sleeping hours later. The hands that shook her shoulders were rough, the face bending over her hard.

"Felly, what are you doing here? They're tuning up at the band stand. We're supposed to be there. What are you doing? Counting your old love charms like a Catholic counts beads?" sarcasm twisted his voice.

Struggling to come out of the dark, deep sleep she had been in, Felly had a momentary desire to strike the hard face above her with a stinging slap. Then she sat up, ashamed, her cheeks reddening as she realized how it must look to Hans to find her laying there with Dan-Pete's necklace draped across her breasts. Hans had heard about her thwarted romance with Dan-Pete, and once when she had worn the firefly necklace and he had thought it very curious, she had admitted it was a gift from Dan-Pete.

"I was...was just cleaning drawers when I...I dropped off..." she fumbled for an excuse, realizing how transparent and false her words sounded even as she uttered them.

"Please...get some clothes on and come," Hans said. "The children have been running wild all afternoon with no supervision. Jake got stung by a bee and someone else had to take care of him. And Seena was behind the barn with a bunch of older boys. I don't have to tell you how that looked."

Felly closed her eyes. I love them. I love them so much. But I'm so tired.

She shook out her dress and then flung its heavy imprisonment back over her head and around her body. The air was still suffocating but it would soon be evening, she could bear it until the cooler air of night.

Hans was already halfway down the stairs calling for her.

She took time to slide the firefly necklace back into its box. A wry little smile curled her lips. She could scarce manage in this nice home with Hans' good salary and she had thought she could live in a wigwam? She closed the drawer with gentle fingers and hurried to join her husband.

CHAPTER 16
Grandma Caroline

***

"For God hath not given us a spirit of fear; but of power, and of love, and of a sound mind."
(2 Timothy 1:7)

The children loved it when Grandma Caroline came to stay. Jason loved his Grandma Caroline. She had a wonderful fragrance about her and the most beautiful clothes he had ever seen, and she treated children differently than most adults. She was differential to children and interested in what they had to say. Jason loved to talk to her because she always thought everything he said was marvelous and wise. Grandma Caroline always looked right into his eyes when she talked to him, and always made time for each of them alone. When she stayed at their house, the four children took turns sleeping with her.

Jason wasn't surprised when Grandma Caroline said she wanted to speak to him alone for a few minutes. But he was surprised when she took him to her room and closed the door and then sat down and pulled him close against her knees looking quite solemn. Usually when they had "alone times," they went for walks together or she took them places in her carriage.

"Jason," she said, her voice solemn, "you are getting to be quite a big lad now, and I know you understand about birthing for you told me how you watched the foal being born in the livery stable. But your brother and sisters don't understand yet. Your mother is going to have a baby today, Jason. She may moan and cry out a little as women sometimes do when they are giving birth, and we don't want to frighten the younger children. Can you take them out and keep them occupied for the afternoon?"

"I can take them picking hazelnuts," Jason offered. "They like to gather nuts and there are still lots of them in the woods."

"That would be fine, Jason. I'll pack a picnic lunch for you, and you take them off to pick nuts."

"Is my mother all right, Grandma Caroline?"

"Your mother will be fine, Jason. Your father has gone for Doctor Bentley and everything is as it should be. Come along to the kitchen now."

The day was fine also. Autumn had come. The deciduous trees were already ablaze. The sun was hot in a cobalt sky, but the breeze which shook small flurries of leaves from the trees and riffled the surface of the lake was tinged with an edge of cold, a chill that tingled the blood and swept away late summer lethargy.

Seena, Saran and Jake were delighted at the prospect of a picnic and nut picking. For a special treat, Jason made a pot of fudge while Grandma Caroline made the rest of the picnic lunch. Jake stood on tiptoe to peer into the kettle, licking his lips with anticipation at the smell of the melted butter and the vanilla. Seena helped pour the fudge into a pan to cool.

Then Doctor Bentley's black buggy pulled up in front of the house and the doctor and Hans jumped out and hurried into the house and past them up the stairs.

Saran's face went white. "Is mother sick?"

"No," Jason said, herding them out to the back vestibule. "We'd all better take sweaters, it's kind of cold. Jake, have you got a pail?"

"Mother is sick, isn't she, Jason?" Saran said biting her thumb. "We haven't seen her all morning."

Grandma Caroline joined them in the vestibule, handing them their picnic basket. "Your mother is fine, Saran. Run off now and have your picnic and your mother will see you when you get back."

The three children looked at each other, still worried. Grandma Caroline wouldn't lie to them, but why had the doctor rushed up the stairs so fast? Once Jason got them started down the lane, their anxiety diminished and then disappeared in the beauty of the day and the interest of their venture.

"I know where there's lots of hazel nuts," Saran confided. "There's a whole grove of hazel bushes next to Per's place."

Jason wasn't sure he wanted to go anywhere near Per's. Per was a squat Dutchman with small, hazy red eyes, a stubbled beard and a sour odor. One night a sobbing neighbor had come running to their house to say Per was beating up his wife. His father had gone with the neighbor to try and help. When his father had come home, he had a big blue lump on his forehead and his mother had to put cold towels on it.

"Did Per hit you?" Jason had asked, his round eyes getting bigger.

"No, he did not. Per's wife did, which teaches me not to interfere in a domestic quarrel. And what are you doing up this late anyway? Doesn't this child have a bedtime?" his father had said crossly. Jason was remembering all this.

"I don't like to go by Per's place," Jason admitted.

"But he's not at home in the daytime," Seena said with certainty. "He works at the mill, and the rest of the time he's in the tavern."

With this assurance, they proceeded on to the place where Saran was sure there was a wealth of nuts. She was right. The grass shook and the leaves which had already fallen stirred and crunched with quick, darting, furry forms with plumed tails, for the squirrels were hard at work getting their share.

The Jacobson children were soon scurrying about like little squirrels themselves. In a short time, every pail was filled. Usually Jason would have been delighted. Now he was not pleased. The day was cooler than they had thought and even with sweaters on, their noses and fingers were cold. The children were anxious to go home now and show their treasure to Grandma Caroline.

"We can eat at home where it's warm," Saran pointed out.

"Aw, that's no picnic," Jason decried, not wanting the mission entrusted to him to fail.

"But you forgot the fudge," Jake complained. "I want to go home so we can have the fudge."

"If we go home they'll put us to work, you know they will," Jason said in desperation. "Why don't we go back to the old barn in our stony field and eat our picnic. It'll be warmer in there. Then I'll run back and get the fudge."

The other children looked at each other. What Jason said was true. Their father was home. He would put them to work at some chores. He hated to see idle children.

Besides, they remembered there was a hay rope inside the old barn which was fun to swing on.

Seena made the decision. "Okay, Jason, but hurry back with the fudge and put the nutcracker in your pocket."

Jason ran all the way back home. The kitchen felt warm and close after the brisk chill of outdoors, and the whole house was so quiet it was eerie. He stood listening for a moment waiting for his heart to stop pounding after the long run. He could hear the wind rattling a few shingles, but there was no human sound.

With a sense of fear, he set down the fudge pan and went to the bottom of the stairs which led to the bedrooms, still listening. Where was everyone? What was happening? Why was everything so quiet?

To his immense relief, Grandma Caroline appeared at the top of the stairway and came floating down to him, a flurry of white petticoats peeping from beneath her pinafore.

"Jason. I thought I heard someone down here."

"I came back after the fudge. I forgot the fudge. Everything is so still."

Grandma Caroline smiled and chucked him under the chin. "Your father and the doctor just left. You have a new baby sister, Jason."

"Can I see my mother?"

"She's very tired now. I think you'd best not bother her quite yet. But if you'd like to see your sister, I'll bring her down."

He nodded and waited, leaning against the stair balustrade for her return.

She came back with a triangle of flannel in her arms. "You're still cold from outside so just look, don't touch her," she cautioned as she folded back one corner of the triangle. "Here's your little sister. A red-haired sister."

When Caroline showed Jason the baby, she told him, "Your papa named this child Rasmeena. That's a big name for such a wee child, but if it suits your papa, your mama will love it too—for she is happy to have another little girl in the family."

Jason couldn't remember Seena being born. But he could remember when Jake arrived, and what he remembered about birth was Grandpa Bay had come the time when Saran was born, and had played the piano and carried each child around for a time on his tall shoulders. But Jason hadn't felt too much one way or the other about any birth event.

Now he looked at the little face framed by white flannel and felt wonder and tenderness touch his heart. She was so small and her eyes were closed like a newborn kitten's. Her perfect little round head looked damp and was covered with commas of red-brown hair. In some mysterious way, she had come from inside his mother. He had come from inside his mother too. This was his little sister.

Jason and Grandma Caroline smiled into each other's eyes.

"Can I go tell the others?"

"You may go tell the others but keep them away for a time yet if you can. Your mother needs quiet and rest for a while."

She snuggled the flannel back around the little face and went back up the stairs.

Jason ran back out into the nippy day, remembering to bring the fudge. By the time he got to the foot bridge over a little ravine, he saw his brother and sisters already coming down the lane towards home.

"Per chased us out of the barn," Jake called, full of indignation.

"He didn't have any right...it's not his barn," Jason said, crossing the bridge to the trio.

"He didn't really chase us out," Seena explained, "he just came and stood in the doorway and looked at us, and Saran got so scared she started to cry, so we all ran."

"His eyes were red," Saran said. Her own eyes were red from her tears and her braids were coming unraveled.

"Never mind, I've got something wonderful to tell you," Jason said. "Let's go over under that tree and eat our fudge and I'll tell you..."

"Let's go home and eat our fudge. I'm cold," Saran said.

"We've got a new baby sister!" Jason said, unable to contain the news any longer.

He was amazed when Seena stopped, looked at him and screamed, "You damn, damn liar! You damn, damn liar! We've got enough kids," and burst into tears.

"I wouldn't lie to you, Seena," Jason protested, nonplused by her behavior.

"Dammit, dammit, dammit," she screamed, stamping her foot so hard dust rose about her ankles.

The other children stared at her unbelieving. Nobody in their family ever swore except Hans and he only when he ran a nail in his hand, or a horse stepped on his foot, or something accidental happened.

"Listen to me, Seena...the baby's name rhymes with yours...Grandma said her name is Rameena...Rameena and Seena... kinda like a song, isn't it?"

"There's already too many of us," Seena said, and then she started to cry.

Jason came and touched his sister awkwardly. He felt surprised and grieved at her pain. "Seena...don't, please, Seena," he said. "When you see her, you'll like her. You will. She's so tiny and she's got red hair."

Seena shook her head. "No, I won't like her. It's easy for you to say, Jason because you won't have to take care of her. I always have to untangle Jake's shoelaces and unsnarl his hair and wipe his chin and cut his meat...and now I'll never have time to play."

Jason couldn't bear the angry tears in his sister's eyes. He had expected her to feel the wonder and mystery and joy he had felt when he had looked at the new baby, wanted her to feel those things. He had never realized until this moment how much he loved Seena, how much he wanted her to be happy.

"Seena...I'll take care of the baby, so you won't have to. I promise," he said recklessly.

She shook her head. "No, you won't, Jason, because you're a boy, and because you always run away and do whatever you want to anyway, and no one can stop you, not even Papa."

Then, perhaps, feeling she had gone too far, she ducked her head and laid it for a minute against his shoulder. "But thank you anyway, Jason, I know you'll help me, and I do love you, Jason, but we don't need any more kids," and she wailed harder than before.

A bit overwhelmed by this forthright announcement, Jason put his arm around Seena and led her over to the tree next to the bridge.

"We're not supposed to go home just yet," he explained. "Grandma Caroline says Mother needs to rest for a while. Let's have our fudge."

He had forgotten to bring a knife so they had to scoop it out with their fingers. Seena wouldn't take any.

"How do babies get born?" Saran asked, licking fudge off her forefinger.

Jason suspected he wasn't supposed to tell because they had sent the younger children away to protect them from the birthing, but he couldn't forebear exhibiting his superior knowledge.

"Well, the baby grows inside the mother somehow. And when she gets too big, she bursts open...you know, just like a pumpkin when it gets too ripe. And then the doctor comes and takes the baby out and sews the mother back up."

Saran's eyes were as round as poker chips. "Did our mother burst open?"

"It's all right, Saran, she's all sewed back together," Jason comforted. He had figured this part of human birth out for himself because animals never seemed to need doctors.

Everybody but Seena ate fudge and fell silent for a while. Jason cracked a few nuts and ladled out the meats to the others.

"You're not the baby any more, Saran," Seena said, looking at her smaller sister, a certain satisfaction in her tone.

Saran and Jake just kept eating fudge, licking chocolate from around their mouths. They didn't seem to be bothered by Seena's resentment of having to take care of them. But later when they started home, Jason noticed Saran dragged her feet in the dust and stuck her stomach out in a funny, strutting way. And Jason realized nothing was ever going to be quite the same, somehow the new baby had changed everything for everyone.

Only later did the children learn the baby was really named Rasmeena after her Swedish grandmother, but Jason called her

Rameena, and in no time, the entire family, even Hans, shortened it to Meena.

CHAPTER 17
Grace Ott's Charming Proposal

***

"But now faith, hope, love, abide these three;
but the greatest of these is love."
(1 Corinthians 13:13 NASB®)

To occupy and amuse himself Adam had taken to writing essays and articles of opinion for *The Century*, a journal devoted to "inquiry, controversy, and instruction in all matters of interest to intelligent citizens."

He was surprised at the end of March of that year to receive an invitation from Dr. Leonard Drunker, the publisher of *The Century* to come to Boston to lecture and expand on a series of essays he had written concerning Darwinism. The English naturalist's theories of evolution had been causing the pages of *The Century* to flare with pros and cons for some time. Adam's essays had been the first to suggest the two viewpoints might be reconciled. Dr. Drunker had been impressed with his insight and was interested in seeing it given a wider hearing.

Adam was long past any desire to be intellectual or to acquire scholarly fame. His articles in *The Century* were signed as Q. Ordinarily he would have refused the opportunity, but the winter had been long, spring had not yet come, and Adam was lonely and restless. The prospect of discourse with a man of Dr. Leonard's intellectual prowess was not without appeal. He accepted the invitation.

When he arrived in Boston a gray, wet April day, an agitated and harried Dr. Drunker met him at the station. Short and portly with mutton chop whiskers and the finest bowler hat money could buy, Dr. Drunker sputtered out his words in such a rapid string Adam had to listen hard to understand what he was saying as the gentleman towed him along by the arm.

"My dear fellow, I am so charmed to meet you. I have looked

forward to this, and to think now I shan't have the opportunity to have the long discussions I had planned for us at all...I am quite devastated...I say, I must apologize to you...so unfortunate...turn this way dear fellow, please. Your observations on Darwin...brilliant, yes, brilliant...a voice of reason amidst conflagrating opinions...oh, I was explaining to you...there...here is the coach which will take you to The Vendome on Newbury Street...best hotel-manor in Boston I assure you and excellent food."

"I did expect to entertain you in my home of course...had looked forward to it, but I'm being called away for the entire week. No help for it. I'm blasted mad this should come up, but I'm sure you are a man of affairs yourself and understand about these things. My associate, Robert Higgins, will look after you. He's a terrible bore but try to suffer him. The lecture will be a great success I know. I'm sure of it. You'll come again. We'll have our discussions yet. There you go dear fellow, into the coach."

The next thing Adam knew he was being driven away while Dr. Drunker waved heartily before running to board the departing train himself.

Robert Higgins turned out to be quite the bore Dr. Drucker had promised. A fundamentalist, he resented Adam's reconciling view of Darwinism and other than to explain his lodging and meals at the Vendome were paid for, and to direct him to the location of the lecture hall, Higgins did nothing further to make Adam feel at home in Boston.

Since the lecture was being held under the impress of the Unitarians, as well as *The Century*, Adam expected a somewhat sympathetic audience. The Unitarians had been formed into a church from the impetus of thought begun by such giants as Ralph Waldo Emerson and prided themselves on openness and tolerance of new ideas.

The audience he faced that cold and windy night in April proved to be anything but sympathetic to his message. Dr. Drunker had done a good job of publicizing the event and a collection of anti-evolutionist groups had come full force to contradict and squash this message of reconciliation before it should gain a foothold in local thought.

There was much heckling from the audience, an experience new to Adam who had hitherto spoken only at churches, the pulpits of which permitted neither applause nor ridicule. He did his best to handle the situation with humor and grace.

"What did you say your name was, sir?" he asked one rude heckler.

"I did not say. But if you wish to know, it is Heidler. William

Heidler."

"Mr. Heidler, my message is opposite to what you seem to perceive it to be. I am not denying a Creator. I am not denying God. Rather I am saying, what compassion, what love our Creator, our God, shows...in the evolution of His creatures. A tiny insect finds it cannot survive without wings, a loving God bestows these wings. Another species beset by enemies is supplied with the mysterious ability to change the color of its body to match its habitat, gaining invisibility. To me, evolution is not a denial of God but a wonderful testimony. He cares about the exigencies of His tiniest creations, mankind too can rely on being loved and cared for, to have our changing needs met."

There were wild bursts of applause and even wilder jeers throughout the evening. By the time the lecture had run its course, Adam was both exhilarated by the duel and exhausted by the effort. He waved away the press of people who descended upon the lectern following the lecture eager to continue the argument or to offer congratulations.

"Bring your objections tomorrow night. We'll give them a hearing in front of the entire audience," he promised. He was surprised then when he had fastened his papers back into his briefcase to look up and find one lone woman still in the now dim and deserted hall.

She came forward at his glance, a youngish woman in a plain brown suit. Her features were not exactly pretty. Her chin was rather short and the word which came to Adam's mind for her cheekbones and nose was—knobby. But she had large, beautiful brown eyes and when she smiled, her teeth (which protruded a little) were extra-ordinarily white. In addition, she had shiny dark hair, so in the aggregate she was extremely attractive, especially when she smiled.

"Rev. Quimby...I had to wait and tell you what a superb job you did tonight under the most difficult of circumstances. Not to have lost your temper once, under such rude and brutal provocation, was so commendable."

He smiled back at her. "Your words are ointment to my wounds. You are then, I take it, a Darwinist...or at least maybe willing to consider it true."

"I'm not sure where I stand," she confessed, "I'm pulled in both directions, which is why I came to the lecture. May I introduce myself? I'm Grace Ott Benjamin. You may have heard of my uncle, Stuart Ott."

"Stuart Ott, the eminent naturalist?" Adam took the slender brown-gloved hand being offered.

"Yes, and therein lies my difficulty. I have been helping my uncle for some time in his study of phylum and I cannot help but perceive that what Mr. Darwin says has foundation in fact, and yet, being of a religious persuasion the evolutionary theory has caused me confusion and pain."

"Miss Benjamin, it is a great pleasure to meet you, and I hope my thoughts on the matter, simple as they are, may prove helpful to you,"

"Oh, they have...tonight meant so much to me...I...well that's why I had to come forth and to tell you."

Adam gathered up his coat and hat. "I cannot tell you how much I appreciate that you did. I will now face tomorrow's lions with new courage," he told her with a smile.

"I'm looking forward to tomorrow night," she said with her wide white smile. She turned to leave.

Adam, watching her trim back retreating down the aisle, found himself calling after her, "Miss Benjamin?"

She turned back, eyes eager.

"Would you care to dine with me? I'm alone in the city and..."

"Oh, yes, yes," she breathed, "I should be delighted...so delighted."

They walked the distance to the Vendome, talking all the way. Adam's exhaustion had evaporated.

He noted his companion's figure, like her face, just missed being conventionally beautiful. She was delicately made but was much taller than the popular ideal for a woman. Adam was a tall man but she had no need to tilt her head to meet his eyes on a level. She had a straight carriage but her figure was marred by a flat bosom that made her look angular. She was evidently of too honest, or perhaps uncaring a nature, to stuff her corsets as more wily females did.

When she took her hat off in the dining room he noticed again how beautiful her hair was and how uniquely it was styled. Though the back was drawn into the conventional chignon, the front hair had been cut in bangs and the side hair too had been cut short so it fell across her cheeks when she looked down or moved her head, which she did all the time. The animation of her expressions was also fascinating to watch. He found himself charmed with her and they lingered over dinner to an embarrassing length. The waiters were giving them sour glances before they at last forced themselves to crumple their napkins and shut off the flow of their discourse.

"It has been such a pleasant evening, Miss Benjamin...would you by any chance be free to do me the honor of being my companion tomorrow night as well?"

She flushed with pleasure. "Oh, yes, I will be free. I would love to."

They parted in a state of the exceptional high excitement which comes from mutual attraction.

On the second night of his lectures, Adam, perhaps because there was now someone he wanted to impress in the audience, far exceeded his first effort. He was brilliant, he was funny, he was scathing and destructive to his critics and opponents while all the time remaining civil and courteous. He turned every barb into laughter at their expense, until even the boldest of his distracters began to lapse into disgruntled silence, not relishing his ability to make them look ridiculous.

The crowd which flowed forward after this lecture was mostly of a congratulatory nature. But Adam felt curiously impatient for his admirers to be gone. At last the final hand had been pressed, the last autograph given, the parting remark rendered and he looked up to find Grace Ott Benjamin waiting.

He could not deny his heart gave a flip. The evening was a replay of the one before except they ranged further afield in their discussions. He found out despite the rather severe, plain clothes Grace chose for herself, she was a seamstress and a designer. She worked with her uncle only in her spare time. Her parents were dead; she had no brothers or sisters, and had been living with her uncle for six years. They were very compatible. He was a widower and his children were scattered to several extremities, so he welcomed her presence in his home.

They talked about the recession ravaging the nation, socialism versus democracy; Mary Baker Eddy and the new religion she called Christian Science, which was causing quite a furor in the nation, especially in Boston; of Blondin who was planning to go over Niagara Falls in a barrel.

Grace was interested and conversant in everything from politics to poetry and the evening again went so fast they could not believe it.

The following day the weather, which had been inclement for all of Adam's stay, relented and became fairer, encouraging him for the first time to venture out to explore the city. He was particularly interested in the contrivances the newspapers were calling horseless carriages. He had seen detailed pictures of them in journals, but now for the first time he found some on the streets of Boston in all their three-dimensional fascination. The owners were always more than delighted to point out all the features and peculiarities of the conveyances and one man even insisted upon giving Adam a short, sputtering ride about the block.

The city was also full of bicycles. On this fair day, they were everywhere. People rode them to work. Messengers used then when carrying messages throughout or about the city. Postmen used them to deliver mail. Children rode them to school. Adam determined at once to buy one, have it crated and take it back for Jason. He spent many hours finding just the right cycle and after riding it about at the shop owner's insistence to "get the feel of it," ended up buying one for himself as well.

Exhilarated with his day's adventures he looked forward to sharing them again that evening with Miss Grace Benjamin. He was disappointed when she did not come to the lecture and berated himself for forgetting to ask her to join him again for supper. He had somehow taken it for granted she would attend. However, he was tired and it felt good to get to bed early.

The next day was his final lecture. The weather turned inclement again. Indeed, it was so nasty out, a veritable downpour of mean lashing rain that for the first time the lecture hall was poorly filled. When again Miss Benjamin was not there at the end of the lecture, Adam had to admit to a sharp sting of disappointment. He would have liked to say goodbye to her and to thank her for making his stay so much more pleasant than it would have been without her companionship.

He was fortunate to get a carriage back to the hotel, but once there he did not feel like eating a lonely supper. He felt bored and restless and decided to venture out again into the stormy weather. He might have treated himself to a theatrical production, but his lecture had lasted until nine o'clock so it was too late. He got soaked waiting for a carriage, since they were much in demand on such a terrible night. He then gave up and wandered for some time feeling the cold and getting wetter before conceding he was not enjoying himself and might as well go back to the hotel and turn in.

He must have walked three blocks in the pouring rain before he turned a corner and collided with a hurrying figure carrying a black umbrella.

He was amazed and delighted when the street lamp revealed the owner of the umbrella was Miss Benjamin. Her face was a study.

"What...what are you doing here?" she cried in a tone almost accusatory.

"What am I doing here? I am trying to get a carriage to take me back to the Vendome. Why, is there something wrong with my being here?"

"Oh, no...no! You're soaking, you're simply soaking. Do come under my umbrella."

He did not have to be asked again. He was soaking. And there they were standing under her umbrella very close together with the rain pouring all around them.

"You're soaking," she said again. "You must come and get dried out. My home is just around this corner and up the street a few doors."

"Miss Benjamin, I'm so glad to have run into you this way. I was very sorry not to have an opportunity to say goodbye to you."

"My house is just a few doors..." she was towing him along now with her umbrella, "please do come and get dried out."

"I don't want to intrude on your uncle. I'm sure any moment now I'll be able to flag a carriage."

Under the umbrella, she looked at him with a tilt of her head. "My uncle isn't there. Please...come."

The house was, as she said, just around the corner and they were by now at the doorstep. He went with her up the steps of the impressive house, large and square with a double front door of etched and frosted glass.

She led him into a world of Aubusson carpets, Havilland china, Duncan Phyfe furniture, silver serving sets. She took him to the library where she said there was a fire. There was, though it needed replenishing. He stoked the fire bed while she took his coat to hang it over a heat register. The house had a furnace as well as fireplaces. He was aware of the impropriety of being there with her alone in the absence of her uncle, and yet he had not been able to refuse her invitation.

She came back with a towel for his wet hair and two glasses of wine on a silver tray.

"This will warm you, if you are not against spirits," she said.

"This is most kind of you Miss Benjamin. I have to admit I was getting chilled." He took the glass she offered. For the first time since they had known each other, they both seemed at a loss for words.

"You were wondering what I was doing here...what were you doing out so late?" he ventured.

"I was with a sick relative."

"Oh...I'm sorry."

"It's nothing. She's something of a hypochondriac."

A beat of silence between them. He fished for another topic.

"I missed you at the lectures."

She turned away from him and went to the window, parting the lace curtains to stare out at the rain. When she turned back, the color in her cheeks was high.

"I deliberately deprived myself of going...because...because..."

"Because why?"

"Because I felt I was falling in love with you," she said.

113

He felt color flare in his own cheeks. "Miss Benjamin..."

She interrupted him. "Then to run into you on the street this way, when I had quite determined I was being a foolish woman. Well it does seem...it seems at the least very serendipitous."

"Miss Benjamin...I..."

She rushed on, "I had been reading Shakespeare this evening, you know the part where he says, 'There is a tide in the affairs of men. Which, taken at the flood, leads on to fortune; Omitted, all the voyage of their life is bound in shallows and in miseries. On such a full sea are we now afloat, and we must take the current when it serves, or lose our ventures.' I think it must be so in women's lives too. I should never think of saying such things to you, except if I don't, you are going to walk out of here and go away tomorrow and I shall never see you again. Rev. Quimby, Adam, I want to go with you."

He stared at her unbelieving.

She left the curtain, coming to him, half supplicating, half defiant. "Must you look so stupefied? Did you feel nothing special between us?"

"I felt a great deal special between us...but you are a young woman, I'm a man in my sixties, disfigured at that. You know nothing of me."

"I know more of you than you realize. I have followed your essays in *The Century* for months. I do not fear putting my destiny in the hands of the man who wrote those words. And as for young, I am not so young, Adam. Look at me. I'm a woman in my late thirties. I disdained all the youths who came courting me in my younger years. They seemed callow and I was determined not to marry a man who would bore me. I wanted a man of intellect. I have found that in you, Adam."

"Miss Benjamin...Grace, I am enormously flattered," Adam said. "I am also astounded. But I must be honest with you. I have had two wives, neither of whom I made happy, and I am still in a certain sense in love with my first wife, though she is forever out of my reach. I have never entertained the idea of marrying again. I must admit you have rather shocked me. But...I-I admire your forthrightness and honesty and I would like to explore our friendship further"

"Explore our friendship further?" She turned a little aside from him. "You are the first man I have ever felt I would like to be with," she declared, her glance as well as her body a little averted. She took a small breath and then looked back at him.

"I'm in my late thirties, Adam. My uncle is very kind but my life is static. I would like a home of my own—children. Time is passing for me. Can you understand that? I'm not interested in or desirous of conventional courtship. I am in short—a maiden lady who is a little desperate. Now you have wrested this humiliating confession from me, please go. Go back to the hotel and think about it—and let me know in the morning...will you?"

"Grace, I did not mean in any way to humiliate you. I..."

"I humiliated myself and I'm not sorry. Please just promise me you will think over what I have said and tell me your decision one way or the other in the morning." She handed him his coat. "It's stopped raining," she said.

* * * *

He returned in the morning as he had promised.

"Grace, I've given it a good deal of thought," he said. "I am not a man of means. What property I have is deeded to my daughter, which I feel I owe to her for the treatment I accorded her in her early years. I'm much too old for you, and in all truth, most of my fire is spent. You will never know how tempted I was by your frank and charming proposal. But in all fairness to you, I must say I would do you a great disservice to hold you to your invitation."

To his amazement, Grace threw back her head and burst into laughter.

"Most of your fire spent...oh, Adam," she laughed so hard it was infectious and he could not help laughing with her. At last, she wiped her eyes and grew serious again.

"Never mind all these reasons why I shouldn't marry you. I want you to answer one question for me with utmost truthfulness. Do you find me unattractive?"

"Oh, no, no. I do not find you unattractive, quite the contrary."

The smiling light came back to her eyes. "In which case, you would do me a great disservice not to marry me, Adam Quimby."

He took her into his arms and kissed her, realizing as he did so he had wanted to do it from the first night. The kiss was his capitulation.

"I packed my bags, just in case," she said. "They are behind the door."

"What about your uncle," Adam demanded, still amazed at the turn of events.

"I wrote him a note," Grace said.

Adam Quimby and Grace Ott Benjamin were married April 26, 1902 at Madison, Wisconsin.

* * * *

Felly looked up at her father and shook her head with disbelief. "A bicycle, Papa? A bicycle? Hans will be furious with you."

Adam flushed red. "Well—you can say it's yours and then give it to him later. I don't know about buying bonnets and stuff like your mother does. This proves it, doesn't it," he said with a helpless gesture. "I did the best I could."

Felly laughed and threw her arms around him. "Oh, Papa there is no one like you, and I do love you so much."

"Firefly," he said as he took her hands from around his neck and held them in his own, his face becoming serious and intent, "I've brought you another surprise—something a bit shocking I fear."

"Whatever is it, Papa?" Felly asked, feeling concern at the sudden somberness of her father's face.

"Fly...I...I married again. Your new step-mother is waiting outside in the carriage.

She thought I should break it to you first. Please...be good to her. She is quite wonderful."

"Married? Papa, it's so...sudden! I had no idea. You never. . ."

"It happened very suddenly."

"Of course, I'm happy for you. It's just. . .just. . ."

"You weren't at all prepared, of course. Come and meet her."

"Wait, Papa. Let me tidy my hair."

A flurry of emotions went through Felly. She had long hoped her father might find someone to share his life with and to make him happy. She had worried about his aloneness. But now that it had happened she was surprised to find, along with an honest joy for her father, other less commendable feelings. She had for so long occupied the throne of her father's highest affection it was not easy to abdicate it to another. And she had always known, even though Caroline was married to Bay, her father loved her mother. She felt a curious jealousy for her mother as well. Someone else would now have Adam's first allegiance. It was not so much her hair Felly needed to smooth as her tumbling emotions.

"Come," Adam said again, and now he was smiling and eager. "She, she's younger than you are, Fly. I know how shocking that is. But that's the way it is."

Felly followed him full of trepidation. Would her smile look forced? Would her voice sound cool? She wanted to behave well but....

The woman sitting in the carriage was sitting with a very upright posture. She was wearing dark clothing. She looked rigid.

"Grace this is Firefly. Fly, my wife, Grace."

The woman turned her head and her dark eyes met Felly's. She leaned forward holding out her hands. All the fear inside Felly melted. She knew at once they would be friends.

116

CHAPTER 18
Hepsie Cat and a Whipping

***

"And when ye stand praying, forgive, if ye have ought against any: that your Father also which is in heaven may forgive you your trespasses."
(Mark 11:25)

Dr. Bentley's wife, Isabel, was standing in her backyard in a state of agitation. "Jason," she called catching sight of him as he came along the street. "Come here."

Mrs. Bentley was an uncertain quality. Sometimes she gave him butterscotch balls and told him delightful stories about the Fourth of July when she was a little girl. Other times she made him help her pull burdocks out of her dog or pull quack grass out of her flower beds and regaled him with long boring narratives about, "Mrs. Patrick, who was Fred Warren's cousin—now that would be a second cousin to my mother's aunt, and I do believe your mother told me your grandmother was also related to the Warren's through my Aunt Virginia's second marriage."

Jason had adventures of his own in mind and he would like to have scampered away but he saw Mrs. Bentley knew he had heard her so he came reluctantly forward.

"My kitty, Hepsie, got up on the roof and now she's too little to get herself down and she's crying and crying and it's driving me crazy. Please climb up and get her down for me, Jason."

Jason hesitated. "Papa doesn't want me up on roofs, Mrs. Bentley."

"Nonsense. I've seen you running around on roofs dozens of times."

"I know. Papa saw me too and he said I'm not to do it anymore. He said it makes the roof leak to walk on it and besides, someday I'm sure to fall."

"Well, this is different," Mrs. Bentley said. "It's my roof and I'm telling you to get on it and get my cat down for me."

Jason still hesitated, remembering his father's anger the last time he had been caught on a rooftop. "My papa might tan me, Mrs. Bentley."

"Well, he would tan you for sure for not doing what I tell you to, if he knew. I'll take full responsibility about the roof. Now you wiggle yourself up there and get Hepsie down."

Mrs. Bentley was used to having her own way and her smoky eyes were sending off sparks by now. Besides Jason could hear the plaintive frantic cries of the little cat, too, and he liked climbing around on roofs, so he didn't argue anymore.

It was easy to get on the Bentley's roof. He had done it lots of times until his Papa caught him and bawled him out. There was a sturdy oak with lots of crotched branches close to the house so it was a simple matter to shinny up the tree and jump onto the roof.

Hepsie arched her back and hissed when she saw him coming, but when she felt his warm hands around her and he had lifted her against his shirt front the little striped cat snuggled against him and purred with relief.

He was just thinking it would be more of a trick to get down the tree with only one hand when Mrs. Bentley hoisted him a basket on a rake handle.

"Put Hepsie in the basket and lower her down," she instructed.

Her plan worked fine. Jason laid on his stomach on the flat part of the roof over the kitchen and lowered the basket to Mrs. Bentley who rescued Hepsie from its depths with a great deal of clucking and fussing.

Jason was just climbing back on to the part of the roof near the oak tree when his father's voice startled him with a thunderous roar, "Jason!"

He hadn't expected to see his father away from the power house at this time of day, and he was so startled he lost his balance and went sliding down the sharp pitch of the roof. He might have fallen clear to the ground and broken something as Hans had predicted except for the good fortune of the flat part of the roof over the kitchen providing a landing.

"Jason, get yourself down here!"

Jason didn't wait to go back by the way of the oak tree. He lowered himself by his fingers from the one-story kitchen roof and dropped. By this time, his father was in the Bentley's backyard.

"How many times have I told you not to be climbing around on roof tops?" His father was breaking off a big switch from a nearby bush.

"But Papa..."

"No excuses. Get yourself home and into the woodshed."

"My dear Mr. Jacobson, please don't be rash," began Mrs. Bentley, who was still holding Hepsie against her bosom, but his father cut her off.

"Mrs. Bentley don't interfere. This is between me and my son."

"Mr. Jacobson...listen to me. You shouldn't punish Jason..."

Ignoring the fluttery Mrs. Bentley, Hans pushed Jason along ahead of him down the street.

"Papa, you don't understand," Jason pleaded.

"Did I tell you not to go up on a roof ever again?"

"Yes, Papa but..."

"Were you on a roof again?"

"Yes, Papa, but..."

"No 'but's'." I'm tired of your constant disobedience, Jason. You go your own way whatever I say and it's got to stop."

They reached the woodshed in their backyard and Hans ordered Jason to lower his trousers. "Do you know what happens to boys who never listen to their parents? They turn into criminals. Well by God, you're not going to turn into a criminal and you're going to start listening to me!"

It was not the prospect of the switch flaying his flesh which broke Jason's heart. It was his sense of justice being flayed. His father's refusal to listen to him, along with his indictment of him as a potential 'criminal,' hurt him more than anything else. He had been hit hard many times but he had never cried. He had borne it stoically, accepting he had done wrong things in his father's eyes, accepting it as the price he had to pay for doing things his father did not understand. But this was different. This time he was going to be unjustly punished and Hans wouldn't listen. When the switch hit his bare buttocks, he burst into a torrent of tears.

Hans was so startled he dropped the switch. The boy had never cried before. In the moment of his bewilderment, Jason pulled up his pants and ran out the door.

"Jason!" Hans bellowed. The boy ran on not heeding his father's shout. Hans would have pursued him and dragged him back to the woodshed for a switching for this new infraction if Mrs. Bentley, who had followed them home, hadn't caught his arm.

Her wagging head was shaking a rain of corkscrew gray curls down around her fat flushed cheeks. "Now you listen to me, Mr. Jacobson. You've no right to hit the boy. I ordered him up on the roof.

I told him I'd take responsibility. Hepsie was on the roof and we had to get her down."

Hans stared at the doctor's wife. "Mrs. Bentley, why didn't you tell me?"

"Well, you wouldn't let me!" Mrs. Bentley said with self-righteous indignation.

He could have struck the woman. Why hadn't she told him straight out that she had ordered the boy on the roof instead of posturing and fluttering about with her appeals. Hans filled his cheeks and blew out a hard puff of air. It was too late now to catch Jason; he would have to talk to the boy later.

"You must watch your temper, Mr. Jacobson, and not be so impetuous," Mrs. Bentley was preaching.

Hans snapped the switch he was still holding in two. Something about the way he did it caused Mrs. Bentley to stop her sermon and retreat to her home.

Hans walked wearily to his house. Why was it these things always happened between him and Jason? God knows he didn't want to be always at odds with the boy. He couldn't just let him have his head, let him go wild, could he? His mouth tightened. His eyes hurt with the tears men do not shed.

* * * *

Tears burning and blurring his eyes, Jason ran an erratic pell-mell course through the back garden, over the commons and up toward the road, colliding with a pair of adult legs in the process.

"Max," he sobbed, looking up to find it was his friend whom he had almost bowled over in his headlong flight.

Max stooped in the dusty road. "Jason, dear child, what is it?"

"Nothing, nothing," Jason snuffled, trying to dart around him, wanting to get away to hide somewhere until he could master these terrible baby tears, wanting his hero, Max, least of all, to see him in such straits.

Max caught his shoulder and swung him back around, "Now come here. I know there is something wrong, of course. You might as well tell me." He took out a fine linen handkerchief which smelled of Bay Rum and pressed it to Jason's cheeks to dam the tears running down.

"What happened, Jason?" So kind, so deep, such a gentle voice, it made Jason's tears run harder. The boy shook his head in shame.

"You can tell me."

"Papa tanned me. He hates me, and I hate him, too!" Jason blurted.

"Ohhh, nooo, no, now, I don't think so," Max said. He stood up

120

keeping a firm hold of the boy. "I think you'd better come back with me. We'll wash your face up a bit and have a little talk...maybe have some hot chocolate. These days are getting brisk, aren't they?"

There was nothing to do but go along with the Colonel and there was comfort in his firm, gentle grip.

Back in the Colonel's pleasant sitting room dominated by the seascape and the grand piano, the late afternoon sun striking little pieces of gold fire from the gilt mirror frames, Jason regained his composure though his heart was more stricken than he could ever remember.

While he washed his face, the Colonel made the hot chocolate from powder in a decorated tin. He made it with hot water from the Samovar since he had no milk in the house and it was not at all like the sweet, creamy cocoa Felly made. It was thin, bitter-sweet, and very hot. It tasted exotic somehow to Jason, and grown-up, as if he were drinking coffee or scotch like the boys in the horse barn.

"Now," Max said, sitting down across from him and smiling, "what is this all about?"

"Papa caned me and I hadn't even done anything!" Jason said with sullen resentment.

Max raised a skeptical eyebrow. "Your father doesn't strike me as a fellow who would do that. Are you sure there wasn't a mistake?"

"No. There wasn't any mistake. He doesn't like me. He's never liked me," Jason felt the tears starting to come again. "He said I was going to be a criminal."

Telling Max about it clarified for the boy the wellsprings of his own grief. He was not crying because he had been caned. He was crying because the vague perception he had carried as long as he could remember that his father did not really like him had been confirmed for him, in the dark woodshed when his father wouldn't listen.

"He likes Jake and the girls, but not me," Jason said.

"I doubt that very much," the Colonel said. "What makes you think such a terrible thing?"

Jason told him about climbing on the roof for Mrs. Bentley and his father not being willing to listen. "And...and he bought Jake a beautiful, shiny gold cornet and he won't let me play it. He has one, and he got one for Jake and they're going to be in the band and play for the parades and play on the bandstand."

Jason was overcome for a moment with the thought of playing on the ornate white bandstand in the park with everyone from all over coming to listen.

"Did you ask if you could play the cornet, Jason?"

"Yes...and he said Seena and I had the piano."

"Well, that's true, isn't it? Now you won't have to share the piano with Jake."

"But they're going to play on the bandstand and they're going to wear purple uniforms with gold tassels on the sleeve and...."

"Would you rather play the coronet and wear a purple uniform or play the piano?" Max asked. "Be honest now."

It didn't take Jason long to decide. "I'd rather play the piano."

"I think your father knows that. You mustn't begrudge Jake having his chance at glory, Jason. You've had lots of applause and special attention and privileges for your playing, you know. You must wish the same for Jake."

Jason's head dipped in defeat. He stared into his chocolate cup.

"However," Max went on, "I think if your father knew how much you might like to play in the bandstand he would quite reconsider about the cornet. Would you like me to speak to him?"

"No," Jason said. "Let him and ole Jake play in the band. I don't care. I hate Papa."

Max came and sat beside Jason on the green settee. He put his arm around Jason and sighed. "No, you don't hate your papa at all, Jason. You love him very much and that's why it hurts so much."

He drew Jason closer and caressed his silky dark head. "Don't think I don't understand, my dear child. I do. And I feel for you deeply. You see, I'm afraid I was always something of a disappointment to my father, too, and my mother as well. I always felt I wasn't at all what they wanted me to be."

Jason looked at the Colonel with wide, rounding eyes. "How could they be disappointed in you, sir?" he asked in a shocked voice.

The Colonel laughed. "Oh, Jason, Jason...I just wasn't what they had in mind for a son. But it's all long ago, they've been dead for years, and there's nothing to be done about it. But that's not the case with you and your papa. You do love each other and you must find ways to show it. By the time I realized I loved my parents and in spite of everything they had loved me, it was too late. We don't want that to happen with you and your papa."

Now it was the old man's voice that had cracked and Jason looked up in amazement to see tears on Max's cheeks. It was his stubby, hot, child's fingers which reached up to brush the tears away.

"I didn't think soldiers ever cried," Jason said.

Max laughed, caught the small fingers wet with his tears and kissed them. "Oh, yes, Jason, soldiers do cry. Perhaps soldiers cry most of all. But we're very good at not getting caught at it. I won't tell if you won't tell, all right?"

"All right," Jason said, matching the grin Max was giving to him. He didn't feel so bad now about his own bawling.

"At least your mother understands you. You have a lovely mother, Jason."

The child nodded, feeling shy though he could not have said why. He wasn't sure he wanted to share the thought of his mother with anyone, not even Max.

"What have you been composing?" The tears were all past, Max's voice was strong and commanding again.

"Well, there's this new stuff..." Jason said with quick eagerness. "Mama can't stand it, but I just love it."

He ran over to the piano and began to run his fingers over the keys. "They call it ragtime. What do you think, Max?"

Max listened a minute and then winced. "I think I'm with your mother." Then he laughed, relented, came over and sat next to Jason and began to improvise on the left hand, nodding in time to the beat.

"It is spirited. Maybe you'll make a convert out of me. Ahh, Jason, we are lucky at that, you and I...we always have the solace of our music."

Jason's hands stilled on the keys, "The solace of music. That's real pretty, Max. Like poetry." The boy looked up at the man with burning eyes. "I love you, Max. More than anyone...except, except my mother."

"I love you, too, Jason," the words came out like a sigh. It's getting dark. You'd better run along home now. We have a regular lesson tomorrow. Work on those runs. They can use a little smoothing."

Jason ran out into the darkness, ran as hard as he could, his heart pumping so fast it hurt. The time had just slipped away on him again. He was going to be late for supper again, way late. He could already see his father's face.

CHAPTER 19
Great Love

***

"My beloved is mine, and I am his:
he feedeth among the lilies."
(Song of Solomon 2:16)

Felly was feeling much better. Pregnancies were always hard on her, but once the baby arrived, her spirits soared with joy and new love. Rasmeena, Meena for short, was, as Jason had told Max, a "sunshine" baby. She was seldom fretful and colicky as the other babies had often been. And Mrs. Howard was turning out to be a treasure.

A garrulous, good-natured woman, Mrs. Howard accomplished prodigious amounts of work in a slow, deliberate manner and never complained. If Felly's spirits had boomeranged back to joy, her physical strength was lagging and she thanked God and Hans every day for Mrs. Howard's strong freckled arms and willing attitude.

There was something else also filling Felly with a new reservoir of contentment and that was her friendship with Max Harrison. She was finding in the old soldier the companionship of the heart she had hoped to find with Hans when she had first married him.

Her father Adam's Grace had become pregnant also, and the two young women were sorry they could not get together as often as they would have liked. Felly had discovered early on that an invisible system of protocol operated at Camp. Her husband's "rank" as chief engineer meant she was expected to socialize with the wives of the doctors, ministers, and Commandant; hobnobbing with "service" people was frowned on.

Whatever Felly's faults, snobbery was not among them. If she had found a compatible soul among the cooks, laundresses, or nursing aides she would have winked at protocol. But what the protocol did was to segregate social doings so Felly seldom came in contact with families' other than that of managers and administrators. An unfortunate thing for her, because the doctors' wives, the Commandant's wife, and the other wives of genteel rank were all elderly women who treated her kindly but somewhat condescendingly. She suffered in their tedious presence and was glad to escape their company whenever she could.

The few younger women who might have been her natural friends thought her aloof and proud. They were jealous of her beauty, her rich parents, and what they considered her fashionable clothes. They scrutinized her at church and made catty remarks among themselves. But if Felly wore her hat tipped to one side, fixed her hair with curly bangs, or wore short lace gloves instead of long white ones, soon all the young women were wearing lace gloves, curly bangs and their hats tipped to the side. Imitation might have been flattering but friendship was not offered along with it.

Part of the malaise of spirit which had affected Felly ever since her marriage, was loneliness. Now she found in Max those qualities her heart hungered for, a love of music, an interest and understanding of literature, a wittiness, a cosmopolitan outlook, an intellect which embraced the abstract. And not the least of their friendship was based on a shared adoration of Jason.

For years, Felly's heart had ached at the distance she saw between Hans and Jason, a distance she felt was disastrous for the boy, and yet she did not know how to bring together her husband and his first-born son. That Max recognized the incipient genius in Jason, that he did all he could to nurture and support the child's musical gift, meant everything to her.

His quiet, beautifully appointed rooms were as much of a refuge to Felly as they were to Jason. There for an hour or so in an afternoon she could lay aside the cares of her own clamorous household. She could be a lady, sitting on a velvet settee, drinking tea from a china cup while she discussed the merits of Flaubert, the nature of God, or the burgeoning new movement for women's rights, with an intelligent companion. And always there was the music. He had such full command of the music, both soothing and passionate. The music of great composers which filled her emotional reservoir and sent her back to her daily rounds, inspired and renewed.

Even as she blessed Mrs. Howard's strong arms each day, she was grateful for and blessed Max's age. She was aware if he had not been a much older man, her frequent and lengthy visits would have created a scandal. His age made their friendship allowable. Even so, she knew Hans was not pleased.

On this particular afternoon spring and winter sparred outside. The tarnished winter sky could not quite hold back a breaking radiance of sun here and there. Snow softened and slid off roof tops like a barrage of distance thunder, or as Max said, "like cannons." Ground already won to spring made dark gaps in the tired landscape of snow. Max opened a window just an inch to let some of the cold sweet air into the too warm room which smelled of cologne, mint tea and the apple wood logs snapping in the fire place.

Max smiled at her as he stirred a dollop of honey into the mint tea he was offering her. "Felly, would you mind if I took Jason with me to Boston this spring? I have tickets for a concert of the celebrated European pianist Paderewski. The boy will never hear a live concert the magnitude of which this one will be. It would enhance my own pleasure a thousand-fold to share the joy of it with him."

"Why, I would be so indebted if you would take him. But the expense and he is so young. I can't guarantee he wouldn't prove a nuisance to you on a trip of several days."

"Nonsense. Jason is a delightful boy to have around. As for the expense, I'm not a wealthy man, but I have the means for this. All I need is your consent.

"Oh, more than my consent, Max. My joy he will have this opportunity, my gratitude. But..."

"But?"

"We must also have his father's permission." Two red spots grew in her cheeks and she looked down.

"Is there any reason to think he would not agree to the trip?"

She stirred her tea. "I never know with Hans, regarding Jason. Their...their relationship is not...not easy. Both my father and my mother have often wanted to take Jason on trips, but his father would never let him go. I don't know why."

"Let us anticipate in this case his answer will be affirmative," he said.

"Yes," Felly said, without conviction.

She did not want to tell Max she sensed a certain resentment in Hans about the close relationship both she and Jason had with the Colonel.

She got up restlessly and went to the window to look up at the half dark, half radiant sky. "It's such a wonderful opportunity for Jason. Maybe I won't ask him, won't risk his saying 'no.' Maybe Jason can just go with you and..."

"No," Max said, "I think you had better ask Hans. I don't want to make an enemy of him."

Felly turned back toward the room and their eyes met and held. She sighed. "You're right. But please, Max, don't mention the trip to Jason until we're sure Hans will let him go. He would be heartbroken otherwise."

"Not a word," Max promised. Then assuming a more lighthearted mien he added, "By the way, I have a gift for you."

"A gift? For me?" She flushed with surprise and pleasure.

"You said you have never read *Tristan and Isolde*. I have an extra copy. It's not wrapped because it's old, a copy I've had for a long time. But nevertheless, it is a gift, yours to keep."

"Oh, Max..." She felt embarrassed. She took the volume, leather bound, gold stamped, well used. "It's so kind of you. I'll treasure it."

"I think you will. A story of one of the earth's Great Loves."

She turned the volume gently in her hands, glancing up at him through her half-lowered eyelashes. "And you...have you ever had a 'great love'?"

She was surprised his face went dark red and a visible tremor went through his body. She feared she had offended him by asking such an intimate question. But the color passed from his face and when he answered there was no outrage in his tone just a tinge of sadness.

"Ah, yes, I have had my 'great love.'"

She sat down again on the settee, spreading her skirts, looking up at him with expectation. But he volunteered no more. Her curiosity made her dare to probe further.

"What was her name?"

He arched a dark brow at her. "How do you know it was a her? How do you know my 'great love' was not war? Or music?"

The two red spots came back into her cheeks.

"Forgive me," he said, seeing he had wounded her. He came and sat beside her on the settee. "We were talking about human love not about abstractions. And I did have such a love. But it was a long time ago, and with the joy and ecstasy great pain was mixed. I don't want to talk about it...even with you, Felly."

The 'even with you Felly,' declared her specialness to him and took away some of the sting of his unwillingness to confide in her.

"What about you, have you had a 'great love'?"

How could she tell him how much she was still haunted by Dan-Pete? Such a disclosure would be a betrayal of Hans. How could she tell him of her passionate youthful ardor for Dan-Pete; about how even now his visage appeared in her dreams, darkly radiant, disturbing, leaving her feeling an aching loss all over again. She was too ashamed to confess she had not long since put such foolishness aside. But how do you put aside a love you have vowed to have forever?

Now it was she through whom a quiver passed, she who felt warmth flood her throat and face.

"Oh, I thought I did," she said with a disparaging laugh. "I suppose it was nothing but childish infatuation, but..." her voice broke off. Now she felt her words were a betrayal of Dan-Pete, a trivialization of what had been a great passion, a passion that still lingered in the depths of her being.

"Then it was a great love," he said. "Most 'great loves' are tragedies. The world's literature bears it out."

They suddenly both felt awkward sitting so close together talking in such choked tones. She gathered her skirts closer to her and he got up and poked at the fire and closed the window which was sending a stream of cold air into the room now.

"Most people think they want a 'great love'," Max said, "but they don't really. They're better off for not suffering it. And 'suffering it' is the right term. A 'great love,' is like carrying a hot coal against your bare heart. 'Great Love' like 'Great Art' exacts a price higher than most of us are willing to pay."

"It's true few people seem to find 'a great love' but that's a hard view," Felly said, her own voice shaken by melancholy. "A hard view, but perhaps true."

He made himself smile. "And perhaps, not true. Maybe the real 'great loves' are the everyday loves, the ones which don't make great literature. The simple, enduring love of common men and women are the true 'great loves,' when you come right down to it.

"A man and a woman, often poorly suited to each other, living together side-by-side day after day, year after year, driven half-mad sometimes by the sameness of the other person and their irritating habits, the wife's shrill laughter, the husband's habit of clicking his false teeth.

"Moments of tenderness, moments of compassion for each other in sorrow, or celebration in times of joy, meted out among other moments of undeniable hatred, anger and impatience. The moments of passion or romance only a flicker of spice now and then, over the whole bland thick pudding of their marriage. And yet...by its very endurance, by its continuance through all these obstacles it is perhaps such relationships alone which deserve the name of 'great love.'"

Tears were standing in Felly's eyes when he had finished. She felt as if he had just blessed her marriage to Hans, given it a stature it had lacked in her heart, burnished it with a fierce irrevocable beauty, which had always been there but she had been too dull to see.

"Yes," she said in a low voice, "but do not ever think this second type of 'great love' costs any less than the first. The coal does not flame as hot against the bare heart, but it smolders longer."

She stood up.

"Don't go yet! Not while we are both so sad," he implored. "Let me play for you."

Why are we both so sad, why? Felly wondered. She sank back on the settee.

Outside the snow fell off the roofs in continuing barrages. Inside, the music, so full of every human passion, triumphed over it all, and left the man who played, and the woman who listened, feeling cleansed and peaceful.

CHAPTER 20
Memorial Day Parade

***

"To sum up, all of you be harmonious, sympathetic,
brotherly, kindhearted, and humble in spirit."
(1 Peter 3:8 NASB®)

The sky behind the trees was silver-white. The dew-drenched grass was silver-green. No birds sang. There was just a faint chattering more felt than heard from the periphery of the woodland. But even as Felly watched, the sun rose higher over the silent, somehow enchanted morning, and dried the greening grass into deep pools of shade or radiant golden strips. Dandelions paved vistas with quick brightness in wide carpets which would have been less despised if not so freely given. Lilac buds drooped, heavy with fragrance.

Another spring had come.

Felly moved on tiptoe through her sleeping household enveloped in a mood of gratitude and contentment. The whole family, except for Meena, was going to Waupaca on this day. There would be the adventure of riding in the streetcar. The tracks had been laid to connect Waupaca with the Grand Hotel, a fashionable resort for people from Milwaukee and Chicago. The hotel sprawled its grandeur just a short distance from their home along the shore, but high on the hill above Rainbow Lake.

Felly and the children had little occasion to ride on the streetcar. Most of their supplies were bought from local merchants, and what did have to come from Waupaca was purchased by Hans.

Hans and Jake were going to be in the Memorial Day parade. And afterward the entire family was going to be treated to ice cream sodas at the new Candy Kitchen on Waupaca's main street.

Part of Felly's contentment this morning was due to the feeling Jason and his father would be drawn a little closer through this happy circumstance of a shared family day.

When she reached the nursery, Meena's pink feet waving in the air announced the baby was awake though she had not cried. The baby was chortling to herself with some secret pleasure. Felly bent over the crib smiling for a minute before she lifted the baby for her morning feeding.

What a pleasure it was to be a mother when you had a Mrs. Howard to back you up. Without Mrs. Howard, Felly would have had to stay home while the rest of the family enjoyed the outing to Waupaca, or else tote the baby along and she knew from experience how tiring and fretful a long day grew for both baby and mother under those circumstances.

She had settled in the rocking chair with the baby when Hans appeared in the doorway, already shaved, his cheeks pink from the blade, wearing a crisp white shirt and the royal purple band uniform trousers with a gold stripe up the leg. Felly looked at her husband, noting his hair was thinning and his waist thickening. She felt a sudden aching sense of love for him.

All of this...the ambiance of the morning, the now well-ordered house, the beautiful children they, she and Hans, had created together. For the moment, the separateness and disparity she so often felt was gone, replaced with a feeling of tenderness and unity.

"Felly," he said crisply, rubbing his hands in relish at the day ahead, "shouldn't you be getting the children up? We want an early start."

She nodded and sighed, but it was a sigh of equanimity born of the knowledge Mrs. Howard had polished all the little white shoes and they were all lined up by the door; that the girl's white waists and the boy's shirts hung starched and pressed and waiting; that the pancake batter was in a pitcher to be poured on the griddle.

"Oh, by the way, Mr. Kennicut will be staying overnight with us."

Even these unexpected guests Hans had a way of throwing at her no longer riled with sturdy Mrs. Howard as her first mate.

She smiled. "Fine."

Within a few minutes, the household was buzzing like a bumblebee.

"Are we going to ride on the streetcar, Mom?" Jake was ecstatic.

"I'm going to have a chocolate soda."

"I'm going to have strawberry."

"I'm going to have banana."

"They don't make banana sodas."

"They do too. Clarence had a banana soda."

"He had a banana-split, silly!"

"What's a banana-split?"

"A banana split is a banana-split, silly."

"Stop calling your sister silly."

But all the conversation stopped, suspended in awestruck pride, when Hans and Jake appeared side by side in their royal purple band uniforms with gold epaulets and their sun-flashing deep gold cornets.

"Can Jake really play in the band?" Jason asked. "He hasn't been practicing very long."

"We'll only be playing two pieces and he knows both very well," Hans said.

Father and son put their cornets into black cases for carrying and Mrs. Howard arrived to care for Meena. She gave the family a cheerful wave off.

"My, you do look fine, Miz Jacobson, scarce older than those pretty girls of yours."

Felly shot her a grateful smile. She wished Hans might have said it.

The streetcar ride was thrilling for the children. The thought of going thirty miles an hour was startling if not fearsome, but except for the wind through the half open windows, they discovered they hardly knew they were traveling at all. It was almost like sitting in someone's parlor while the landscape outside rushed mysteriously by. Felly, of course, had ridden on trains so the experience was not so new to her.

The cars were jammed with other people like themselves, dressed in their best, headed to Waupaca for the Memorial Day celebration. Through open windows, the scents of lilacs, apple blossoms, and warming earth mingled with the smell of starched, bleached and blued clothing, shoe polish, plus a whiff of salami and fried chicken from some of the picnic baskets tucked under the seats.

Felly saw the shy look Seena gave the handsome conductor from under her lowered eyelashes. She guessed what a romantic figure he must seem to the girl, with his blue uniform, brass buttons and air of authority. She was glad it would be a few years before she would have to take such glances seriously, for Seena was going to be a beauty and beauty brought its own problems and perplexities.

She glanced at her younger daughter. Saran's attention was all for the passing cows and bright glimpses of ponds as they rode into town. She was so like Seena and yet she just missed the beauty her sister was endowed with. Her face was squarer; her nose was blunter. But there was a simple goodness and strength in Saran which always reassured Felly. This daughter would be all right!

Her eyes moved on to Jake. His face, always ruddy, was rosier still this morning from excitement and heat from the heavy band jacket. Like Saran, his forehead was pressed close to the half open window so as not to miss any of the panorama. Of all her children, he was the most self-contained. Secrecy was not quite the word, but he kept his own counsel. Still he was aggressive enough when his rights were involved. But he seemed to need less affection and reassurance than the others. He was impatient of her caresses, and would twist and bolt away to be at other things. He was most like Hans of course, and perhaps he drew his assurance and self-sufficiency from his father, she mused.

Her eyes touched Jason. Jason, how special and precious he was. Not more special or precious than any of the others, but somehow more accessible to her, more responsive. He had gone through the quick spurt of growth that springs children upward after the age of seven, and it had left him gangling and fragile looking. He neither looked out the window like Saran and Jake, nor covertly watched fellow passengers like Seena. She could see by his expression he was lost in some inward dream. Yet at once he sensed her eyes on him and the dreamy look evaporated. He smiled at her, his eyes sparkling. As she smiled back at him, her heart caught. Oh, Jason, Jason...let it be all right with him, God.... Why did she feel always this extra concern for her first born, as if he were in some invisible jeopardy?

Lastly, her eyes sought her husband. He sat across the aisle from her; they had divided the children the better to shepherd them. His profile was strong and proud, somehow chaste in the clear spring sunlight. Hans...all these years married to him and yet he was still a mystery to her. And she to him?

"Wau...PACA," the streetcar conductor called in ringing voice. The swift journey was over and the cars were jolting to a halt, the passengers chattering and stirring, gathering children and belongings.

Already the streets were thronged with people anticipating the parade. The women had traded their black alpaca skirts for white linen, many wore straw bowlers which were the fashion this spring and some carried parasols unfurled against the sun. Most of the men were spiffed up in suits, celluloid collars and new ties, and Felly felt sorry for them for the day already was hot for early spring.

Far down the street, there was the sound of instruments being tuned. Several beautiful teams of horses went stomping by swishing their tails like the fringe on a Spanish dancer's shawl. They would be part of the parade, as would the fire wagon, freshly painted red with gold emblems; and there was to be a cordon of veterans from the Camp carrying flags and banners. But it would be an hour before the parade and Felly had shopping she wanted to fit in before it commenced. She hurried the children ahead of her.

"I need to get pickling jars, and grosgrain ribbon, Hans, and I promised Mrs. Howard I'd look for some paisley print for her. Are you and Jake going down by the parade formation right away? Where should we meet after?"

Before he could respond to her rapid questions, she halted on the sidewalk. "Oh, Hans...look." She clutched his arm and directed his gaze to a blouse in the window of the mercantile. "Isn't it beautiful! It's just like the one I saw in *The Ladies Home Journal*, straight from Paris."

After decades of high collared blouses with leg of mutton sleeves, Paris was showing soft crepe de chine blouses this spring with crystal pleated sleeves and bertha collars. The one in the window was a flowered rose and blue print, colors Felly thought particularly suited to her.

Hans snorted, but good naturedly. "It's all right, I guess. But you'd better hurry along if you're going to get your errands done before the parade. How do you expect to carry pickle jars home on the street car? Can't they wait until I come with the team?"

"We can put them under the seat."

"Well don't buy them until after the parade so you won't have to tote them all day," he advised. "Here, my dear, there is something I want you to do for me." He took out his wallet and doled out a bill. "Please go on up to the drugstore and get some Slone's liniment and some more Clover Leaf salve."

She tucked the bill into her purse. "All right. I'll do it as soon as..."

"Do it first, or you'll forget," he said, giving her a firm little push in the right direction. "We'll wait for you after the parade by the bandstand."

Jason started following his mother as a matter of course, but his father's voice summoned him back.

"Yes, Papa," he said surprised.

His father put some crumpled bills in his hand and nodded back toward the store they had just passed.

"Your mother's birthday is coming up. You go get the blouse she liked, you know her size. Jake and I must get down to the parade formation. You tell the clerk to just put the package under the counter and I'll pick it up another day when your mother's not along."

Jason didn't know his mother's size but he knew Millie, the clerk in the mercantile, would. He flushed with pleasure at his father's confidence in him and went off with some importance to the errand.

"Jason..." his father called after him, "you go find your mother then and stick by her. Don't be running around wild. You hear?"

"Yes, Papa." Jason was disappointed. He wanted to sneak into the pool hall because there was an upright piano in there and an old black man named Rudy Seegar who knew how to play rag. Hans liked a beer and he liked to play pool and once or twice he had taken the boys in with him. Felly didn't like beer, and she didn't like pool, and she didn't like rag. Jason adored his mother but having to stick with her on a holiday was a bore. She would just run around until parade time looking at candles and buttons and such stuff, he knew.

He kicked a board in the mercantile porch with disgust, but then cheered up as he felt the bills in his hand. It wasn't often he had dollars to spend just like a grown-up. Besides, it made him happy his father was buying something pretty for his mother.

He had barely got his charge accomplished when his mother herself came strolling into the store with Seena and Saran in tow.

Jason and Millie exchanged conspirator grins thinking about the secret package under the counter.

"What did Papa want?" his mother asked.

"He just wanted to tell me not to run around wild," Jason said.

"Oh."

A short time later, they all stood on the curb and watched as Hans and Jake marched past in the parade in full glory, right in the first row, their cornets lifted brazenly to the sun, epaulets glittering, their gold-striped legs in perfect cadence. A rum-tum-tum, rum-tum-tum and Sousa's *Stars and Stripes Forever*, which they had heard practiced ad infinitum, issued in glorious strains from the two Jacobson horns and were made magnificent to the family by the support of all the other members of the band.

Jason felt a wistful tug again as his father and brother went past, but it was lost almost immediately in the splendor of the horses and the town sheriff who was dressed up like Buffalo Bill riding a western pony. Then came a beautiful girl with painted cheeks and gold spikes in her hair who represented Miss Liberty.

Later they sat on white wire chairs in the cool ice cream parlor. Seena had a chocolate soda, Saran had her banana-split, all the rest of them had cherry fizzes. It had been a splendid day. One all too soon to be ruined.

CHAPTER 21
Felicity's Birthday

***

"But if we hope for that we see not,
then do we with patience wait for it."
(Romans: 8:25)

Hans himself could not have said why he disliked both of his double sets of in-laws, though he understood his resentment of Adam a little better than he did of Bay and Caroline. Hans liked his life. He was proud of himself, proud of his achievements, proud of being important at the Grand Army Home and the surrounding area. He loved his wife. He loved his children. The only serpent in his Eden was that from the first he knew Felly was not as happy as he was. There was at times an inner restlessness, a sadness in her which cast shadows over the sunshine of his existence and made a rage boil within him because he did not know how to combat it.

There were moments when he wished he could take a knife and cut into her heart and remove whatever was the locus of her discontent, the way Dr. Bentley removed a diseased appendix. He was not a violent man but there were other moments when his impotence to make her happy filled him with such anger he wanted to shake her. What was the matter with the woman?

He gave her everything...children, love, a beautiful home, a servant, and still there was something he could not read in her eyes. There was a sigh in the dusk, there was a way she had of turning her head and arching her neck which gave her an expression of repressed longing he could not bear, because he loved her so much.

Then Adam would come, with Grace or without, and a transformation would come over her. Her eyes would sparkle; her cheeks grow pink. The laughter Hans could never seem to find in her, Adam evoked at will. The silences which stretched so often between him and his wife never happened between Adam and his daughter.

136

She would stay up half the night to talk to her father. Their words and laughter tumbling over each other like cataracts tumbling over rocks, sending up rainbow sprays.

And the final exacerbation was Jason's response to Adam. Hans felt at times as if the mysterious sadness and discontent within Felly had taken material and concrete form in the boy. He could not reach Jason. The boy was both desirable and elusive to him. The unbridgeable gap between them was maddening. And more maddening yet was to see the leap of joy in Jason's eyes when Adam came. Here there was no gap to bridge.

Adam, Felly, and Jason...it was as if they heard a music he could not hear. As if they occupied a terrain on which his feet were forbidden, as if they constituted themselves an elite to which he could never aspire. There were moments when if he had not been a civilized man he could have killed Adam for no good reason except the pain in his own heart.

Caroline was harder to hate. His mother-in-law gave off a radiance of love to which most people responded like plants to sunlight. She wanted to offer this warmth to him. At times, he was almost seduced by it, by her kindness and generosity, and her love of his children. But always his heart was hardened by what to him was her unforgivable sin. She could not seem to refrain from pouring extravagant gifts upon his wife and children. Hans was convinced Felly's unhappiness was her mother's fault.

Caroline had spoiled her rotten. Spoiled people were always unhappy and discontent. And now, his mother-in-law and her husband were trying to wreak the same havoc upon his children. The danger of loving Caroline would pass and his hatred would burn bright inside of him.

His resentment of Bay was less intense. He would not have admitted to himself but it was centered on the fact his own candle dimmed in the glow of the other man's personality. Hans was an important man in his community. Bay's importance stretched throughout the state and even to the national level. Senators came from Washington to confer with Baird LaSeure. The man seemed to make money with no effort. Gold coins seemed to roll to his feet. People sought him out for his charm as well as his money.

And the final gall, though Hans could not have articulated it, was that Caroline adored Bay. Felly had never once looked at him the way Caroline looked at Bay. The unarticulated, even unconscious anguish of that was part of the reason Han's face grew so dark when he saw his in-law's expensive new horseless carriage sitting beside his house.

"Jason," he barked, "take the horses back to the stable and see they are watered and fed. Jake, get the wood in. Seena and Saran, you get into your old clothes and get the garden weeded now while it's cool."

"Hans," his wife protested, "Mother and Bay are here. They've probably waited all day to see the children. Can't they-"

"They've had all day for holidaying. It's time to get to work," Hans said, his tone cold and brusque.

The children were eager to see their grandparents but they knew they did not dare disobey their father. They did not understand why Hans was always so short-tempered when their grandmother came or why he always found so many chores to keep them busy. They did not understand, yet they did understand somewhat. Children understand a great deal more than adults realize, and in some things, they understand and see more clearly than their parents.

They trooped into the house, except for Jason who had to go directly to the stable, for a brief greeting and quick kisses from Bay and Caroline, then fanned out to do the chores set for them by their father.

The day had been so good. Why did Hans have to ruin it by being so jealous and irascible, Felly thought, her own pleasure in her parents' visit spoiled by Han's grudging hospitality. Her mother and Bay, who were always so good and so loving to them all, did not deserve this kind of treatment. Her throat ached, and despite her best efforts, there were times when tears stood in her eyes.

Oh, damn Hans, damn him. Why was it every time she started feeling tender shoots coming up in her heart for him, he had to tramp them out, stomp on her sensibilities and feelings until he seemed a stranger, an alien to her...even worse...an enemy.

She felt her mother's concerned glance on her. "Felly?" There was a question in her mother's tone.

She managed a smile. "I'm sorry Mother, I missed what you said."

"I was telling you what a beautiful baby Rasmeena is, as if I had to tell you," Caroline laughed.

Felly laughed, too. "All the same, I love to hear it."

"I expected to find her taking a few steps but not to find her walking already. And she says so many words for only nine months. You talked early, too."

"She and Mrs. Howard jabber to each other like mad. I expect she may end up having an Irish brogue," Felly said, forgetting her tension with Hans in the joys of her newest baby. "Anyway, I'm glad she kept you entertained this afternoon. I didn't expect you until Sunday."

138

"We came sooner because we have to go south on business for a few weeks," Caroline explained. "It may even be over a month before we get back, so we brought your birthday things a few days ahead."

"Grandma! Grandpa Bay!" Jason had finished his chores. He spun in like a small whirlwind.

Caroline held her arms out wide and he rushed into them.

* * * *

The following day they had the birthday party. Kemink had sent a birthday cake topped with white frosting cascading down the sides, decorated with snippets of fresh flowers, and slivers of pink ribbon adorning the base of the large cake plate. With Jason to turn the crank, Mrs. Howard spent the morning making ice cream. Mrs. Howard also baked a goose and there were fresh strawberries from the garden.

The fine blaze of the candles made bright points of light in the eyes of all the scrubbed and smiling children around the table. Felly blew them out with one triumphant swoosh and everyone clapped.

Hans watched his wife unwrap one gift after another. A pearl-embedded locket from her sister-in-law. A tortoise comb and brush set from Adam and Grace. An exquisite embroidered set of bed linen from Danny and Emily. A leather-bound journal from Jimmy. Sundry little gifts which the children had made themselves or bought with pocket money: hot pads, a crocheted key chain, writing paper, toilet water. Even Mrs. Howard had brought her a bouquet of peacock feathers to put in a jar in the foyer.

As usual there was a whole pyramid of packages from Caroline and Bay. Hans watched Felly draw out kidskin slippers, doeskin gloves, a music box which also held jewelry, a matched set of books by Emerson...and then the blouse. His heart lurched.

This blouse was not a Paris copy. It had to be an original. Even Hans, who knew and cared little about fashion, could see at a glance the blouse he had bought was to this blouse as a paper-mache brick is to a real one. The same crystal pleated sleeves, the same Bertha collar, even something of the same colors, except the colors on this blouse shimmered and glowed with a subtleness which made Hans think the colors on the blouse he had purchased were crude and raw by comparison. Instead of tucks in the front, this blouse had delicate smocking, instead of glass buttons, tiny pink pearls.

Felly gave a cry of delight, "Ohhh, ohhh, ohhh." She leaped up to embrace her mother and Bay.

At the same moment, Hans leaped up also and strode out of the room, slamming the door behind him. All the happiness and excitement in the room melted as if it had been a structure of air and sugar like the cotton candy at the county fair.

Felly could not keep back her tears. The children grew solemn and sad watching their mother sob. Caroline and Bay, upset and embarrassed themselves, tried to soothe her. Mrs. Howard tiptoed back into the kitchen, shaking her head. Jason went in search of his father.

There had been many times when he had felt his father had done injustices to him, but this time it was his mother who had been hurt. He went hurtling after his father like a small bristling warrior. Unsure what he would do when he confronted the dragon but determined to do something; if only to say in words what he knew his father already knew, "You ruined Mother's birthday. You acted awful."

He would say it even if he got beat for it. He would not let his father get off with acting as if nothing had happened.

He ran panting after the older man with his longer stride. He could see Hans' bright head glinting in the sunlight. He was headed toward the boathouse the family was allowed to use.

When Jason reached the boat house there were black and red spots in front of his eyes from running so hard in the hot sun and it took a moment before he could see in the dim shed. Then he saw his father savagely tearing open the box Millie had wrapped with such care the day before. He drew out the flimsy blouse and his great hands rent the cloth. The sound of the ripping cloth was almost like a human cry to Jason's trembling soul.

"Papa...what are you doing!" he cried in anguish.

"You can damn well see what I'm doing. You've got eyes in your head."

"Papa..." he was heartbroken. He had been so happy over the blouse for his mother. "Why, Papa, why? You could have taken it back for another style. You could have..."

Hans pushed past him onto the dock and threw the shredded remnants of the blouse into the lake, where they floated like strange gossamer flowers. Then he turned back and snarled at his son, "Not a word of this to your mother, do you understand?" When Jason stood stunned and mute, he caught his shoulders and shook him. "Do you hear me? Not a word!"

Jason, his throat too choked to speak, nodded. All the brave words of censor he had vowed to deliver to his father had evaporated. He stood as if hypnotized watching all the little bits of flowered crepe float away. A breeze stroked his hot forehead. Somewhere a crow chortled.

Finally, he turned and watched his father's broad back retreating toward the house. Hans would go back in and act as if nothing had happened, Jason knew, but the day had been ruined. Maybe something more than just the day, something more precious and delicate than the blouse, but something just as impossible to put together again, something he didn't have words for but existed nevertheless.

Jason wished he could run off by himself. He remembered with nostalgia, as if he could no longer ever have them again, those childish days of ant hills and grasshoppers, unimpeded and injured by human emotions. And after the first wish for aloneness, he wished for Max. Max never acted crazy like his father. He was never irrational and unreasonable. Max always understood.

He withstood both those temptations, the desire to be alone, and the desire to flee to Max, and plodded back to the house. He would go in and smile at his mother, and even if she still had tears in her eyes, she would smile back, and they would both feel better.

Three days later her real birthday, Felly waited to see if Hans would give her a gift. He did not even say "happy birthday" to her.

"He can't bear to have my family give me pretty things," Felly confided to Mrs. Howard, "But he never gives me anything himself. It's as if he doesn't want me to have pretty things."

A change came over Felly Jacobson. All her little fripperies disappeared. She no longer styled her hair in dozens of innovative ways. She took to wearing it pulled back into a severe bun. She no longer affected the newest sleeves, a brooch worn in an unexpected way, a wisp of veil or ribbons used with a flair which was the essence of style. Summer and winter, she wore plain white waists with dark simple skirts, which she covered with gingham aprons for household chores.

The women in the church noticed. Even those who had been jealous of her, who had said snide things behind her back, felt an inexplicable sense of loss. Something exciting had been lost from their lives. They looked at Seena hopefully, but she was just a very pretty young girl in simple dresses and braided hair. Perhaps in a few years.

Hans noticed the difference too. He put it down to the fact Felly was growing older and probably didn't think it was seemly to dress up so much. He also noticed that even with her hair drawn back severely and her clothes plainer than Mrs. Howard's, the eyes of other men followed his wife when she went to town or moved down the church aisle. Framed by her severe, still dark hair, her face was like a cameo, and he could hardly bear to look at it, for unhappiness was written there for everyone to see.

CHAPTER 22
Broken

***

"And he spake a parable unto them to this end,
that men ought always to pray, and not to faint;"
(Luke: 18-1)

Soon after the Fourth of July, a sullen heat set in. The air was nitrous, so heavy with suspended dust the sky had a rusty tinge. Flower petals curled and drooped, the knee-high corn shriveled and rattled like skeletons in the occasional hot breeze which swept from the lake.

The great central pump at Camp throbbed and pulsated trying to meet the increased demands as residents attempted to save their gardens and lawns from the searing heat. Hans had his children bring buckets of water from the lake to pour around the tomatoes and pepper plants, so as not to add to the strain on the pump. He let the children bathe in the lake too instead of having house baths. Their hair was gummy with lake water and Seena got an earache, but their skin felt scoured and clean.

Even so Hans worked overtime keeping the pump going— sometimes at midnight he was still in the engine house. He seemed to enjoy the challenge, remaining cheerful even though brown circles grew beneath his eyes and his eyes themselves were bloodshot like an old drunk's.

On the eighteenth of July, a dry hot wind rose, towing in clouds like small dirty sheep. All day the wind blew and the clouds piled up until they were a great roiling gray mass that shut out the rusty sky.

"There's going to be an awful storm," Mrs. Howard said, sweat standing on her hot face. "I've always been awful afraid of storms, Miz Jacobson."

The wind crackled through the grass like the fissure of hidden firecrackers, buckets blew over and rolled, and in the garden, the limp

142

cucumber leaves lifted and flipped like tiny green elephant ears. Felly and Mrs. Howard ran all over the house shutting windows, sure of the coming deluge.

Mrs. Howard looked out the last shut window at clothes blowing into corkscrews on the clothesline. "We'd better get the clothes off the line."

The women went out together and struggled with the frenzied, dancing clothes. Their hair came loose, their skirts whiplashed around their legs. The moment they got in the house again, Mrs. Howard looked at Felly.

"Miz Jacobson, can I go home to my kids?"

Felly had never been afraid of storms herself. She had rather liked the excitement and beauty of inclement weather, but there was something about this day which was making even her unnerved.

She gave Mrs. Howard her approval and then went in search of her own children, brushing back the strands of hair the hot wind strung in her eyes. She made them all get out of the milky warmth of the lake and follow her back to the terrible still air inside the house.

She had barely got them back into the house when the first colossal branch of lightning ripped through the gray-wool sky. The thunder which followed shook the house so hard even Jason gave a little cry of fear.

Poor Mrs. Howard, Felly thought. Her housekeeper had passed on her fear of storms to her children Felly knew, and she could imagine all of them huddled together under a table prostrate with terror.

Felly carried in a pitcher of lemonade for her own brood and took Black Beauty down from the shelf to read to them. But the lightning was so persuasive and the thunder so loud and continuous it was impossible to make herself heard. In the end, they huddled together with silent endurance, not much better off than Mrs. Howard and her household.

The rain broke like a dam and for thirty-six straight hours poured down on shriveled gardens and shrunken lakes and melba toast earth. The electricity went out. Electric lines snapped by the storm whipped wildly in the wind, shooting white fire like giant sparklers. Felly was frightened for Hans who had to work round the clock trying to repair the lines and restore the power.

He bobbed into the house for brief seconds, wearing an oiled slicker, to gulp cups of coffee and to put on dry socks.

Darkness came and morning again and darkness, but it was hard to tell the difference, they had to burn candles to see in the day as well as at night. Sometimes Hans and his crew succeeded in restoring the electricity for a brief time and then all over Camp the lamps would go on and the world would turn light as if in hope. Then the lines would go down again.

Felly made all the children kneel several times during the day and pray "for Papa's safety." She lamented and repented of every harsh thought she had ever harbored in her heart against Hans and tried to forget the stories she had heard of men charred to cinders through contact with broken electric lines, or men who had plunged to their death from slippery wind-lashed poles.

She wanted to hold him, to cling to him during those brief moments when he came for coffee or a ham and bun to thrust into his slicker pocket. But he would have none of it. He was bursting with adrenaline and the urgency of getting on with the job. His growing whiskers were jeweled with rain, his hands were raw and cold. He slipped irritably away from her clinging hands and left her to make fresh coffee, to soothe the children who were now growing more restless than afraid, and were saddened to see their parents at odds. All Felly could do was comfort them, and pray for Hans and the men working with him in the storm.

She prayed for forgiveness for not cherishing him more during the years. She begged God for his safety and promised if he came back to them whole and unharmed, she would be more charitable of his shortcomings, more loving, more tender.

On the third morning, the wind stopped. The lights came back on. But Hans did not come home. She paced the floor assuring herself that if anything terrible had happened to him she would have been notified or summoned. She tried calling but telephone lines were still down.

The children, shut up for so long together, were quarreling and fretful. Even Seena and Jason who usually got along were being spiteful to each other all day long. Felly sent them all to bed early, then pulled a dark cloak over her pounding heart and went off to search for Hans, unable to bear the suspense of her anxiety any longer.

She filled a jug with hot coffee and went to the engine house. Perhaps there was still a great deal to do she did not understand. If she could just see he was safe, she would be reassured and could go home and sleep in peace. She slopped through ankle deep mud and under dripping branches to find the engine house dark and deserted.

She looked around feeling helpless. The darkness of the night looked even blacker against the gold and white brick of lights from electricity restored in Camp. Flung out and spangled all around her was the result of Hans' work to keep and restore the power.

And God said, "Let there be light" ...and there was light, Felly thought, for the first time understanding a little the love Hans had for his work. But along with the stir of pride for what Hans' skill meant to Camp, was a sense of desolation. Where could he be? Her heart thumped. Could something have happened to him? Where could she look? Should she go to the main building? The Commandant's? Surely, if something had happened the Commandant would know.

She started threading her steps in that direction, but on the way, she passed the pool hall. Singing and laughter were spilling from the building. She knew Hans liked to play pool. She hesitated and then walked a few steps back. It wouldn't hurt to glance in the door. Maybe there would be someone she knew, whom she could ask about Hans.

The smell of warm bodies and fresh drawn beer came through the door to her. For a moment, she blinked against the bright lights.

"Who put the overalls in Mrs. Murphy's chowder? NOBODY ANSWERED SO THEY YELLED ALL THE LOUDER! WHO PUT THE OVERALLS IN MRS. MURPHY'S CHOWDER?" A lusty bellow of disparate, slurred voices was coming from a tangle of men around the bar, and one of them was Hans. There was beer foam on his moustache and he had a mug lifted high and was waving it in time to the song, his other arm thrown across a companion's shoulder.

Felly let the door slip from her cold fingers and close. She ran through the mud, stumbling over tree branches strewn by the storm. A sense of rage engulfed her. How could he do such a thing to her? How could he go to the pool hall and never bother to come home and let her know he was all right? Didn't he know how worried she had been?

Halfway home she stopped, winded, and held on to a tree catching her breath, and trying to calm her emotions. Only a few hours before hadn't she "bargained" with God if he would let Hans return safely to her and the children she would cherish him more, be more tender? Shouldn't she be thanking God her prayers had been answered, he was safe?

Felly literally ground her teeth trying to master her conflicting emotions. Father, why, why is it always like this between Hans and me, she cried. The only answer was the sound of dripping rain and the hoot of an owl.

She walked on, drained of both energy and emotion. By the time she got home, her cheeks were cold and red from the dripping trees and her hair was soaked. She put on the beautiful birthday nightgown Emily had embroidered for her and toweled her hair. She was brushing it dry when Hans walked in the door of the bedroom.

He looked at his wife in her swirling white gown, her fresh brushed hair glinting in the lamplight about her shoulders, and his reddened eyes lit up.

"By damn, Felly, you're still a gorgeous woman," he said.

She was not interested this night in testimonials to her beauty. She wanted understanding, an apology. He threw heavy arms around her and she stiffened.

"Thirty-six hours of the damnedest storm this area has seen in twenty years, Felly, and me and my boys we had the lights on again before it stopped dripping. Do you realize that? Dya' realize what we did?"

"I was very proud of you, Hans," she said, her voice cold, "until I went looking for you because I was so worried when you didn't come home, and found you in the pool room having a high old time. Didn't it ever occur to you to come home first and let me know you were all right?"

"Do you care, Felly? Have you ever cared?"

"Hans!" Her rage was mounting again

"Show me you care." His heavy arms wound tighter, capturing her like a prison, his hot mouth covered hers, wet, smelling of sour beer; the odor of three days sweat rose from his armpits, the harsh new beard scraped her cheeks. She struggled away from him.

"Not tonight, Hans. You know we aren't supposed to..."

He pulled her back hard against him, his hot, wet kisses on her neck now.

She pushed against his shoulders with her hands. "Hans, at least go wash first. You stink from sweat."

His face went red as slaughtered beef and his arms slackened, allowing her to go free momentarily, but he instantly grabbed the front of her gown and pulled her back.

"You think you're too good for my sweat, Felly? Good honest sweat working for you and my children. You've always felt you were too good for me, haven't you?"

The fragile cloth of her nightgown ripped and tore in his angry grasp. Felly went white with shock. She tried to draw her ripped gown back over her breasts. "Hans..." She was still expecting an apology. She was stinging with embarrassment and shocked over his rough behavior.

He picked her up bodily and slammed her on the bed.

"No!" she cried out, and then he was on top of her.

It was dawn before she could get free. She stood in the thin morning light holding the torn fragments of her gown together, her face white and transparent as new ice.

"I will never come to your bed again, Hans," she vowed.

He raised up on an elbow, sardonic and unrepentant, the wild beard on his jaws red in the early light, his swollen eyes barely open like clam shells.

"If the mountain does not come to Mohammed, Mohammed will go to the mountain."

She washed in cold water. She stared in the mirror at a face she had never seen before. She could hear the children stirring. She dressed and went downstairs. She kindled the fire in the cold stove. Put water on to boil for the children's oatmeal, and set plates on the table. Life went on. But inside her was a maelstrom.

I won't have my children raised by such a man, she thought. I will go to Danny. Danny will take us in. I will manage some way. My mother did.

For the first time, she felt a twinge of hatred toward her father for old sins, understood what it must have been like for her mother.

Yes, dear good gentle Danny. She wanted her sons to grow up like Danny, not like Hans.

The children came down. She tried to make her voice sound normal. It was necessary to keep very, very busy. She did not sit down with the children to breakfast. She set bread, she scoured the work table until it was bone white, she started cleaning the pantry.

Hans came down. His eyes were still red but he was clean-shaven and had on a white shirt.

She did not speak to him. She waited rigid, her back to him. But there was no word of apology.

"Is there any coffee?" he demanded.

She poured his coffee. She fried his eggs.

The children had finished their breakfasts; they were ready to drift off. He made them stay at the table with him while he ate and read the paper.

She stared off across the lake. If he had at least made some effort to say he was sorry. He wasn't sorry. Her heart felt like a block of granite inside of her.

Danny and Emily would take her in she knew, but it wasn't fair to Danny. He had enough burdens already. Her mother and Bay would open their big house to her family without hesitation she knew that too, but she hated to inflict five, lively, demanding children upon their tranquil golden years.

Her father and Grace too would take them in, but again they had their own new baby and another on the way. Felly's fierce pride rebelled against having to admit the failure of her marriage, her own failure to her marriage. And there was something more. She glanced obliquely at Hans. Whatever he was, he loved his children. She had to give him that, and she knew he would never let her take them away from him without a battle. She was afraid of him.

Mrs. Howard arrived. She wondered at Felly's abstraction and wild industriousness. She was acting in the middle of the summer as if it were spring cleaning, turning closets apart, scrubbing walls. Mrs. Howard took care of Meena, canned green beans and tried to stay out of her way.

All day, Felly planned escape, to Danny, to her mother, to her father, but at the end of the day she knew she would not leave. She moved her things into the baby's room.

The children were too young to understand the import of the move, but in the months which followed, they felt the currents and cross currents of stress which girded the house. They avoided their parents all they could, drawing together for support or finding shelter in the ample oak tree of a woman, Mrs. Howard.

Felly had a lock put on the nursery door. It would not have been necessary. Mohammed never came near the mountain.

Mrs. Howard liked her job at the Jacobson's and so she bridled her usually gossipy tongue, though in the privacy of her own marital bed she surmised to her husband, "Either she found out he had been stepping out on her, or else she's just plain tired of having children. She hemorrhaged bad with the last one you know."

Felly fluctuated between spurts of maniacal ambition and periods where she did not seem to care if the beds even got made. Sometimes for weeks on end, she would do nothing but read books, play the piano or walk alone. Without Mrs. Howard, the household would have fallen apart.

Twice she went to visit Grace and Adam for a week at a time. Another time she visited her mother. But each time when she came back nothing was changed.

She went often to see Max. She found a peace and solace in his quiet, refined room. She did not know how she could have gotten through those troubled months without Max. He sensed and sympathized with her inner turmoil without ever probing. She would close her eyes and let his music wash over her. It was as good as the prayers she no longer seemed able to pray.

On the surface Hans seemed his usual ebullient, self-satisfied, energetic self. But his temper had ever a shorter fuse and the children, even Jake, stayed clear of him all they could.

CHAPTER 23
Boston

***

"And thine ears shall hear a word behind thee, saying,
This is the way, walk ye in it, when ye turn to the right hand,
and when ye turn to the left."
(Isaiah 30:21)

In early November, Jason's trip to Boston came up. As Felly had feared, when she brought it up, Hans barked a quick, "No!" and went back to reading his newspaper.

"Either Jason goes to Boston, or I go, and I will never come back," Felly said.

The newspaper trembled, then dropped to the floor. Hans unfolded like an erupting mountain. "You've wanted to leave me since the day you married me, haven't you!" He left, slamming the door so hard it cracked.

Jason went to Boston.

* * * *

They left on the night train because it was less expensive. Jason sat on the edge of the prickly plush seat and stared out with excitement as red crossing lights smeared past the window because of speed. He thrilled to the sound of the train whistle when they went around corners. All his resolve could not keep him awake past midnight. The rocking motion of the train was so rhythmic, he soon lost the battle between leaden eyelids and will power. He spent most of the night with his head on Max's knees, Max's gentle hands smoothing his hair and cradling the bumps.

He came to at dawn as they pulled into the Boston station. Once off the train, he stared, still heavy-eyed, at the melees of cabs, carriages, cars and people already strung in and about the terminal. In this one place, there were more people than he had ever seen in his entire life put together. Max smiled at his widening eyes.

"There is a little restaurant I know of down a few blocks," he said, taking Jason's hand and handing the boy his small valise.

Jason's first impression of Boston was of brick, of a dark and solid old city. In the early November light, the brick and cobblestone streets looked wet and black, buildings loomed on all sides soot-smudged with forbidding facades, and here and there a dim window glowed.

But even as he ran along, struggling to keep up with Max's long stride he felt a tension of excitement in the older man's hand and he saw the city begin to change and come alive. There were lights on in most of the shops of the street they had turned onto. The smell of cold iron, wet brick, and diesel oil, which had filled his nostrils at the terminal, was replaced with a wonderful aroma of warm bread, of fresh ground coffee, and perfumed women.

The lighted windows were cornucopias of wonder. Max let him stop and stare at everything. There were toy shops with electric trains whizzing through tunnels and miniature villages, dolls of every description with pink painted cheeks and glassine eyes that stared back at him as if they could really see. He vowed on the spot to grow up quickly so he could make money and buy one of the wonderful dolls for Meena and one for Saran and Seena, too.

There were bicycle shops with hundreds of glittering vehicles, some of them hung on the walls. Jason noted with satisfaction none of them were grander than the one his Grandpa Adam had bought for him.

There were bakeries, each with more resplendent displays in their windows than the last. Sugar buns glittered with sugar, bread in more exotic shapes and sizes than he could ever have imagined hung in braids or sat on lace doilies and silver trays, pumpernickel, rye, sesame, Russian, French, German. Wedding cakes rose tier on tier, masterpieces of bells and doves and swirls and flowers each with a culminating wonder on top the cake. Jason liked those with the little brides and grooms on top best and secretly picked out one he would have at his own wedding.

Even the tobacco shops were wonderful, with wooden Indians with painted cheeks in the windows and huge Meerschaum pipes with such deep curving bowls they made Jason think of saxophones, and tiny pipes with carved ivory stems.

"Hungry?" Max asked, smiling at his excitement, his own eyes alight. "Here we are." He held back a blue glass door and ushered Jason into a room with black and white marble floors and chandeliers which cast a crystal dancing light over small tables with pale blue cloths and thin young women in black uniforms with ruffled white aprons and little white caps pinned into their hair.

Max ordered croissants and café au lait and while they waited for the food to come he coached Jason in saying the strange words, laughing at his first attempts.

No," he said, "Croi-sants. You must say it through your nose like the French do. The French speak very nasal."

"Crow-sents," Jason said, trying to speak through his nose and it was wonderfully funny to both of them.

When the croissants arrived, tender and flaky with melting butter, Jason thought he had never tasted anything so delicious. He was not as pleased with the café au lait until Max added sugar to it, and then he liked that too.

Over breakfast, Max planned the itinerary of their day. First, they would go to the hotel where they had reservations and would leave their bags and freshen up. Then he would take him to the Museum of Fine Arts. They would walk so Jason could see the sights along the way. They would have lunch in a neighborhood beanery because "you cannot come to Boston and not have baked beans and brown bread," Max said.

There were antique and import shops with marvelous things from other lands Max wanted Jason to see. Afterwards they would rest at the hotel for a time so they would be fresh for the concert. They would have just tea beforehand because after the concert Max said they would be so exhilarated they would not be able to sleep at once and they would have a midnight supper near the concert hall where concert goers dined fashionably late.

On the way back to their hotel, Max pointed out Symphony Hall where the concert would be held. He made Jason note architectural details on other buildings they passed: Corinthian columns, Spanish style dados, and on a bank building Medieval gargoyles. Jason's head swiveled, his eyes ached with trying to take everything in. The air was zingy and their cheeks were red and their fingers cold inside their gloves by the time they reached their hotel.

The lobby of the Bradford Hotel was so elegant it made Jason feel like tiptoeing. The carpeting was maroon and gray patterned and there were gleaming brass railings on all the staircases, urns, and vases in glass cases along the walls. But Max was "comfortable," not rich, and the luxury thinned floor by floor. They arrived on the sixth where their room was and found it pleasant but not plush. Their room was not large, but had a single bed for Max and a cot for Jason. Jason discovered when he went into the bathroom the hot and cold faucets had handles like lions' heads painted gold and there was a knotted hemp ladder which could be let down from the window in case of fire.

Jason was sure he was far too excited and full of anticipation to sleep and chattered on about the day, but Max groaned and growled, he was a tired old man and needed the rest whether Jason did or not and the least he could do was to lie down quietly and not bother him. Jason laid down on the cot and tried to close his eyes and the next thing he knew was Max's hand shaking him, as the church across the street pealed its sonorous bells at six o'clock.

Max spent a long time getting ready. He wore the scarlet-lined cape many people at Camp thought was affected, and put a pearl stickpin in his stock. He had dove-gray gloves, a fine top hat, and finished with a heady cologne, which he also sprinkled on Jason. Jason thought he looked magnificent and strutted along beside him swelling with pride when people's heads swiveled to give him a second admiring glance as they made their way to Symphony Hall.

The boy envisioned in his mind what the hall would be like. Red-wine carpets, cut-glass chandeliers, gold-crusted balconies, all of this Max had told him, but when they went inside he was still stunned and unprepared for the opulence which greeted them. The very air seemed different, cool and sweet and tinged with exotic aromas he had no name for but which reminded him of the scent of dewy carnations Grandma Caroline had once worn on her shoulder, and into whose heart he had thrust his nose.

Confidently, Max led him to their main floor seats. On the bare stage, the piano waited, black and shining as a whale's fin. Jason could scarcely breathe. In his mind's eye, he saw himself grown wearing a suit with satin lapels, walking into the center of light, sitting down at the piano.

As if he had looked into his head and his secret dreams Max leaned close and whispered, "Someday, Jason...if you work hard...you will be up on that stage."

A spark sprang through the boy's heart.

The great hall was filled now with stirring, laughing people. Jeweled fans waved; diamond necklaces and dowagers' brooches sparkled like strange icy flowers; furs slid off white shoulders; elegant men pulled off their kid gloves with effete grace; their fragrances were lost in a thicket of pomades and perfumes and powders. At last the house lights dimmed and it was as if a baton had been lifted shutting off all sound. For one expectant moment, it seemed even breathing had been suspended, and during that silken hush, Paderewski, the Great Master, appeared and walked across the stage to the piano.

The man was fragile, childlike, completely unprepossessing. He sat down before the piano. His head strained backward for a moment; his hands poised in a curious claw-like movement above the keys...then they crashed down and he became a god.

After the first Bach Prelude, Jason's mouth was so dry he could hardly swallow and the spark in his heart had become a conflagration. He understood for the first time that music was emotion and the willingness to deal in the emotion brought power. He broke his own mesmerism long enough to note the rapturous faces about him lifted toward the stage, lifted by the strange power in this man to carry them into a realm beyond their daily cares and struggles, into a realm of epic effort and transcendent beauty.

When it was all over, when the last tremulous note had gentled into silence and the little man got up and walked away and was brought back by their applause and walked away again, Jason was so drained with emotion and exultation his legs felt weak.

Max peered at his face and smiled, satisfied. "Now...you will work," he said.

The house lights came back on, the great stirring and chattering and laughing began again, and Jason moved through the press clutching Max's hand, his eyes somnolent, but his ears and heart still pounding with the music, his fingers aching for white and black keys. He had been working at home on one of the pieces performed. Now he knew, knew how to put in the transition which had eluded him.

They reached the exit doors and the steps outside. The air was full of flakes of snow, huge, the size of goose feathers. They came floating like cold kisses onto their noses and eyelids.

"Oof!" Max said, "The sidewalks will soon be slushy and we've no boots. We'd better hurry."

With their laughter echoing, their lungs jabbed with the cold air they were gulping, they ran all the way to the nearest chowder restaurant; went in with epaulets of snow on their shoulders and star-shine in their eyes. Forgoing the more elegant dinner plans, they were happy to be out of the slushy weather.

The warm homey scent of chowder engulfed them. The windows were steamy. An old woman with a greenish-black coat rubbed shoulders with an elegant young man who had just come from the concert. Fishermen with beards stared at the young man's companion with her long white gloves and up-do hair, and the lovely woman smiled back.

Jason thought he had never been so happy in his life. He caught Max's hand and held it against his cheek. "Max...I love you so much...so much. I will never forget tonight."

The older man's eyes went watery. He looked down and a stain of blush crossed his cheeks. "I admire you, too, Jason perhaps more than I should. It's nice to watch you growing up."

Just then the waiter brought their chowder, and the old soldier and the talented young lad were content, for this one night, to be in heaven, in Boston.

CHAPTER 24
Forgiveness

***

"And be ye kind to one another, tenderhearted, forgiving one another, even as God for Christ's sake hath forgiven you."
(Ephesians 4:32)

The water of Rainbow Lake was no longer blue. It had not yet iced over but the waves chopping against the shore were cold, reflecting the dark, snow-threatening sky. The scarf Jason had around his neck lifted and slapped in the wind and his mother's black skirt and white petticoat riffled and clung to her legs as they walked and climbed.

"And there was one shop with nothing but China stuff in it," Jason said, "there was a statue of a dragon as big as a dog and a samurai sword and an opium pipe."

"Chinese things not China stuff," Felly corrected.

Jason was telling her all about his trip to Boston. Sometimes she encouraged him with a word or two but the joy and excitement with which she would once have hung on every word were not there.

Part of Felly always seemed distracted these days. Even though she had felt despondent for a long time, she had not turned her thoughts to Dan-Pete for solace. Jason had noticed his mother had not been the same for a long time and it worried him. He had spoken about it to Max.

"Pregnancies often drain women a great deal," Max had said. He often talked to Jason as if he were a grown-up, discussing things other adults would never have thought of mentioning in the presence of a child. That was one of the reasons Jason adored him. Max never talked down to him.

"But Meena's over a year old," he protested.

Max considered his comment. "Well, perhaps it's just a cycle. All nature goes through cycles, you know, Jason. I think people do too. Your mother is probably just in a wintry cycle. It will pass. Spring will

155

come for her again."

All the same, Jason could tell by Max's eyes he was worried about Felly, too.

He and his mother had reached a bluff overlooking all of Rainbow Lake and they sat down on a siding to rest. His mother's eyes were grayed like the winter waves, and she looked far off. Two small tendrils of hair had escaped; her scarf blew against her cheeks. Jason, sitting beside her, fell silent. For a long time, they sat together in the cold wind not speaking, until his mother roused herself like someone coming out of a sleep.

"Jason, you haven't told me about the concert, you haven't told me the most important thing of all."

Jason didn't want to tell her about the Paderewski's performance. It wasn't fun to talk to her when she was like this.

"I'm cold," he said, "I'll tell you another time. Let's go back."

Felly sighed and agreed. "Yes, it is cold," and she stood up and took her son's hand.

They descended from the bluff and walked again along the shoreline, close to the choppy, querulous waves. The lake smelled different than it did in the summertime. There was a smell of cold wet sand and rotting leaves.

"Snow will come soon," Felly said.

Jason grunted agreement. He was lost now in his own thoughts and dreams no longer trying to communicate with his mother. As they rounded the boat landing, his mother's voice lifted in surprise, "Why, Jason, look, what's that? Flowers in November?"

He followed her pointing finger with his eyes. Something pink and fuchsia was bobbing in the weeds near the shore. They moved nearer and his mother knelt in the sand and parted the weed stems to look closer. She pulled something out.

"Oh," she said, it's just a piece of torn cloth. It looked like flowers." But she did not drop the wet, torn piece of cloth back into the lakeshore. She stared at it frowning, perplexed, smoothing the wet cloth out on her knee. "I've seen this somewhere before."

"It's your blouse," Jason said. His father had warned him never to tell, but it didn't seem to matter anymore now. "The one Papa bought you when we went to Waupaca. The one he tore up because Grandma and Grandpa got you a better one."

She made a strange little noise. The expression on her face frightened Jason. He wondered if, after all, he had done the wrong thing in telling her.

But she looked at him with an expression he couldn't understand,

156

her lower lip trembling. "Oh, Jason, why didn't you tell me?"

"He told me not to...not to ever...maybe I shouldn't of now..."

"No," she said, "no, it's good you did. It explains so much, so much."

She released the little scrap of cloth back into the water as if she were releasing a small fish. It bobbed free of the weeds and floated like a tiny pink, fuchsia and lavender bouquet. Jason felt uncomfortable. His mother's face was impassive but he felt as if some great upheaval was going on inside of her and it frightened him.

"Mother...is...is everything all right?" he pleaded.

She was still kneeling in the sand. She caught his hand and brought him down to her level. Her loving gentle fingers were in his hair, cupping his face, caressing his cheek. Her eyes, no longer abstracted, were looking into his with such emotion it was like pain touching him.

"Oh, Jason...darling Jason, be strong when you grow up, and good, and pure. Don't ever let the gifts God has given you tarnish. Use them to bless others. And take care of your sisters. Promise me you will always take care of your sisters."

It sounded like she was saying goodbye. He became terrified. "Mother," he cried, grasping her in his young arms. "What is it? What's wrong!"

"Jason, there's nothing wrong...nothing," she soothed him. "Indeed, I think things will be better now." But her voice sounded sad to him and tired.

She stood up and brushed the sand from her knees, and smiled. "I'll race you back to the house!"

"You know I'll win."

"I've got a head start!"

She ran ahead of him like a girl. He felt his heart tearing inside of him and did not know why. He let her get as far as the tall pines before he ran after her. He wanted her to win, at least the race.

* * * *

Hans had gone to Appleton for the day. He was late getting home. There was a light coming from the half open door of his bedroom as he came up the stairs. He moved wearily, pushed the door open wider and halted, stunned. Felly was in his bed, her hair loose around naked shoulders.

He stood for a long time with the door still in his hand. She waited, her heart beating erratically within her. She would not have been surprised if he had turned and walked away.

Felly?" he breathed. It was a question her presence answered. Their eyes met and he came to the bed.

He took off his clothes and getting into bed, he began to weep convulsively. He lowered his head to rest upon her breasts, his tears falling hot on her skin.

"Oh, Felly...I'm sorry...I'm sorry...I'm so sorry..." After all these months, he was finally able to say it. "I was drunk..."

"I know," she said, "I know..." She was crying, too.

Then they made love as they had never made love before and when it was over he fell asleep like a child with all the tension smoothed and gone from his face and one great hand still curved around her waist. She did not sleep at all, but now and then she brushed the hair from his forehead with the tender gesture she might have used with one of her children.

* * * *

In the morning, the children sensed something had happened in their house. They did not know what, but there was a gentle tenderness about their mother which had not been there for a long time. It was not that she seemed happy, just softer. And Hans...it was as if Hans had been given an injection of joy and lightning. He tickled Meena until she nearly had hysterics, swung Jake to the ceiling and went off whistling.

Mrs. Howard went upstairs to change the linen and was arrested at the door of the master bedroom. She saw the two pillows crumpled together, she saw the wildly disarrayed coverings. She looked wise and began humming to herself.

* * * *

Felly was afraid. She did not know what she was afraid of which made the fear even more terrible. She had found out the truth of the old saying that to understand all is to forgive all. During the moment at the lake when she had finally understood Hans' side of it, when compassion for his hurt had overwhelmed her, it had been easy to forgive him. And it had been a great relief to let go of the burden of her own anger, but at the same time in letting go of her anger it was as if she had laid down her last defense.

Defense against what? She could not name what she needed to be defended from, yet the nameless fear was there. She was totally vulnerable now to whatever the danger was.

Each night she clung to Hans as she had never clung to him before to assuage her terror. She slept with her arms tight around him, her head burrowed in the curve of his shoulder and neck. Again and again, her closeness aroused him and she woke and met hunger with hunger. They had never had such madness before. It was terrible and wonderful.

They both knew what was going to happen. It was inevitable. Yet they seemed helpless to alter their course. It was as if they were swept up in an irrevocable destiny which they could not fight. They were moths fluttering toward the flame, caring nothing but for the ecstasy of the hot, sweet light.

They lay with their half-open lips touching, their skin warmly wet. "Hans..." "Felly..." And it would begin again.

* * * *

Felly stared out the dripping window. Rain had come instead of the expected snow. She could feel Dr. Bentley's anger crackling in the room even before she heard the irritation in his voice.

"Dammit, Felly, what in the hell is the matter with Hans? He knows how you hemorrhaged last time. I told him no more babies for at least three years and preferably never!" It was a measure of his wrath that he swore. He was not a swearing man and on the few occasions when he did swear it was not in front of women.

She turned from the window and looked at him. "I cannot explain it, Dr. Bentley."

He digested her words in silence for a moment, noting how beautiful she still was at fifty, the full pale lips, the luminous eyes. His own almost forgotten sexuality stirred. How could he blame Hans?

"I told you both," he said. He felt old and weary. "Well, it's done and we must make the best of it. I want you to go to bed at once Felly. Flat on your back. I don't want you to lift a finger for nine months. I want you spoon-fed. You never were built for bearing babies."

"But Dr. Bentley..."

"Dammit, Felly, don't argue with me! We're talking about your life. Do you want to live, or don't you?"

"But..."

"You've got Mrs. Howard."

"She has her own family. She..."

"I mean it, Felly. Go home and go to bed. I know that's not easy for you, but you must do it. We'll see how it goes. If things seem to be coming along well, I may let you up a little more after the first few months. But it's essential now, not just for the baby but for your own life. Those girls of yours are growing up. Seena's almost a young lady. It won't hurt them to help."

She sighed. "All right. All right, Dr. Bentley." She summoned a smile, picked up her coat and purse. At the doorway, she turned back. "Dr. Bentley...when you see Hans, don't scold. He already feels bad enough." She went out closing the door soundlessly.

He beat his fists for a moment on the desk. Sometimes he hated being a doctor.

****

Over and over, Hans cried, "Forgive me, Felly...forgive me."

She kept saying, "There is nothing to forgive."

And he knew she meant it, but all the same the barriers had gone up again between them. He could not reach her. She was embarked on a voyage and he could not sail with her.

Day after day, she lay alone in the upstairs bedroom. He brought her every gift he could think of, flowers, ribbons, books, sweets. She accepted the gifts politely without joy. She was gentle but inward. The gates had been closed against him again. And after a while the pain was too much, and he grew hard and no longer cared. He went back to his life and he shut the pain of her bedroom out of his mind. He refused to think of it, or of her. She was so restless at night, he slept in the nursery to spare them both.

CHAPTER 25
Foreboding Fear

***

"Mine eyes fail for thy word, saying,
When wilt thou comfort me?"
(Psalms 119:82)

Jason had promised Seena when Rasmeena was born he would take care of her. To Seena's surprise, and perhaps a little to his own, he kept the promise to the best of his ability. Especially now their mother was confined to bed and Seena had to take over so many of the things Felly had formerly done, Jason took Meena everywhere with him.

Her red hair had turned red-gold and her eyes were seraphic blue but there was nothing angelic about the child. She was a clown, a mischief, a hoyden, and to all of them in the worst moments of family depression, a salvation. Meena always made them laugh. Meena always broke the tension.

Her clowning was deliberate. Even at fourteen months, she was aware of her power to make them laugh, and she did her antics on purpose. The fact her mischief was on purpose was terrible, and still they could not resist her.

They did not dare to dress her in the delicate, ruffled, dresses Aunt Emily sent. She was into everything from axle-grease to cow manure. She loved the world and investigated it with the same eagerness which had once propelled Jason. Finally, in desperation, Mrs. Howard made her some sturdy pinafores which could be changed like a bib several times a day. As soon as she could walk, she wore her shoes out with alarming regularity.

During vacations, Jason took her on the rounds he had established for himself as a younger child. Even now in the bitterest cold of December, he bundled her up to the tip of her little red nose, packed her into a sleigh with pillows for support, and pulled her behind him.

161

He still practiced the piano in Entertainment Hall. Meena loved the music and the vast open spaces of the polished floor. She ran and ran and whirled and danced to the music until she was dizzy and fell down. And Jason looking over his shoulder at her laughed at the sight of the little whirling top of mufflers and mittens and leggings.

When she had worn herself out dancing, he carried her down to the stables and let her pet the horses and feed them sheaves of hay and pieces of apple. She shrieked with fear and delight when the big velvet noses scoured her tiny hand for the last of the treat. He made a shoot for her to slide down the hay but found it would work better in summer for the hay was cold and stiff now, not slippery as it should be. But she loved to sit on the horses, with Jason steadying and crooning to her.

Off they would go then to the main building. Some of Jason's old regulars had died, but there were always others coming. Some of the old men were bitter and withdrawn and cared nothing for children, but to most of the residents of the Old Soldiers' Home, both men and women, Meena was a sunbeam. She broke the overcast of their day, brought sparkle and delight back to their eyes. They looked forward to her visits, kept treats for her and fashioned toys.

The last stop was always the dining hall where the cooks petted and made over her and gave her cookies. Everywhere she went she was given prodigious love. But it was clear to everyone, Meena loved Jason best. How could he then do anything but adore her?

Jason was the one who rocked her to sleep at night in the nursery humming little melodies; Jason who lifted her from the crib in the morning kissing her sweet little neck and carrying her down to breakfast; Jason who fastened the garters to her long black stockings and brushed the snarls from her hair, sometimes having to chase her throughout the house to get the job finished.

On school days, she knew just when Jason would get home and she would go and stand with her little nose pressed against the cold glass waiting for the first sight of him. When he looked up and saw her waiting, his heart whelmed with joy and his footsteps quickened. As soon as she caught sight of him, she would run squealing to the door just in time to be caught up by him and tossed into the air. There was always something good in his pocket saved as a treat for her.

Mrs. Howard watched and marveled. All her children had fought like little wolves and still did. The relationship between Jason and Meena was beautiful...and unnatural, she thought. She muttered to herself about it, but was glad enough to have Jason take so much of the child's care off her hands. With Felly ill, the two households had become quite a burden even for her sturdy shoulders. More and more

162

heavily, the Jacobson household leaned on her.

"Mrs. Howard, could you come back after supper for just a couple of hours? We hate to ask...but Saran can't get the gussets in her Christmas costume alone, and Seena's hair needs to be cut"

A knock on the door at midnight, a scared little voice coming out of the dark, "Oh, Mrs. Howard can you please come! Jake's throwing up all over and Papa's on a trip and even Jason doesn't know what to do. Doctor Bentley's helping with a baby."

"Mrs. Howard, I feel terrible to ask you to cut into your weekend, but I'm in a position where I have to entertain a few people. Could you please come on Sunday for just a couple of hours? I'm not asking you to put on a dinner, just to pour some coffee, a few sweets?"

She could never refuse Hans anything when she considered his earnest red face, his light, burning, gray eyes. She could not say why but she felt so sorry for Hans. Useless to explain to him those "few sweets" would take all morning to make. Useless to remind him the "couple of hours" always stretched to four or five by the time the last crisis in the household was put to rights, the last cup hung in the cupboard.

She loved her "second family" but she worried she was beginning to short change her own five children and take advantage of her own husband's jolly good nature. She decided to ask her niece Maggie to help her and perhaps learn to take her place.

* * * *

Mrs. Howard was grateful Grandma Caroline was coming. Now with Christmas upon them, all the extra baking, decorating and present making and wrapping for both households was threatening to sink her. She had rapped Jake on the ears and shouted at Saran and made her cry which wasn't like her.

There was something about Caroline LeSeure...Mrs. Howard squinted trying to define it, but couldn't. Caroline seemed to enjoy everything she did. She never hurried. She smiled, spoke softly, nothing seemed a burden, yet in her wake, peace and harmony seemed to come. Babies stopped crying, jam pots didn't spill, the cat stayed in his corner and didn't get into the pantry butter, all the children were on their best behavior, there were flowers on the dining table and candles were lit, the house stayed clean.

Mrs. Howard did not understand it; she only knew she welcomed the benign presence.

* * * *

Caroline sat at the foot of Felly's bed, her face reproachful. "Fly...why didn't you tell me? You know I would have come at once."

163

Felly sighed and plucked at the ruffles of her nightgown. "I didn't want to worry you. Dr. Bentley says I'm doing fine. Much better than he expected. It's just...just I'm so bored lying here day after day."

"And afraid."

Felly looked up into her mother's eyes, surprised. "How did you know?"

"How could I not know? From a human point of view how could you not be afraid...after Meena's birth?"

"From a human point of view?"

"From one point of view, God's, we are always safe. That is what none of us as mortals can fully realize, not one of us. We are all afraid to varying degrees."

Felly shook her head, thinking of all the people she knew who were not safe; thinking of the veterans without legs, suffering from old wounds and degenerative diseases, thinking of retarded and crippled babies, thinking of derelicts and drunks, thinking of suicides and murders, thinking of outwardly peaceful households inwardly riven with passions and pain. Who really was safe? How could her mother think anyone was safe?

For the first time, she voiced her doubts. "Mother, I...I didn't ask you to come, because I was ashamed."

"Ashamed?"

"Ashamed of being weak and sick again, of being pregnant again. At home, you always harmonized everything and I took it for granted. I took it for granted but I never understood it. Danny understood it but I didn't. I was ashamed, I thought you would think I had let you down somehow—because, because I don't understand. I don't think I'm safe. I don't think anyone is safe."

Caroline hugged her and smoothed her hair as she had done when Felly was a little girl. "Oh, Fly, you have nothing to be ashamed of and nothing to be afraid of. Listen to me, dear. Listen."

She told Felly again of how her arm had been healed of a malformation when she was a child after all the doctors had said she would be crippled for life. Felly could just barely remember the many rounds to the doctors. She remembered long train rides, strange rooms, strange faces peering at her, and strange fingers poking at her. She remembered the antiseptic smell of hospitals and doctor's offices. She could not remember the healing. She could not even remember a time when her arm had not been all right.

"Healing came when I realized you were already perfect," Caroline said. "You are still perfect." Felly shook her head, but a new strength did seem to pour into in her mother's presence.

Bay came for Christmas Eve and Felly got out of bed, went downstairs to open presents and join the festivities with the rest of the family. It felt wonderful to be out of bed, to be in the center of the family again. She had not realized how alone she had felt, how isolated, how afraid. Here the warmth of all the people she loved seemed to surround and protect her. She looked up at Hans, remembered their nights of passion and blushed like a girl. For the first time, she felt love for the new child stir in her.

She began to go downstairs for meals and then to stay down a few hours longer every day. She felt good. In January, she confessed to Dr. Bentley and asked for his official approval.

The doctor checked and rechecked her, then granted his approbation. "You're doing much better than I anticipated," he admitted. "Your weight gain is moderate, and I'm pleased to tell you that the baby's heart beat is strong. You're not anemic. The rest has done you good. I think it's safe for you to come down a few hours a day as you have been doing, but with caution. With caution, you understand! I don't want you beating rugs and hanging out sheets."

"I promise," she said.

The doctor looked down, embarrassed. "And...no relations with your husband. You understand?"

"Yes, Doctor." Sadness swept through her. Hans seemed remote to her, lost for the time being. She knew it was her own fault, but everything in her was focused on getting this baby born. She knew she held her other children at arm's length now too. It was as if she was balancing on a high wire and dared not be distracted.

Felly and Caroline had one last cozy talk in the carriage on the way to the train.

"I used to feel sorry for you, Mother, all those years of raising Danny and me alone. Once I had children of my own I became awestruck you not only took care of us, but all those others. But ..." she gave her mother a roguish glance from the corner of her eyes, "it occurred to me you were lucky in a way, all those child-bearing years without a man to get you pregnant."

Caroline laughed, then grew sober. "So many women burdened with child after child, far beyond their strength to care for, it isn't funny. Have you heard of Margaret Sanger? Have you heard of the work she is doing?" It isn't that big families can't be wonderful and a blessing for strong men and women. But for less sturdy souls, too many women die young and leave girls who are children themselves to try and cope with all the demands of a household. Men unable to cope desert their families. Well, I don't mean to get up on a soap box.

"I've read a little about Margaret Sanger," Felly said, "didn't they put her in prison for helping women prevent pregnancies?"

"Yes, they did, and someday it will be considered a scandal." Caroline said. "What she is doing so needs to be done." How did her mother's concern match with the idea everyone was safe? Felly wondered. But they didn't have time to talk about it.

They had arrived at the station. Caroline took her daughter's hands. "Bay wants me to go to Europe with him. I've never gone and there is so much he wants to show me. We'll be back before your baby is born, but please promise me if anything goes wrong in between, anything, you'll get in touch with me. I'll come home on the first ship. Promise or I won't go."

"Now, who is being anxious?" Felly teased. "Besides you always told me distance didn't matter. That healings have nothing to do with being close or far, everything is within God's power in thought."

"It is. All the same, promise."

They held each other longer than usual in parting, heart beating against heart. As Caroline boarded the train, she waved and called, "I promise."

She stood a long time watching the train go down the track until it was nothing but a distant blue blur, and even afterward, she stood for a long time looking after it.

CHAPTER 26
The Music Inside his Head

***

"Fear thou not, for I am with thee; be not dismayed;
for I am thy God: I will strengthen thee; yea, I will help thee;
yea, I will uphold thee with the right hand of righteousness."
(Isaiah 41:10)

The winter had not been a good one for Hans. Something was wrong in the power house. Unexpected outages and blackouts kept occurring. For a long time, he could not find the source of the problem. When he did at last locate a faulty breaker, he had a devil of a time getting it replaced, several times having to travel to Chicago in person to get the correct part.

The weather was bitter. Long stretches of below-zero temperatures made all the water and sewerage problems attendant in so large an institution as Camp more acute. Some of the main lines froze in the ground and broke. Holding tanks froze and grew sluggish. Effecting solutions became more exasperating working in howling winds and freezing sleet.

In addition, he was worried about Felly. He became bad-tempered with everyone, even Mrs. Howard.

Jason did not know the reasons for his father's short fuse, he only knew he was often the brunt of it, and more and more tried to stay clear of his reach, which worsened things for him. Managing to be always out of reach of his father's anger meant he was never there when his father wanted him.

"I can't understand you, Jason," Hans exploded. "You know your mother can't do the work she did before and everyone in the household has had to pick up additional burdens and has done so with cheerfulness and good will, except you. You're always running off. You're never here when you're needed. I thought you loved your mother."

167

Jason had no defense against this bitter diatribe. His father never seemed to notice how much of Rasmeena's care he had assumed, never noticed the wood box and kindling box were always full for Mrs. Howard; never noticed the groceries were carried home and the ashes were taken out without a prompting; never noticed he helped Saran with her math or helped take the sheets from the line. What his father noticed was the snow was not shoveled from the walk and he had forgotten to pick up the cream from the dairy.

"Do you think because you are some la-de-da musician you are absolved from the gritty details of normal living?" Hans thundered. "Well, think again, my boy. You are no more privileged than any other human being and you had better start picking up your share of the burden of existence or someday you'll find yourself in the gutter. The world takes care of no one. If you don't hold up your end, you go down."

Once he had seemed insulated from his father's moods. No longer, each word hit his heart like a poisoned arrow and stuck there quivering.

"Well, what do you have to say for yourself?" Hans would demand.

"I'm sorry," Jason would say, "I'm sorry."

He knew nothing else to say, but in his secret heart, he was not sorry. He felt himself unjustly accused. His only "sorry" was he had such a man for a father. He compared him with Max and wished the Colonel was his father instead.

Max was always supportive and helpful with his problems except in his relationship with his father. He was careful not to encourage Jason's indictments of Hans. He managed to change the subject as soon as he had assured the boy these kinds of things were a part of the growing up process and someday he and his father would be great friends. Jason thought this was the one false note he detected in his friend, because he knew by Max's own admission he and his father had never been reconciled.

Things came to a boil in early spring. An episode of flu hit Camp and half of Han's usual crew were sick in bed. In desperation, Hans took Jason with him to the power house and set him to some of the more routine chores. At first, Jason was nervous and frightened. He knew he had no expertise in matters like this and Jake, though five years his junior, could probably have executed them better. But then he began to feel rather pleased his father had entrusted him with the responsibility and had even got him excused from school for a few days, He began to feel pride he was managing all right and had won some approval from his father.

This pleasant state of affairs ended on an unexpectedly warm day at the end of April. Spring was beginning to throb everywhere. Violets and tulips perfumed the air and made Camp a visual paradise. There was a hum of bumblebees and a new outburst of bird song. The lake, so newly released from its sheath of ice, smelled sweet.

The routine tasks in the power house, once mastered, had become boring to the boy. His mind wandered, his senses registering all the seductions of spring. He began to become acutely aware of the sounds of outside, the stirring branches, the bird cries, in counterpoint to the sounds within the power house, also throbbing, also pulsating, but regular, predictable, measured. A wild excitement began to pour through him, a composition was forming in his mind, a symphony of music which would draw from these two disparate, yet somehow, complementary sources—nature and the works of man.

The music inside his head became so compelling he could not bear it. He had to run home and note it down before it was lost...lost as other things like this had been lost to him. Feverishly he scribbled with a stub pencil, ran his fingers trembling and searching over the ivory keys, feeling freshets of relief and joy each time his fingers succeeded in evoking the sound in his head. He meant to take the pencil and paper back to the power house with him, but he forgot all about the power house. Forgot everything but the need to help the music in his head be born into reality.

A shadow fell across his paper. A cold presence loomed behind him. He looked up startled, realizing what he had done. How many hours had he been here? How long had he deserted his post?

"Papa," he cried, to the ice and stone face above him. "I'm sorry. I didn't mean to..."

This time he was sorry but his father was in no mood for apologies or forgiveness. No scolding words came. His silence and contempt were more terrible than any words he could have flung at Jason. Ignoring the boy's floundering apologies, he turned on his heel and walked out.

Jason ran after him. "Papa...Papa..."

Hans never turned his head. Jason followed him as far as the power house door. Then he saw Jake inside doing his job. The job he had run away from, the trust he had failed. Never in his young life had Jason felt such desolation.

So often at moments like this he had run physically, trying to escape his dilemmas through the roar of the blood in his head and veins, the bursting physical pain of heart and lungs shut out the more violent pain of bursting music in his heart. He could not even find that solace on this day. He crept away, filled with shame, remorse, self-loathing.

The fiery cherubs had now been set far above him. He had been expelled for his sins. He would never be his father's son again. He had not wanted Hans as father. Now it had happened. Hans was no longer his father. He felt it. He knew it. And he was unprepared for the hell into which he descended. He had never realized he loved Hans, that he needed his father and needed to be his son.

For several hours, he hid himself, set alone in a cramped position enduring his agony, not even able to cry. But eventually he went to Max, not expecting or hoping for absolution, but needing at least confession.

He handed Max his crumpled music, told him in a few disjointed words what had happened. Max listened. He gave him cold water to wash his face, and some lemonade to drink. Then he sat down and began to play Jason's composition. He played as always with exquisite beauty. Listening, tears came at last for Jason.

"It's...it's beautiful, isn't it, Max?" he said, confused, trying to comprehend why creating this beautiful thing had become such a heinous and unforgivable sin. Hating it because of what it had done to him, loving it because he did not really have to ask Max if it was beautiful, his whole being knew it was.

"Yes," Max confirmed. "It's very beautiful. The most mature and wonderful thing you've ever done."

He came and knelt in front of the crushed and abject boy, took his hand. "Jason, someday your father will understand. I promise you. In the meantime, the gifts of the gods are not given without price. You will just have to do the best you can. But for you, Jason...and I want you to understand this very clearly, there is no real choice, you must always decide for your music and not for the power house."

Jason tried to accept Max's words, grateful, so grateful, for his friend's understanding and caring, but some part of him warred with the last statement. Something whispered to him there were things even greater than his music which he must not lose. His head ached with trying to understand and not being able to. He wiped his cheeks with his sleeves but the flow of tears kept coming and coming.

"Enough," Max said in his old soldier commandant voice. "This masterpiece must be celebrated, and on such a day, we can't do it inside. We're going on a picnic. And we're going to have champagne! Great celebrations deserve champagne. Do you feel old enough for champagne?"

Jason shook his head no, in silence. He felt small, diminished, shamed.

"Anyone mature enough to write such music is mature enough for champagne," Max decreed. "You get a bit of ice from the ice house and I'll prepare us a feast for a picnic." Then seeing the boy was so down he did not even want to move, he said, "I'll get the ice. Wait here."

He came back with ice and all the treats he knew Jason liked best, and with sharp commands and quiet endearments he managed to pry the boy into his jacket and out of the house and back into the splendor and exhilaration of the spring day. A cool afternoon breeze brought the smell of the lake, lifted and sang in the budding of the trees, squirrels sashayed ahead of them as they made their way down a path to a secret clearing Max knew about.

Max had brought exquisite crystal glasses and he made a great ceremony of drinking the champagne. The bubbles tickled Jason's nose and made him grin.

"See," Max said, "and you thought you would never smile again."

Their conversation was desultory because Jason still felt sad and depressed. For a while, they just sat and listened to the sounds of the wind and the lake lapping behind the trees which hid it.

"Nature is healing," Max said. "Sometimes if you just lay down on the earth you can feel it healing you."

Jason had tried to eat the lunch but had felt too sick at heart to enjoy it. He brushed the crumbs from his jacket and laid flat on the earth, begging it to heal him as Max had said. But when he sat up, nothing felt changed. His hurt clung on like a sandbur. He noticed Max was still nearby, and he turned toward him. Max looked at him with sympathy and a loving smile.

"Besides Jason, you have a wonderful mother who does understand what your music means and knows you must have time to pursue it," he went on as if their earlier conversation had never stopped

"All of us have genius of one kind and another, but few people ever develop it to its full extent. And many times, those who do are able to because of someone who believed in them. Most great men and women had someone to shine their brilliance back to them. You have that, Jason.

"Leonardo da Vinci was one of the greatest men who ever lived. He invented machines which were never built until hundreds of years later, he wrote, and of course he painted, painted masterpieces. He was the son of a duke or some such high positioned personage. But because he was illegitimate, he could not live with his father. He was brought up in the simplest of circumstances and raised by an old peasant woman his father selected. And it was this old creature who fanned his greatness. She thought the sun rose and set in him, and because of her worship, he had the courage of high self-esteem.

"Even Thomas Edison, who is causing the world to be turned on to electricity, was considered dim, but his mother believed in him and fed him with the belief and we all know now he's a genius."

"And you...you believe in me, don't you Max? You believe in me and my music."

"You know I do."

Jason wished his father would love him as Max did, and try to understand what he felt when music coursed through his mind and distracted him to the point where nothing else was of interest or of any matter to him.

Then the sun went beneath a cloud, and in the moment of grayness he saw Max as an old, old man, ravaged by time. He seemed thinner, even gaunt. Gone was his dashing hero, the man he wanted to become.

Jason was shocked by seeing his best friend's face become a death head, the eyes sunken, withered flesh clinging and outlining the skull beneath. His smile seemed tinged with evil. The boy had a sudden terrible revelation. Yes, his mother was his champion. Whenever he put his music first before everyone and everything and his father grew so angry at him, his mother stood up for him. But what happened then was anger between his parents. Sometimes their quarrel lasted for weeks or even months, and the whole family suffered. And now he could see, it was his fault! And the Colonel aided and abetted him in causing all this to happen. He had told him today not to obey his father. "...you must always choose your music over the power-house." He must not see the Colonel anymore, ever.

He doubled over in a terrible anguish. How could he give up his friendship with the Colonel? Who would understand him, encourage him, sympathize with his compulsion to compose and perform music which each day now seemed to ooze from every pore of his being. His mother loved him and as Max said, understood, but she seemed of late to have gone off into some castle of her own where he could not reach her. Without Max...

The thought was too terrible to endure. Max no longer around to bandage his sorrow when Hans tore into him, with scathing rebukes and criticism. Who else would hold out a faint hope his father could change. Jason could not stop the tears which came; and he could not hide from his dearest friend. But he must, he must give him up, and his music too.

"What's the matter, son?" Max, with his usual sensitivity, became aware of Jason's deepened distress. He reached out to take the boy's hand. But Jason wrenched it away, and with a convulsive sob jumped up and began to run away.

The Colonel struggled to his feet, confounded. "Jason...," he called, "JASON!" But the boy kept running.

* * * *

Jason didn't stop running until he reached a small sunlit clearing now covered with early spring flowers, buttercups, violets, with velvety dark leaves beneath their namesake color petals. He threw himself into the grass and blossoms. Lying there where no one could see him from near or far, he spent his tears until, exhausted at last, he fell asleep.

Nearly everyone at Camp was by then searching for him. His father found him just before dusk. The boy was so exhausted and feverish he did not even know his father. Hans' heart smote him. Spring flu season. What if he lost his firstborn son with no reconciliation between them? He gathered Jason into his arms and carried him home and up the back stairs to his bed. He covered him with a sheet, bathed his face with cool water until the boy seemed to fall at last into a real sleep.

Hans tip-toed out, amazed at the imprint upon his heart of the form of the difficult little boy he had found so hard to love until he carried him the great distance home. Camp was a mile from where he had found his son, burning with fever and incoherent, and brought him back to his distraught mother. Jason was slight for his age, but he was fourteen now and it had still been a great labor.

Carrying Jason in his arms, he had looked down at his face again and again and realized how much he looked like Felly, and repented of his harshness of the past, flooded with love for this child so much like the wife he adored. Jason no longer seemed a rival, he saw how young he was and needing of his father's strength.

Hans had also to calm Felly. He held her in his arms all night until she at last fell asleep as the morning star began to pale in the dawn sky.

For a week, Jason suffered with flu like symptoms. He was excused from all work. Mrs. Howard brought him pudding and his mother got up to rub his chest with camphor. In a week or so the danger of a real illness passed. Everything seemed to be back to normal. But Jason avoided the Colonel. He felt the happiness of his whole family rested on his ability to forgo being with him.

Max was all tangled up with his music, and in Jason's troubled young mind, his music was the barrier between himself and his father, a scourge on his entire family. To see Max was to give into his temptation. Max was his siren song. Max was his betrayal of his father, his desire to have the old soldier as his father instead of Hans, a desire to put his music before everything else and be all the selfish things his father accused him of being. A terrible guilt had affixed itself to his love for Max.

CHAPTER 27
Struggles; Heart, Mind, and Body

***

"Watch ye, stand fast in the faith, quit you like men, be strong."
(1 Corinthians 16:13)

Felly knew Jason was troubled about something. He had nightmares, and had taken to stuttering when anyone spoke to him unexpectedly. He no longer quarreled with Jake or teased Seena and Saran.

Once Felly would have probed for his problem and tried to help him with it, but she was overwhelmed with a struggle of her own, an inner dialog with fear and the possibility of death.

As she embarked on the sixth month of her pregnancy and the delivery loomed closer and closer, bringing risk to herself, she became passive. In some curious way, she could not understand, death had become seductive.

"To have it all over with...to be done with the long struggle..."

She did not know what voice within her whispered such thoughts, but the whisper was there. It offered peace, surcease, escape from those things in her life about which she felt helpless, and therefore hopeless; especially the deep pain both she and Hans felt of needing each other, reaching out to each other, and yet forever eluding each other. Showering each other with sparks as they swung away, each into different preordained orbits.

Some healthy, more vigorous part of her was shocked at these sibilant whispers and fought back. Of course, she wanted to live! She wanted to preserve her own life, the life of the child within her, and be there for the other children she dearly loved. The other voice was madness. She would not listen to it. It was just part of a depression which sometimes accompanied a woman's pregnancy. It would pass. It would pass.

Her inner heart had become a battleground of such intensity even

175

Jason's problem, her darling Jason, could not take precedence. A serpent had crawled inside her and she must not take her eye from it for a moment or it would strike. The rest of the landscape was a blur.

For six weeks' flu raged in Camp through May and into June. In the Jacobson household, everyone except Felly had it in varying degrees; Saran the hardest. Felly stayed alone in her room, isolated from the disease and others, lonely and soul searching. Mrs. Howard or her niece, Maggie, both nursed the sick and ran the house for Felly. When most of Camp was over the siege, the Colonel came down with it. His illness was severe and he spent many days in the hospital.

A few people in Camp, the older, weaker ones, had died of the flu, but the Colonel, who for the most part was still in good health, survived and got well enough to return to his own home. However, he was still in a weakened condition and Felly volunteered to Dr. Bentley she would send food to him from their own table so he would not have to take his meals at the Central dining room.

She said it without much thought, thinking Jason was over there so much anyway it would be no trouble for the boy to take the Colonel his food. But when Jason was handed the tray to take to Max, he went white.

"I can't," he said, "I can't."

"What do you mean you can't," Hans said, "If anyone has been kind to you it's that old man. And now when you could do something for him...'you can't'. Well, you can. You take the tray and get yourself over there." Despite his new tenderness toward his son, he felt he had to bring the boy up right, and insist that he fulfill his responsibilities.

Jason sent a wild, pleading glance at his mother. Dr. Bentley had recently told her she seemed to be doing well enough she could start spending moderate time on her feet and being with her family. She was feeding Meena peaches and did not look up. He took the tray and went back through the kitchen. He knew Saran was starting to clear the table and would come into the kitchen in a minute. When she appeared, he said in a gruff way unlike him, "Saran, you take this tray to the Colonel or I'll box your ears."

She looked at him in surprise and laughed, then stuck her tongue out at him. "Phoo on you, I've got dishes to do. I heard Papa tell you to do it."

"Please, Saran, please!"

His desperation bewildered her, and made her curious. "Why don't you want to go to the Colonel's?" she demanded, thinking this strange indeed, and becoming aware Jason hadn't gone to the Colonel's for a long time.

A cold voice came from the doorway. Hans was standing there his face flushed with anger.

"Jason, you take the tray to the Colonel at once. Saran has enough to do without you sloughing your chores off on her. Now you go. I mean it."

Jason stumbled away with the tray. There was no help for him. His father could not know he was sending him into the heart of temptation. How could he explain to Hans he was trying to let go of his betrayal of his father, trying to be the son Hans wanted, and trying not to love Max more.

There was no help for him. Step by step, his feet carried him to the Colonel's. "Who's there?" Max called from the bedroom, as Jason entered. That rich evocative voice, what memories it stirred for Jason. Boston, how wonderful Boston had been. On slow feet, he advanced to the bedroom.

Max was sitting up against two white pillows wearing red silk pajamas. He looked a little wan and gray, as did everyone recovering from flu, but otherwise quite his usual impeccable self. When he saw Jason, his face lit up so it smote the boy's heart.

"Jason," his gladness rang in the room.

He asked Jason to play for him. "I want to hear the new things you are composing," he said. Jason played for him, how could he not?

"Not as great as the composition you composed in March, but interesting," Max said, "Playful, a little discordant. You're experimenting. That's good. Come in here. I want to write down some interposing chords I would like you to try in the last movement. We haven't done that, composed together, have we?"

Jason went into the bedroom bringing Max a pencil and score sheet. Soon the shiny dark head and the luminous white one were bent together in absorption over the sheet.

Jason went back to the piano and tried it. "It's great, Max! Rills, I love the rills." For a long time, Jason had fun fooling around with the new kind of music.

That night when he brought the supper tray Max peered at it and made a face. "I hate tapioca. Eat this for me, Jason." He patted a spot beside him on the bed.

Jason climbed on the bed beside him and ate the pudding. Soon they were chatting in the old warm, loving way. Jason felt flooded with happiness. It was so wonderful to be back in the Colonel's elegant rooms, feeling all the old good things. But the joy did not last, as his spoon clicked the bottom of the dish, guilt assailed him. He was also back to wanting to put his music first, to wanting Max for his father.

177

Firefly

His face flushed with pain.

"I can't stay, Max, Papa said to come right back home," Jason half lied.

"It's always good to see you, Jason," Max said, with such tenderness, Jason wanted to throw his arms around the old man and tell him how much he loved him.

"I'll...I'll bring you breakfast," Jason said, and ran off.

He continued to take the trays, but Max, perceiving his reluctance, never urged him to stay, as he used to do.

And so, the summer passed. Jason did not give into temptation again until the last of August. He had turned the practice session with the rills into a piece he thought was spectacular and he couldn't bear not to show it to Max. He stopped in before school, knowing it was going to make him tardy, yet helpless before his desire to share his new music with the one person who would understand his excitement.

When Max did not answer his rap, Jason became concerned and cracked the unlocked door a little.

"Max?" he called.

He was relieved to hear the Colonel's answering, "Jason!" though the Colonel's voice sounded odd and cracked. He hurried into the bedroom, and the sheets of music fell from his fingers. The death's head Colonel was back. An ancient, grey-faced man lay, heaving upon a crumpled sea of soiled sheets.

Jason wanted to run, but this was Max, his beloved friend. He forced himself forward, inch by inch. A hand came out of the tangled sheets and gripped his arm with a ferocity which denied any weakness.

"Jason, thank God, Jason," a voice which did not sound like Max croaked.

"I'll get the doctor!" Jason cried trying to dislodge the biting fingers.

"No... stay with me. Lift me up, Jason. I can't breathe."

Jason was not a muscular boy. He was small to begin with and he had been very good at avoiding the kind of chores which might have built muscular strength. He struggled with all his might to lift the inert, sweat soaked Colonel to a sitting position and get pillows propped behind his head. The Colonel too was panting when the boy managed to complete the maneuver, but his hand still clung to Jason's arm, even as the boy tried to pull it free.

"Stay with me Jason, promise me you will stay with me..." The words came with great effort.

"I've got to get you a doctor," Jason's words came out as a squeal.

"Stay with me, promise." The eyes in the ravished face were still

178

the eyes of Max.

"I can't...I've got to get you help!" Jason tried again to extricate himself from the clamped hand.

"Promise me..."

The words were so weak Jason stopped pulling away, he cradled the old man's body the best he could.

"I promise," he said.

"Promise..." the old man whispered again.

"I promise."

Max's mouth was moving now like a fish pulled out of water, in gasping breaths which allowed no words.

Jason had almost given up on prayers of late, feeling cynically God never answered anyway, but now prayers came bleating into his brain. "Help me! Help me!"

His strength was failing. He didn't know how long he could go on supporting the heaving, gasping man in his arms.

* * * *

Felly was ashamed. She felt she had neglected the Colonel in her absorption with herself. She hadn't visited him for weeks except for a brief "look in" while he was in the hospital. Now the early apples were ripening on the tree in the backyard. She had Maggie make pies and an extra tart which she determined to take to Max herself. Dr. Bentley had said it was good for her to walk a little if she didn't walk too fast or too far.

The first days of autumn were beginning to flick the edges of the trees with a gold or red leaf here and there. The air had that ideal balminess which sometimes came between the heat of summer and the cold of approaching winter. The children had started back to school. She could hear lazy, laughing voices from the schoolyard when she passed. The bottom of the pie pan was still warm against her hand as she walked and the cinnamon laced scent of apples seeped from the top.

She was just balancing the pie tin on one hand to knock on Max's door when she realized the door was agape and she heard strange, choking sounds. Her heart lurched with fear. Something was wrong with Max? She rushed in without knocking, calling, "Max...?" What she saw made the pie slip from her fingers and crash on the floor.

"Mother," Jason breathed. She could not know at that moment she was an answer to his fevered prayers.

She ran to help support the Colonel and cried out to Jason.

"Run, run for your father." She was almost screaming at her son.

Jason didn't move or answer.

"Go, Jason, quick...get Dr. Bentley...your father, anyone...!" Felly began to weep, holding the Colonel against her shoulder. "Jason, go, go get help!"

Jason's face was as white as the Colonel's. "I can't. I promised him...'

"It doesn't matter, go, go! Hurry."

"I promised."

In a rare fit of anger at her firstborn Felly shoved the weight of the Colonel back on Jason, "Your father's right, sometimes you're worthless! I'll go!" She turned to leave, almost slipped on the pie mess on the floor, righted herself and began to run. Her body felt inept with the burden of her pregnancy. She wanted to streak and seemed able only to lumber. She forced herself to pick up pace.

By the time she got to Dr. Bentley's, she was gasping and reeling, clutching her huge stomach with both hands, strands of hair coming down around a red, sweating face.

"My God, Felly..." the doctor exploded, and then his scolding was stopped by her message.

* * * *

Almost upon the moment of his mother's leaving, the fierce grip on Jason's arm loosened, the Colonel gave one last gasp. His mouth collapsed, and he was gone. Jason's best friend had left the world. He sobbed like the child he still was, and added to his enormous pain was his mother's scathing words, "Your father's right, sometimes you're worthless!" His mother had not only confirmed what his father thought of him, but she concurred.

Out of the abyss of his grief a new rebelliousness was born. Let them think what they would of him, he had kept his promise. He had stayed with the Colonel until the end.

He overcame his horror of the cadaver and continued to hold the old man's body in his arms until Felly and the doctor returned.

* * * *

Hans too, had been invigorated by the beauty of the day and came home from work feeling less tired and irritable than usual. He made his way first to the staircase to run up and see Felly and found Jason coming down. His son's face startled him. The most haunted, anguished eyes he had ever seen looked at him from a white mask.

"Jason..." he said. The boy would have rushed past but Hans put his hands on his shoulders and turned him around. "What's wrong, son?"

Jason was mute. Han's heart catapulted inside of him. "Is, is your mother...!"

Jason shook his head.

Hans felt relief pour through him, but he continued to hold his son.

"What is it Jason?"

Jason seemed incapable of forming a single word. Even this did not make his father angry. He caressed his son's shoulder and said, "All right. It's all right, Jason. We can talk later. I must see to your mother. We'll talk soon."

Hans started up the stairs and found Felly standing at the top of the stairs holding on to the newel post. Her face was whiter than Jason's had been.

"Felly..." he said, "what's wrong, Felly?"

She was staring at her feet.

A thin trickle of crimson was leaking down the stairs. The long-feared hemorrhage had begun.

Hans Jacob Jacobson nearly broke his neck leaping down the stairs to go for Dr. Bentley.

CHAPTER 28
Reconciliation

***

"...with all humility and gentleness, with patience,
showing tolerance for one another in love,"
(Ephesians 4:2 NASB®)

The lights burned all night long in the Jacobson house. In the morning, Dr. Bentley came out of Felly's room wiping his hands on a towel, his brow furrowed like an old hound dog.

"God must be with you, Hans. She hasn't lost the baby yet, and we've got the bleeding stopped. But..." he threw the towel down and shook his head, "I won't be responsible from here on out. I don't know what's going to happen. If you're a praying man, you'd better get to your knees. And you keep her in bed, you hear? She's not to get up even to go to the bathroom."

He strode off, angry with life, angry with the stupidity of people. She had been doing well and now he could guarantee nothing.

Maggie, who came in regularly now to help Mrs. Howard, was even more disgusted than Dr. Bentley. She hadn't appreciated being kept up half the night washing bloody towels and running to the ice house for ice. And now she would have to tote bed pans. If I had a husband like Hans Jacobson and a beautiful house like this and lots of money, I'd never be so foolish, she thought. You can bet I'd take care of myself and not take any risks.

Hans sat beside his wife all morning.

"You're going to be all right. The baby's all right." He took her hand and kissed it. He laid his cheek against hers. "Felly...what happened?"

She stroked his hand, but she could not tell him what happened, how she had run like a mad woman to get Dr. Bentley, forgetting her own condition, forgetting the baby. She knew Hans would blame Jason for not going instead, and the boy was in enough pain without being scolded. She felt some resentment at Dr. Bentley. How could he get so angry with her when there was nothing else she could have done under the circumstances? She did appreciate that the doctor had not told Hans what had happened. Dr. Bentley had been too busy to mention the Colonel's death. She told Hans about it now, reserving the things she thought it best for him not to know.

"Ahh," Hans said, "so now I know what's the matter with Jase." All the same, he felt, as always, shut out. He sensed a great deal more had happened his wife and son were not sharing with him. But he did not bolt away from Felly in anger, as he once might have. He remained at her bedside, holding her hand.

"Rest, Felly...rest," he whispered, "Get well for us."

She closed her eyes and after a long while, he tiptoed from the room.

He met Maggie in the hall. She had just come out of the bathroom. She had clean towels over her arm and her cheeks looked moist and pink.

"Poor Mr. Jacobson, you're all done in," she said, "and have to go to work yet, too. I've run a hot bath for you and set you a mug of coffee to drink while you're soakin'. Lots of cream and three sugars just as you like."

Hans gave her a tired smile. She might be something of a sassy little flirt, but she has a good heart, he thought.

* * * *

Felly's strength was slow to come back. She felt listless and wasted, and she was upset Jason had not come to her. She remembered the words she had hurled at him in her distress when he would not fetch the doctor and felt sorry and anxious to assure him of her love and the love of his father.

But the boy eluded everyone.

"He was here a little bit ago, but he's not in his room now, Mama."

"He was on the porch last I saw him, Miz Jacobson, but he doesn't seem to be around now."

"I think he went down to the stable."

Jason did not want to face anyone. Late at night when everyone else had gone to bed, he crept into his bedroom and lay on his side dry-eyed and empty.

When he awoke in the morning, he could hear Seena and Saran and Jake bustling about. They were all excited about being back in school. Had he ever been so young, so innocent and safe? After a time, he heard Rasmeena laughing and got up to resume his commitment to look after her.

* * * *

September came in with a rush of rain. Instead of autumn beauty against a cobalt sky, they had dank wet leaves dangling limp against a bullet-colored sky. Rain raced and smashed against the upstairs windows where Felly lay propped grey and wan against her pillows. Over the tops of the trees she could see glimpses of the lake, lashed with rain.

She still felt weak and depleted, but she got up, washed and dressed, determined to find Jason herself. She could not rest until things were right between them. He would not be in school because it was Saturday.

She was buttoning the last of the buttons on her jacket when Maggie passed by with a pile of fresh linen. The girl halted at the doorway and stared.

"Miz Jacobson, what are you doing up?" she asked. Her eyes and voice accused.

Mrs. Howard might have said the same words and Felly would have accepted them as genuine concern, but somehow there always seemed an edge of insolence to the tone of Maggie's voice when she spoke to Felly. She had to tighten her lips to keep from saying, "That's none of your concern."

She went to the mirror and began to smooth her hair. "I'm not going far and I won't be gone long," she said, resenting having to make explanations to this girl. She turned and stared into Maggie's eyes. "You are not to tell Mr. Jacobson. Do you understand?"

"I was told you're not to get up. You're putting me in a very awkward position, Miz Jacobson," Maggie said in measured tones, her green eyes were as cold as Felly's were and did not waver.

"You are not my jailer, Maggie," Felly said, and brushed past her, vowing as soon as she was strong enough to replace the girl.

Maggie followed her to the head of the stairs and watched her slow, cautious progress down. Then she gave a toss of her head and took the linens in to make the beds.

As Maggie whipped sheets about, she debated whether she ought to call Mr. Jacobson. Felly was still a power to reckon with, Maggie knew. If she got her back up she might dismiss Maggie and Maggie didn't want that to happen. She liked this job. On the other hand, if she didn't tell Mr. Jacobson, he might blame her and she would get the sack anyway. She had a moment of pure hate for her mistress for putting her in such a position. She went into the hall and started to crank the phone when a saving thought hit her. She put the receiver back on the hook with a little shrug of her shoulders. She could just tell

Mr. Jacobson Felly had sneaked off without her knowing it. Maggie had gone to market!

She gave a last sharp tug on a spread and went to get the wicker market basket. "Please, Father," she prayed, crossing herself at the door, "let Miz Jacobson be back in bed by the time I get home!

Maggie had crossed herself in the Catholic manner as Felly passed her. The gesture stayed with Felly, as she stepped outside, disquieting her. Why did she let that girl bother her so?

Felly took in eager gulps of the fresh air. Sunlight touched her cheekbones. She lifted her head, and arched her neck, staring up into the wet, still pretty, fall foliage. Oh, it was good to be outside again...so good. For a while walking through the beautiful damp world, she forgot about Maggie, and the Colonel's death, and even her anxiety about Jason. The trees were all dripping, water was running in little eddies and cross currents in the gravel course ways, a few spears of sunlight shot like special benedictions through an overcast of clouds.

Looking every place, she could think of where he might hide, Felly finally found her son in the old boathouse where she knew he often went to be alone. He was sitting on a barrel, whittling. His face was bleak, his eyes empty. He jumped to his feet when he saw her.

"Mama, you should be in bed!"

"You didn't come to me, Jason. I've been worried. I said some mean things to you the day the Colonel died. You know I didn't mean them. I love you so much...you mean everything to me..."

He noticed for the first time there were strands of silver in his mother's hair. There were half-moons of darkness beneath her eyes.

She held out her arms to him. He could not refuse to go into them. He burrowed his head against her, hiding his face. For a long time, she held him, and he had to admit in his heart; however harsh his mother's words had been, he knew she did love him.

He could feel her hot tears against his cheek.

"Jason...forgive me for my careless words. I was so worried for the Colonel. I loved him, too, you know."

Jason drew back and looked at her. Her face was hot and wet from her tears, her lips twisted with pain.

"I loved him because he understood you...was helping you...cared about you. I am so sorry you had to see him have the seizure. I think I know a little how you feel. But darling, he was an old man—an old, old man. He was ready to go and my dear child, you were one of the most loved people in his life—it was you whom he last looked upon. I'm sure that is what he would most have wanted."

"That's why I had to stay with him, Mother. I promised him not to leave."

"I understand now, Jason. Please forgive my quick words. Tell me you still love me.

"I love you, Mama, I will always love you."

He always would. But it would never be quite the same. She had been a goddess to him; more beautiful than anyone else, stronger than anyone else, purer than anyone else. Now she, too, had become mortal. She could no longer save him. Not in words, but in a feeling, he knew those few moments in the boathouse had changed their relationship forever. He could no longer look to her, instead she looked to him for comfort. He would have to take care of her, and he was filled with an even deeper despair because he did not feel he had any strength to give.

All the same, he tried to comfort her. "Come, Mama. It's all right. I'm sorry I ran away. It's all right. Sit here a minute and rest."

He led her to the barrel and helped her sit down. "We have to get you back to the house. Back in bed."

He wiped her face with the tail of his shirt. And when her breath seemed to have quieted, he supported her the best he could as they started back up the hill to the house.

* * * *

When Maggie got back from marketing, she left the things on the kitchen table and climbed the stairs, peeking almost clandestinely into Felly's bedroom. To her relief she saw her mistress, though still fully clothed, laying on the bed, her eyes closed, a hand flung across her forehead. Maggie's relief made her feel kinder toward Felly.

She advanced into the room and said in a softer tone than usual, "Miz Jacobson, would you like me to help you get back into your nightdress?"

Felly was exhausted and she caught the kinder note in Maggie's voice. She nodded and was grateful to have Maggie's strong, competent hands remove her day clothes and get her into a fresh gown.

Hans did not get home until eight. The house seemed wonderfully light and radiant after the cold, dark walk home. A delicious smell of roast meat and fresh bread greeted him. Through the arched doorway, he could see Seena bent over her schoolbooks, her cheeks rose-touched and her lovely blond hair burnished by the lamplight. He could hear Jake practicing his horn. Saran was sitting before the fireplace putting Meena's pajamas on her, tickling her and playing with her as she did so. Jason was at the piano, as usual.

Maggie came to him with a swish of her skirts and began helping him take off his rainwear.

"Thank you, Maggie..." he said touched by her attentions, "I smell something wonderful."

"Your favorite...roast," she said, smiling up at him. "I've kept it hot."

His heart swelled with all he had. He closed his eyes. God, please let me keep it. "Thank you, Maggie," he said. "I'll be down soon." He ran up the stairs to see how Felly was.

* * * *

Felly gave birth to a little girl at midnight. The baby was still-born.

When told, Hans, his eyes ragged red holes in his face, breathed, "Felly?"

Dr. Bentley shrugged. "I don't know, Hans. I just don't know. She has surprised me before with her reserves of strength." He could hold out no more hope than that.

This time he had not been able to fully stop the hemorrhage, he explained, perhaps it would stop of itself. There was nothing more he could do. His head throbbed. He no longer could care. He wanted his bed. He wanted sleep. He was an old man and sometimes he thought God put too much on his shoulders. He laid a hand on Hans' bowed head and left.

Maggie had been listening in the hallway. She ran ahead of the doctor to let him out, then she ran into the kitchen and threw herself down in front of the kitchen stove, her hands clasped and raised in prayer.

"Please, let Miz Jacobson be all right...please...please," she cried out loud.

Hans came to the kitchen door to ask for a cloth to wrap the little body in. He saw her on her knees, heard her cries. From the rock-bed of his own grief, he was touched. What a good little person Maggie is, he thought.

"Maggie...they're coming for the baby. Do we have a heavier cloth to wrap about her?" he asked, voice husky, every word difficult.

She scrambled to her feet. She found the pain in his eyes hard to bear. All the way up to the hall closet to get the cloth, she begged God not to let her feel the way she felt about Mr. Jacobson.

CHAPTER 29
Letting Go

***

"Then shall thy light break forth as the morning, and thine health shall spring forth speedily: and thy righteousness shall go before thee; the glory of the LORD shall be thy rereward."
(Isaiah 58:8)

The Commandant came to visit Felly. He stood at the foot of her bed, awkward and upset. She was still very weak. They hadn't wanted him to go into her room. He had felt terrible insisting.

"Mrs. Jacobsen, "he said, "I feel awful to bother you at a time like this, but the Colonel...the Colonel left in his papers instructions that you should have his piano and books. We need your signature verifying you have received them."

It horrified him to think she must know he was being so inopportune because he feared she might die before he could secure her signature, and then be put to a great deal of trouble to have it transferred to Hans.

"We're...we're going to give him a twenty-one-gun salute. We're going to bury him with the highest honors," he said, as if his promises would somehow restore his goodness.

Mrs. Jacobson signed his paper without comment. Her shaky letters spiraled downward, then her hand hung limp off the side of the bed, and she turned her head away from him.

The next day the Colonel was buried with military honors and the twenty-one-gun salute. Those of his old comrades who were still alive sat in the tavern afterward and toasted him, recalling what a great man he had been.

The following day there was a service for the Jacobson's stillborn child. Death always comes in threes, the superstitious in Camp whispered. They waited for the third death. With a grieving heart, Felly Jacobson hung on.

＊ ＊ ＊ ＊

As soon as Felly had gone into labor, Hans had sent a night telegram to her brother Danny. Danny dropped everything at Harbour Hill and came at once, the next morning. He was shocked when he saw his sister.

"Has Mother been sent for?"

She shook her head. "Don't...Danny. Don't send for Mother, don't spoil her trip."

The first few minutes were difficult. Danny was having a hard time controlling his emotions at seeing her so wasted, but she clung to his hand, light filling her eyes. She was so glad to see him it became easier and soon he was talking and laughing and reminiscing with her as if they had never been apart.

She wanted to know all about Emily, the children at Harbour Hill, and Jimmy, and Kemink.

"Kemink wanted to come," Danny told her, "I'm afraid I talked her out of it. She's in her eighties now, you know, and although she is generally in good health, she gets a little heavier every year and it's a great hardship for her to travel."

"Dear Kemink..." Felly murmured, "what loyalty...what love she has always given us."

Danny pulled a tissue-wrapped package from his valise. "She...she sent a present...for...for Rasmeena," he finished in a burst of inspiration. Actually, the Indian doll he removed from the tissue had been meant for the new baby, but Danny did not want to remind his sister of the loss.

Danny laid the small doll beside her and she touched the black yarn hair and the real buckskin leggings with her forefinger. Thinking about Kemink and seeing her gift made her think of Dan-Pete and the gift he had given her so many years before.

Seeing Danny again was wonderful, precious. I want to see Dan-Pete one more time, she thought. In spite of her haunting dreams, she realized the years had stolen him from her. She could no longer remember the exact shape of his face or the sound of his voice. But in her mind, she could still see his shining dark head beneath her window on the morning she was to have married Robert Anderson...what a far-away life that seemed now...but she could still remember the smoky taste of his lips when he had kissed her on the terrible night of the Peshtigo fire when he had risked his own life to save hers.

Dan-Pete had been as much a brother to her as Danny. She needed to see him one more time

"Danny..." she whispered. He could see she was already growing tired. "In my top bureau drawer, there is a box..."

With the help of her description, he found it and brought it to her. She had him take the firefly necklace out.

"If you ever need me...send this to me and I will come..." Dan-Pete had said. The amber stones hung like drops of frozen honey in the sunlight of the bedroom.

"Please see Dan-Pete gets this...."

Danny promised and then bent to kiss her. "I'll let you rest now..." He could see even this brief visit had taxed her strength.

She clung to his hand a moment longer, spoke like a sleepy child. "Danny...you've always been such a good brother...so kind."

He tousled her hair. "And you...you've always been...a...a firefly." He kissed her one more time.

In the hallway, he blew his nose and then went at once to telegraph his mother in England.

* * * *

Caroline sat up so abruptly in bed it woke Bay from a sound sleep. Her face was utterly devoid of color in the blue-light reflections from the long narrow hotel windows. She clutched his arm.

"Bay...we must start home at once." The urgency of her tone cut through his sleepy grogginess.

"But, Caroline...we're having such a good time...what is it?"

They had lingered for several weeks in England where Caroline was having a wonderful reunion with her sister, Ann, whose husband, Bromley, had died several years before. They were planning to spend six weeks in Switzerland enjoying the mountain air, the flowers, the beauty of the Alps, and were looking forward to later being in Italy, Florence and Rome.

"Fly...something is wrong with Fly."

"Darling...you've just had a nightmare."

"No," she said. "No. Please, Bay, please...make arrangements for us to go home."

He held her close. "All right, darling...all right. The first thing in the morning..."

"No," she said, "now, right now, Bay. Oh, please..." she was out of bed, dressing, starting to pack things in their steamer trunk.

He tried to calm her, to reason with her. Then he saw the look in her eyes, and he began to dress himself. "I'll find out how soon we can sail."

She had their trunks all packed, was dressed and waiting when he returned at four in the morning.

"We sail at eight, the best I could do," he said. "Let's rest a bit, get some breakfast, then I'll pay our bill and we'll have our things taken to the dock."

"I can't sleep...I can't eat...Bay." She was pacing the room. He had never seen her so agitated.

"This isn't like you, Caroline," he said. "Through all our life together you have met every crisis with strength. And we don't even know there is a crisis. Why don't we telegraph?"

"Bay...I know. I don't know how I know, but I know," she said. "But you're right...the way I am acting doesn't help. We should try to rest. I should pray."

At six o'clock, a telegram was delivered to their door. It was from Danny, explaining Fly was in bad condition following the birth and loss of her baby.

Bay stared at his wife. "How did you know?"

She shook her head. "I don't know. Please, Bay, please let's get our things to the wharf."

He did everything he could to expedite their progress toward home. By eight, the ship was sailing, and Caroline was straining at the rail as if by the sheer power of her will she might push it more speedily through the waters.

* * * *

Felly was growing weaker each day. Jason and Hans took turns sitting with her around the clock. She spoke very little but when she roused and saw them there, they could see by her eyes she was glad of their presence.

Maggie did everything she could to help. She did not grumble at the extra work Felly's care brought upon the household. She was solicitous of Hans, bringing him coffee at midnight to break his long vigil, insisting he get food down to keep up his strength. Sometimes in the evening, she came and sat with him in the sick room, playing solitaire at a little table in the corner, the lamp shining on her red hair. Sometimes she told him the events of the children's day to take his mind off his wife's weakening condition.

Once when Jason came to take his father's place, he heard them laughing, and his cheeks burned with anger at the thought Hans could sit at his mother's bedside when she was ill unto death and laugh...and with another woman yet. From that moment, he hated Maggie.

There were times when Hans had to attend to the work at Camp, there were emergencies his subordinates could not handle, and Jason was forced by physical necessity to sleep for a few hours. During those times, they had to entrust Felly to Maggie, but Jason did so fearfully, grudgingly.

191

On one such afternoon Maggie left Felly's bedside to answer the door. She came back carrying a necklace with strange golden stones.

"Miz Jacobson..." she spoke in a loud voice because it had become hard to break through the lethargy of Felly's illness. "There's a man downstairs to see you. He's an Indian...but he's all dressed up like a white man, he looks respectable enough. He says he is a relative. Miz Jacobson...do you hear me? He gave me this..." she dropped the necklace on the bed beside Felly. "He wants to see you. And Mr. Jacobson called. He's on his way home."

Dan-Pete was coming. He was finally here. Felly tried to pull herself up on the pillows, but she was too weak.

Then Dan-Pete was above her, lifting her to a more comfortable position among the pillows, kneeling beside her, and taking her hands in his.

The boy she had known was forever gone. The man looking at her with such tenderness wore his hair in the Indian way in a braid. The dark hair was grizzled with gray now, but it made his large, dark eyes seem even more beautiful. She freed one trembling hand and traced his full lips.

"Dan-Pete."

"Firefly."

Something strange was happening to her. Seeing him again jarred old memories. No more than a memory, it was as if she was *there* again in the past.

She remembered...she remembered...she had run after him that night at sunset, followed him into the woods, declared her love, and he had told her it could never be, told her she could never live in a teepee, bathe in an icy stream. Told her he was Indian, she was white...that old Sashwatka had died, and his tribe had elected him, Dan-Pete, as their chief. Told her it was an honor he had to accept, a place she could not follow. Told her his people needed him and he needed his people.

She was there again, there in all the anguish of her love and need... He turned away from her.

"Dan-Pete!" she screamed. "Don't you walk away from me. Do you think I'm so shallow, so frivolous, so nothing that I couldn't stand up to everything anyone might throw at me? Your mother and my mother lived alone on the frontier. Do you think I'm made of so much lesser stuff? Dan-Pete, believe in me," she ended in sobs.

The next moment he was holding her in his arms, but even as he held her tight and hard against his body, his head was arched back as if he were in unbearable pain.

"Firefly, don't do this to me. If you truly love me, help me to do

what I must do."

"At your side, in your arms, I will help you..."

He shook his head, looking down at her with an expression in eyes that became branded on her heart. "If I stay with you, I will never be able to do what may be required of me."

"Dan-Pete," she whispered, "are you trying to tell me that you expect to be martyred or some such terrible thing?"

"I don't know yet what will be required of me, Fly. I only know I will not be able to do whatever it is that I must, if my heart stays in the wigwam with you."

"You're saying that you love your stupid Indian struggle or whatever it is, more than you love me!"

His lips were barely touching hers. "Fly" his eyes were filled with tears. "If you love me, help me to do the things I must, and to be what I must be."

"I do love you!"

"Swear to help me."

"I can't."

"I can fight anything else in this world, Fly, but I can't fight you, because you are my own heart. If you say to me this moment, stay, I will stay"

She looked up at him. She could feel the hot, wild current of his body, the thrashing struggle of his soul and young though she was, she saw, however dimly, that if she told him to stay she would destroy him and the thing in him that she loved. She hesitated and then with great effort said, "I swear by my love" she got the rest of the words out between uncontrollable sobs, "to help you by letting you go to be what you must be."

All those years that she had been so angry with him for leaving her...she had forgotten those last words, that he had given *her,* the choice, and that *she* had sent him away.

He was kissing her hands. She drew them away and placed one on each side of his face. She reminded him of those last words and apologized to him for her long anger and anguish.

"I was only sixteen, and I loved you so much, but I did the right thing, didn't I Dan-Pete?"

"You did," he said, "you did."

"Can you imagine me in a wigwam?"

"No, I could not, and still cannot imagine you in a wigwam."

They were both laughing and crying together.

"I'm sorry I didn't keep my end of the bargain up very well." She felt so weak now she felt as if she were fading away to some other dimension but there was something important she had to tell him. Oh, yes, it came to her.

"Thank you so much for coming, my dear brother. But I must ask you to go now, my husband is on his way, and he wouldn't understand. I love him, Dan-Pete, I don't want him hurt."

"That's good, Fly. That's *good*." He kissed her hands one last time.

A great feeling of peace flowed between them, a closure.

He took the firefly necklace from his pocket and tried to give it to her. She closed his fingers around it.

"Please keep it in memory of me."

* * * *

A hand was holding hers, a small, strong, desperate hand.

"Jason...?"

"Yes, Mama, yes..."

"Jason..."

Jason's face was all squinched up, he didn't seem to understand her. Why was he crying every time she saw him? She drifted back into the darkness. She was so hot. Her body felt parched.

She wanted her mother. She wanted Caroline as she had wanted her when she was a child. She began to call for her mother over and over again. "Mama...Mama..." but it was Jason who answered. Then there was daylight around her again.

She laid her hand against his cheek. He was so beautiful. She loved him so... She remembered then what she wanted to say to Jason.

"Jason," she said, "Your father is such a good man. Don't quarrel with him. I love him, Jason. I love your father very much, I always have. Take care of your sisters. Tell Seena...tell Jake and Saran...tell Rasmeena...I love each of you...so very much." She drifted away again.

Hans came in to relieve Jason, his large hand cradled his son's shoulder. "I'll sit with her now, Jason."

The boy shook his head. "I don't want to leave her."

"You have to sleep, Jason. You've been here for hours."

The boy shook his head. "I can't leave her. She's so bad. She might...she might...while I'm gone...she might..."

"Jason, if there is any change, any change at all, I'll call you," Hans promised. "Come now, son, you're falling right off the chair."

"You promise?"

"I promise, Jason. You'll be just across the hall. If there's any change, I'll call at once. You've got to rest if only for a few minutes."

Reluctantly, Jason let himself be led to his bedroom. Hans pulled the boy's boots off and drew a spread over him before returning to Felly's side.

He sat hunched close beside his wife, exhausted himself, his eyes burned and blurred, trying to stay open.

* * * *

Felly's eyes were open but she felt so tired, so tired. Please, please...I want to be free...no more, no more...She called again for her mother. And this time her mother came. She felt flooded with joy but also dazed, bewildered." Mother...? Please, Mama...I want to go...please let me go..."

She could hear her own moaning, feel the sounds of it hot in the back of her throat, and a hand on her forehead, a hand she knew.

"Mama?" The childhood name ached up through her moaning.

"I'm here, Fly, darling, I'm here," her mother said.

Her mother was there in the room with her. She saw her hazily in a red-gold light from the turned-down lamp. Caroline was propping her up on pillows, giving her water to drink. Her mother's hands were cool. Her mother's hands were...healing hands.

Felly shook her head in protest. "No. Let me go, Mama. I'm so sick. Let me go. Don't try to heal me."

"My darling daughter, you can go if you want to, but you've struggled so hard to live, I don't think you want to go. Your children need you, and Hans, he loves you so."

Her mother was coming more into focus. Her face, her beloved face, was there above her. Some of the great lassitude seemed to recede from Felly.

"He does. He does, doesn't he?" she acknowledged.

"Yes, Fly, he does, terribly, terribly."

"I love him, too, Mother."

"I know."

"Somehow, something jumbled, didn't work," her voice faded, she felt herself sinking back toward the darkness. He'll be all right. We all die...even healers...even Jesus..." Her last words were barely more than a wisp of breath.

"Yes, we all die when the time is right for us. But you have a choice now, Fly. If you want to live, you have to see yourself well. Do you remember when you were a little girl and you could never use your left arm? How it hung, withered and useless from birth?"

Felly groaned a little, her mother had told her the story so many times how could she forget? Then something happened, she did begin to remember, not a story but as if she were there again. She felt a strange surge of strength go through her, a joy. The whole family was in the sitting room of her aunt and uncle's mansion in Chicago. Her aunt Ann was holding an embroidery hoop so the little Firefly she embodied could draw a needle with crimson thread back and forth with her "good" hand, and as naturally as if her other hand had always worked, she had taken the hoop and held it herself. Her mother noticed and exclaimed in shocked delight, and then all the family was gathering around her crying and laughing and hugging her. The elation of that moment shot through her again.

"See yourself well and strong, Fly. Know God never withholds healing. It comes as soon as you can ask for it with faith believing. Jason needs you."

Jason. The name tore into her heart. Yes, her first born son needed her, more than all the others he needed her. The music in him must not be lost.

"Do you think you could drink some tea? Just a few sips?"

Felly held on to the joy she had been feeling. "I'll try."

"Yes," Caroline said, a long quivering sigh came from her. "Yes."

* * * *

The next morning Felly could get down a few teaspoons of oatmeal and cream. When the doctor came to examine her, he announced the hemorrhaging had stopped.

"Her fever's gone. I think she's got a chance," he said. His clouded old eyes were wet.

Her mother, who had come into the room with a basin of warm water to bathe Felly, smiled. "Yes," she said, "yes."

Firefly's childhood healing had not been as instantaneous as it had looked the afternoon in Chicago. It had taken many months of anguished searching until she had found the touchstone of knowing her daughter was perfect, of accepting the healing before it appeared.

Caroline understood Fly was still weak, not yet ready to jump out of bed and take the reins of her household back from the bossy red-headed helper named Maggie. But Caroline was filled with the peace of certainty, a healing had taken place and all would be well. It would be safe for her and Bay to return to their own lives within a few weeks.

CHAPTER 30
Maggie

***

*"Come unto me, all ye that labour and are heavy laden,
and I will give you rest."
(Matthew 11:28)*

Adam Quimby was in a rage. "Why didn't you call us? You knew her condition. She might have died, but not a word to us. It's unforgivable! Unforgivable!"

Hans sat on a kitchen chair, his arms hanging through his knees, accepting the verbal blows like a dumb, stolid, beaten ox.

"She asked me not to call you. She was afraid you would be frightened by the way she looked. She wanted to get better first."

"You knew she might not get better. You knew she..."

Grace laid a restraining hand on her husband's arm. "Adam."

"You telegraphed Danny!"

"I sent the telegraph before she knew. I was going to call you in the morning. She made me promise. I had to promise her. I couldn't deny her anything she wanted right then."

"I will never forgive you. Never!" Adam pounded his fist on the table, his face contorted and red.

"Adam, stop it!" Grace said with authority. "He's had enough. Can't you see what you're doing? Felly will never forgive *you*. What matters now is she is getting better."

Adam looked at the bent head of the man seated in front of him. He looked into his wife's calm, imploring eyes and forced himself to silence, but his face was still quivering.

"Go to Jason, Adam," Grace said. "Go to the children. They need you. They've been through a frightful time."

The kitchen was very quiet after Grace led Adam out. The sight of Hans sitting so cowed, his eyes glazed, a rampage of whiskers marring his jaw, along with the melancholy ambience of the sound of burned wood falling in the fire box, the ticking clock, the dripping rain from the eaves outside, were almost too much for Maggie to bear.

She knelt in front of Hans. "Mr. Jacobson—you must take care yourself, now. Your missus is going to be all right." She pleaded, "She wouldn't want this. You've got to eat something...bathe, get dressed."

His eyes flickered at her urgings. A sigh swelled his chest. "Yes, Maggie, yes, you're right," he said. But still he sat. He had been holding himself together for so long for Felly's sake, now it seemed she was going to be all right, it was as if all the starch had gone out of him, and he had given into his exhaustion.

"Come on, Mr. Jacobson, come on," Maggie pleaded, "I've run you a hot tub upstairs. While you bathe I'll fix you some food." As she stood up, she put her arms around him and tried to draw him up with her. In so doing she lost her balance and would have fallen backward if he had not caught her. She gave a silly little laugh as one sometimes does in such a situation.

At that unpropitious moment, Jason came into the room. What he saw was Hans with his arms around Maggie, and Maggie giggling. The shock on his face was like another blow to his father.

"Jason," he cried, "this is not the way it looks. Maggie was just trying..."

"I hate you, Papa, I hate you!" Jason exploded. "All this time while Mama was sick you and her...her and you..."

Maggie fled the room.

"No, Jason, no, it wasn't that way," he sank back on the chair.

"It was. It was. I heard the two of you laughing and having a good time while Mama was lying there, almost dying. I heard you. You never loved Mama, never. You've always been mean to her and made her cry, and you never wanted her to have anything pretty."

Hans' face went from pale to livid—dark with rage, and he charged from the chair with a sudden roar. "Never loved your mother? Never loved your mother?" He grabbed Jason's shirt front and threw him back against the wall, holding him there like a squashed bug, Hans' eyes flashing with anger. For a moment, Jason thought his father was going to kill him. "I adore your mother and I always have!"

Then his grip went slack, he let Jason go, and slumped back in the kitchen chair, his head between his knees. "It's your mother who never loved me. She's mooned all her life for some Indian she fell in love with in her childhood. It is she who's never loved me."

Jason stared. His father was crying. He had never seen his father like this. Terrible paroxysms of guttural sobs were issuing from beneath his humped back.

"Papa, you're wrong," Jason said in a hushed voice. "She does love you. She told me so. Not long ago. She told me you were such a good man and she loved you a whole lot and I shouldn't cause you problems."

Hans shook his bowed head.

"She did, Papa. Honest."

Hans lifted his head, his eyes red and wet. "You're just saying that."

"No, Papa. She did."

Hans took out his handkerchief, wiped his eyes, and blew his nose. Jason could see his father finally believed him and it mattered.

The boy was filled with a new humility. He had witnessed his parents' relationship for years, thought he knew what it was like, but standing in the damp, dreary kitchen, he realized how little he had really understood. Whatever had been between this man and the woman who was his mother was far more complicated and diverse than his childish mind had fathomed. For the first time, his heart broke for his father as well as for his mother.

"Papa," he said, "I'm sorry. I'm sorry about the things I said."

Hans clamped a hand on his shoulder. "I know, son, I know. I am sorry for many words I've said to you, too, Jason. I'm going upstairs now to get cleaned up and to be with your mother. "

He turned back by the door. "Son, I want you to apologize to Maggie. It was not the way it looked. She has gone way beyond the bounds of duty to help this family. I want her treated with respect."

The intensity of his father's new emotion had convinced Jason the charges he had made against him were not true, but the apology to Maggie stuck in his throat. He did make it, but it was a grudging apology, and he continued to harbor hatred in his heart for the saucy, red-headed hired helper.

* * * *

When the family assembled for supper, Grace and Bay, with the sensitivity of the fine people they were, drew back and watched as Adam and Caroline knitted hands with their relief at the doctor's prognosis their daughter had at least the promise of recovery now. Long ago, they had loved with all the ardor of their youth and from their love had come this daughter who they both desperately wanted to survive.

Adam brought Caroline's hands up to his lips and kissed them. "Thank you, Caroline, without you she might have..."

Caroline just bowed her head at his words, embarrassed. It always embarrassed her when people subscribed healing to her. She knew she was an element but not the cause.

Grace and Bay both loved Felly and would have been devastated by her loss, but they knew, deep as their concern had been, it did not have the well-springs of the fear Adam and Caroline had suffered. A thousand memories, both sad and happy, thronged about them for the moment when they stood together, before releasing each other's hands. They joined the others at the table.

"Amen and amen...and amen," Hans intoned finishing the blessing.

Grace felt her stepdaughter had become her best friend, and she still felt concerned about her. However, she had been human enough to peek up at Caroline and scrutinize her during the prayer, this woman her husband had not wanted her to meet. This woman her husband had known and loved and shared his young lifetime with long before he ever had set eyes on Grace.

Caroline had felt her gaze. "Grace," she said, "Firefly has told me so much about you. She loves you very much."

Grace could not help staring at the other woman's face. She saw white hair, tissue-paper cheeks, an elegant woman, but with the beauty of a fading rose, no one to be jealous of. Why then did she feel her first stab of jealousy? What power did this woman have that after half a century and years of separation Adam still said, "I will always love her" but otherwise wouldn't talk about her?

Bay reached forward and laid his hand over Caroline's. He, too, always felt uncomfortable when Adam was around, even though he was certain of Caroline's love. He still couldn't like Adam, even though the man was said to have "changed his spots."

Grace managed a smile. "Thank you, I love Felly, too," she said to Caroline. "Please pass the potatoes."

* * * *

Mrs. Howard cut another pan of cake into squares and filled the cups on another tray to send into the dining room. Her feet hurt and she was looking forward to when all of Felly's concerned relatives would go home. And Maggie wasn't helping her. The girl was sitting in the corner by the chimney. Her curly, exuberant hair was now pulled back in a tight bun, the freckles on her nose stood out on an unnatural pallor.

Mrs. Howard lifted a piece of cake onto a saucer and poured a cup coffee and took them with her to the corner where her niece sat. "Maggie, child, you're all worn out, too, I can see. It's not easy helping in a household with sick people. I suspect you've had little rest."

Her aunt's kindness brought tears to Maggie's eyes. It was true, she had taken care of everybody else, been up night after night; no one had taken care of her. Or cared.

Mrs. Howard set the cake and coffee down in front of her niece and sat down on the window seat. "What will you do now, Maggie?" When or who said Maggie wouldn't be working there anymore? Did I miss something? The last anything was said was when Hans caught her when she fell, but he did not fire her. Jason didn't like her, but still she wasn't fired...? And Mrs. Howard also, when was it decided she would be leaving for sure?

"Dr. Bentley was impressed with how well I did on this job...he's offered me a position at the hospital."

"How wonderful!" Mrs. Howard said. "Do you want to move in with us, Maggie?"

"I dunno," Maggie said, her lips pouting, "I dunno if I even want to stay here." Stay here? Where is here? In the Jacobson home or near Camp? Her long lashes swept down.

"Why it's a wonderful opportunity for you," Mrs. Howard chided. "You're just worn out, Honey."

"Probably so, "Maggie said. From where she was sitting, she could see into the dining room through the open kitchen door. Her eyes sought the pale hair of Hans Jacob Jacobson, circled now by smoke rings from his cigar, a habit that upset Miz Jacobson.

All day her eyes had sought him out, in the parlor, on the stairway, in the kitchen. Not once had Hans Jacobson looked back at her, noticed her, or thanked her for the long hours she had put in to assure his wife's survival. Her lower lip trembled and it was difficult to keep a convulsive sob from rising in her throat. Miz Jacobson was going to live and all of Maggie's hopes were crashing around her.

It wasn't that she had wanted Felly to die! A swarm of guilt descended on her. Hadn't she even prayed Miz Jacobson wouldn't die? It was just...she had been so sure she would.

CHAPTER 31
Contrition?

***

*"And the Lord direct your hearts into the love of God
and into the patient waiting for Christ."*
(2 Thessalonians 3:5)

"Hans, if you want us to take any of the children, or all of them until Fly regains her strength, we have plenty of household help. We would love –"

Hans shook his head at Caroline. "Thank you, but I want to keep my family together."

"If there is anything, Hans –"

"I know."

Caroline kissed his hard-red cheek. She knew he had always built barriers against her. She had not understood why and it had always made her sad. She thought of Jesus and how he had lamented he would have liked to gather Jerusalem to him as a hen gathers her chicks under her wings, and Jerusalem would have none of it. At last, things were different. Hans could not seem to tell her enough how grateful he was she had come and helped Felly get better.

Caroline and Bay hugged and kissed and said their goodbyes to all the children. She hated leaving them, but she respected and agreed with Hans the family should be kept together. They would find some way to get along until Felly could take over again.

Grace was more practical. When Hans went into the nursery to fetch Meena he found her packing the child's small garments.

Hans shook his head. "I'm going to keep my family together, Grace. I appreciate your willingness, but no. Meena stays with us."

Grace went on laying garments in her valise. "It isn't you who would suffer from such a decision, Hans, it's Seena. The burden will fall on Seena. She's still a child herself and the burden is going to be heavy enough as it is."

202

Hans thought of Seena standing in her long nightgown, her face pinched and white. He thought of how she looked studying at night, her long fair hair lit by the lamplight, her face so earnest. His heart turned over inside of him. His children – oh, his children. His first thought was always for Felly. But Grace was right. Too much was demanded of Seena now.

"And Meena and Felly would also suffer from such a decision," Grace went on. "You can't keep Seena home from school to take care of her. Mrs. Howard is a wonderful, loving woman but she has come to an age and time when she wants to devote herself to her own family. There is no one else in camp who would bring to Meena the love and concern Adam and I will give her, Hans. Meena is used to being with us. She plays well with Jan."

Hans turned away, his face rigid. Grace laid a hand on his shoulder.

"I know how hard this is for you, but we aren't going to steal Meena from you forever. We'll only keep her until Felly is strong again. We're so close, Hans, you can come and get her weekends so she doesn't forget where she belongs."

He knew what a great kindness Grace was offering, but at the moment, he hated her, because he could not withstand her logic. He knew Meena would be better off with Adam whom he had never liked. And he had to do what was best for Felly, regardless of his feelings.

The decision was not popular when it was announced to the other children, either. Meena was fun and made them laugh. They needed her. With Seena, however, her reluctance to have her baby sister gone was intertwined with relief. It was going to be enough to try to keep track of Jake. Grace and Adam left with Meena and the Jacobson household settled down to trying to cope.

In the weeks which followed, Saran and Seena tried hard, but they had school work as well as housework. They managed to keep the surface of the house presentable but dirt gathered in corners, meals were burned, clothes scorched, sheets not changed. In the frustration of their failures, they fought with each other and blamed each other. There were rages and tears and actual hair-pulling at times, all the while each of them trying to shield their mother so she would not try to take over beyond her ability.

Jason tried to exert control so Hans did not come home to pandemonium night after night. Then the girls turned on him.

Jake escaped to his bedroom and practiced his horn or went down to the pool hall and shot pool. He always gave the impression of being like a duck, with events sliding off his back like water, leaving him untouched. It aggravated the rest of the children and yet they envied him and respected him for it, too.

Mrs. Howard gave them an occasional hand. She would come over with a cake or fresh-baked bread or do a pile of mending. But she told Hans he must hire a girl to help since she could no longer take care of his household.

Hans hired one of Old Per's daughters. She was slovenly and lazy. He let her go when she started a grease fire and almost burned the house down. He hired a pleasant middle-aged lady from Waupaca who promised to be everything they were looking for. She turned out to be a lush. He hired an elderly lady who admitted she would not be able to do much heavy physical labor but she could direct and assist the girls. Saran and Seena ended up waiting on her. The kindly old soul suffered from lumbago. Hans gave up and the household went back to struggling on their own.

Maggie Grasslee had accepted the nursing position offered by Dr. Bentley at the hospital. Like Mrs. Howard, she also took to popping in to "give a hand".

Maggie was energetic and she did know how to do things well. Seena and Saran might have forgotten their first antipathy toward her and been grateful for her assistance if it hadn't been for Jason.

"She has her eye on Papa," he said with venom. "I hate her. She doesn't care two hoots for any of us. She just wants to get in good with Pa."

As a result, Maggie got scant thanks for the help she offered, and indeed Saran and Seena were often tart with her.

Christmas was difficult. Felly's recovery was slow. She came down to the kitchen and helped make cookies, wrap presents and put a few decorations on the tree, but everyone could see it was a great effort and she was still too weak to be up. She had always made a big production of Christmas. This Christmas seemed meager by comparison.

Hans had decreed there would be no houseful of company. Even though he knew Caroline and Grace would pitch in with the work, he felt a boisterous holiday would be too much for Felly. The children felt cranky and bereft. No fig pudding, no grandparents coming to visit, no sleigh rides in the snow to sing carols and deliver presents to the old soldiers, no new dresses or shirts made by their mother's hands. None of the "special" gifts she had always squirreled away for each child.

In the midst of the festivities, such as they were, Maggie arrived, her arms full of packages. Even hostile Saran and Seena had to admit she looked ravishing. Her hair was done in a cascade of shining ringlets. She had on a claret dress, a daring color for a redhead in a time when pink and russet tones were considered off-limits for the titian haired, but a color which made her skin look alabaster and turned her eyes to emeralds.

She had selected the presents with great care. There was a music book for Jason, a pair of long pants which would be Jake's first, and matching dresses for Saran and Seena that Maggie had made herself.

Hans was embarrassed. It had never occurred to him to buy a present for Maggie. His embarrassment was exacerbated by his children's ungracious acceptance of their gifts.

"I'm long past this music," Jason told her, "mostly I compose my own – or I play rag. Why don't you give this to one of your nieces or nephews who is still learning the basics?" He shoved the book back at her.

"Jason!" Hans was outraged.

The other children had not been effusive when opening their gifts, either. Maggie's face was the color of her dress. She jumped up from the settee where she had been sitting. "Well, I must go. I only stopped for a minute. I'm sorry you didn't like the book, Jason. I'll do like you said, give it to one of Aunt Mabel's youngsters. Well – Merry Christmas to you all, I must fly. Got a heavy date, you know."

She rushed into the vestibule and was fumbling into her wraps when Hans followed.

"Maggie," he said, "you were so fine to come and try to make our Christmas better, and I'm so ashamed of Jason. There's no excuse, none. But I think it was probably the incident in the kitchen. Somehow, he's got the wrong idea –"

She folded her hand around his. "It's all right. It's not your fault, Hans."

He saw tears seeping from under her eyelashes and his heart was wrenched anew. "You have been so splendid to us, Maggie."

Her wet eyelashes lifted. She looked into his eyes. "And you are a splendid man, Hans Jacobson." She stood on tiptoe and pressed her strawberry lips against the corner of his mouth.

He felt a tremor go through him, followed by shame. He hated himself for the sensation she had aroused. He opened the door, and was glad to see her go.

In the parlor, a shocked Felly, was chiding her children for their rudeness.

"How could you be so cruel to someone who was trying to be nice to you? To someone who has done so much for us?"

Jason wanted to blurt out to her the things he had seen and felt between Maggie and Hans, but he managed to hold his tongue, and pretend to be sorry for his behavior.

Hans came back into the parlor, disgruntled and angry. Whatever possibility there might have been in resurrecting Christmas was shattered.

No one took the tree down for weeks. It stood in the corner turning brown and dropping needles into a pile over the forgotten wads of tissue paper beneath it. The children had all been reprimanded for their treatment of Maggie, but underneath their forced contrition, they were well pleased with their performance. They congratulated themselves they had finally discouraged Maggie to the point where she would not bother them further.

CHAPTER 32
Entertainment Hall

***

*"And forgive us our sins for we also forgive every one that is
indebted to us. And lead us not into temptation;
but deliver us from evil."
(Luke 11:4)*

February came in mild. It snowed almost every day but the flakes
were tiny and benevolent. With no wind to make them violent, they
settled on everything like a silent white blessing. Some days the air had
almost a spring-like warmth to it which melted the new snow and sent
a fresh sweetness into the air. The gentle weather was fortunate for
Felly. Dr. Bentley had insisted she must walk outside every day to
regain her strength. To begin with five minutes a day, but the goal was
to get up to a half hour as she recuperated.

Felly went dutifully at first, then came to cherish this quiet time
alone with nature. More than in any church or chapel, she began to
feel a connection with God. Her near brush with death and her
mother's healing invocations had stirred an inner change in her which
kept unfolding. The panorama of the natural world took on new
significance to her.

The little chipmunk stopped its scurrying through the snow to
stand up on its hind legs to contemplate her with a cocked head, the
continual sifting of the snow from heaven, the hieroglyphics of a
multitude of life forms written in the whiteness about her all filled her
with awe. The flower-like footprints of house cats, the crosshatches of
bird feet, the delicate punctures made by deer feet, the distinctive pad-
like marks made by running dogs, the skidded tracks of rabbit feet
leaping in confused directions, the squirrel and mouse imprints, all
testified to a raging flood of life all about her.

The God she had been taught about in church still mystified her.
The traces of blood and evidence of carnage she also saw sometimes in

the snow sobered her. The sheer magnificence of the trees, sedges, clouds, sun, wind, animals convinced her all of this could not have happened by accident. There had to be an intelligent, evolving mind behind it all. She was finding a connection to this, something she had never felt before.

Sometimes the disclosures of her contemplation were painful. She saw her faults with a new clarity and a sense of shame. The life stretched behind her seemed now, with her new vision, to have been one of self-pity. All the work with the babies, the house, the cooking, and the constant demands from Hans had seemed such an overwhelming burden. She had not been used to so much physical labor, and burdened with one difficult pregnancy after another she had resented and wilted beneath the load. She felt indicted now by her resentment and self-pity.

She had been too little to remember all her mother and Kemink had gone through to survive alone in the wilderness when her father had deserted her mother, Danny and herself. She did remember the stories Danny and Dan-Pete had told her and the occasional narratives from the two women. They had had no time for self-pity. Their very survival and that of their children had depended on courage and determination to survive.

What they had gone through was different from the daily drudge of her challenges. A band of ruffians had stolen most of their food and destroyed what they could not cart away. Kemink had broken through the ice while working the trap-line, which brought in their only income, and came home so near death. Caroline was on her own to save her friend's life and provide for their children. She might sometimes have despaired but she never gave up or quit.

Later there had been the terrible Peshtigo fire which had taken thousands of lives and destroyed hundreds of acres of forest, and her mother had not simply wrung her hands but had converted her home and barn into a make-shift hospital to care for the injured and dying. She did remember that. She had been old enough to be pressed into service.

Felly's self-pity had also been connected to her refusal to give up the feeling of abuse she felt because her love for Dan-Pete had never been fulfilled. The saving grace of her illness had been the moment she sent the man she had loved so much away because his presence might have caused Hans pain. That act told her who she really loved—Hans, the father of her children, the man who adored her despite all her vanities and failures. She would always love Dan-Pete but no longer in a way that threatened Hans.

This realization of her love for Hans surged through her and opened her heart in new ways as she walked through the snow. She would return home with color starting to blossom in her usually waxen cheeks and her eyes moist and radiant with gratitude for what she had.

Hans felt the difference in her. He had always loved her with a desperate love, but part of her had seemed forever unreachable to him. He had fought and fought to break through the barriers of her heart and always seemed to blunder, to come off seeming loutish and undeserving of her love. His ever-deepening despair had caused him rage, further damaging their relationship, fueling his resentment against Jason, who he could see had instant access to his mother's heart and soul.

Now it was as if she were opening whole chambers of herself to him which had been off limits. As always, his own reciprocity seemed inadequate and clumsy in its expression, but he was nearly in tears at her new tenderness, and that she had been spared to him. The surfeit of his emotions was hard to handle. She was still so delicate, so frail, he felt as if she might crumble beneath the terrible assault of his affections.

Something else had changed in Felly. She laughed more. And she made him and the children laugh more, too.

Dr. Bentley had ordered Felly to eat liver. She had lost so much blood she was now anemic and liver would help restore her health he insisted. Felly hated liver. But she was determined to get it down because she wanted to get well. She deliberately made such terrible, funny faces eating the liver, it made the whole family laugh, and of course, she laughed, too.

Hans noticed Felly's new willingness to laugh extended to many things. Household disasters and tense situations which once would have left her white-lipped and withdrawn were now treated to ridicule and good-natured laughter. Laughter did much to ameliorate whatever had gone wrong. His whole household became more relaxed and peaceful.

When Hans awoke in the morning and found her lying beside him, lily pale, her dark hair spread across the pillow, his heart ached with love for her. His heart was also filled with fear. Fear she would yet escape from him, fear that death still waited in the wings ready to pull her away. He wanted to gather her up in his arms and crush her against him. Instead, he would brush a kiss gentle as a whisper against her hair and rise as soundlessly as possible so as not to wake her.

For several weeks the dark, cold winter weeks during which colds, flu, and pneumonia were again rampant in Camp, Maggie did not come near the Jacobson household. Her extra duties at the hospital were enough to cope with. But with the advent of the almost spring-like weather in February, Maggie appeared at the Jacobson door again.

She came bearing curtain stretchers, pails and cleansers, announcing she had come to help Felly and the girls get a start on spring cleaning. She showed the girls how to set up the frames on which to stretch the lace curtains after laundering, and how to mix a dough-like cleanser to take marks off the wallpaper. She herself whipped the carpets and stood on a footstool to attack ceiling cobwebs.

Again, her efforts brought scant thanks. Saran and Seena would have preferred to bumble through the cleaning themselves than to have her commanding them about like a drill sergeant. And Felly felt upset someone else had to do the things she felt she should be doing.

Hans found himself coming home to the smell of roasting duck or bubbling stew, to fresh washed curtains and sparkling windows, to the smell of lemon furniture polish and flowers on the table. He was not dumb. He began to get the portent and he was not at all comfortable with it.

He did not find Maggie unattractive; few men would have, and he still considered her "such a good little person." Felly was not snapping back as fast as all of them had hoped for and he resented Maggie's attempts at a forced intrusion into his family, knowing it made Felly feel badly she could not do more. Besides he knew his children did not like Maggie, and her coming by like this made him feel indebted. He suspected she was sweet on him, which also made him feel uncomfortable.

What she needed, Hans decided, was a swain nearer her own age. One evening when he came home to find her dishing up chicken and dumplings, he said, "Maggie, you're too good to us. A lovely young woman like you should be out having fun, out finding a young man to have a family of your own. There's a dance tonight at Entertainment Hall. I insist you put on your prettiest bib and tucker and go."

Maggie flushed and shook her curls. "I hate going alone and Aunt Mabel and Uncle Hal don't like to go."

"Jason will take you," Hans volunteered. "He's getting to be quite a presentable young man."

Jason choked on his dumpling. He was not above enjoying Maggie's good cooking despite his animosity.

Maggie grew still redder "I adore Jason, but you know, well the truth is he can't abide me. I wouldn't put him through it. But ..." She looked up with sudden radiant hope, "You wouldn't take me, would you Mr. Jacobson?" Then growing woeful, she answered her own question. "No, of course not. I'm sorry. There'd be gossip and all that."

Hans considered the risks. There would be gossip, but on the other hand Maggie was a born little flirt and he was sure once he got her to the dance, men would flock around her and he'd be off the hook.

"I'll tell you what, Maggie, "he said, "I'll check with Felly and if she thinks it's okay I'll take you, with the understanding once there you're on your own."

"Ohhh, yes," Maggie breathed. "I'll go get ready."

"Wait until I've talked to Felly," he said. Felly had eaten earlier and was upstairs getting ready for bed.

Saran and Seena glowered. Jason crumpled his napkin and left the table without seeking permission.

Felly, brushing her long hair in front of the mirror, listened as Hans explained his plan, and nodded. "You're right, darling. She's done so much for us, and she needs to be around some people her own age. I think taking her to the dance is a good idea."

She too was hoping Maggie would find some other avenue of affection other than the Jacobson family. In the past, she had not liked the girl, but in her new softened consciousness she felt love even for Maggie. The young woman had stuck by them during the hard, bedridden time of Felly's illness. While she preferred not to have the forceful girl in her household, Felly wished Maggie well.

* * * *

Things were already swinging at Entertainment Hall when Hans arrived with Maggie. She looked like a princess in a cream lace dress with pearl combs in her hair and tendrils of curls escaping at the nape of her neck.

"Won't you please dance just the first dance with me, Mr. Jacobson?" she begged, blinking her long eyelashes at him. "To get me started? I feel so shy."

The polka music was enticing and Hans loved to dance. "Well, why not?" he thought to himself. He was not doing this behind Felly's back. He knew he would be in for some good-natured ribbing from some of his contemporaries. He guessed he could bear it, comforting himself that after the first dance with Maggie he would retreat to the corner of beer mugs and cigar smoke and let the young men take over. His friends would see his intentions toward Maggie were not romantic.

He did not reckon with Maggie's full potency or his own long restrained needs. When he put his arms around her for the first dance and felt her warmth and softness he went weak. He pushed her back from him. She looked up at him, her eyes round and questioning. His cheeks burning, he drew her to him again, his heart thudding, his legs stiff and awkward; he who had always been the best dancer at any doings moving stick-like, stumbling over his own feet.

"You'd better get another partner, Maggie, I'm all out of practice," he said.

"You just need a beer to get you relaxed," Maggie said. She slipped from his arms and came back with a foaming mug.

This was different. Felly had gotten so she wouldn't even go to the dances because it made her so angry when Hans drank too much beer. Hans took the glass and quaffed it in two gulps. He took Maggie in his arms again. He did feel more relaxed. He gave himself up to the exciting sensations of having Maggie in his arms. Might as well enjoy it, he told himself.

The beer was the first of many during the evening and the dance was not the last with Maggie. The young men did flock around her just as Hans had known they would, but it was quite clear to everyone in the Hall she had eyes only for Hans and after the fifth beer Hans no longer cared.

He had always loved to dance. It had been a long time since he had come to a dance to enjoy himself. He found himself having the best time he'd had in years. He gave himself up to the pulsating, pounding music, to the beer, to the sensuous pleasure of Maggie's soft breasts against him, to the heady feeling of knowing other men envied him.

He got so drunk he could not remember taking Maggie home, in truth, she had taken him home. He awoke the next morning with a killing headache and a sense of shame. He was angry at his own shame. Why should he have to feel guilty for an evening of fun? He hadn't done anything wrong, he assured himself. He loved Felly, only Felly. He found himself sitting on the edge of the bed with a lump in his throat.

It had been months since he had been able to hold his wife in his arms and make love to her. He had never loved Felly more than he loved her now, but she was physically off limits for the time being, and perhaps always, but his desire for her never waned. Sometimes his physical need and yearning for her burned his flesh like nettles. Yet he was terrified even to touch her, remembering how their passions had overcome them in the past and knowing any new pregnancy could take her from him forever.

No matter how he reasoned with himself, the sense of shame, like the bad taste in his mouth and the headache which kept lumbering back and forth across his brain, persisted. Some subterranean part of his brain admitted he had hungered for Maggie the night before. It made him hate her.

Oh, God, would he ever be able to hold Felly in his arms and make love to her again? Did part of him have to die?

CHAPTER 33
Temptation

***

"And lead us not into temptation,
but deliver us from evil;"
(Matthew 6:13)

The gossip which sped around Camp after Hans appeared at the dance with Maggie was not malicious. Most people wished Hans and Felly well, but there is something in human beings that relishes a scandal. All the same, Saran and Seena wept over the innuendoes and the laughter, and Jason, who had been getting on much better with his father since the revelations in the kitchen the morning his mother began to get well, grew sullen and alien again.

The Commandant had always liked Hans and, seeing the struggles of the family, he had offered to have the family's laundry done along with the veterans and to open the dining hall to them for their meals. Hans had appreciated the kindness but had declined, not wanting to "institutionalize" his family, hoping to keep things as normal as possible.

Now he reconsidered and accepted the Commandant's offer. If they were taking their meals in the dining hall, Maggie could not be coming over all the time to fix meals, making him feel indebted and embarrassed.

No more would Saran and Seena have to pry frozen sheets from the line in the winter months and then finish drying them on racks in front of the parlor stove. No more would they have to worry about getting the starch too thick and scorching Hans' white shirts. No more would they have to try to get a roast or chicken simmering before they hurried off to school. Baskets of clothes came back from the central laundry, white, starched, folded and mended. In the evening, the family walked to the main dining hall and ate at a table by themselves but surrounded by the babble of a hundred other diners.

Felly had resisted the new arrangement at first, but then accepted it as preferable to having Maggie hovering about. She renewed her own efforts to regain her strength.

Hans was at pains to let Maggie know of the new arrangements. Soft, fragrant, and exciting she might be in his arms. But it was Felly he loved, now and always. His gratitude for her recovery was almost religious in nature. Nothing must disturb or hurt his beloved wife. Nothing.

He ran into Maggie at the post office a couple of mornings after the dance. She smiled up at him and shifted the paper bag she had in her arms.

"Good morning, Hans. I just came from Pete's. He had some marvelous lamb chops, this thick. I know they're your favorite so I bought a few. I'll come over tonight and show the girls how to do lamb chops just the way you like them."

Other people in the post office were watching from the corner of their eyes, their eyebrows rising.

"Maggie – I'm glad I ran into you. We're taking our meals in the dining hall and sending our laundry out, so you won't have to worry about us anymore. And – to tell you the truth, I'd appreciate it if you didn't lend a hand with the rest of the housework. I want the girls to learn to be self-sufficient. They're becoming all too willing to take advantage of your generosity," Hans said. He was sorry to be so blunt, but he knew Maggie would understand nothing else.

A lesser woman might have been crushed by this obvious rejection. Maggie lifted her chin and shifted the grocery bag again, there were sparks in her green eyes.

"Well, I'm glad to hear you've found a way to get the laundry and meals done, but quite frankly, Mr. Jacobson," she not only lapsed back to the more formal name but frosted it a bit, "those children of yours need more than just food and clothes. They need some discipline and direction. They are spoiled, inconsiderate, and ill-mannered."

Hans' cheeks burned, more because the little scene between him and Maggie had become "theatre in the real" – people were lingering over their mail so as not to miss the next rally, and because he knew Maggie's charges were not without foundation. He had once been a strong disciplinarian, but since Felly's illness, his heart had ached so for his children he had not been able to bring himself to scold them or punish them to any degree.

"You are quite right, Maggie," he said, his neck stiff, his voice cold. "I will try to do better with them in the future."

Maggie's cheeks also were high colored now and her eyes over bright. "I don't mean to offend you, Hans. I hope I haven't hurt your feelings," she said in a softer voice. "They are wonderful children, even if they are spoiled. There are so many ways you can be proud of them. And of course, I adore them or I wouldn't have done everything I could possibly do to help you with them."

At the reminder of his debt to her, the muscles stood out in Hans' cheeks. "Maggie, you have been wonderful to us. We will never forget the things you have done. Believe me. If there is anything we can ever do for you, let me know."

It was an exit speech. He tipped his hat and tried to leave. It was also a tactical error.

She blocked his departure and sweetened her voice. "Why, Hans, how kind of you. In fact, there is one tiny little thing you could do for me if you would?"

"Of course, Maggie." What else could he say?

"I know you go to Waupaca once a week. Could you take me along? I hate riding the streetcar."

Maggie alone with him every Monday, beside him in the car. Hans swallowed. "I'd love to take you Maggie, but I'm on official business on Monday. I don't feel it would be right to –"

The Commandant happened to be in the post office and had sorted through his mail five times so as not to miss any of the repartee turned with a beaming smile.

"Ah – I couldn't help overhearing, Hans – no problem, no problem at all. You can let Miss Grasslee ride along with my blessing. I can't see it would interfere with your business at all."

Maggie had won. She turned her dazzling smile on the Commandant, thanked him, and swished out, her chin high.

The Commandant went home whistling, feeling well pleased with himself. After seeing Hans and Maggie together at the dance he was convinced in his own mind Hans was sweet on her. He surmised his obvious attempts to discourage the young lady in the post office had been due to a sense of duty to his family and probably a notion he was too old for her. The Commandant was aware Felly was an invalid and Hans was still a vigorous man. He had faced such conditions himself and felt pity for his friend. What was a little dalliance now and then? Was one supposed to turn into a monk? If a young woman was willing...well?

****

Maggie proved to be a pleasant companion on those Monday excursions. She always looked beautiful and she was full of bright, witty chatter all the way to Waupaca, often making Hans laugh with her sharp observations. She always enthused and was excited over the

216

car, which pleased Hans, who was one of the few car owners in Camp and proud of it.

They usually got home around dusk. On the trip back, they were both tired after a long day and she was as pensive and quiet as she had been lively in the morning. Maggie always had several packages which she sat next to the door instead of between them, so it necessitated her sitting close to Hans. He was acutely aware of her physical nearness and it irritated him when she would clutch his knee or grasp his arm when they went over a bump or turned a sharp corner. If a man clutched a woman's knee, she would slap him, he thought, but women can get away with anything.

The first of March looked like it was going to come in like a lion. Though they had no snow, the temperature was dropping below zero at night and the sky was heavy with menace. Most people had already put their cars on blocks for the winter. Hans wanted to make one more trip with his but he discouraged Maggie from coming.

"It looks as if there is a storm coming and it's going to be bitter cold, you'll freeze before we get home," he said.

"Oh, Hans!" she said, with a wail of disappointment, "I need to get so many things to make Easter baskets for Aunt Mabel's children, and you said yourself we wouldn't be going again until spring. I'll dress warm and bring a car blanket."

He gave in. He had become used to her companionship on the weekly trips.

All day the sky glowered, emitting a few stinging flakes, but it was not until they were headed for home that the snow started to come down in earnest. By the time they got to the third crossroads they were in a blizzard. Hans had to keep stopping to scrape snow from the windshield.

Maggie was terrified. "Oh, Hans, we can't even see the side of the road – oh, please, let's turn around and go back to Waupaca. This is terrible!"

"I would turn around if I could, Maggie," Hans said, "but we're more than half way there and I'd get stuck trying to turn around. Keep your eye out for a farmhouse. We'll stop at the first one. We can't be far from Rob Johnson's place."

The storm swirled around them like white demons chasing each other in the darkness, obscuring any sight of a cheery farm light. Maggie sat crunched against Hans, half sobbing, her teeth chattering as much from fear as from the bitter cold. They reached a steep hill, and in spite of Hans' best efforts, the car could not make it up the slippery incline. Again and again, he tried. Then the engine sputtered and died. The car wouldn't start again.

Maggie was in a panic. "Oh, Hans – we're going to die – we're going to die!"

"No, Maggie, we're not going to die," Hans said, prying himself loose from her hysterical embrace. "I know where we are now. We're at Lyman's Hill and there's a schoolhouse at the crest."

He pulled his collar up and his wool cap down lower over his forehead.

"Hans –" Maggie sobbed, "don't go out in this. Don't leave me. You can't see where you're going – you'll get lost in the storm and die. It happens all the time. Oh Hans, if we're going to die please stay with me and let us die together."

Hans again unwound the arms strangling his neck. "I'm not going to get lost, Maggie. I've got a rope in the back. I'll tie it to my belt and to the bumper of the car so I can find my way back. Now you just try to be calm and courageous and sit here and wait for me."

"Oh, Hans, please don't leave me." Her wail followed him off into the storm.

Though the incline was sharp, the distance up the hill was not great and when Hans had struggled to the top, he was rewarded by a brief break in the storm that allowed him to see the Lyman School was within a few feet as he had hoped. The front door was padlocked and his cold-stiffened fingers could do little. He felt his way around to the back of the building and forced the woodshed door.

The schoolteacher had been in the building until five o'clock so there were still warm ashes in the stove. It only took minutes to have a good blazing fire going. Hans took a few minutes to warm himself and still his own chattering teeth and then he went back after Maggie.

Maggie had rallied her courage. She sat wrapped in the car blanket, still shuddering and sobbing, but she had not given way to total panic. "Oh, thank God!" she cried when she saw Hans's dark figure looming through the storm.

Hans secured the car robe around her, forming part of it into a hood around her head and pulling it low over her forehead. "Come on, Maggie – it's not far," he encouraged.

Supporting Maggie with one arm and cradling a sack of groceries with the other, Hans negotiated the hill again.

Fortunately, Hans had found some kerosene lamps earlier in the day before they left for Waupaca. When they stumbled in the door Han's quickly found and lit the kerosene oil lamps. Soon the oil lamps helped warm the room and permeated the room with the most wonderful fragrance Maggie had ever smelled; on this night, it was the smell of safety, the smell of life. They were not going to die after all.

Hans stoked the stove and they huddled around it, warming their stiff red hands while water drew to a boil for coffee. Hans cut slabs of cheese, put them on slices of bread and set them on the top of the stove to toast and melt. Soon they were dining on food which seemed as marvelous as any they had ever eaten.

They talked about the danger they had been through, of their good fortune in being near the school, of their own school days. The school clock ticked with loud monotony. The room grew warm.

"You might as well put the car robe on the floor and lie down and get some sleep," Hans advised Maggie. "It's going to be a long night."

He found a discarded sweater in the cloak room and rolled it into a pillow behind her head. She lay with half-closed eyes looking at Hans outlined by the kerosene lamp light.

"Hans – are you going to sit up all night?"

"I imagine," he said. He had found a book to read. "Catch up on my ancient history."

Maggie slid out of the car robe. She came and stood in front of him.

"Oh Hans, you were so brave tonight, so calm, such a hero. All the things a woman wants in a man." She put her arms around his shoulders. "There's no reason for you to have to sit up all night. Come lie down with me."

Her warm strawberry lips found his mouth, not the corner this time but full on his lips, and began moving them back and forth as she laid her body against him.

He made a sound like a maddened bull and shoved her away. "Dammit, Maggie, enough of this! You've been trying to tempt me for weeks. I love Felly. I loved her from the moment I saw her. I will always love her and I'm not going to betray her. As for you, I'm done with you! Once I get you home, I never want to see you again. Do you understand?"

She staggered against the momentum of his shove, trying to stay on her feet, then sank, wilted, back to the impromptu bed he had fashioned for her, giving into uncontrolled sobs.

Hans fell asleep to the ragged sounds of her sobs and the wind still raging overhead.

In the morning when he awoke, stiff-necked and sore from sleeping in the chair. Maggie was already up. She had regained her dignity. She spoke to him in tones as cold as the sheets of ice that coated the schoolhouse windows.

"I want to come back and work for you, Mr. Jacobson," she announced, "because your wife needs me. I'm very good at what I do and you know good help is hard to find. And if you don't agree to keep me on, I will give Miz. Jacobson a very different version of what happened last night and she will believe me."

Hans had never hated anyone as much as he hated Maggie Grasslee at that moment. He refused even to speak to her. Had things been different he would have refueled the schoolhouse stove and made some coffee and toast for them. As it was, he gathered up the grocery sack and car robe and left without inviting her to follow.

The morning outside was calm after the storm. A few crows talked to the wind and Hans could hear Maggie's feet crunching through the snow behind him. Hans did not open the car door for Maggie when they got to the car, but he allowed her to slide in while he cranked to get it started. He finally got a spark, and after he had driven for a half hour, he finally spoke to her.

"Very well, Miss Grasslee, you may return to my employment for the sake of my wife's need of you. But this decision rests upon impeccable behavior from you, and I will no longer drive you to Waupaca, understood?"

"Understood," she said in her new cold voice, but inside she was seething with emotion. She was still sure that Felly was too frail to survive, and Hans' rage was caused by the fact that he had desired her the night before. She told herself that in the end, she would win. She would be Mrs. Hans Jacobson yet.

CHAPTER 34
Mrs. Grasslee

***

"Treat others the same way you want them to treat you."
(Luke 6:31 NASB®)

Hans had given in to Maggie's threats for two reasons. Felly was starting to do too much around the house. He did not want a setback to her efforts to get well. His wife did need Maggie. Secondly, although he considered Maggie's threat to tell malicious lies to Felly a hollow one, he was sure Felly would take his word over Maggie's lies, he still did not want his wife subjected to such a disgusting scene, sure to cause her upset and pain.

At first, Felly resisted the idea of having Maggie back in the house, but when Hans said it meant they could bring Meena home, she agreed.

Not the least of Maggie's pleasure in forcing Hans to reemploy her was feeling she had some power over Hans now, and she would use it to deal with those snippety Jacobson children. I did everything I could to be kind to them, Maggie thought, and they did everything they could to be mean to me. Now it was her turn to be in the driver's seat. Hans dare not refuse to back her up.

She blamed the children's behavior on Felly. Felly had been far too indulgent a mother and too absorbed in herself to keep the tight rein children need. Well, things were going to be different now! Maggie was determined Hans Jacobson's children were going to be models of decorum and industriousness.

Poor Maggie, she entered a hostile camp and the war was immediate. It was a guerilla war. The attacks on both sides were almost always covert, since neither Maggie nor the children wanted to do anything blatant enough to make them the villain in Hans' eyes or to upset Felly.

For all their care in being subversive, Hans was aware war was waging. The tensions and undercurrents in the house were palpable. Hans felt wearied by his children's harassment of Maggie. He no longer thought of Maggie as "a good little person." He was disappointed in her and sick of her, so he was not on her side either. Was there never any peace in life? As long as the war remained covert and Felly seemed unaware, he said prayers of gratitude each night.

Nor was there any doubt the household ran more smoothly. They no longer had to go to the commons every night to eat. Delicious meals appeared without seeming effort, there were always clean clothes, and orderliness. And the most enormous benefit was being able to bring Meena home. His family was intact again, which meant so much to him he even felt kinder toward Maggie, and tried to remember how good she had been to him through the terrible darkness when he thought Felly was dying.

The rest of the family was delighted to have Meena home again too, their little sunbeam. Their natural joy was even more enhanced by the fact Meena was a trial to Maggie. Now three, a spirited, adventurous child, she was in to everything. She led Maggie a merry chase and wore her to a rag. And since Meena was Hans' darling, Maggie did not dare retaliate with too severe a punishment or restriction.

Jason loved to put Meena up to doing things which caused Maggie chaos. Maggie was quite aware Jason was the inspiration behind such events as a bread and jam party for the six kittens, and blanket and sheet tents in the parlor on the afternoon she was expecting the sewing circle. She suspected he was the mastermind for the "cooking projects" in the kitchen which included broken eggs and dried-on flour and water which took Maggie hours to clean up.

Maggie was convinced Jason was the instigator of most of her misery. She surmised Jake didn't much care if she had come to live with them. He liked her cooking and whatever Pa did was all right with him. Seena and Saran were hostile but Maggie was sure she could win them over if it were not for Jason, who poisoned them against her.

Jason did poison his sisters against Maggie. He was the ringleader in trying to cause her grief, but Maggie's own behavior didn't help.

She knew she was a good cook and it piqued her the children relished the meals she made but not once would give her a word of praise and they often contrasted them with Felly's cooking, in favor of their mother's version. Even when she fished for a compliment, they would refrain from giving her the satisfaction of saying, "– yes, the cake was wonderful," or "the soup was delicious."

In retaliation, she made a large batch of wonderful maple-nut fudge and set it on the dining room table on a sliver dish with a lace doily under it, accompanied by a large hand-lettered sign: "FOR THE HOWARD CHILDREN."

The children came home from school and eyed the situation. They knew the candy had been set there to tantalize them.

"She doesn't care two figs about Mrs. Howard's kids," Jason declared. "She's just doing this to be spiteful to us." With a sweep of his hand, he knocked the sign to the floor. "We like candy, too."

All the children dived in and grabbed a handful from the plate. Maggie, coming down the stairs, caught them in the act.

"Stop!" she screamed. "Can't you read? Didn't you see my sign? Put that candy back!"

Nobody put the candy back. Jason and Saran even took more.

"You just wait – I'm going to tell your father!" a red-faced Maggie screamed.

They knew she wouldn't tell Hans. Her ruse had been too transparent. Hans would see through to the spite of her act as well as they had. They knew it and she knew it. She never told Hans. She did determine when spring came and school let out she was going to find some way to get rid of Jason for the summer.

During the winter, Maggie's father died. Maggie's mother, Mrs. Grasslee, was old and heavy-set. Even simple chores were too hard for her. In the spring, Maggie asked Hans to send Jason to stay with her mother for the summer to help fix her chicken house, repair a leaking roof, and take care of the garden for her.

"It would do Jason good to have a change," she argued, "and I know the other children would settle down if Jason went away for a bit."

Hans and Felly talked it over and agreed it might do Jason good to get away. Ever since the old Colonel's death, Jason had been too quiet and withdrawn. He was skin and bones and his eyes had a glazed look.

"Does she have a piano?" Jason asked. "If she doesn't, I'm not going."

"We'll get your piano hauled down," Maggie promised.

The promise was not kept, but on the first day Jason arrived at Mrs. Grasslee's house, he found a fine old brass cornet which had belonged to her husband and he contented himself by practicing on that all summer.

Mrs. Grasslee lived in a shambling house on the edge of town so there were no neighbors to protest to Jason's ever-lasting "tooting," and Mrs. Grasslee was a good old soul who never complained about anything. Her husband had been a charmer who had kept everyone entertained at the local tavern but had never done much about earning a living. Mrs. Grasslee had been the main supporter of their eight children. She raised chickens and sold eggs, took in washing and sewed a fine seam. She had loved her husband and her children, but now the children were scattered and her husband gone, she did not complain. She was tired and it was good to have just herself to think about for a change.

Mary Grasslee's hair, which once must have been as fiery as Maggie's, had faded to a pinkish-grey, her round face and two chins were dusted with a Milky-Way of freckles. She laughed a lot. Some people in the Neenah area thought she was a bit dotty. Mrs. Grasslee was interested in spiritualism and she wasn't above "having a drop."

As much as the Jacobson children disliked Maggie, they adored her mother from the first visit. Mrs. Grasslee arrived with a pail of beer and a bucket of herring. When Hans got home, he found everyone having a party in the kitchen, drinking beer and eating herring and brown bread. Even Meena had a little mug of beer. Hans knew Felly was upset, but Mrs. Grasslee's intentions were so good and the children were having such a happy time, he could not scold. He sat down to the beer and herring.

It turned out Maggie was right; it did do Jason good to get away. The summer he spent with Mrs. Grasslee was a happy one. He fixed her chicken house and mended her roof, helped in the garden, and painted her front porch; and never had he had so much approbation, except from Max.

"Well ya look at those tomatoes – I swear Jason ya've a gift for growin' things. I've not seen the likes. 'Tis a very angel ya are, fixin' the roof like ya did. 'N what a fine job. There's nothin' ya set yere hand to but it comes out well. It's some lad ya are."

She loved to hear him play her "dear departed's" old horn. She would sit with her eyes closed, rocking a little to the beat, tears flowing down her cheeks. "Ahhh Jason, ya've a gift for so many things but 'tis music is yere genius. Ya go with yere music and someday ya'll be somebody, ya'll see."

While encouraging Jason to dream big dreams, Mrs. Grasslee had no patience with Maggie's pretensions. She had none of her own and she was impatient with her daughter's "airs" as she called them.

"Maggie's always tryin' to be sumthin' she ain't," she said, shaking her head with disapproval. "She's that bright 'n pretty, if she'd just be herself she'd be all right."

When school started again in the fall, Jason was sad to leave the shambled down house and the warmth and love which had enfolded him at Mrs. Grasslee's. All summer long, he had practiced for hours on the old horn. When he got home, he picked up Jake's cornet, lifted his head high and began to play for Hans. The notes came out pure and golden, soaring, "trembling up from the gut" as one old black man had once put it to Jason.

Hans listened, his face impassive.

When Jason finally laid down the horn, he said to his father, "Do I play as well as Jake?"

Hans was an honest man. "Better, Jason – far better. I have never heard anyone play the cornet more beautifully than you just did." He was unaware that his younger son was within hearing distance, but Jason was not.

Jason could not understand why the moment did not seem sweeter to him, but he knew he had taken something away from Jake which couldn't be restored, and he was sorry.

CHAPTER 35
Maggie and Jason's Showdown

***

*"Therefore let us not judge one another anymore, but rather
determine this—not to put an obstacle or
a stumbling block in a brother's way."
(Romans 14:13 NASB®)*

Maggie was not happy to have Jason home. While Saran and Seena had not turned into adoring friends during the summer, they had been less intransigent without Jason to egg them on. The minute he was home, she could feel the undercurrents growing stronger again.

"Jason hates me, Hans," she said. They were having coffee early in the morning before Felly got up. "He does everything he can to make me miserable."

Hans sighed and lowered the paper he was using to shield himself from Maggie's desired intimacy. "He doesn't hate you, Maggie. He's just a confused, unhappy boy," Hans said.

But he feared Maggie was right. Maybe Jason did hate her. Maybe he would have hated anyone who tried to take Felly's place. But what could he, Hans, do about it? Sigh after sigh swelled through him.

Hearing Hans' sighs, Maggie felt afraid. If only she could press close to him and kiss him and touch him. She could not forget the night in the schoolhouse. He did love her, no matter what he said, he did! She was sure of it, and she lay awake at night scheming ways to make him confess as much to Felly.

The covert war between Jason and Maggie came to a showdown in November. Two members of a prestigious bank were coming to discuss a loan with Hans and the Commandant which would allow them to do some needed construction and repair at the Camp. They were bringing their spouses and since the Commandant's wife had been an invalid for many years, he wanted Hans to host a dinner to impress their prospective benefactors. He knew Felly was an expert at this sort of thing and she had Maggie to help. Maggie, however, insisted she wanted to do it all on her own. She wanted to be the one to plan. She wanted to select the menu. She wanted to choose the table settings and decorations.

Maggie brought her desire to Felly, being humble and pleading about it. "It's my heart's desire to turn out a real elegant dinner party, Miz Jacobson. I'd so love to do all the plannin' and decoratin' and of course the cookin'."

When Felly did not respond at once, she added, "Of course, I'd come to you to see if my choices suited you."

Felly had always hated giving dinner parties, and so she welcomed Maggie's ambition to take over the task and gave the girl her blessing in the matter.

Maggie had it in her mind Felly turned out elegant, marvelous dinners without effort. She was determined to outdo Hans' wife.

In truth, entertaining had not been effortless for Felly. With a house full of demanding young children and often no help, it had often been a strain. But Maggie was right, the elegance had come easy for Felly. Except for the early years of her life she could not remember, she had been raised with fine china, linen, silver, and candles – all the niceties of polite society. She knew what to do and how to do it.

Maggie had been raised in an "Irish shanty" where the family had eaten in the kitchen off faded oilcloth from chipped crockery and drank their milk from jelly glasses. For her, elegant entertaining was a challenge she was determined to master.

One of the things which had gotten the Jacobson children's ire up was they were banished from the dining room table. She fed them supper early in the kitchen so the adults could dine by candlelight later in the dining room.

Hans did not like this arrangement, but his work often brought him home so late it was hard for the children to wait. And it was nice to have some time with Felly without all the boisterous children interrupting their conversations. What was not so nice was most of the time cheeky Maggie ate with them, so the topics could not be intimate. And worse, since Dr. Bentley insisted Felly needed to go to bed no later than nine, when Hans was real late, Maggie had Hans to herself.

Before Felly's illness, the evening meal had been the time of family sharing, the time when all the family members returned from their individual adventures of the day to relate and discuss them with the rest. Hans believed the family table was where parents could help children deal with their problems and impress values upon them. The reason Jason's habitual lateness or absence had so enraged him was because he felt so strongly about the importance of the family table. He appreciated the succulent meals Maggie prepared, the flowers and candles, her efforts to please him, but he would have been more than glad to trade them for having his children back around the table. But he did not protest, Felly still needed Maggie's help and he did not want to wrangle with her.

In the carefully prepared meals she had served to Hans, Maggie had been practicing the art of entertaining, and now she felt confident enough to host this special important dinner party. She pored over the women's magazines for menus, hors d'oeuvres, place cards and centerpieces. She dutifully brought her decisions to Felly, but overrode any suggestions Felly gave her. She wore herself to a frazzle the week before, cleaning and polishing every crevice of the house. She screamed at the children if they left the slightest evidence about the house which revealed people lived there. She had chosen a menu way beyond what was reasonable to prepare, the piece de resistance of which was roast squab.

Even Seena and Saran acknowledged the table was magnificent. Maggie had made small gold and lace fans as place cards, there were gold-colored candles in silver candlesticks and an extravaganza of a centerpiece made from a series of crystal bowls piled with golden oranges, yellow lemons and hot-house flowers. The napkins were folded like winged doves and a single golden blossom floated in each finger bowl.

Her greatest triumph however was in the kitchen. While Jake played cornet for the guests, Maggie took the perfectly browned squabs (pigeons) from the oven and placed them in a circle around a mound of brown rice. Between each squab, she placed a half-peeled orange and a candied kumquat which she had to send to New York for along with a sprig of parsley. Then she stood back with clasped hands to admire her masterpiece. It was as beautiful as any picture in the women's magazines.

At that moment, Jason came home. He reached over her shoulder and plucked one of the squabs from the silver tray. Maggie gave a shriek, which was fortunately not heard in the dining room because it coincided with a high A Jake had just hit on the cornet.

"Give that back!" she hissed. But Jason's teeth were already tearing into her perfect little squab. She took after him. Laughing, he ran outside and vaulted to the woodshed roof where he continued to eat the squab while she hurled invectives at him.

"You rotten, rotten, ROTTEN boy!" Maggie screamed, until she realized her face was becoming fiery red, her careful hairdo was coming down, and the guests might hear her outside screaming like a fishwife. She would have killed Jason if she could have gotten her hands on him.

She went back in and tried to rearrange the squab so the missing one did not show. The rearrangement looked messy and there was the irrefutable fact: there were eight people to feed, the two visitors and their wives, Hans and Felly, and the Commandant and herself. Eight people, seven squabs. Well, Maggie could do without. Maggie pinned up her loose curls but she could not make the fire go out of her face. Red and flustered, she bore the main dish in but the evening was ruined for her.

Her poise was not equal to what had happened. She was so distraught, apologetic and nervous, the guests were all glad to make excuses and leave as soon as possible.

Maggie sat red-eyed looking at the ruins of her dinner party. She tossed her dinner napkin at Hans like a gauntlet and motioned him into the kitchen. "Hans, what Jason did was deliberate – vicious. I've had all I can bear. Are you going to let him get away with this? I demand you call him down here and take some action. Or do I have to walk out? Are you going to stand up for me or not?" She was half screaming, half crying.

"Jake, go get your brother," Hans said to the boy who had followed them. He felt weary and old. He knew Jason's action was indefensible but in truth he was as disappointed in Maggie's behavior as in Jason's. The stupid dinner party had been important because the financial loan had somewhat depended upon it, but the loan was going to come through anyway, so who cared about a missing squab? Yet he knew he had to call Jason into account.

Mollified he was going to call Jason to task, Maggie subsided to sobbing and sniffling. Felly had come into the kitchen too, to try to console her upset servant who had worked so hard on the event only to have it end in disaster.

"The table was lovely and the dessert was delicious, Maggie. Please don't take on like this."

Maggie would have no part of Felly's comforting. "Your son ruined everything. Everything! And you know it!" she spat out.

Jason appeared, pale and sullen. He had been shooting up like a twig without branches, his new height made him look more fragile. He needed a haircut. In his childhood, Hans had looked at him and saw Adam Quimby. Now more and more when he looked at him he saw Felly staring at him out of Jason's face. Never more so than in the flickering lights of the golden candles still burning on the table. His heart turned over.

"Jason," his voice faltered. "What do you have to say for yourself?"

Jason looked down and didn't answer.

"You realize you ruined Maggie's effort to make our dinner tonight outstanding?"

"Yes, sir."

"Are you sorry?"

There was a long silence during which Maggie's sobs grew louder. Finally, reluctantly, "Yes, sir."

"Would you like to devise your own punishment, Jason?"

"No, sir."

"Do you realize you should be punished?"

"Yes, sir."

"First, I want you to apologize to Maggie. Then for the next six weeks I want you to help her in the kitchen to make up for what you did to her tonight."

Jason never had to apologize. Maggie leaped to her feet, livid.

"Oh, this is it! I have had more than I can bear. Do you hear yourself, Hans? 'What do you have to say for yourself? Would you like to devise your own punishment?' And then – then to punish him by having him help me in the kitchen! You know it would be as much of a punishment for me as for him."

She stormed to the closet and began dragging out her coat and other wraps. "I helped you in good faith – came here wanting to give your children the discipline and care they had been lacking for so long – but you have done nothing to support me, Hans! I cannot go on like this. You take over, Felly! Wake up and do something about all of your spoiled and selfish children!" she cried.

Hans had to restrain himself from slapping her across her mouth. Felly had gone ash white.

Maggie struggled into her coat. "Either I'm deserving of your respect and support – or I'm not. It's up to you, Hans. I'll be at Aunt Mabel's if you want me."

She slammed the door behind her.

After a moment of heavy silence, Hans said, not without bitterness, "Do you see what you've done, Jason?"

Jason made a strangled sound and bounded away up the stairs. For the second time in his life he felt as if his father had driven a spike through his heart, and it made it no easier as he knew he deserved his father's words.

Seena ran up the stairs after him. She found him in his room throwing his clothes into a valise. "What are you doing, Jason?"

"You've got eyes, Seena. I'm leaving home. There's nothing else I can do. There's no way I could spend six weeks in the kitchen working with her."

"But she left, Jason."

"She'll be back. You know she will, Seena."

"Yes."

He pulled out a drawer and began throwing sheet music into his valise.

"Jason – it was mean to eat her squab."

He sagged against the bed. "I know. That's why I must go. I guess I'm a bad person. You heard what Pa said. I've always made Pa unhappy."

"I guess – I guess maybe you do have to go, Jason, but please, don't go tonight. It's started to snow outside something fierce. I think it's going to turn into a regular blizzard."

"I have to go. I have to go tonight."

She came and put her arms around him. "I love you, Jason – I wish you wouldn't go."

Jason had always loved his sisters dearly. He even loved Jake though he got no affection back from his brother. Seena had never expressed her love so openly. He was touched and had to blink back tears.

"I'll be all right, Seena. I'll write to you. Don't tell mother until I'm gone. Please Seena, don't tell her until tomorrow, or Pa'll come after me."

She was crying, using her sleeve for a handkerchief to wipe her eyes. "Where will you go, Jase?"

He slipped away from her without answering and went down the hall to look at Meena. She was asleep, the light from the open door catching in her red-gold hair, glowing on the tender down of her round little cheeks.

"Goodbye, little darling," he whispered, "I will come back for you some day."

Jake was in his room cleaning his cornet. Through the open door, the brothers looked at each other as Jason passed but they did not say goodbye.

Saran was clearing the table. Jason wanted to say goodbye to her, but he could not risk encountering his father.

He slipped out the front door into a whirligig of snowflakes. He lifted his face to their coldness with eagerness. His face was so burning hot he felt as if he were on fire. The biting sting of the snow felt heavenly.

He realized after a few steps he had forgotten his boots but he wasn't going back into the house for them. He walked off into the cold and darkness, fighting a desire to look back at the golden lights of the house.

****

Sitting at Mabel Howard's round kitchen table, Maggie played game after game of Solitaire, listening to the heavy tick of the clock. At midnight, she threw the cards down and began to sob afresh.

"He's not going to come, Aunt Mabel – he's not going to come!" She had hoped that Hans might rush after her, beg her to come back. Though she was aware the words she had flung at Felly had probably burned her bridges. This time her sharp tongue had gone too far.

Mabel stopped stirring the cocoa she was making at the stove and came and held her sobbing niece. "He'll come tomorrow – you'll see," she comforted. She didn't know the words Maggie had thrown at Felly.

Hans did not come. He had had enough. If Maggie was going to tell Felly lies about the night at the schoolhouse, Felly and he would deal with it. He could not have Maggie in his house anymore.

CHAPTER 36
Bawdy House

***

"Oh my God, I am ashamed and embarrassed to lift up my face to You, my God: for our iniquities have risen above our heads and our guilt has grown even to the heavens."
(Ezra 9:6 NASB®)

As Seena had predicted, the snow turned into a blizzard. The soft, thick flakes which had felt so refreshing to Jason when he had first stepped from the house had been picked up by a shrieking wind and driven to madness. The boy, groping and stumbling through the raging holocaust of whiteness, realized he was lost.

When Jason had left the house, he was bitter, hurt, full of pain, but within his anger and pain had also been rebellion and self-confidence. He would show his father! He had no doubt he would conquer the world on his terms and return to a father made contrite and conciliatory by his success. Furthermore, he would be able to shower largess on his grateful and adoring sisters and his beloved mother.

Never had it occurred to this confident young man the world might be too much for him at the tender age of fifteen. Some of this confidence had been based on the inner assurance Maggie's kind old mother would take him in and provide him with a secure base from which he could launch to conquer his world. The irony of going to Maggie's mother for refuge did not penetrate his egotistical young mind.

Seldom has a neophyte been so swiftly disabused of his powers. The boy's flaming confidence lasted for the streetcar ride to Waupaca and the train ride from Waupaca to a way-station near Neenah. When he had got off at the deserted station into the blowing snow, the conductor shook his head and urged him to get back on the train.

"I've scarce a mile to go," Jason called back. His words were so whipped by the wind the conductor could not even hear them and it was then, as the train rushed away from him, Jason felt the first sag in his bravado. Something akin to terror rose in him as he faced the full force of the screaming whiteness.

Only a mile to go and he knew the way like the back of his hand he had told himself. Too late he saw no landmarks were discernible through the rage of snow. He had to brace himself to keep his footing against the fierceness of the wind and the sinking realization came – no boots, I have no boots.

He tried the doors of the deserted station house but they were locked. The young lion became a little boy close to tears. He cursed the conductor for his callousness in allowing him to get off. Then since there appeared to be no other choice, he rallied his courage and set out in the direction of Mrs. Grasslee's house. I'll make it, I'll make it – he encouraged himself. The bridge wasn't far from the station and the bridge was large and substantial, even in this storm when he got closer he would be able to see the bridge, and once he found the bridge, Mrs. Grasslee's home was a stone's throw from there. Surely, he would see her light.

With such exhortations, he urged himself onward – and onward and onward, for no bridge loomed, no comforting light beckoned. The storm swallowed him, chewed on him with needle teeth, and at length he could no longer deny to himself he was lost. All the stories he had heard of people freezing came flooding to his brain and he had to struggle against rising panic at each step.

He set his jaw hard against the rattle of his teeth and vowed to himself he would not give in to panic, he would keep his head. He would think this out. He tried to think of the stories he had heard of people who had not frozen when they were caught in a blizzard, or people who had been cool enough and clever enough to save themselves in some way. His brain seemed as tired as his gasping, struggling body. All he could remember was some of them had burrowed into the snow, but something inside of him cried out if he stopped and tried to find refuge in the snow, he would die.

He stumbled on until the panic he had fought overwhelmed him. His feet– he could no longer feel his feet! He was walking on stumps of numbness. Oh, my God, his feet! Even if he survived now, he would have no feet. He would be like the veterans he had seen in the hospital. He began to bawl like a young calf, stomping as hard as he could on his unfeeling feet.

He began to fall to his knees. He couldn't see anymore. His eyelashes were half frozen together. Every bawling, sobbing breath he took was like an icy lash to his lungs.

His fingers were going numb too. Never had he been in such pain and terror and never had life seemed so desirable and sweet.

"I want to live – I want to live!" he bawled. "I don't want to die!"

His own words forced him to struggle back up onto the numb stumps which had once been feet and to lurch forward. "Please God – please help me. I want to live. Mother – Mother, help me!" he cried out to Felly.

He had reached the crest of a hill and almost as if in instant answer to his prayer he saw through the crusted ice that lined his lids a glimmer of light. He clawed at his eyelids, ice-crusted mittens trying to free his vision – and yes – oh, thank God, yes, there below him were the lights of a house. He half staggered, half rolled down the incline in his eagerness.

Thank you, God, thank you – thank you, Mother, oh, my dear mother, thank you –

To Jason it seemed when he at last got himself dragged to the door he pounded forever and was going to die after all before anyone came – though to the people in the house it seemed they heard his muffled pounding and answered at once.

The door swung inward to light and warmth, to a young girl with a haze of gold around her head. "Ellie-Bee," she called in a shrill voice, "Ellie-Bee!"

Then a dozen hands seemed to be pulling at his frozen clothes while black and white blotches kept bursting in front of Jason's eyes.

The woman kneeling in front of him had the brightest copper-colored hair he had ever seen. Her eyebrows had been drawn on with a pencil and she would have been as pretty as the picture on a candy wrapper except she had a waddle of flesh under her chin and bags beneath her large blue eyes. She began prodding and pushing at his feet which were ensconced in a bucket of water. She grunted as she rose, rubbing her back, then chuckled and winked at him.

"Nothing's froze, young lad. You're not even going to lose a toe, though I would say you got here just in time. You have got some frostbite there."

He remembered disgracing himself by sobbing like a child in gratitude at his rescue. Someone brought a warm cloth and washed his face and someone else combed ice crystals from his hair, someone put quilts around his shoulders and got his feet dried. He was clutching a hot drink that burned and glowed inside of him with a welcome fire. "Brandy," someone said and Felly's Puritan upbringing of him stirred but did not deter him from finishing the rest of the liquid. Medicine, he decided. His mother would have given it to him with her own hand.

The black and white explosions were receding. Except for the fact that feeling was coming back into his feet like the sting of a thousand bees, he was beginning to feel quite normal and to be able to look around him with some interest.

He was in a large parlor of an old farmhouse. A huge stove, its pot-belly glowing red against the fierce cold of the storm, dominated the room. There were a few pictures hung high on wires: one of a semi-naked Goddess whose pearl-like flesh stood out against the darkish, brownish pattern of wallpaper. There were several horsehair settees and a clutter of rocking chairs, but the thing which riveted Jason's eyes was a piano. Not the sturdy upright ubiquitous among wealthier families in the area, but a beautiful little rosewood spinet.

He pulled himself up on his stinging feet and tried a few steps. This seemed to be a houseful of girls. They all kept looking at him with bold eyes, which made him feel very shy. He stared at the piano.

The copper-haired woman who had told him her name was Ellie-Bee Neffer followed his gaze with a little smile. "You like my piano?"

"Ohhh, yes," he breathed, "I've only seen one other like it. It belonged to my grandmother."

"Do you play?"

His eyes kindled. "Would you mind?"

She laughed. "No, my little frozen trout, if you think you're up to it, go ahead." She poured more liquid in his glass. "But you'd better drink some more of this. We don't want a case of pneumonia on our hands."

He gulped the burning liquid.

She laughed again. "If you gulp it down like that lad you're liable to pass out on us."

The whole roomful of girls laughed. Jason's cheeks felt hot as a fire poker and his head was beginning to buzz now almost as much as his feet.

"If you don't want us to go on calling you our little frozen trout you might tell us your name," Mrs. Neffer said.

"Jason –" he said, surprised his voice sounded so thick. "Jason Jacobson."

"Ja - son - Ja - cob - son" one of the girls said, mocking the slight Nordic lilt Jason had picked up from his father.

Everyone laughed again. Normally, Jason would have felt stung and angry. But the girl who had mocked him was smiling at him with such a warm smile, and he was so grateful to the household for rescuing him from the storm, he accepted their raillery with good grace. He covered his embarrassment by taking refuge at the piano.

He winced as pain shot through him when his full weight came on his feet. "You're sure my feet aren't frozen?" he asked Mrs. Neffer, terrified.

She nodded. "I've seen plenty of frozen feet, Jason Jacobson, and yours will be all right."

He sagged down on the piano bench and closed his eyes for a minute against the buzzing in his head. The room whirled a bit when he opened them and he heard all the girls laughing again.

Mrs. Neffer came and stood on the other side of the piano, leaned her elbows on the top of the spinet and stared into his eyes. "Were you running away, lad?"

"I was going to a friend's," Jason said, which wasn't a lie, but the steady gaze of Mrs. Neffer's large blue eyes elicited the truth. "My father and I had troubles. I'm on my own." He hated the little crack in his voice which came with the words.

A sadness came over Mrs. Neffer's face. "Aren't we all," she said.

One of the girls came and sat on the bench beside him, the one who had mocked him. She was also the one who had let him in the house, the one with the haze of golden hair around her face. He had never sat so close to a girl before. She smelled like powder boxes and bouquets of flowers. Having her sit so close to him was doubly embarrassing because she had on lacey wrapper which came apart when she sat down and he could see the black satin knickers and salmon pink chemise she wore underneath.

Jason could not help noticing these young women were in dishabille. One had on a very short black slip with a flowered kimono which she left loosely open. Another had on a long white nightgown which would have seemed proper enough except you could see right through it; and none of these young women seemed to take the slightest care of their modesty to close buttons or to tie ties.

If Saran and Seena ran around like this, I'd smack them, Jason thought, and then became ashamed of himself. After all, he'd gotten all these girls out of bed for his emergency, and since it seemed to be an entirely feminine household they probably weren't used to having to be modest.

"Well, Ja – son Ja -cob-son, let's hear what you can play," the girl sitting next to him purred.

"What – what's your name?" Jason asked.

She had a sweet, full mouth, and when she smiled, there was a dimple in the corner of her cheek. "They call me Comfort," she said, "and you're so cute I'd love to comfort you." She petted his cheek and all the other girls giggled and laughed again.

Jason concentrated on the piano keys and tried to clear the buzz in his head. He wished they would quit teasing him. Being the butt of someone else's jokes was hard on his pride. His fingers crashed down on the keys and he ripped into the "Maple Leaf Rag."

The girls gave a cheer, and in a minute, they were all around the piano, clapping and stamping to the music.

Mrs. Neffer leaned further over the piano. "My God," she said. "You're good! You're terrific! You're on your own, you say?"

Jason nodded, his hands wild and joyous on the keys.

"Would you like a job?"

His fingers halted in mid-air with surprise.

"We have entertainments most every night. I'll give you five dollars a night to play on Wednesday and Thursday – and room and board if you want it."

Jason's confidence came roaring back. He'd been gone from home for only a few hours and already people were recognizing his talent. He grinned a wide grin. "I'd sure appreciate the start, Mrs. Neffer."

The girls were crying out for their favorites. He played on and on. He felt hot and dizzy and exalted and consumed by the music. Then he started to tremble all over and would have slid from the bench if Comfort hadn't put her arms around him and steadied him.

"Ahhaaa," Mrs. Neffer said. "This night has been a little bit more for you than you realize, my young Mr. Jacobson." She came around and supported him from the other side. "Have you had anything to eat today?" she asked.

"Not much," Jason admitted, thinking back to those fatal bites of squab he had eaten on the roof so many hours ago.

"Audre," Mrs. Neffer commanded. "Take Jason back to the kitchen. Get something warm in his stomach and then put him in the East Room."

The girl addressed as Audre led him down a dark hall to a large high-ceilinged kitchen covered with yellow wainscoting. He noticed the girl was pitifully thin with lank hair and she was not all dressed in pretties like the other girls. She had on a dun colored wrapper and the buttons were buttoned.

She slammed kettles on the stove and stoked up the fire without any special enthusiasm. His buzzing mind tried to make sense of this Audre. She couldn't be a sister to Comfort. They were too different. He had noticed all the girls were too different to be sisters.

"Is this – is this some kind of girls' school?" he asked as Audre shoved a plate of steaming stew and homemade biscuits in front of him.

She frowned at him. "How old are you?"

"Sixteen," he said, padding a few months.

"You sure aren't very smart for sixteen," she said.

After that ungracious comment, he ate in silence and did not try to engage her in further conversation. The food was great. He ate all of the stew, even the turnips, and he had never liked turnips. Then he followed Audre's spare little shanks up the stairs to the East Room.

"Will – will you tell the others, thanks –again?" Jason said.

She nodded and left.

Jason sat down on the bed, so tired it was difficult even to take off his own clothes. His eyes fell upon many strange items on the dresser as he struggled with the buttons of his shirt, and a shock went through him.

Why – why this is a bawdy house! Despite his weariness, he leaped from the bed and began to struggle back into his trousers. What would his mother think? – Him in a bawdy house! What would Grandma Caroline think?

Then his ears heard the wild shriek of the storm still raging around the gables of the old house and when he pulled aside the curtain the snow was like white fur against the window. He let his pants sag back to the floor.

He wasn't going anywhere. It wasn't possible. And besides – wasn't it God and his mother who had found him refuge here?

He slid between the sheets, the deep comfort of the quilt. A dull burn of embarrassment heated his whole body. "You're not very smart for sixteen." In God's truth, he wasn't – but Joe and the other boys at the stable had told him about bawdy houses and they had said there were all kinds of pictures of naked women and mirrors and red velvet carpets – and this, this was just like any old farmhouse.

Jason's tired, buzzing brain refused to bother with it anymore. He turned on his side and slept.

CHAPTER 37
Mrs. Neffer

***

"It is of the LORD'S mercies that we are not consumed, because his compassions fail not. They are new every morning: great is thy faithfulness."
(Lamentations 3:22-23)

Jason awoke to wintry sunlight and a strange room. Both his head and his legs throbbed. He remembered the night before and how stupid he'd been not to know he was in a bawdy house. His face grew hot remembering how the girls had patted his shoulder, ran their fingers through his hair, patted his cheeks, mocked and teased him. They treated me like a damn poodle, he thought. He flung the quilt aside to examine his legs. There were some white-looking patches that frightened him, but when he stood up everything seemed to be working as well as usual.

His ice-encrusted work shoes had been left downstairs to dry out along with his frozen stockings, so he tiptoed on bare feet down the long-carpeted hallway and stairs. He had slept a long time. It was already 11 o'clock but none of the girls were up yet. Mrs. Neffer greeted him.

She was seated at the kitchen table going over some account books. She did not look so pretty this morning in the wan sunlight with her eyebrows washed off and her hair in curl papers. She looked like any pleasant stout farmwife, except a cigarette dangled from her lips. Jason stared. He had never seen a woman with a cigarette in her mouth before.

"Good morning, my little Frozen Trout," she said. "How are you this morning?"

"I've got white patches on my legs," Jason said, worried.

She laid down her pencil and bent over the leg he proffered for her inspection. "You're going to have a little proud-flesh which will

240

slough off, but you're all right. You're not going to lose any digits," she assured him. "Get yourself a cup and saucer, there's coffee on the stove." She bent back over her ledgers.

The coffee must have been on since dawn. It was black and bitter.

"Mrs. Neffer – about playing the piano for you –" Jason faltered.

She looked up, waiting.

"I – last night – I didn't know – I didn't understand – this was – was –"

"A bawdy house?"

Her bluntness caused Jason to rattle his cup in its saucer. His face turned scarlet.

"Oh, please Mrs. Neffer – I don't mean any disrespect...you've been so wonderful to me...I don't...", he floundered trying to find the right words.

She laughed and blew a cloud of blue smoke. "Oh, stop suffering, Jason. I understand. You're a nice boy and even though you're estranged right now from your family, you don't want to hurt them. You can't play the piano in a house of ill repute."

"You're wonderful," Jason said with a rush of love for this kind, tough, but motherly woman.

She took a sip of coffee and a drag on her cigarette. "Are you ready to go home now, Jason – or are you still 'on your own'?"

Jason's mouth tightened. "I'm still on my own."

"Uh-huh. Well I think then you should meet David."

"David?"

"David plays the piano for us two nights a week. He's very good. Not as good as you are, but very good. He's also young and on his own. I think he can help you."

Audre came into the kitchen at this moment. She looked better in the light of morning, less sullen, fresh faced, but she still had on the dun colored wrapper. Jason's curiosity about her was renewed.

"Audre, make Jason some bacon and eggs," Mrs. Neffer said.

"Good morning, Audre," Jason said.

"Hi." She threw a skillet on the stove. Jason had never heard anyone make so much noise cooking as Audre.

"Is Audre your daughter?" Jason asked Mrs. Neffer, still trying to fit her into the scheme of things at this farmhouse.

"My daughter?" Mrs. Neffer chuckled. "No, you might say Audre is an apprentice. She wants to get into the trade when she gets a little more meat on her so she's appealing. In the meantime, she's our cook."

Jason felt his face get red again. He hid behind his coffee cup.

"We'll never get out of here with the car today – maybe not for a week. I have urgent business in Appleton and I think we can make it with the horse and cutter. Then I can take you to meet David. He has a room at the YMCA and I think he'd be glad to share it with you. What do you think, Jason – think we can get through those drifts?

Jason peered out the window. "At least it's not snowing," he said.

Audre's bacon and eggs were as good as the stew of the night before. Jason's shoes were dried and oiled, his socks laundered. These people sure were good to him, he thought as he laced up his shoes, even if some of them did treat him like a poodle. He felt ready to take on the world.

While he ate breakfast, Mrs. Neffer got dressed. She took Jason out to the stable where it turned out there was a man on the premises after all, a black man she called Lute. Lute dragged out the sleigh and hitched it to the horses.

"Think they can get through the drifts?" Mrs. Neffer asked Lute.

Lute nodded. "Snow's dry 'n powdery. Wants me to drive, Miz Neffer?"

"No, Lute, Jason will drive," Mrs. Neffer said.

Jason's heart swelled. He had been around horses enough and he was confident he could handle them and it made him feel fine and grown-up when she handed him the reins.

There was so much snow there was no way to discern where the road was, which worried Jason at first, but the horses seemed to know the way by heart and made every right turn by themselves. Sometimes beasts knew more than people, Jason marveled.

With her hair, out of the curl papers, peeping out from under a fur hat and her eyebrows drawn back on Mrs. Neffer looked quite ravishing again. Reflecting on how much he liked her, Jason felt full of confusion. Prostitution had almost been equated with murder for sinfulness in the sermons he had heard all his life. Yet the girls seemed so happy and giggly and Mrs. Neffer seemed to him kinder than most Christians he knew. Wasn't anything he'd been taught in his childhood true?

He tried to voice some of his feelings. "Mrs. Neffer – you're – you're about the most Christian person I ever met."

The snorting sound she made told him she did not take this as the compliment he had meant it to be.

"I mean – I mean –" he stammered, "all my life I've been told places like – like you have, are – wicked, and..."

"They are wicked, Jason," she said.

"But you – you are so – and the girls are –"

"Most folks are just folks when it comes down to it, my Little Trout, and it doesn't hurt you to realize that. But don't throw away what you've been taught. All the bad things they say about whorehouses are true."

"But the girls seem –"

"Every girl back there is a sad story. And I am a sad story. And most of the men who are our patrons are sad stories in one way or the other," she said.

Jason drove in silence digesting this for a time. As is often the case after a storm the day was dazzling. Even the wan sunlight kindled such a sparkle in the drifts and ice-hung trees his eyes watered from seeing the glory. He thought about what Mrs. Neffer had said and he thought about the sadness and tragedies within his own family.

"I guess maybe everybody is a sad story, Mrs. Neffer," he said.

"Ahhh," she said. "Yes. You are too young to know it yet. You should still be full of dreams and illusions at your age. How old are you, Jason, fourteen?"

She had made him feel such a man when she had handed him the reins of the horses, now with a few words she had turned him into a little boy. He felt a bit crushed.

"I'm sixteen," he said. "Well – nearly sixteen."

"Yes, for you the world should still seem a bud about to blossom."

"It does," he said. Excitement was coursing through him on this tingling, brilliant morning. He felt adventure and greatness lay before him. "Maybe everyone is a happy story, too," he said.

"Maybe," she said, without conviction. "Turn here."

They had reached the outskirts of town and she concentrated on directing him to the bank where her urgent business was. Appleton was astir with proprietors out on the sidewalks shoving away the snow and breaking icicles from their eaves. A truck with a wooden snowplow was clearing streets.

Jason stayed in the sleigh and kept the horses quiet while Mrs. Neffer completed her bank errands. He was glad when she came back because his legs were starting to throb again even though she had tucked a thick rug around him before she left.

"Now to the YMCA," she said. "We must catch David before he takes off somewhere."

Mrs. Neffer asked for David at the desk and the clerk sent a message up. Within moments, a young man came flying down the stairs buttoning a crisp white shirt as he came.

He was a few years older than Jason, sturdier, taller, and as blond as Jason was dark. With his blondish wavy hair, classical features and quick smile Jason thought he was one of the best-looking men he had ever seen.

243

"Mrs. Neffer?" David seemed surprised. "Is something wrong?"

"Nothing's wrong – I've brought someone to meet you. This is Jason Jacobson. He's a young musician on his own – like you. I want you to hear him play. Is there a piano?"

"In the basement." David showed them the way, flashing down the stairs ahead of them.

Jason kept a more decorous pace with Mrs. Neffer.

David rummaged through the dog-eared sheet music that cluttered the piano. "Here, give this a try."

Jason grinned when he saw it was rag. He ran his fingers over the keys to get the feel and tone of the scarred old upright and then he launched into the music with a vengeance.

"Yeow!" David said with delight. He pulled up a chair and started improvising a counterpoint bass.

Jason threw in some extra rills and a series of runs. David didn't miss a beat. They played a dozen rags attracting a knot of clapping, finger snapping onlookers.

"M'gosh, you're good!" David said.

"What about you?" Jason said.

"What do you do besides rag?"

Jason switched to some classical music and then to one of his own compositions.

"What was the last one? I've never heard it before – it's fantastic." David said.

"Something of my own," Jason said. "I call it 'Rainbow'."

"You compose, too?" David's tone was without jealously, rather one of celebration. "Oh boy! You 'n me are goin' places, buddy!"

"Just as I thought," Mrs. Neffer interjected. "Gaston and Alphonse, David and Jonathan."

"What?" They turned blank stares on her. They had forgotten her presence and had lost awareness of the admirers gathered around them.

"Do you want a roommate?" Mrs. Neffer asked, looking at David.

"I want this roommate!" David said.

"He doesn't have a job. Probably no money."

"I can get him work," David said.

"All right. Then you're all set, Jason," Mrs. Neffer laid a hand on his shoulder. "I'm going then. I have more important things to do than to listen to a couple of loony piano players all morning. I'll see you Thursday night, David."

Jason leaped off the piano stool and ran after her.

"Mrs. Neffer –"

She turned back, brows lifted in inquiry.

"I just want to thank you – for everything. You saved my life, you know."

"Oh God, don't put such responsibility on me," she said, rolling her eyes.

"I won't ever forget," Jason said. "I'm going places. Someday I'll pay back all your kindness, you'll see."

She waved away his words with an impatient little gesture. "Just keep your nose clean, Jason, and make people happy with your music," she said.

David came up beside Jason and the two young men watched as Mrs. Neffer's ample bottom swayed up the stairs.

"She's a great ole broad," David said.

Jason would have taken exception at having Mrs. Neffer spoken of in those words by his new friend, but David's tone was so affectionate and admiring he let it pass.

"You hungry?" David asked. "I know where we can get a great bowl of soup for fifteen cents."

Jason had breakfasted late but the minute David spoke of food he decided he was hungry again. They went off down the street together pulling on their wraps as they went, spewing out words as if there were a deadline on the information they wanted to share.

Jason thought he'd never had a friend he liked as much as David, except Max – but nothing or no one would ever exceed the memory of that relationship. As the excitement of the day waned, Jason felt a wave of guilt engulf him. Was he betraying his values? Had he lost them in the pain and snow of yesterday?

CHAPTER 38
The Movie House

***

"For I know the thoughts that I think toward you, saith the LORD,
thoughts of peace, and not of evil, to give you an expected end."
(Jeremiah 29:11)

After the boys had finished their soup, David took Jason back and showed him the room. There was one long window with a rusty fire escape. On either side of the window was a narrow metal bed painted white. There were two dressers and a closet, and that was all. But the light green walls looked freshly painted and the cord bedspreads crisply laundered.

"We share the bath down the hall with four other guys," David said. "I'm neat. How about you?"

Jason could see David was neat. The room looked like a monk's cell. The only evidence of David was two military brushes on one of the dressers.

"I'm not this neat," Jason admitted. "In fact – well, I can be pretty messy sometimes."

David laughed. "Either I'll shape you up or clean up after you and charge you for it!"

"Mostly it's my music sheets which get messy when I'm composing and I wouldn't like anyone straightening and going through those."

"Well you must have had to put up with your mother or the maid doing it at home," David said.

"No," Jason said. "My mother always left my music alone."

His face went bleak. At the mention of Felly, he had some realization of what his mother might be going through. The whole circumstances surrounding his running away had to be stuffed away for now, as soon as he got a free minute he'd write to Saran.

Other awful memories ached back. Felly starting to hemorrhage after she ran to get the doctor for Max because he wouldn't, the dishpans of bloody sheets soaking in the washroom. He had almost killed his mother – he loved her so much, but he had almost killed her, and the baby had died, the little girl who would never be now.

David stared at his white face. "Hey – don't take it so seriously. If you want to pile your side sky-high, it's all right." He laughed his good-natured, charming laugh and bounced down on the bed. "Just don't let any of it drift down to my side."

Jason bounced down on his bed and within a few minutes David's breezy talk had carried him away from the dark closets of his soul and he was laughing again.

David said his real name was Bernstein, not Berg, and he was Jewish.

"I can't believe it." Jason said. "You don't look Jewish at all. Where's your hooked nose and your curly black hair?"

"Well, you don't look Scandinavian, either," David laughed. "Where's your blue eyes and blond hair and wide cheekbones?"

The boys agreed they would have to change identities. Jason would be the Jew. And David would be Nordic.

"Except –" David said, "we may not look our origins, but we sound them. I talk a mile-a-minute, like Jews often do. And you – you have the slow, almost musical lilt to your voice of the Northlanders."

"Why did you change your name? Are you ashamed of being Jewish?" Jason asked.

"If I were ashamed, would I have told you?" David said. "Why should I be ashamed of being Jewish? We're a proud people. We are like cats. Throw us anywhere and we land on our feet." But there was a slight edge of abrasion in David's tone which told Jason he had faced harassment in the past for his origins.

Jason shrugged. "We're all in the same boat. Why shouldn't we all get along."

"I changed my name because I was mad at my father," David said.

"I'm mad at my father, too," Jason said.

They compared notes for some time on the knot-headedness of their fathers, each insisting their own father was the most knot-headed. They ended up laughing and with the sheepish realization they both respected their fathers despite their "knot-headedness" and wanted to "show them."

Jason wanted to know where David thought he might get work.

"Have you ever seen a flick?"

"What's a flick?"

"A motion picture."

"Oh, yeah. We had a projector at Camp once."

"Come on," David bounced off the bed. "We're going to the flicks!"

"What about my job?"

"That's it. I think you can get a job playing for the flicks."

The next thing Jason knew they were half-way down the block toward the theatre. He was learning that if you traveled with David, you were always putting your clothes on as you went.

The movie house was an unpretentious wooden building on a back street but it was gay with bright posters of current and coming attractions and there was already a line queued up to get in when the door opened. The day was cold, so Jason was glad a man with a moustache and rubber arm guards on his white shirt opened the doors within moments of their arrival.

Inside a white screen stood in front of a blue velvet curtain. Camp-meeting-type chairs were set up in rows to view the screen. To the right on the side was a roped-off area where a piano sat on a small platform. When everyone had bought their ticket, filed in and settled, the lights dimmed. The rustling and chattering stopped. There was a moment of hushed expectancy just like at the great opera house in Boston when the house lights had gone down and people had waited for the maestro to come on stage.

Then an overhead blue-white light pierced the dimness and settled on the screen crackling it to life at the same moment the man with arm garters scurried to the piano and began a triumphant overture.

Within minutes, Jason was lost in the magic on the screen. David had told him to pay attention to what the piano player did, but Jason forgot all about the piano player as the story unfolded. The picture was titled *Rebecca of Sunnybrook Farm* and it starred Mary Pickford. Never had Jason seen such handsome men and such attractive women. At the end of the reel, he snuffled along with most of the others in the theatre as it became apparent the heroine and hero might never be able to live happily ever after. In a final burst of music, things came out all right.

David laughed and handed Jason his handkerchief. "You never paid any attention to the piano player at all. But it's okay. It's a double matinee so you can stay and watch it again – but this time keep one eye on the piano player. I'll be back after you in a bit."

Jason waited while the theatre emptied and refilled and sat through the feature a second time. This time he made himself aware of the piano player as David had instructed. It became evident to him that without the piano player, the "flick" would have been dead. The music was what breathed the emotion into the flickering shadows on the screen. Staccato arpeggio notes spilled over each other in moments of excitement, pianissimo romantic etudes set the mood for tender scenes, and crescendos came with crisis.

I could do it, Jason thought. It would be fun. Having made this assessment, he soon found himself lost once more in the movie, finding even deeper meanings in it the second time.

David returned and slid in beside him just at the snuffling stage. "Well, what do you think?" he whispered. "Think you'd like to play for the flicks?"

"I know I could do it," Jason whispered back with excitement. "And I'd like to – but what makes you think they'd hire me? The guy they've got is good."

"I happen to know the other guy who plays here is going to quit."

"How do you know?" Jason asked.

David laughed, "Because I'm the other guy."

"Why would you quit?"

The movie was over and the people were starting to file out.

"Shhh," David said. "The guy at the piano is Mr. Barret. He owns the theatre and I don't want him to know I'm quitting just yet. Come on, I'll introduce you."

They waited until the last straggler had left and then approached Mr. Barret who was storing the music he had played in the piano bench. He was a sour-faced man with a large Adam's apple and thinning hair. He looked at Jason with stony eyes when David introduced him.

"He's great on the piano, Mr. Barret. He's wondering if you could use him as another player, because, well, I've taken another job."

Mr. Barret's cold eyes examined Jason. "Follow me," he said. He stomped ahead of the boys up a flight of dusty stairs to the projection booth.

There were large wheels which held the film. Barret began to rewind the reel he had just played. He barked a few instructions Jason tried to understand.

"You think you can do it?" Mr. Barret put it up to him.

"Yes, sir," Jason said, though he wasn't completely sure.

Barret wound up some cords, flicked some switches, and unplugged some sockets. Then without a word, he started back down the stairs. David and Jason followed.

He flung a sheet of music onto the piano rack. "Let's see what you can do."

This Jason was sure he could do. He sat down with confidence

Firefly

and ripped the music off with virtuoso style.

Barret gave no sign of being impressed. "We'll give you a try," he said with no enthusiasm. He rummaged through some papers in a case he was carrying. "This is the score for next week's picture, *The Birth of a Nation*. It's an epic film. You learn this by tomorrow night and we'll see how well you can coordinate the music to the pictures."

"Does this mean I've got the job?" Jason asked.

"If you work out," Barret said. His voice was harsh and dry. "As for you, Berg," he said to David, "you coulda given me more notice."

"No problem, Mr. Barret," David said. "I'll stay on until my friend is competent to take over."

Barret gave a little snort. "Here's the key then. You be sure you're back by seven sharp tonight to have the doors open, can't keep people waiting in this cold."

"Yes, sir."

The two young men left with dignity but as soon as they were two blocks from the theatre where they were sure Barret couldn't see them or hear them they broke into hilarious laughter, stomping and laughing and holding their sides. They weren't sure themselves what was so funny but it had something to do with the wry, sour, dryness of Mr. Barret and their own youthful exuberance and their relief Jason got the job.

Jason leaped through the snow flinging his arms up in celebration. He had been on his own less than two days and already he had a friend, a job, a "home". He felt like he was King of the World, as if everything he desired lay like crushed diamonds in the snow waiting for him to claim it.

"You crazy kid," David said. "You never even asked him how much money you'd get."

"How much money will I get?"

"Seven dollars a week, it's not much, but then you won't be working full time. Two shows every night and double matinee on Saturday and Sundays. He plays for the weekend evenings himself."

To Jason seven dollars a week of his own money sounded like a fortune.

"Why are you quitting, David?"

"Like I said, I found a job which offers more money. It's exciting, Jason. This fellow I know has invented a new musical instrument. It's not an organ and it's not a piano, it's sort of a cross. He calls it a Pianorg. I'm going to demonstrate them and sell them. I know I'll make good. I'm a natural born salesman. My grandmother always said, 'David – you've got the gift of gab'. In fact, I've sold two already."

"Well...great! But what if you don't sell any for a week or two? I mean – it won't be steady –"

"I made more on commission for those two Pianorgs than I made working at the flicks for six weeks," David confided. "Besides, it's fun playing for the flicks at first but after a while it gets boring. You'll see. By the time you start to get bored, we'll find you something else to do."

They were convinced life would have to yield its sweets to them. They were invincible. They celebrated with a fifteen-cent piece of apple pie and grown-up coffee before David went back to open the theatre. When you were on your own there was no one to make you eat liver and string beans, you could live on dessert if you chose.

The next few days were busy ones for Jason. He soon found out his new job entailed a lot more than just playing the piano. He had to be at the theatre at six in the morning to practice the score for the next week's feature and to fire the coal boiler in the basement.

The coal boiler became a demon to him. He was afraid of the big gray monster which ruled the subterranean area beneath the movie house. The creature was voracious. It wanted more, more, even more shuttles of coal but even when its stomach glowed red with a super abundance of fuel its temper did not seem to improve. It made strange growling sounds, it burped and sent dark clouds of coal-tar-smelling exhaust up through the registers. Jason was convinced from its menacing rumblings, someday it was going to explode. Yet he was dependent upon its beneficence. Until the old monster huffed and puffed some heat into the building, Jason's stiff, cold fingers could not come out of his mittens to practice.

He found he was janitor, ticket taker, and projectionist besides being piano player. For seven dollars a week, he was the attendant for double matinees every weekday except Thursday and for the two shows at seven and nine, five nights a week. The last show never ended until 11 and then there was still cleanup and the ticket take to count and deposit again in the safe. It was after one before he got settled in to sleep and then it was up again at six. Add to this, Mr. Barret was no charmer to work for and the seven dollars no longer seemed so grandiose.

Especially when Jason began to realize three pieces of apple pie cost him forty-five cents. Being on your own meant you could eat pie if you wanted but it also meant you had to pay for it on your own, too. Two dollars a week went for his room and he soon realized eating out cost too much and he had to opt for an additional three dollars a week for board even though the food was bad. Familiar sounding things like bread pudding and chicken pie bore no resemblance to the dishes which came under those labels at home.

251

Still, in spite of the hardening edges of reality setting in, Jason still felt like the Prince of the World, if not the King. He loved the movies that came each week to the Bijou and never got bored seeing them over and over. To his own surprise he had mastered the projector without much trouble and it was a magical moment when he flicked the switch which sent dreams and excitement and glamour on a blue streak of light to dance on the white screen below.

Mr. Barret had some printed announcements which came on the screen before the feature which allowed just enough time for Jason to scurry down the stairs and seat himself in front of the piano in time for the overture which went with the studio logo. If the film broke or tangled during projection, Jason would have to leave the piano and leap up the stairs to remedy the situation. It never annoyed him when this happened. It made him feel important.

At the end of the first three days of his new job he had just settled himself into bed when he leaped up yelling, "M'gosh!"

"What is it?" David cried, alarmed.

"I promised my sister I would let her know I was all right. I forgot all about it," Jason said.

"For Pete's sake," David grumbled. "I thought the house was on fire." He smothered his head under the covers.

"Dear Seena," Jason began on the back of an old music sheet with a stub of pencil borrowed from David's drawer. "Tell mother not to worry about me. I'm doing terrific. I have a job as a pianist. I'm making good money and having a good time. Maybe I'll come home and see you at Easter if things are all right with Pa. Love, Jase."

* * * *

Although Jason's new adventures were a wonderful distraction, pangs of guilt and sadness in the way he left home still tugged at his heart.

CHAPTER 39
Chaos to Calm

***

"Be angry, and sin not;
let not the sun go down upon your wrath:"
(Ephesians 4:26)

While Jason established his new life, shock and chaos reigned at home. Poor Seena, added to her grief at Jason's departure and her anxiety for his safety, Hans' anger came down on her like an avalanche.

Her father, unaware Jason had run away the night before, was stunned when he found his son gone in the morning. Seena had to admit she knew Jason had run away.

"Do you mean to tell me you knew he was walking out into that storm and never told me?" Hans bellowed.

"But, Papa," Seena sobbed. "It wasn't snowing so heavy when he left."

For the first time in her memory, Hans used physical force on her. He shook Seena so hard her braid unraveled. "Don't you realize he may have frozen to death? It was twenty below zero last night!"

"Jake knew, too!" Seena cried, trying to spread the blame.

But her father, his anger already vented, made no effort to find his younger son and reprimand him. He was already pulling on his overshoes and grabbing for his wraps.

"Have you any idea where he was going?"

Tearful, Seena shook her head.

"Get on the telephone. Call Mrs. Howard, call your grandfather, call everyone you can think of where he might have gone."

"Where are you going, Papa?"

"I'm going to catch the street car conductor and see if Jason went to Waupaca."

The telephone calls brought negative responses; they also brought a houseful of anxious friends and relatives into the parlor by noon.

Hans returned just after the noon whistle. Yes, the conductor did remember Jason taking the street car to Waupaca, and the ticket agent at the train had a record of him buying a ticket to Appleton, but the train conductor vowed the boy had never gone to Appleton, he had gotten off midway at the cold and deserted station near Medina Junction. The conductor said he had pleaded with the boy to stay on the train but Jason had not heeded him.

Hans, Adam, Jake, and a half dozen other male friends filled vacuum flasks with coffee and got out horses and cutters to break through the drifts and search in the vicinity for Jason.

Seena had spent the afternoon red-eyed and weeping in her bedroom, not even Felly could comfort her. If Jason was dead, it was her fault.

Since Mrs. Grasslee did not live far from where Jason had disembarked for the train the men searched first in that area although Mrs. Grasslee had already reported by phone Jason had never showed up at her place. The searchers inquired at every farmhouse along the way where Jason might have taken refuge. No one had seen him. They went off in the other direction with the same results.

They even inquired the following morning at the farmhouse where Jason had found sanctuary. But it was Lute who answered the door, everyone else was sleeping, and due to the nature of Mrs. Neffer's business she had instructed him over and over he was never to reveal the names of gentlemen who came to the house. Common sense would have dictated this was an exception but Lute hated white people and it gave him some satisfaction to stick to Mrs. Neffer's rule on this morning.

Most of the searchers gave up. They tried to talk sense to Hans and Adam.

"If the boy is safe you'll get word sooner or later. If he's out there somewhere under these snowbanks, we'll never find him until thaw anyway. There's nothing we can do now but go home and wait."

All day Hans and Adam floundered back and forth through the drifts sticking long search poles through the snow, faces pained and grim.

At darkness, even they gave up. They came home with their eyes terrible in faces as reddened and scorched by snow glare as if they had been out in July heat.

Adam was in his seventies now and the night and day of searching had taken their toll. Grace was furious at him for putting himself through such an ordeal and angry at Hans for not insisting he return home.

"He's got pneumonia," she cried, pouring buckets of hot water over his feet and packing his chest with camphor. "If he ends up in the hospital Hans, it's on your head!"

Hans had given her a sardonic look. "No one ever made Adam Quimby do anything he didn't want to do, and your husband didn't want to come home."

Caroline and Bay arrived at this point. Bay had wanted to join the search at once but Hans had asked him to remain in Appleton and check out the hospitals, jails, rooming houses, and hotels.

Bay reported he had come up with nothing. Again, the answer had fallen through the search net. The most likely boarding house a young man with little money would resort to was the YMCA. Bay had called there first, but there was no one registered by that name.

In a house full of strain and exhaustion, Caroline noticed the new strength in Firefly. Her daughter was not becoming hysterical.

"Fly," Caroline offered, upon learning that Maggie was no longer employed. "Let me take Meena back with us to Appleton for a few weeks. Saran and Seena must go to school and you can't perform your other duties and take care of the child, too."

"It would be better for her to come home with us," Grace interjected. "She is used to us and has our Jan to play with there."

"You're going to have your hands full with Adam," Caroline said. "And I would like some time to get acquainted better with our little granddaughter."

"Saran, get Meena's things together," Hans had directed, making the decision for Felly. "All the rest of you – go home. My friends are right. There is nothing more we can do – except wait." He had turned his back on everyone and went up the stairs.

Felly, with the help of Saran and Seena, got both sets of grand-parents off. She had her daughters' heat blankets to wrap around Adam for the trip home and tried to soothe Grace's wounded feelings because Hans had chosen to send Meena with Caroline and not her. They had Meena's things together and assisted Caroline in providing cake and coffee for the other concerned people to soften Hans' abrupt dismissal.

Caroline cradled Felly's face in her hands for a moment before leaving. "Dear child," she said. "Don't suffer. I know Jason is all right. I can't explain it but I know in the same sense I knew things were not well with you long before I got home from Europe. Jason is all right."

Felly embraced her mother. "I believe you, Mother."

Seena began to sob with relief. She could not have said why but she took her grandmother's words as inexorable. For the moment, she felt better.

Caroline wiped away Seena's tears with a lavender-scented handkerchief and said, "You must come and spend a week with me soon, Seena – and you too, Saran. Your Aunt Rosalie would so love to take you on a shopping spree and have some good times with you."

When everyone had gone, the two young girls stared at each other. The emptied room felt cold, dark and void, and already they missed Meena.

Felly had put an arm around each daughter. "I'm so proud of you," she said. "You helped so much."

Seena started to spring tears again.

"Jason is all right," their mother declared with authority. "I just know it. And you must know it, too."

She took them upstairs and tucked them in bed as she had when they were little. Her calmness and faith had helped them, and exhaustion and sleep took over.

****

Seena was not the only one who shed tears that day. Maggie Grasslee had soaked her aunt's pillow. The Howard residence had been one of the first Seena called and Mrs. Howard had urged her niece to speed at once to the Jacobson's to help.

"Hans hasn't made one effort to call me – to apologize – to ask me to come back. His entire concern is for Jason," Maggie protested. "No, I will not go over there and try to help find that nasty Jason."

"Maggie," Mabel had scolded. "Hans isn't afraid you are under a snowdrift somewhere. He doesn't know what's happened to Jason. Of course, he's concerned."

"How does he know I'm not under a snowdrift? Has he called to ask?" Maggie responded, her mouth bitter.

"Maggie, are you in love with Hans Jacobson? Is that what this is all about?"

"Yes!" Miserable sobs ensued.

Mrs. Howard shook her head in disapproval.

"You don't understand! You don't understand," Maggie said. How could she tell her aunt about what had happened in the schoolhouse – she couldn't and wouldn't, but it was at the core of her despair. She had convinced herself Hans loved her, not his sickly wife. She was certain he had desired her that night. He had been so mad and mean because it was hard for him to reject her, she reasoned. His silence and indifference were lacerating.

Her aunt's palpable disapproval did not help. In the afternoon,

Maggie packed her bags and went home to her mother. She would not have Hans think she was waiting at the Howard's for some word from him.

Mrs. Grasslee accepted her daughter back with a secret sigh. She loved this stormy petulant child as she loved all her children, but her peace, her little rituals were shattered. Maggie wept and stormed and denounced Jason and what could Mrs. Grasslee, who thought Jason was a wonderful lad, say?

She offered hot cocoa and apple cake, which her petulant daughter swept aside. She offered silent listening if not sympathy, and grunts and nods. And Maggie, sensing not even her own mother was wholehearted in offering comfort, went into fresh tantrums and vowed she was going to kill herself. No one loved her, no one cared.

"Your Pa always did say you was a porch climber," Mrs. Grasslee reflected.

"I tell you I'm going to kill myself and all you can say is I'm a porch climber?" Maggie cried.

"Well, you always have to be something you're not. And I guess I'm just trying to say you can't be happy that way."

"Is it so wrong to want to be more? To rise in the world?" Maggie cried. She wanted to run away from her mother too, but there was nowhere to run. She stared at her mother for a minute in helpless frustration, and then she went into the little back bedroom and sat swollen-eyed, dry-lipped, gazing into space.

****

Hans Jacobson had wept, too. Felly found him sitting on the edge of their bed, his shoulders heaving. She knelt before him and he clutched her into his arms, clinging to the warmth and sweet scent of her.

"Oh, Felly, Felly – It's my fault Jason went off into the storm. If something has happened to him, you'll never forgive me. I'll never forgive me."

When had the boy ever been his? He had always been alien, and yet – Hans realized the depth of his bitter love for this dark, difficult son. Jake was so easy, as were Saran and Seena and Meena – so difficult with Jason. Yet, he loved the boy no less than the others, and the more his passion, love, and need of Felly deepened, the more it seemed to him his love for Jason deepened, too. Jason, the child so like his Felly. The others were copies of him.

His big hands clutched Felly's delicate frame. "Oh, Felly, I love you so much. I want you so much." His pain poured out of him, he couldn't stop it.

She caressed his face. "We can make love, Hans."

"No. Another pregnancy would kill you."

She lifted his chin and looked into his eyes. "My poor darling. Didn't Dr. Bentley tell you? I'm not capable of getting pregnant ever again."

The realization sank in slowly. "He's sure?"

"He's sure."

A new shame surged through him. He was overwhelmed with desire for his wife at this moment. What kind of man was he when his son might be dead beneath the snow, to be feeling his own appetites?

"Jason is all right, Hans. I just know it." Felly unbuttoned her nightdress.

Sex, like food, was one of the great comforters of life. She took her husband in her arms, needing him as much as he needed her.

****

The anxiety for Jason, her grandmother's words had soothed, came flooding back to Seena. That night she dreamed of Jason, blue and frozen, sticking like an icicle out of the snow and woke shaking and drenched with sweat. Her usually rosy face was pale and shadows gathered beneath her eyes. The dream continued to haunt her.

One good thing did come out of this period. One night after school, Johnny Knightengale, stopped her.

"Seena," he said with an awkward sincerity. "I heard about your brother. I never knew Jason well but I always admired him because of the way he could play the piano and everything. I'm really sorry. I can tell how much it upsets you. Is there anything I can do for you?"

Color came spilling back into Seena's cheeks. She had mooned over Johnny Knightengale for months, as had most of the girls in the eighth grade. He was tall and fair and sweet-tempered. His uncle owned the Ford agency in Waupaca and people said he "had a future." It had never occurred to Seena he might notice her.

"Just saying what you did helps," she stammered. Then she ran away so he wouldn't see her confusion. But his kind words did help. Sometimes in the darkness at night, she forgot for a little while the terror about Jason and thought instead of Johnny Knightengale, a sweet lassitude spreading through her which relaxed her and let her drift into sleep without nightmares.

****

Seena stood at the mailbox, a bundle of newspapers and periodicals under one arm, holding a square envelope with familiar writing in her mittened hand. A gasp of joy and relief came from her, sending out a great plume of steam in the frozen air and then she ran over the icy yard and up the front steps shouting, "Mama, Papa – Papa – Saran!"

Her father was at his desk doing accounts, he half rose as she burst through the door and flung the other mail on the dining table.

"Papa – it's a letter from Jason. He must be all right!" She pulled her mittens off and tore the envelope open with her teeth. "He's all right – he's got a job – and he's doing fine."

Hans grabbed the letter from her hand to read it for himself. Then he crumpled it in his fist and threw it on the floor. Seena stared in astonishment as her father walked through the house and went out the back door without even a coat on.

"Papa – aren't you glad? Papa?"

In the backyard, Hans smashed his fist into the woodshed. All the boy had put him and many others through was for the moment overcoming the tortured love he felt for him. Damn selfish boy. Didn't he have any idea the agony he had caused them all? He looked down at his bleeding knuckles. Well, it's enough he's alive. Nothing else matters. He's alive! He bowed his head before his God and gave thanks.

"Papa?" Anxious, Seena was at the back door holding out his coat to him. He went back into the house and ran up the stairs to tell Felly.

"Aren't you going to call Jason, Papa? Aren't you going to tell him to come home?" Seena called after him.

Hans's jaws were tight. "Seeing he's doing so well, let him be," he said. A renewed coldness had settled over his heart. A coldness not even the rejoicing Felly could pierce.

"Hans, all you asked for yesterday was for him to be alive. Can't you just give in to the joy of that?"

"I have thanked God, but why didn't Jason call us? Why did he let us live through such a hell of anxiety and pain when he could have picked up the phone and let us know he was okay? Hard to forgive, Felly, very hard. Adam and I were out there for hours sticking a damn pole in the snow, thinking any moment we might find him dead in a snowbank..." His voice broke off.

Felly took him in her arms. He had a right to be angry with Jason, and it would wear off, she knew. Despite the certainty she had felt all along that Jason was okay, she shivered with relief. Her son was alive. Her intuition had been right. The rest would pass.

She called the YMCA and managed to get Jason on the phone. During their long and tender conversation, she explained how it was with Hans and chided Jason for his behavior. He in turn told her of the terror of his night in the snow, and of how his faith in her love and the belief in God she had instilled in him had upheld him and got him through. He was contrite and promised to write a letter of apology to his father. Which he did, but Hans remained angry and hurt.

When Seena wrote to Jason, she ended the letter, "Papa's still pretty sore. You better not come home for a while. You better wait until Easter. Love, Seena."

****

"I'm glad Jason's all right, I was just as worried as you were, Seena," Saran said. "But I'm mad at Jason, too."

"Mad at him?"

"Sure. Because of Jason everything's on us again. We have to help fix the meals and launder the clothes and help with the heavy cleaning and take care of Meena when she comes home."

"Do you want Maggie to come back?" Seena asked.

The two sisters considered in silence, then Saran began to giggle.

"No!"

"No!" agreed Seena.

She threw a pillow at Saran, and in a moment, they were pursuing each other in a raucous chase all over their bedroom until they collapsed in laughter, releasing some of the tension of the previous week.

Life without Maggie was harder, but it was also better. Once again, they could sprawl in the living room with their homework, eat in the dining room with their parents, leave their things scattered without being scolded, and have their friends over. They knew their mother was happier, too. Maggie had been both a help and a burden.

CHAPTER 40
Lottie Carthington

***

"For thou, LORD, has made me glad through thy work;
I will triumph in the works of thy hands."
(Psalm 92:4)

As it turned out, Jason did not get home for Easter either. The city of Appleton was planning a big celebration of a new bridge being built. There was going to be a parade; the mayor and governor were going to speak. There would be a street dance from nine until midnight, and most of all, what excited Jason and David, a contest was being sponsored by Mr. and Mrs. Hubert Carthington for words and music to be used as the city's anthem. The prize was one thousand dollars, an unbelievable sum. And it was to be presented by the governor of the state.

The young men were sure they could win. As David put it, how much competition could they have? The winner had to be a resident of Appleton or the surrounding area. True, there were some fine musicians and composers at Lawrence University, but they tended to be longhaired and too dignified to participate in a popular promotion like this. There were some bar piano greats, like old black Rudy, who were a magnet to serious musicians from all over the country. But Rudy was alcoholic, nearly blind, and as old as the Piltdown man who was shaking the country with evolutionary arguments. Rudy lived in his own hazy, smoke-filled world of dreams and it was doubtful he would compete.

"So, it's us against a handful of other talented upstarts, eighty housewives, and two businessmen," David construed the odds. For several weeks, Jason and David spent every spare moment working on the city's anthem. They worked half the night, spurred on with coffee and dreams, crumpled music sheets overflowing the wastebaskets and growing in pyramids on the floor. After the first night, the other residents of the boarding house complained so much they had to search for another piano. Mr. Barret reluctantly agreed to let them use the piano at the movie house when they promised if they won the prize they would mention the Bijou and its treasures in their acceptance speech and would also give several performances of the anthem at Saturday matinees.

They found it wasn't easy to come up with just the right tone. The first piece Jason did was the most beautiful, but it was too sonorous for an anthem people were expected to sing. The next one was too rollicking and the third one sounded too much like, *The Battle Hymn of the Republic*, and the fourth sounded too much like a Sousa march. They wanted to do something highly original, something which bore their own imprint.

When they finally got the music right to their satisfaction, the lyrics were a problem. David had a witty facile mind which came up easily with catchy phrases but in the end his efforts always proved too clever, too tongue-in-cheek. An anthem had to have a certain amount of dignity even if they were determined not to make it pretentious.

They went to work bleary-eyed, their young cheeks fuzzy with tender unshaved beards. They rushed home with fresh inspiration.

"I've got an idea – if we reverse those two phrases in stanza six!"

"Jase, it's come to me you've got to add two more notes on the end. Here where it goes tra-la, tra-la – just make it tra-la, tra-la, la, la. See?"

Then it was done and they couldn't have been more satisfied. They were sure it would win. The song had as Jason said "heart" and as David said "pluck". It was rousing, easy enough for everyone to sing, and stirring enough for city pride. They were already mentally spending their thousand dollars.

"I'm going to buy me a Dusenberg with my share," David said. "And a cigar about a block long and then I'm going to go home and sit in the driveway and bleep my horn 'til my old man comes out. What're you going to do with yours, Jason?"

"I'm going to go home with my arms so heaping with presents. Saran and Seena's eyes are going to bug out and it will take Meena a week to unwrap all of hers. And maybe I'll buy me a diamond stick pin for my tie."

"Of course, what we should do is move out of this lousy place and buy a Ford," David said, coming down to earth a little.

"What we should do is stay in this lousy place and use the money to support us so we have time to write new hits and get famous," Jason said.

Jason's romance with the Bijou had dimmed. He was, as David had predicted, now bored by the scores he had to play many times, and it was no longer so thrilling to sit through the same movie all week – add to that the monster in the basement, sour Mr. Barret, and the long broken up hours for small pay, it seemed heaven was not having to go to the Bijou.

"After I've driven around in my Dusenberg for a while," David said, going back to his first dream, "maybe I'll sell it and use the money to go to Europe. They say you can live real cheap over there. We could probably live over there for six months and not work. Eat goat cheese and roam the country, and play in little wine bistros."

"Grow a moustache and come back world-weary," Jason laughed.

They spent almost as much time dreaming about what they would do with their contest money as they had writing the song. "We're going to win!" they kept assuring each other.

Yet despite all their bravado and confidence when a letter arrived in the middle of April informing them they had won, they were stunned and incredulous.

"We won!" they kept saying to each other in disbelief. "We did – we won. Can you believe it? We won!"

The letter informed them that Mrs. Hubert Carthington would meet with them at a fashionable restaurant to explain to them how the music would be presented and what their part in the ceremonies would be. The actual check would be presented to them after the governor's speech before the ball at night.

They pooled their meager funds to have a girl who lived down the street steam-press their suits for them. They polished their shoes to a spit, each had their hair cut, and took off for the Blackwell, the plushest restaurant in Appleton.

Looking around at the waitresses in little black dresses with what looked like embroidered white crowns on their heads, chandeliers, and the real silver on the tables, David said, "I sure hope this Mrs. Carthington is picking up the tab or we're going to be doing dishes."

Then Mrs. Carthington herself swept in – and "swept in" are the only words you could ever use for Charlotte Carthington's entrance. Not quite five feet tall, heavyset with a pigeon bosom, she seemed to sail on hidden streams of music, head tilted back, hat plumes waving, and a feather boa streaming out behind her, a heaven-like scent of Parisian perfumes enveloping the air about her.

"My dear boys," she cried out in a throaty, enthusiastic voice which turned heads all over the restaurant. "My two geniuses, you are my two geniuses, aren't you?"

263

They nodded, nonplused by this apparition. She was the ugliest woman either of them had ever seen. She had a neck like a bull and no chin. Her tangled wavy hair looked like it had once belonged to a tired teddy-bear and her nose – her poor nose looked as if it had been attacked with a potato masher. They could not help but stare.

For her part, not at their first meeting or at any time in their long association afterwards, did Lottie Carthington ever give any indication she considered herself anything but a great beauty. She exuded charm and self-confidence and her expressions, gestures, and airs were all those associated with a woman who is beautiful and knows it. Her appearance and her performance were so incongruous, she attained an instant fascination and, curiously, people came to trust her at her own estimation, as if she were a great beauty.

"Just goes to show what money can do for you," David asserted later.

Jason demurred. "There are lots of wealthy people who are shy and reclusive and don't have any self-esteem," he said. "Money is too easy an explanation for success."

In time, the young men learned Lottie had not been born with her unfortunate physiognomy. A train accident in her youth had resulted in her unfortunate facial deformities. A fortune had been spent trying to rectify the damages, but when it became clear nothing further could be done, Lottie had found the courage and resilience somehow and decided she would not allow her misfortune to rule or ruin her life. In her own mind, she "erased" her condition and like the lines of Omar Kyaham she was fond of quoting, "replaced it with one nearer to her heart's desire."

At the moment, she was pulling off her laced kid gloves to reveal plump hands sparkling with jeweled rings. She took Jason's chin in her hand and tilted it up to her.

"You are not only geniuses but so adorable too!" she enthused. "You're good looking, too," she threw a bone to David. "But a bit smug. I've always liked these lean-faced, dreamy-eyed ones."

A half-dozen waiters materialized to pull out Charlotte Carthington's chair and dance attendance. She ordered food and wine with French names without consulting her companions, then went on with her praise of Jason's looks as if she had not been interrupted.

"Yes – you're absolutely darling – remind me of my Hubie when he was young, and being so good-looking won't hurt your musical career, believe me. Oh, you're going to be lionized."

The two young men forgot all about how ugly "Aunt Lottie" was, as she insisted they call her. For an hour, they basked in her predictions of fame and greatness awaiting them and her effusive compliments, and felt they had never been in the company of a more enchanting woman. The French filet mignon and dessert Napoleons did not hurt either. After weeks of Mrs. Whitney's cabbage soup and soggy bread pudding, eating at Blackwell's was heaven.

Aunt Lottie explained they would be included in the grand parade. They would ride on the float with the Celebration Queen, Miss Appleton. Their composition would be performed with "Pomp and Circumstance" by the city band all dressed in scarlet and gold. The lyrics would be printed in the newspapers prior to the big event and be handed out on flyers on the day, so the public could sing along.

They would have the opportunity to meet the governor, but she decided she would publicly present their award following the mayor's address. In the evening, they would attend and be special guests at a banquet and ball at the Carthington's where they would receive their check. White tie.

The two young men looked at each other. Neither of them had ever worn a tuxedo in their life, and they were not even sure about the difference in formality of white and black tie, but it was a style to which they desired to become accustomed. They would rent tuxes somehow. After all, they were soon coming into a thousand dollars. Five hundred each!

Lottie left them with a sense of all of this just being the beginning for them. She affirmed their secret fantasies. Part of Lottie's power and success as a social arbiter was money, but ninety percent of her personal charm was her genuine kindness and her relish for life. She left her young companions walking on clouds in the tree tops.

The only drawback was they would not get home for Easter, but that scarce seemed to matter since when they did go home it would be in triumph, bearing gifts and trailing success.

Lottie Carthington's home turned out to be on the same street as Caroline and Baird LeSeure's mansion. Jason knew he could have entered the Carthington's world at any time through his grandmother's door, but to have made it on his own was ten million times more satisfying.

His grandmother had come to see him at the rooming house several times. With her regal bearing, her furs and pearls, her angel hair, she was an anomaly in that modest establishment. People hung over the banisters to peer at her. And David had opined with a low whistle, "Your grandmother is some classy woman, Jason. How come you don't stay with her?"

"I could," Jason said with a slight sigh. "My step-grandfather would even arrange to start me in his business; they've offered a number of times. But I want to be a musician and I want to do it on my own terms. Grandma Caroline is wonderful, but she's different..." He groped for the words to describe what she was and couldn't quite find them. "She would expect me to be better than I want to be right now," he finished lamely.

"Oh, she's one of those," David said.

Jason was unfairly angry at David for this slight disparagement of his grandmother. "No, she's not one of 'those', whatever you mean. She's..." And again, words failed him to describe his grandmother.

"She's...she's sort of a healer. People come from all over with all kinds of problems and she helps them somehow. She doesn't advertise or anything, people just find her. She sees me as more wonderful than anyone else ever has or ever will. I can't explain it, David, but it touches me and humbles me. I can't be as wonderful as she thinks I am – not yet, anyway, and I don't want to disappoint her. Does that make any sense?"

"I guess so," David said.

Jason did go to see his grandmother now and then, but only because he loved Caroline and did not want to hurt her feelings by refusing her invitations. His uncle Jimmy was in California but he enjoyed his Aunt Rosalie, too. She was a beauty, with shining blond hair, wide cheekbones, and a soft and vulnerable mouth; though somewhat tall for the tastes of the day, towering an inch or so above Jason. At thirty, she was still unmarried and men were still vying avidly for her favors. She fascinated Jason because she was so warm and charming and outgoing – always so interested in what he was doing and sympathetic to his viewpoints – and yet he felt she never let anyone really know her.

Their conversations were always about him, never about her activities or thoughts or feelings, and when he tried to shift in that direction, she would laugh and get up and find something else to do. So seemingly open, but so truly mysterious, he thought to himself and became more and more interested in probing beneath the sweet surface. The more he probed the more uneasy she became. She started avoiding him, which amused Jason and made him more determined to shatter her defenses.

But for the most part his own life kept him too busy to spend much time at the LeSuere mansion.

David was finding it harder to sell Pianorgs than he had thought it would be. Weeks when David made no sales, the two young men scrimped by on Jason's Bijou salary. They learned to darn socks and put cardboard in their shoes to cover the worn holes in the soles, they walked instead of taking the streetcar and they had to settle for Whitney House cabbage with no apple pie. They went without the small pleasures of a Sunday paper or a cup of restaurant coffee.

When David made a sale then they shared equally in the largess. They splurged on new suits and banana splits and foraged the local music stores for new sheet music and paper. They went to the theatre and had supper at Blackwell. The money disappeared like morning dew and they went back to the penury of Jason's salary until David's next bonanza.

The small hardships were real enough but still it was a happy time for them both, full of expectancy and excitement of things to come. And now with the winning of the Appleton anthem award and the coming of Lottie Carthington into their lives, they felt the thrilling exhilaration of being on the way.

CHAPTER 41
Rejoice

***

"Rejoice in the Lord alway: and again I say, Rejoice!"
(Philippians 4:4)

The changes which had been going on in Felly were noticed not only by her family but by the whole Camp community. As suddenly as she had once assumed an austere hairdo and stark clothing, she now let go of her austerity. She took her daughters to Waupaca and all three of them got bobs and one of the new permanent waves. Hans at first grieved for the loss of her beautiful, long hair, but as the permanent grew out it became soft, almost wind-blown looking curls around her face and he came to love it.

Felly was also the first to wear one of the new shorter skirts which exposed a woman's ankles. She bought pretty, high-heeled slippers and real silk stockings and wore the skirt to church. She had very fine ankles indeed, and everyone was shocked, appalled and, against their will, delighted.

She had a way of pulling an old blouse or dress out of her closet and changing the sleeves or the collar to make it fit current fashions. She was also the first woman in Camp to wear a cloche hat and lipstick.

There was the usual original envy, gossip, and disapproval. But once again Felly had become their fashion arbiter. Soon all the women were wearing shorter skirts, a smidge of lipstick and cloche hats, and craning their necks to see what she would come up with next.

As she began to feel better she started going to church again, helped with the junior choir, and would often go down to the main hall to play for the old soldiers. She played their favorite hymns and the battle songs of long ago. They loved them, and her. She started a poetry circle and attended quilting bees.

"It's as if she rose up out of the grave and was transformed," Mabel Bentley pronounced.

And so it was. Felly was beginning to feel alive again. More alive than she had ever felt in her life. She breathed in every nuance of each day with reverence and gratitude.

Making bread for her family became a sacred ritual she enjoyed. Bathing Meena was a fun time for both her and her youngest. She started taking the toddler along on her walks and together they investigated an inchworm, the way squirrels buried their nuts, how frogs hopped, and why Jack-in-the Pulpits had that name.

She required Seena and Saran to help much more than before her illness, but now she made it more fun for them. In the evening, she would often play the piano and the three of them would practice singing harmony. Then when there were unpleasant tasks to be done the three often sang together and the burden lightened. They made a ritual of rewarding themselves after hard workdays with a batch of fudge. At night when the dishes had to be done, two of them worked while one of them read to the others. They were halfway through Dickens.

Jake had always been his father's boy, but now she took time to read stories to him, play checkers or help with his homework, even if it meant leaving dust in the corners, carpets not cleaned or dishes stacked. She was rewarded with glimpses of his burgeoning curiosity and his genius with machines.

Her greatest gratitude was for the new sweetness between Hans and her. Sometimes she felt as if she were almost holding her breath because it was better than she had ever dreamed it could be.

Not that the stings of fortune no longer occurred. They did. The milk boiled over on the stove, Hans smashed his thumb, a beloved puppy got run over by a car, an important document got lost, Felly sprained her ankle, Jake's appendix had to be removed. There were the usual disruptions and upsets which occur in any household. What was different was her ability to accept and embrace it all with grace if not with equanimity. She would think of Kemink and her mother and resolve to be a woman of courage, and the problems and challenges would somehow shrink.

Felicity sat in a rocking chair on the front porch at dawn enjoying the warmth of the blue ceramic cup of coffee she held in her hands. She shivered slightly from the cool fall breeze and pulled her pink shawl closer to her. She felt peaceful as she watched the morning the sky being washed with splashes of the yellow and orange as the sun rose.

Autumn was her favorite season. She enjoyed the changing palette of tree colors and the mixture of fragrances in the air from the harvested crops of corn and potatoes, and hay.

As she watched geese flying south for the winter, she thought about the seasons of her own life. Her youthful resolve to be married to Dan-Pete gave her a twinge of remorse.

Being older and wiser now she realized her childhood bond with Dan-Pete was a gift that had served them well in providing joy, friendship, and love in the springtime of their life. However, life, like the seasons, involves letting go to make room for the next cycle of life. She acknowledged to herself that to her own detriment, because of her selfishness, she had failed to completely let go of Dan-Pete until late in her life.

Her previous angst and longing for his love had changed over the years to feelings of pride and respect for him. Felicity knew in her heart that Dan-Pete's had done the right thing to honor his Indian heritage. She smiled briefly as she thought of his tenderness and kindness to her.

Felicity realized the path of adversity during her life with Han's had forced her to push beyond her selfishness. Turning to her mother during difficult times for solace, Caroline's gentle ways and adherence to her faith helped Felicity over time to develop her own faith in God, spiritual resilience and inner strength.

Fly had accepted in her heart that she might never know gentleness and true joy with Han's. At times, she had thought their disappointments and resentments might never be healed. She had spent many hours in prayer for reconciliation and happiness. She had worked hard to appreciate him, embrace his love and acknowledge his steadfast commitment to her. As her thoughts and behavior towards him changed, Felicity felt her prayers were being answered as Han's seemed to be making equal efforts to be more patient and thoughtful.

Her heart was content that all was well with the Jacobson family. She was grateful that the relationship between Hans and Jason had softened. Hans had finally given Jason the verbal affirmation of pride and acceptance that Jason's heart had yearned to hear for so long.

Rejoice!

CHAPTER 42
Homecoming

***

"Beyond all these things put on love,
which is the perfect bond of unity."
(Colossians 3:14)

Early on a March morning there was a hard thumping on the door of the room Jason and David shared and an irritated voice announced, "There's a lady downstairs says she's got to see you."

The boys' two ruffled heads appeared from tangled covers to stare at each other in amazement. What lady could be seeking them out?

Jason leaped out of bed first and ran to the door. The thumper was already half way down the hall and he had to run to catch up with him.

"What lady? Who?" he said, grabbing onto the thumper, who turned out to be the night clerk, a fellow called Slats.

"Cartington, something like that. Let go of me, Jase. I been up all night and I'm worn out."

"Cartington? Ohhh, Carthington." Jason let go of Slats and hurried back to David.

"Lottie's here," he announced to his pal. "Why would she come here?" She had always instructed them to meet her at restaurants before.

David tumbled out of bed. "Must be something important."

The boys splashed themselves with cold water, sleeked their hair back, and dressed in the most respectable outfits they could put together. They both felt nervous, afraid something might have gone wrong. Had they been eliminated from the contest money after all?

They found Lottie pacing back and forth on the worn, flowered carpet of the small reception office of the YMCA. As usual she was a sight to behold. She wore a white suit with a pink blouse foaming out at the neck and sleeves and a huge, fuchsia pink hat which bobbed with roses. She looked totally out of place in the rather dingy lobby. In fact, it had never seemed dingy before, but her resplendence made it so.

The day clerk was looking at her with goggled eyes.

"Oh, there you are!" she cried when the two rather pale young men came racing down the stairs. She held out her arms as if she were going to gather both into one monstrous embrace. Then she noted their apprehensive expressions and folded her arms back around herself.

"Forgive me for coming so early and unannounced, but I have such good news for you!" her voice dropped. "And unfortunately, bad news as well."

They stared at her, waiting. It seemed to both their combined heartbeats sounded like tom-toms in the room.

Lottie put her hands like a steeple beneath her chin and smiled a broad smile. "You're not going to believe this, but I sent your anthem to the producers of the Chicago WGN radio show and they were so impressed they want you to come in for an interview.

"They are planning a two-hour Sunday morning program and they want someone who cannot only play the piano but who can compose as well. The position will pay seventy dollars a week, and you will get unbelievable exposure!"

The boys let out a holler, which seemed to come from one throat, grabbed each other and began to dance up and down. It was all they could do not to grab Lottie and swing her into the dance too. She was laughing happily at their antics, and they could see she felt included.

Then they remembered there was bad news, too, and they calmed down and waited for the other shoe to fall.

"The bad news?" David coaxed.

Lottie looked down at the tips of her elegant boots. "I'm afraid, my dears, they only need one of you. They will determine which one when you audition for them."

The two young men looked at each other, their elation evaporating.

"No," Jason said. "We've been through too much together. They take us both or they take neither of us."

David laid his hand on his friend's sleeve. "Let's take the audition, maybe they will want both of us when they hear us and see us."

Lottie's kid-gloved hands flew apart like two birds taking flight. "It's a wonderful opportunity, Jason, I wouldn't take it lightly."

Jason nodded, not wanting to seem ungrateful for Lottie's efforts in their behalf.

"Could we take you out to breakfast somewhere, Mrs. Carthington? We can hardly express our gratitude."

"Call me Aunt Lottie," she reminded them, her laughter trilling in the small room. "And no, you cannot take me out to breakfast, I have another engagement. However, when you come back with the job, we shall all go out for a fabulous dinner to celebrate."

She began giving them addresses, directions, and times for the upcoming interview. Following this, she kissed each of them on the cheek, enveloping them with the sweet, powdery scents that were her essence, and departed.

The boys went back up to their room in a subdued mood despite the exciting news they had just received.

"We're not going to be split," Jason said with finality.

David rearranged the brushes on his dresser. "Jason, I want you to take the interview. I want you to have it. I'm good, but I know quite well you're better."

"Nonsense! I could never have written the anthem without you. We're not going to be split!"

David stopped pushing his brushes around. "No, we'll never be split. We're always going to be buddies and partners. We'll always work on music together, but this one's for you, Jase. Seventy dollars a week, ten times what you're making now. You have to take the interview."

They wrangled all day and into the night and into the next week. In the end, Jason went alone to take the interview, and when the producers were more than enthusiastic and he was awarded the job, his joy was tinged with sadness.

He wrote to his mother, "Whether Papa wants me to or not, I'm coming home for a visit." He kept his big news a secret to spring on his family when he arrived.

The anthem check had been given to the boys, and with the prospects of his new job, Jason felt well able to go on the spending spree for his family he had always envisioned.

"You'd better seek Rosalie's counsel," David suggested. "She'd know more about what young girls might like."

Jason shook his head. "No. I want to pick everything out myself." And he did.

He shopped for his father first. Hans had long ago bought a fine cornet for Jake, but his own was old and worn. Jason picked out the brightest, shiniest, most expensive cornet he could find, encased in a red velvet container, and had it inscribed with Hans' name. He also bought him an expensive barometer and a set of gold cuff links.

For Jake, there was a new bicycle, even though the one Jason had received from Grandpa Adam was still in good shape. And he bought him a ukulele. The instrument was becoming very popular with young people, and besides, David had taken to selling them along with the Pianorg.

He roamed the stores for a long time selecting his gifts for his three sisters. The new fashions seemed to him not as pretty as the ones his sisters usually wore. Sailor dresses with huge collars and bright red ties seemed to be the rage. The shop girls assured him his sisters would love the outfits, so he succumbed to their advice and bought each of his sisters one of the sailor outfits complete with the flat-topped straw hats with ribbons which went with the garments. Even Rasmeena would have one, and he could imagine her looking darling in it.

He also bought each of his sisters a dress which seemed to him more in accord with their usual sweetness and lady likeness, white lawn dresses with embroidered bodices, the waists tied with wide satin ribbons, blue for Seena, pink for Saran.

He bought them each a mother-of-pearl brush and mirror sets for their dressers because he had once heard Seena long for one. He bought them kid gloves like Lottie wore and sweet powders. He bought them silk stockings and gold lockets.

For Rasmeena, there were also an array of dolls and toys, including a small red wagon to haul her teddy bears around.

For the whole family, he brought baskets of fruit and boxes of chocolate, and tins of the finest nuts.

The present for his mother was the hardest. Nothing he could think of seemed fine enough for the love he wanted to express for her. In the end, he bought her earrings with real diamonds in them. A gift he thought would last forever.

Then armed with all the riches of his excess, he along with David set out for The Grand Army Home in King. They had decided, despite their new riches, they had better not buy a car just yet; however, Lottie had insisted they borrow hers. They came chugging and roaring into the yard in a brand new Dusenburg.

The glories of spring were all about them. Baby chicks, still in their downy yellow fluffiness, greeted them in a yard starting to erupt with Felly's perennials, lilacs, irises, tulips, and hyacinths. The dog, Mac, came running out and wiggling with happiness to greet Jason, welcoming him as only a dog can.

Jason had convinced David to come with him by telling him how beautiful his sisters were and how he would fall in love with them at once.

When Seena, and Saran with Rasmeena in her arms, appeared on the back porch, their pale hair shining in the sun, their faces radiant with welcome, David whistled softly and punched Jason in the arm. Should they look surprised because before he said he would keep it a secret he was coming...

"Golly, you weren't exaggerating – your sisters are beautiful. I'm in love."

Then Felly appeared, her arms wide open.

"Gosh, even your Mom is beautiful," David whispered.

Felly did look beautiful with her new windblown curls, her face beginning to fill out again and color returning to her cheeks.

A moment later, Jason was entwined in their arms, all laughing and hugging and crying at the same time. Jason broke away to introduce David and to start pulling packages out of the car. Only then did his father come out and stand on the porch, not smiling.

Jason halted at his task, unsure of his welcome.

"Father?"

"It's good to see you, son," Hans said. "Come in."

In the yard, there had been nothing but joy for Jason, but when he walked into the familiar rooms inside, his love for his family became overwhelming. He set Rasmeena, who was in his arms, down and darted back to the car. "To bring in more presents," he said. He stood for a long time under the trees swaying in a gentle wind until he regained enough composure to return to the house.

There was the revelry of all the presents. There were "ohhs" and "ahhs" and squeals of delight. Each family member declared their gift was the best present ever.

There was the announcement of Jason's new job, which brought more squeals and hugs and praise and excitement from his sisters and mother.

There was the dinner Seena and Saran had helped produce. They did not yet have the culinary skills of Felly or Maggie, but they had done well. There was pot roast with carrots and potatoes, a salad made of dandelion greens, and a cake with coconut frosting.

David's spirits were somewhat dashed when a fellow named Johnny Knightengale arrived. It was evident he already had his drubs on Seena, and he was not only good-looking but he also had a ukulele and began to show Jake how to chord.

In the afternoon, the whole family made ice cream together, taking turns turning the crank, and sang silly songs in accompaniment to the ukulele. "Come Josephine in my flying machine and up we'll go!

Up we'll go!" or "Camp Town ladies sing this song, du da, du da..."

It was a warm, loving, beautiful day. The boys could not spend the night because they needed to get Lottie's car back to her. But it had been everything Jason had dreamed of. As dusk grew near and their departure close, he walked with his mother up to Rainbow Lake. When they passed the boathouse, he remembered how he had felt Felly would never be a source of strength to him again and reflected how wrong he had been. He knew now a mother's strength flows into the very marrow of a loved child's being and is there for their lifetime, and he told her so.

"Your father has given you gifts, too," she said.

He reflected on how hard the relationship between himself and his father had been, but he nodded. "Yes, accountability and humility, Pa made it his goal to never let me get a big head."

They both laughed.

He tried to teach her how to skip a stone across the water. She was so terrible at it that they laughed some more until they were both bent over holding their ribs. But in the end, she finally threw one stone that skipped smoothly over the surface of the lake. The small feat was a great satisfaction for them both, a benediction of their time together.

****

At the end, there was one private moment with his father.

"Your mother is very proud of you, Jason," Hans said.

"And you, Father?" Jason's throat felt tight.

"I'm proud of you, too, son. I should have told you years ago how proud I am of you. Will you forgive me for my stubbornness?"

Tears tumbled like a waterfall down Jason's cheeks as he said, "Of course I forgive you Pa. I love you."

It was the best moment of Jason's entire life.

CHAPTER 43
Vindication * Boston Symphony Hall

***

"Beloved, I wish above all things that thou mayest prosper and be in health, even as thy soul prospereth."
(3 John 1:2)

November 1937, twenty years later.

The first icy wind of winter was siphoning through Boston. Laced with the whiteness of a few snowflakes, its sharpness was exhilarating. Jason drew a deep breath of it into his lungs as he stepped from his rented limousine. For a man in his mid-40's he was still almost as slight as he had been as a boy, but his expensive black overcoat gave him large shoulders, and the white silk scarf tucked around his throat, elegance.

He caught a glimpse of himself in a darkened store window and smiled. Not quite as flamboyant as the old Colonel, but he would do.

Cars inched by on streets which were no longer cobblestone, queues of cars, with golden headlights and ruby taillights. Many of them, he knew, were there because of him. He could see them turning to where there would be parking. There was the oogah of horns as the congestion around the area grew. His stomach tightened, and finally he allowed himself to look up at the building before him.

Symphony Hall.

The journey had been long, but he was there. He could have gone in the back way to the dressing room reserved for him, but he had wanted this moment. He stood there until his hands became so cold he had to jam them in his pockets; stood there until he realized people were recognizing him and staring. He slipped away along a side street and made his way to the back of the building.

His dressing room was full of flowers, their dewy scent greeted

277

him. Later, he would look at each tag to see who all his well-wishers were. Now, he slid out of his overcoat and looked at himself in a mirror lined with light bulbs. His hair had become grey, but he approved. As a boy and young man, his dark, almost-black hair had added to an intensity he projected. The grey hair softened his visage. His aging face was a softer face, less hungry and haunted, he decided. All of this was acceptable. What pleased him most was his suit with satin lapels, just as he had dreamed of as a boy.

He flexed his fingers until they warmed and became pliant. There was a rap on the door and then a face appeared through its opening. "It's time, sir."

His moment was upon him.

There was a rush of applause as he walked across the polished wood of the stage to the grand piano awaiting him. In a moment, there would be only him and the piano, all the rest would recede from him. The house lights, though dimmed, had not yet been turned down, and for this brief instant he became aware of the building and the audience waiting for his music.

Memory swam back to him. The great hall was filled with stirring, laughing people. Jeweled fans waved, diamond necklaces and dowagers' brooches sparkling like strange, icy flowers; furs sliding off white shoulders, elegant men pulling off their kid gloves with effete grace; the camellia smell lost in a thicket of pomades, perfumes, and powders.

The ornate gas lamps had been replaced with crystal chandeliers ignited by electricity. But the sense of opulence and grandeur remained. In the audience, jeweled fans no longer waved, electric fans circulated air warmed to just the right temperature. The women's gowns were simpler, many like slips or strapless, but they still sparkled with jewels, and their perfumes rose to him like the scent of the flowers in his dressing room.

He seated himself at the piano and the house lights went out. The rustlings, the stirrings, the whispers stopped. He experienced the same moment of expectant, breathless silence he remembered when the old maestro of his childhood had sat down at his piano on this same stage. Only this time, the expectancy was for his music, his gift. He closed his eyes, lifted his hands, and brought them down on the keys.

Jason played as he had never played before, played the music he himself had composed. And all his life's blood was in it, everything; the frogs leaping out of Rainbow Lake in his childhood, the smell of his mother's cheek when she kissed him goodnight, his sisters running downstairs in their white nightgowns, his envy of Jake's wonderful brass horn, his father's strength and sternness, the old soldiers petting and loving him; the rude, rich, mealy odor of the stables and the beauty of the horses; and summer storm clouds that swam in Rainbow Lake. All of it flowed out of his sometimes crashing, sometimes tender stroking of the ivory keys.

He gave his audience the champagne picnic with the Colonel, their heads together while ecstasy rose in the boy who was learning he could make music. He gave them his terror and heartbreak at the Colonel's death. He gave them his desperate love and need of his mother, and the vast vacuum her illness had created. He gave them the rejections of father of son, and son of father, and the great chasm of yearning which had nevertheless been between them. He gave them his mystical Grandmother Caroline who appeared throughout his life like some fairy godmother, lifting darkness and chaos for a time, only to disappear and leave their troubled household to resume its passionate wayward journey. He gave them his father shredding the flowered blouse and throwing it into the lake. He gave them Seena crying out she didn't want a baby sister. He gave them Rasmeena with all her ability to lighten the family with laughter. He gave them his two grandfathers and his wonderful bicycle.

He gave them his own cruelty to Maggie, his waywardness and selfishness. He gave them his mother's ravished face the day in the boathouse. He gave them the snowstorm he nearly died in, and the paper-thin gaiety of the whore house.

He gave them the moment his father had said, "I'm proud of you."

The last note died away and then there began a thunder of applause, an applause that kept on and on. He stood up and bowed and then left the stage. The applause was insistent and he returned to walk to center stage to bow again.

Then his eyes darted quickly searching the audience for his mother and father. In the first-row center sat Hans and Felicity. Hans was smiling, clapping and nodding his head in approval. Felicity was also smiling and clapping voraciously. She was well into her years now and frail, but Jason thought how elegant she looked.

Felicity wore a long sleeve black velvet dress with a high collar and a silver rhinestone pendant around her neck. A small black hat with red velvet petals topped her perfectly coiffed white hair. Her face was filled with joy, her lips were parted in a smile and her eyes...her eyes were like fireflies. Fireflies sparkling on a dark night.

Seena, Saran, Jake, and Rasmeena were all waving from the row behind mother and father.

Even though his Grandfather Adam, his Grandfather Bay, his

Grandmother Caroline, and Kemink had passed away years before, he felt their presence with him tonight. Jason's throat swelled with tears as he thought of his childhood friend and companion the Colonel wearing his flowing cloak.

They were as real to him as any other people in the hall, more real. Tears began streaming down his face so hard, he had to keep bowing and bowing to hide them.

His mother's love and faith in Jason, and unforgettable Max, had given him the courage to be on this stage, the courage to make music, music that would last beyond his own life, music that would bless generations. The continuing swelling, surging applause told him that. People were on their feet in a standing ovation. He knew this moment was the epitome of his life, there would never be another one like it, and it was in some way a vindication of a girl once called Firefly.

The End

Appendix I
Tomorrow River Country
– Wisconsin

For more information on the book, "Tomorrow is a River" and Tomorrow River country in Wisconsin, refer to the following website:

www.TomorrowRiverCountry.com

Kim Vroman-Pence lives with her husband, Robert, and their two dogs Django and Hope in Plano, TX.

Appendix II
Tomorrow River Map

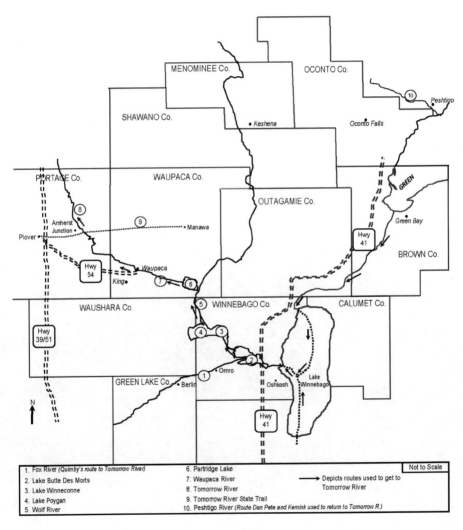

1. Fox River *(Quimby's route to Tomorrow River)*
2. Lake Butte Des Morts
3. Lake Winneconne
4. Lake Poygan
5. Wolf River
6. Partridge Lake
7. Waupaca River
8. Tomorrow River
9. Tomorrow River State Trail
10. Peshtigo River *(Route Dan Pete and Kemink used to return to Tomorrow R.)*

→ Depicts routes used to get to Tomorrow River

Not to Scale